The Villa

The Villa

ROSANNA LEY

Quercus

New York • London

Quercus

New York • London

ISBN 978-1-62365-118-3

Library of Congress Control Number: 2013913497

This book is a work of fiction. Names, characters, institutions, places, and events are either the product of the author's imagination or are used fictitiously. Any resemblance to actual persons—living or dead—events, or locales is entirely coincidental.

Manufactured in the United States

10 9 8 7 6 5 4 3 2 1

www.quercus.com

To Caroline with love

Chapter 1

Tess didn't open the letter until later, when she was sitting on the beach.

In a hurry to get to work that morning, she'd barely glanced at the envelope, just grabbing it from the mat before kissing her daughter Ginny good-bye.

Now Tess plucked the letter from her bag. Read her name, *Ms. Teresa Angel*, and her address in bold, confident typescript. Stamped and postmarked London.

Ginny had left for college—an unruly streak of long legs, jeans, red shirt, dark hair and eyes—while Tess had set off for the water company, where she worked in customer information. A euphemism for Complaints, since who really needed information about water? (Turn on the tap, out it comes; better still, drink the bottled variety.)

This was her lunch break, and she'd come—as she often did—to Pride Bay, five minutes away by car, to eat her sandwiches by the sea. It was an early spring day, and breezy, so she, too, was sandwiched—between a row of pastel-painted beach huts and the high mound of tiny ginger pebbles of West Dorset's Chesil Beach. This gave Tess some shelter, and she could still just see the waves. She didn't have to be back in the office till two thirty. She stretched out her legs. Flextime. What a wonderful invention.

Tess eased her thumb under the seal of the envelope and tore it open, sliding out a single sheet of white paper. It was so thick and creamy she almost felt she could eat it.

Dear Ms. Angel, she read. *We are writing to inform you . . .* her eyes scanned over the text . . . *following the sad passing of Edward Westerman.* Edward Westerman? Tess frowned as she tried to make sense of it. Did she know an Edward Westerman? She was pretty sure she didn't. Did she even know anyone who had just died? Again, no. Could they have got the wrong Teresa Angel . . . ? Unlikely. She read on. *Concerning the bequest . . .* Bequest? *On the condition that . . .* Tess's mind raced . . . Hang on a minute. *Sicily . . . ?*

Tess finished reading the letter, then immediately read it again. She felt a kind of nervous fluttering like moths' wings, followed by a rush—of pure adrenalin . . . It couldn't be true. Could it . . . ? She stared out at the sea. The breeze had picked up and was ruffling the waves into olive-gray rollers.

She must be dreaming, she thought. She picked up the letter and read it through once more as she finished her sandwich.

Well. What on earth would her mother say . . . ? Tess shook her head. There was no point thinking about it. It was a mistake. Surely it had to be a mistake.

It was clouding over now, and Tess felt chilly despite the woolen wrap she had slung over her work jacket when she left the car by the harbor. She checked her watch, she should go. But if it were true . . . If this wasn't some sort of joke, then . . . *Sicily* . . .

Tess tucked the letter back into her bag and began to put the jigsaw pieces together in her mind. Her fierce and diminutive mother Flavia was Sicilian—though she had left her home and her family when she was in her early twenties. Tess just wished she knew why. She had tried often enough to find out the full story. But Muma had never wanted to talk of her life in Sicily. Tess smiled as she got to her feet and picked up her bag. She loved her dearly, but Muma was stubborn, and Sicily was out of bounds.

Tess thought back to the few details she'd managed to glean over the years. Her mother's family had lived in a small cottage, she'd once said, on the grounds of a place called the Grand Villa. That had been owned by an Englishman, hadn't it? Could that be the Edward Westerman mentioned in her letter? She did the math. Edward Westerman—if he was that man—had lived to a ripe old age.

But why would he . . . ? She paused to empty her shoes of tiny pebbles; it wasn't easy to negotiate Chesil Beach in heels, even though Tess was used to it. She headed back to the harbor, past the bright, tacky stalls selling fish-and-chips, cotton candy, and ice cream, and past the fishing boats with their nets hanging out to dry, the scent of the gutted fish ripe and heady in the air. Pride Bay, despite its name, had little to show off about. But it was part of her childhood, and it was home. Best of all for Tess, it was by the sea. And the sea was in her blood—she was addicted to it.

She mentally replayed the contents of the letter on the way back to the car, and as soon as she was sitting in the driver's seat of her Fiat 500, she retrieved it, smoothed it open, and reached for her cell phone. One way to find out.

"This is Teresa Angel," she said to the woman who answered. "You wrote to me."

Tess drove back to work on autopilot, the still-fresh phone conversation running through her mind. This was the kind of thing that could change your life, wasn't it? But . . . She paused. She was thirty-nine years old; she wasn't sure she even wanted change. Change could be scary. Her daughter's life was changing fast, and she found that hard enough to handle—after all, what if Ginny went to university hundreds of miles away and then emigrated to Kathmandu?

But on the other hand . . . What would happen if her life stayed the same? What if her lover, Robin, never left his cold and fragile wife, Helen, as he kept promising to? What if she had to work for the rest of her life dealing with complaints at the water company. It was inconceivable.

CHAPTER 2

TESS DROVE PAST JACKAROO SQUARE—DECORATED with pots of red-and-white spring geraniums—and the deco Arts Centre. The town center was a little shabby, but it came to life every other Saturday with the farmers' market and the Morris dancing. The town used to be a rope-making center, but now most of the old factories had been converted into apartments, offices, and antique warehouses.

Sicily . . . She shook her head in disbelief as she took a right and parked behind the water company building. She walked round to the front entrance. The person she should call first was her mother. Hmm. Tess pulled out her cell, selected *Robin*. Telling her mother must be done face-to-face. But she had to tell someone.

"Hello, you . . ."

Tess loved the intimate way he spoke to her. As if he were about to take off every item of her clothing one by one. She shivered. "You'll never guess what."

"What?" He laughed.

"I got a letter this morning. From a solicitor in London."

"Oh, yes? Good news or bad news?"

Tess smiled. She was due to see Robin after work, because on Thursdays Ginny stayed late at college. Twice a week was the average, three times was good, four unprecedented. All their time together was snatched. If she wasn't on flextime, Tess sometimes thought, she and Robin would never be able to see each other, never have late Monday lunches (making love) or early Thursday evenings (ditto). What would they do then? But she wouldn't dwell on that now. "Good," she said. "I think."

"I like good news," he said, a smile in his voice. "What is it?" She could imagine him doodling on today's datebook page, maybe drawing a fish face with bubbles. He'd started doing that when she signed up for her first diving course. It told her that actually he was a bit jealous. Which she quite liked.

"I've been left a house," she said. She could say it out loud now. She went to sit on the wall by the hydrangea bushes. There was a sharp edge to the breeze that she liked—a sort of *hey, it's spring*, wake-up call. *Something's got to change . . .*

"What?" he said.

"I've been left a house," she said again. "In Sicily." Yes, it was really true.

"Sicily?" he echoed.

She couldn't blame him for being surprised. She was still trying to get to grips with the thing herself. Why would Edward Westerman have left her his house? She didn't even know him. And what would she do with a villa in Sicily? It wouldn't exactly fit into her lifestyle. Her life was in Dorset—wasn't it? With Ginny. With Muma and Dad, who lived only a few streets away from her Victorian townhouse in Pridehaven. And with Robin—at least, when possible.

"Yes," she said. "A villa in Sicily." The Grand Villa . . . Just how grand was grand . . . ?

"You're joking, Tess."

"I'm not," she replied, the truth finally sinking in now. "I know it's weird. But someone's left it to me in his will."

"Who on earth . . . ?" he asked. "Some ancient admirer?" Robin was ten years older than she. Was he an ancient admirer, too? Ginny would think so. If she knew.

"A man I've never met. Edward Westerman." His name was rather romantic. She explained some of the background to Robin—at least, the little she knew so far.

"Bloody hell, sweetie," he said.

"And that's not all." Tess shifted her position on the wall. Thought reluctantly of her in tray. "There's a condition." It was, she'd been told by the solicitor, a stipulation of the bequest. Always in life there was a catch. Have a child with a man you trust, and he will leave you and emigrate to Australia. Meet someone gorgeous, sexy, and funny and fall in love with him, and he'll be married—to someone else.

"What's that?" Robin still sounded as shell shocked as Tess felt.

"I have to go there."

"To Sicily?"

"Yes. I have to visit the property. Before I can . . ." She hesitated. Dispose of it, was the way the solicitor had put it. "Sell it," she said. How much would it fetch anyway? Enough to pay off her mortgage? Enough for a holiday or two? *Enough to change her life . . . ?*

Sicily . . . It almost seemed to be calling to her. That might not seem surprising in itself, to be drawn to a warm and sunny landscape, but Tess had been brought up by Muma, whose eyes darkened in pain or anger, or both, if you asked her about her home country, her childhood, her parents, her life there. Until finally you accepted the fact. Sicily was off-limits. The thing was though . . . what Tess realized now was that she had never really accepted the fact. And already a thought, a hope, an idea, was winging through her brain. She felt the surge of nervousness return, that moth-wing excitement, that thrill.

"Wow," said Robin.

Tess watched a bee heading purposefully for the yellow cowslips grouped in front of the hydrangea bushes. It dived in headfirst. She understood how it felt. "I know." It was mind boggling. And then there was the mysterious under-current. The stipulation. She had to go and see the villa—before it was truly hers. But—why?

"So you'll be off to Sicily, then?"

"Mmm." There was nothing to stop her going—apart from what Muma might say, of course. She was owed holi-day time from work, and Ginny . . . Well, Ginny would prob-ably be glad to have the house to herself for a week. For a moment, she thought of Ginny's music on full volume, Gin-ny's friends invading the house, and Ginny going out when she liked and for as long as she liked—when she was sup-posed to be studying. Her friend Lisa next door would keep an eye on her, though. With Lisa and her parents close by, nothing too dramatic could happen, could it?

"Soon?" Robin sounded different, as if he were suddenly taking her more seriously.

She wondered what he was thinking. "I suppose." A couple of smokers had emerged from the entrance of the building. They lit up.

Tess glanced at her watch. She was unwilling to go back to her desk and the complaints. And she was also tempted by that new seriousness in Robin's tone. "Is there any way . . . ?" She let the words hang. If your lover is married, he can't go away with you—not without copious amounts of planning and lies. She knew that. If your lover is married, you can't share your life with him. He shares his life already—with someone else. He's never yours—not even in those brief, exciting moments when you think he is. And if you think otherwise, you're fooling yourself. *Aren't you?*

"Maybe there is," Robin said. "Maybe I can come with you."

Tess's heart jumped. "It would be perfect," she said. She couldn't keep the thrill out of her voice, and one of the smokers glanced at her curiously. She turned away, facing the hydrangea bushes. "Just perfect. A villa in Sicily, Robin. Imagine. To see it with you would be so special." *Careful, Tess, you're gushing.* Mistresses must remain cool at all times. That was the deal. Still . . .

"It would be fabulous, sweetie." Robin's voice was low again. "There's nothing I'd like more."

Tess waited for the *but*. It didn't come. "So could you?" She held her breath.

She hadn't meant to fall in love with him. They'd first met in the café in the square where the coffee was strong and the pastries to die for. She'd noticed him because he was attractive—if dressed a touch conservatively for her taste—and because his voice, when he spoke to the waitress, was low and sexy. But she wasn't in the market for a relationship. She was an independent woman with a daughter to care for, and Ginny was her number one priority; she always had been. Tess was the only parent she had. Tess had seen friends try to introduce a new man into their equation of single mother and children and witnessed how impossible it was to juggle everyone's demands. When Ginny left home . . . Well, perhaps. But until then, Tess had dates, and she had male friends. But serious relationships . . . ? No, thanks.

Even so, twice a week she went to the café in the square for lunch, and it seemed that he did, too. She always had a book, he a newspaper. Twice she caught him looking at her when he was supposed to be reading; once he smiled.

One day there were no spare tables, and he appeared at hers with a cappuccino, a panini, and an apologetic grin. "Would you mind? I shan't disturb you."

He had, though. Pretty soon they were swapping work stories—he worked in the finance company two buildings away—and discussing whatever was in the news. He didn't mention his wife—not then. But he did suggest another lunchtime meeting in the pub farther down the street on the following Friday. Why not? Tess thought. She had enjoyed his company. And it was only lunch.

After that, he'd suggested a drink one night after work, and after the drink he'd kissed her. Sometime later, after she'd cooked him a meal—chicken with pistachios . . . she wasn't her mother's daughter for nothing—and he'd seduced her on the couch (Ginny was staying with a friend), he'd told her he was married.

By then, she was already half in love with him. He had kind of crept up on her. And it was an old cliché, but she couldn't turn back even if she wanted to.

Tess watched the smokers throw down their cigarette butts and grind them underfoot. Still chatting, they disappeared through the glass swing doors. Tess brushed some water from a budding hydrangea with her fingertip. Earlier, it had rained, a sudden burst, a mad shower over almost before it had begun; a rinse of the sky, it seemed like. She checked her watch again. She should go in. But something told her this moment could be the one she'd been waiting for.

"Why not? Why shouldn't I come to Sicily with you?" he said again.

Tess caught her breath.

She was grinning like an idiot as she blasted her way into the building and leaped into the elevator. It was really going to happen. She had been left a villa in Sicily. And she was going there. With Robin. Her smile faded as the elevator went *ping* and the door started to slide open. Now she just had to break the news to Muma . . .

CHAPTER 3

"I DON'T UNDERSTAND." FLAVIA SAT DOWN HEAVILY. She had always had so much energy, but these days it sometimes swept away from under her without warning, and she was scared by how weak she felt. She was getting old, of course. She was, in fact eighty-two, which was quite ridiculous. Because she didn't feel old. She didn't want to have to struggle to remember things. She wanted everything to be clear.

She tried to order her thoughts, but with Tess looking at her in that probing way she had, it wasn't easy. She steadied her breathing. So, Edward Westerman was dead. That in itself was not surprising. He must have been well into his nineties. He was the last. First Mama, then Papa, and then Maria, two years ago. She had lost touch with Santina; had no choice but to let her go. And now. Her last link with Sicily gone. She put her hand to her head. There were beads of sweat on her brow. The last link. She felt a wave of panic.

"Are you all right, Muma?" Suddenly Tess was all concern. She came over to where Flavia was sitting in the old wooden kitchen chair by the table, and bent forward, a gentle hand on Flavia's shoulder. "I'm sorry. I didn't know it would upset you so much. Were the two of you close?"

Flavia shook her head. "No," she said. "Not really." He had been an Englishman—her employer. She was a young Sicilian girl. And it was so long ago. Though there had been a bond . . . Edward had been the first man to speak to her in English, and he had made it possible for her to come to this country when she was twenty-three. Like her, Edward had felt an outsider in his homeland, and so he'd gone to live in Sicily—though it was years before she understood why. Puzzles were like that—you could have all the pieces in front of you and yet still not see the overall picture.

"What, then?" Tess said.

Flavia smoothed her apron with the palm of her hand. *Iron out all the creases and all will be well* . . . She couldn't exactly say what had floored her. The mention of Edward, perhaps, the memories, the fact of his death.

Then she realized with a jolt what it was. "Why did they contact *you* about his death?" she demanded. "I don't understand. What does it have to do with you?"

Tess stood next to her, all long legs and blonde-brown unruly hair, looking like the child she once was. "He's left me his house, Muma."

Flavia blinked, frowned. "What?" She struggled to get her bearings. "Why would he do such a thing? He, of all people . . ." He'd understood how it was for Flavia. He himself had broken with England, hadn't he? Well, hadn't he . . . ?

"I don't have the faintest idea," Tess said. She hooked her thumb into the belt loop of her blue jeans. "But I thought you might."

Flavia rose slowly to her feet. There was supper to cook—a distraction. She was not too old to cook—never too old for that, though these days she stuck to the one course and the occasional *dolce*. She and Lenny now lived in a modern house on an English estate of identical houses, and it was very different from Sicily. But *la cucina* was still the most important room. Her kitchen, her food . . . That could always make everything safe again.

"Well, now," she said. Every time in her life that she'd imagined herself free of Sicily, something from that place snapped at her heels. Now it was Edward and Villa Sirena, house of her childhood. Not that Flavia's family had lived in the Grand Villa itself, of course, but . . . What could she say? "He had no children," Flavia began. "Perhaps he felt . . ." What had he felt? Responsible? Had he left her daughter the villa to make up for some imagined wrongdoing? She shrugged, aware that this wouldn't satisfy Tess. Tess had been born curious; she never let things go. Now this. It was as if Edward had known how Tess would be.

Sure enough . . . "But he must have had relatives, Muma." That innocent, blue-eyed gaze . . .

"Maybe not." His sister, Bea, had died some years ago and she, too, had been childless. Thanks to Bea, Flavia and Lenny had run the Azzurro restaurant in Pridehaven; run it until they retired just over ten years ago. She missed the place—but everyone had to slow down sometime.

"Or friends?"

"Who knows?" Flavia began to slice the eggplant, the knife cutting smoothly through the slick, greasy skins and pulpy flesh. They needed time to degorge; otherwise they would be bitter.

Edward had—of course—had friends. Arty friends, but more especially, men friends. Sometime later she'd understood why, as a girl, she had felt at ease with Edward, even when alone with him. It was significant, too, she realized, that she had been *allowed* to be alone with him. These days, naturally, his homosexuality would not mean so much, but then . . . In England, the activities he indulged in would have been illegal, but in Sicily, in a small village in a grand villa, it was easy to hide and be safe. Easy to have lots of houseguests, lots of parties. English eccentricity was accepted, even while it was not understood. And Edward had inspired great loyalty in his staff by giving them a living and treating them well.

"Perhaps he became a recluse," she said. Perhaps he had been lonely. She could imagine that. "It happens. Especially to artists and poets."

Tess—on her way to fill the kettle—shot her a disbelieving glance and flicked a tangled curl from her face. "What about the people who cared for him at the end?" she said. "What about whoever took over from Aunt Maria?"

Maria . . . The knife hovered above the purple skin. Her sister's death had been sudden and shocking for Flavia. They had not been close, and this made the loss even sadder. It was too late now. Maria had come to England only once in her lifetime, when Tess was just eighteen, and the visit had not been easy. Their lives had been so different, she supposed; they had traveled in such opposite directions. Flavia had become anglicized long ago; she even thought in English now.

Maria was timid—dark and vigilant as a rat. She was shocked at the way Flavia was bringing up her daughter . . . *You allow her to go out alone? Dancing?* She was distrustful of the relationship Flavia had with Lenny—their casual teasing, the way Flavia cheerfully left him to get on with the dishwashing after supper. And she found it hard to accept that

Flavia had become a businesswoman—running her own small restaurant, managing her own accounts, her own staff.

"England is different from Sicily," she said to Maria—over and over, it felt like. "If you stayed for longer, you would find out. There is a freedom here that you have never dreamt of."

"Perhaps so, perhaps so." And poor Maria would sigh and frown and wring her hands. "But Signor Westerman is alone. He needs me." And Flavia suspected that, truth be told, Maria wouldn't want such freedom. Her sister had not been blessed with children, and she had lost her husband many years ago in a traffic accident in Monreale one night. "What was he doing there?" she'd moaned to Flavia on more than one occasion during her visit to England. "I shall never know."

Perhaps, Flavia thought, it was better not to know. They were talking about Sicily, after all.

"Our family looked after Edward for many years," Flavia said now, throwing the rounds of sliced eggplant into a colander for salting and keeping her voice level. First Mama, Papa, and Flavia, then Maria and Leonardo. "This must be his way of showing appreciation." Was that how it was? Or had Edward Westerman known how it would tear at her? She suspected that he would.

Tess dropped tea bags into two cups, looking enquiringly at Flavia as she did so. "Muma?"

"Please." Tea was an English taste that had taken Flavia twenty years to acquire. It would never get you going like an espresso, but it had its uses.

"But why not leave the house to you?" Tess persevered. "You knew him, at least. I've never met him."

"Pshaw." Flavia dismissed this notion. "I am an old lady. No doubt he thought I was dead."

"Muma!"

Flavia shook her head. She didn't want to be having this conversation. She had tried to put Sicily behind her. Since leaving for England she'd never gone back there. At first, because to go back would mean too much pain, too much compromise. And then . . . because she'd wanted to punish them, of course—her father whom she had never forgiven, her mother who in her eyes had betrayed her almost to the same degree, and even poor Maria—because she was just like them, because she could never understand that the only way to make things different was to fight . . .

"Muma?" Tess's arms were around her. Flavia could smell her daughter's honeyed perfume and the faint orange-blossom scent of her hair. "You're crying."

"It is the onions." Flavia wiped her eyes with the back of her hand. "You know they always get me that way."

"It's not just the onions."

Such intensity she had, this daughter of hers. Flavia closed her eyes for a moment, the better to drink her in. Wild, beautiful Tess, who—like Flavia—had also been let down badly in matters of love. Who loved with too much passion, who always expected too much . . . And who had an irrepressible young daughter of her own. But not a man to share her life with. Flavia discounted Robin. She didn't even want to think about him. When she thought about Robin, she wanted to crush the life out of him with her bare hands.

"No," she agreed. "It is not just the onions." It was the past, always the past. Sicily was a dark country. And when it was in your blood, it never quite let you go.

"Did you like Edward Westerman?" Tess moved away, long limbed and elegant even in jeans, to pour boiling water on the tea.

Flavia went on chopping onions, garlic, and chilies. She was making a tomato sauce for *melanzane alla parmigiana*, one of her granddaughter's favorites. "Yes." She had liked him, yes, because he embraced the unconventional. And because he had shown her what was possible.

"Only, you've never talked about him much." Tess's sly look from behind a wisp of hair suggested that Flavia hadn't talked much about any of them.

This was also true. She had not told Tess why she had left Sicily in 1950, nor why she would never go back. She had not allowed the memories of her upbringing to surface and seep into her English life. She had been unable to forgive. Flavia held on to the countertop, just for a second, to rest.

"Let me help you, Muma." Once again, Tess was at her side.

"I am not yet totally decrepit," Flavia said, feeling her breathing get back to normal. She sprinkled oil into the pan. "There is still life in the old wolf, you know."

"Dog," murmured Tess, putting the mugs of tea on the table.

"Dog, wolf, whatever," muttered Flavia, adding the garlic, onions, and chilies. Her daughter was pedantic—it was the Englishness in her. Now she poured oil for the *melanzane*. She had her own methods, her own way of working. And there were—of course—some matters in which Sicily would always be triumphant. Olive oil, for example. In Sicily, the best oil was pale and golden; here it was green and more refined. Here, people thought you odd if you used it to moisten bread or toast—they preferred to use animal fat. In this respect, Flavia had not adopted English traditions.

Tess was watching her. She seemed restless, long fingers fidgeting first with the buttons on her shirt, then with her teaspoon. "Can't you tell me anything else about him?" she complained. "This benefactor of mine?"

Flavia clicked her tongue. The oil had reached the correct temperature, and she lowered in the eggplant. Into the other pan she tossed the tomatoes she'd prepared earlier. What you did not know could not cause you harm. "Grate me some *parmigiano*, hmm?" she said over her shoulder to Tess.

"Muma?"

Flavia sighed. But her daughter deserved to know something, she supposed. "He used to read to me," she said. "Poetry."

"His own poetry?" Tess's eagerness as she turned to face her was a reproach. Once again, Flavia felt the weariness engulf her.

"And other poets. He liked Byron and D. H. Lawrence." She smiled. Edward Westerman had told her about these writers, and the young Flavia had listened with wonder. Edward clearly approved of Byron's lifestyle. Ah, yes, he had introduced Flavia to a world that was a million miles away from her life in Sicily. She paused, about to throw some sweet-scented basil into the pan, hearing again Edward Westerman's melodic voice, quite low, intoning the words, half of which she hadn't been able to understand. But the music of the words—that, she had understood.

"He sounds interesting." Tess had retrieved the cheese from Flavia's larder—fridges were too cold for certain foods, something some English people never seemed to understand—and was grating it into a small white dish. "Enough?"

"Enough."

Tess wrapped the Parmesan up again in its waxy paper, and Flavia took the dish from her. She noted the dreamy look on her daughter's face. "Well?"

Tess sat down and cradled the mug of tea in her hands. "I can just see you as a girl, that's all." She didn't add—*for the first time.* But she put out a hand, and Flavia felt her daughter's soft touch on her arm. "It's nice."

Yes, yes. She knew, and Lenny was always telling her: *It's unfair not to talk to her about what happened. It's your story; she's your daughter. It's all long past. Can't you tell the story and let it go?* But Flavia wasn't sure that she ever could tell the story. And how could she let it go?

Things became more complicated as you grew old. What was black and white acquired many shades of gray. She took a deep breath. "Edward helped me come to England," she said. "That may be why he has left you the house."

Tess frowned at the contradiction. "To encourage *me* to *leave* England?"

Something inside Flavia dipped in panic as she took in the possibility. "You wouldn't, would you?" She stared at her daughter.

"No . . . oo." But Tess was looking out of the window into their small garden, complete with patio furniture and lawn, shrubs, and annual plantings that were all, Flavia had discovered a long time ago, prerequisites of an English garden. She didn't mind—it was Lenny's department; even now he was out there pottering around. The window was ajar and the breeze was fluttering the yellow curtain like a bird's wing.

Flavia recognized her daughter's look and she did not like it. She was far away—imagining being somewhere else. Why? Was she so unhappy here?

"But..."

"But...?" The eggplant had caramelized and was seconds away from being overcooked. On autopilot, Flavia whipped round, lifted them from the oil. No, they were fine. She tipped them onto paper towels to drain and tasted the bubbling tomato sauce. Flavia made all her sauces with fresh tomatoes; until she retired she had mostly grown her own—in two huge greenhouses rented from a nearby farmer. The quality of the tomatoes depended on the soil and the climate. At least here they were by the sea; the salt in the soil brought out the sweetness. And Flavia only used her tomatoes when they were as ripe as the setting sun. Ah. Her mother had taught her that good cuisine depended on two things—simplicity and using the best, freshest ingredients. She had never lost sight of that. Still... "But?" she said again.

"But I'd like to see the place," Tess said. "Obviously. Especially now that I own it." She turned to face Flavia. "And I'd like to see where you grew up, Muma."

Furiously, Flavia stirred the sauce. The heat of it seemed to be on her face, in her blood. When she had been pregnant with Tess, she had spent the morning before she went into labor making a huge pot of Bolognese sauce. "Nesting instinct," the midwife had said, when she told her. Flavia didn't know about that, but she thought that even when she died, there would no doubt be a lump of dough wrapped on the side and waiting for rolling, some ripe tomatoes, and basil halfway toward a pan...

"I see." She tried not to sound clipped and brittle. As if her heart weren't twisting inside. Why shouldn't Tess visit the villa? What was Flavia so afraid of? That Sicily would stretch out a gigantic claw and drag her daughter into its cruel ebony center? She was a foolish old woman, she decided.

"Anyway, I have to go," Tess said. She seemed unaware of the effect her words were having.

"Why?" Flavia's heart was thumping inside her chest. Her knees almost buckled, and she held on to the side of the stove. Just for a second. She would be all right in a second. "Why do you have to go?"

"It's a condition of the bequest. I have to visit it, before I decide what to do with it."

Before she decided what to do with it? The panic bloomed. Still Flavia continued to stir. The sauce was a good color. All her life, cooking had helped her, food had seen her through. The tomatoes had thickened, grown more pungent, the sweet aroma of tomato and chilies rising from the pan. "I see," she said softly. And she was beginning to.

"I've looked the area up on Google Earth," Tess said matter-of-factly, as if she were talking about a day trip to Weymouth. "It's beautiful. You never said how beautiful it was."

Flavia grunted. She had never said exactly where it was either, had she? She dragged her baking dish out of the cupboard. She realized that somehow, sooner or later, she might have to say a whole lot more.

"Isn't it, Muma?" Tess's voice was pleading.

"Yes, it is beautiful." She began with a layer of sauce, then Parmesan, then eggplant. Sauce, Parmesan, eggplant . . . *Don't go there . . . Don't go there . . . Don't go there.*

"I'll keep an eye on Ginny," Flavia heard herself say. "If you want to visit Villa Sirena," she paused, "before you put it up for sale." *Sauce, Parmesan . . .*

"Thanks, Muma." Tess's voice was lighter now.

Because if your daughter is here, you will come back. Flavia didn't say it out loud, though. She opened the oven door and slid the *melanzane alla parmigiana* inside.

After supper, and after Tess and Ginny had gone home, Flavia snuggled up in bed under their rose-pink quilt next to Lenny. During the evening they had all talked of other things, but half of Flavia's mind had remained settled on the past.

Now she recounted her earlier conversation with Tess to her husband.

"Bugger me," he said with characteristic candor. "She's just been left a house in Sicily, and she never said a word until now?"

"She hasn't told Ginny yet, that's why." Lenny's body was warm and comforting. It always had been. Flavia wondered what would have become of her if she hadn't met Lenny. He had always loved her, despite everything.

"Why hasn't she told her?"

"I don't know." Perhaps Tess had inherited her mother's secretive streak. Flavia shivered and felt Lenny's embrace tighten. At seventy-nine he was still a fit and healthy man— thank God. "Perhaps she is waiting for the right time," she said.

"Like you?" It was the softest of murmurs, but Flavia recognized the words almost before they were out of his mouth.

"I have had my reasons," she said.

"And now?"

Flavia nestled closer into his shoulder. He was so comfortable; there was a place that felt snug and just right. And Lenny knew her so well. He had recognized instinctively that something had changed.

"She is going there," she said. "I cannot stop her."

Lenny was stroking her hair. It was snow white now of course, not almost black, as it had once been. "It doesn't hold the same darkness for her as it does for you, poppet," he said. "It's your past, not Tessie's. She just wants to see the place where you grew up. That's normal enough."

Flavia sighed. Put simply, that much was true. But something else was true. A place could hold you, it could change you, it could exert an influence on you. And the secrets of Sicily went back a long way. Ah, well . . . She was old. What did she know?

"What are you so frightened of?" Lenny persevered. "What on earth do you think could happen to her, my love?"

"I don't know." Flavia forced a laugh, though it sounded a touch hysterical.

"Are you frightened for her?" Lenny's touch on her hair was soothing. She felt herself relax, felt her mind drift. "Or for yourself?"

And just before she slipped into sleep, she realized the truth of his words. *For herself* . . . If she was going to do anything, she would have to do it soon. She was eighty-two years old. How long did she have left? She had to face it. Tess was going to Sicily. It was time.

CHAPTER 4

GINNY HAD FALLEN IN LUST WITH HER HAIRDRESSER. She'd even been sneaking in to have her bangs done for free between scheduled haircuts. She watched him in the mirror as he lifted a strand of her dark hair and frowned.

"What?" she asked. He didn't pluck his eyebrows, did he? She wouldn't be surprised. They were perfect crescent moons.

"Have you been deep-conditioning, like I said?" He rolled his eyes as he rubbed the lock of hair between his thumb and forefinger, and she giggled.

He had wicked eyes. Wicked as in evil, that was. Almost navy. And almost-black hair. His fingernails, now strumming through her long crowning glory, were painted metallic green. It was such an awful waste that he was gay. All the best-looking boys were gay—it was a known fact. She and her best friend Becca were into the same style. They liked boys with dark hair and long bangs who wore vampy eyeliner, slightly smudged. And they liked boys who were tall.

Ginny was six feet in her sneakers, Becca six feet two. This was no laughing matter. Until recently, Ginny had hunched her shoulders and worn flats. But since she'd discovered Becca at college, high heels were the way to go— the spikier the better. Together, the two of them were a superior race. Warriors. Amazons.

"Sounds cool," said Ginny. Ben was telling her about the night out he'd had at Barney's on Friday. She felt a honey shiver every time he touched her hair.

At times like these, Ginny could almost forget about the Ball. Almost, but not quite. It was rolled up very tightly and was lodged below her throat and above her breastbone. Like matting. She wasn't sure how long it had been there— maybe a year. Sometimes it seemed to shrink a little until it resembled indigestion, and she almost thought a couple of antacid tablets might take care of it. But other times it grew, rolling around inside her as if gathering moss or momentum, until she could hardly talk and barely breathe. That's when it got scary.

She hadn't told her mother about the Ball. She didn't want to be dragged to the doctor to talk about periods or sex or something equally embarrassing. Her mother would assume she had bulimia or was on drugs (two of her pet subjects) or was just crazy. Ginny would be examined, maybe put on happy pills. No, she didn't dare tell. If she closed her mind to it, really hard, it might roll away.

"D'you ever go there?" Ben asked. "To Barney's?"

"Nah. It's a bit chavvy." Becca was still only seventeen, and her fake ID wouldn't get her into a place that was managed by a friend of her dad's. And it *was* full of chavs. Boys in hoodies and overweight tattooed girls in micro-tops, white flesh bulging. No class. No style. Very, very sad.

"Yeah." Ben continued to chip and snip. "That's true."

It was a nice motion, Ginny thought to herself. Sweet.

She'd like to bump into Ben when she was out some-where. In fact she fantasized about it regularly. In the fan-tasy, she wore her black close-fitting minidress with the wide zip at the front that went from cleavage to hem and was perfect with her red stilettos. This was the dress that her mother described as "fun," her expression dubious as she no doubt angsted about the number of men who might try and unzip her daughter that night. In the fan-tasy, Ben was amazed at her transformation from gawky college kid to red-hot girl about town. *You are so fit,* he murmured, as he bent closer. *So hot . . .* Oh, yeah, and he wasn't gay.

Yesss . . . But Ginny couldn't go out very often right now, because she was supposed to be studying for her exams, and Mum was being *sooo* boring about it.

She shifted minutely in the seat. Her legs were bare this afternoon (they were her best feature, so she and Becca had decided on the high-cut denim shorts), and she didn't want to stick to the black leather chair. She'd spent an hour shaving her legs until her skin felt raw, so she was pretty confident there were no visible prickles. Her underarms felt suspiciously damp, though—she must remember not to lift her hands above her waist, just in case.

"So . . . Where else d'you go?" she asked. Even though he was a lost cause.

"Parties, I guess," he said. "Last week I broke up with my girlfriend. My friend Harley threw a rave to celebrate."

"Pardon me?" Surely she was hearing things? *Girl-friend . . .?* Ginny gripped the arms of her chair.

He repeated what he'd said.

"Cool." Inside, Ginny was squealing. He'd had a girl-friend. He—at least for the moment—wasn't gay. Unless he was in denial? This was amazing news. She couldn't wait to tell Becca. "High five," she muttered.

"Sorry?" He was absorbed in the bit next to her right ear. She hoped she didn't have any visible ear wax.

"Nothing." She tried not to stare at him, but when you were having your hair cut, you had to look at something, and there wasn't a lot of choice. Mirror. Hair products. Her own face. Ben. No contest. "Sorry about your girlfriend," she added.

"I'm not." He grinned at her.

Ginny pulled in her stomach. The Ball was still lurking. But at least she was thin. And according to her mother, she had inherited Nonna's "black Sicilian eyes." Which had to be sexy, didn't it? People were always telling her she should be a model, and they were probably right. She should leave college (though Mum would kill her), move to London, and sign up with some agency. How hard could it be?

But she wouldn't. Ginny tried to swallow and felt the usual lump in her throat. She wouldn't do it, 'cause she couldn't do that sort of thing, she just couldn't. And she'd have to go to uni, because, well . . . they all expected her to.

Snip, chip . . . Snip, chip . . . Ben was appraising her in the mirror. Ginny felt hot. What was wrong with her? She couldn't even talk to him now that he wasn't gay. His fingers were brushing against her neck, and goose bumps were traveling the full length of her body. Which was, anyone would have to admit, a long way. So was she hot or cold, or what? Jumping jackals—it must be what.

What was it like, she wondered for the zillionth time. What was it like to do it? To really do it with a boy? Most of her friends had got to at least second or third base; Becca all the way. But then—as Mum had pointed out—Becca was a bit *up front*. Ginny didn't really want to imagine Becca . . . But there again, sometimes when you looked at her, you couldn't help but imagine, which was probably what her mother meant. Becca wasn't thin, but on the plus side she had what Ginny wanted more than almost anything, more even than Ben's hands on her neck (though not more than the Ball to disappear). Boobs.

Ginny had a private theory that third base was more intimate than fourth, but she didn't want to voice this in case there was something else she didn't know about. After all, until you'd done both . . . Was she the only girl of her age in Pridehaven who hadn't done it? Sometimes she reckoned this was very possible. And it was her own fault. It was just that all the boys . . . Well, she didn't care for any of them. But she did want to be over this. She wanted, she supposed, to know it all.

"Maybe," Ben said, as if he could read her mind, "you and I should go out for drinks sometime."

Was he asking her out on a date? This gorgeous boy with hot lips who could make shimmering turquoise eyeliner look macho? Ginny tried to stay calm. But suddenly it felt as if all the best things in the world—those jeans in Topshop that she couldn't afford, chocolate biscuits from Marks & Spencer, Kentucky Fried Chicken in a bun, and cookie-dough ice cream (okay, mostly items of food, she realized that, but, hey, that was her problem and she'd deal with it)—had all happened in one fabulous wave at Hide Beach in full sunshine when she had no spots on her face, was wearing her zebra-print bikini, and the Ball had disappeared behind a far-off goal line . . .

"Yeah," she said. "Maybe we should."

He finished the jagged bit of her bangs. "Cool. Let's exchange numbers."

"Okay." Ginny watched as he fluffed it out with his fingers. "I'm having a party soon," she added. Her mother had only told her last night that she was going away. But how long did it take to plan a party? In this case, about twenty seconds.

"Will you be okay, Ginny?" her mother had asked. "It's only for a week. You'll have Nonna and Pops down the road. And Lisa next door. You could stay at Nonna's if you don't want to be on your own."

Hovering unicorns. How old did she think Ginny was? Ten? She loved having the house to herself, though it didn't happen often. Her problem would be that Nonna and Pops *were* down the road (although they were lovely, and Nonna was a great cook) and that Lisa *was* next door.

"Who're you going on holiday with?" she asked her mother innocently.

As intended, this brought on the guilt. "Oh, Ginny, I'd love to take you with me. Only you're in the middle of studying for your exams and . . ."

"It's okay." Ginny shrugged. "But I might have a few of the girls round one night. That's all right, isn't it? We'll probably have pizza and watch a movie." If her mother knew she was having a gathering, then if it got out of hand, or *when* it got out of hand, or *if/when* any of her minders noticed that it had got out of hand, then everything would be far easier to explain. She firmly subdued the twinge of remorse that popped up whenever she deceived her mother. Ginny loved her, of course she did. And she knew how much her mother had done for her, what she had sacrificed, all that stuff. But she also wanted to punish her sometimes. Just for . . . Well, for nothing really. That was just the way things were.

"Of course it is." Her mother looked vague. "Who . . . ?"

"And who did you say you're going with?" Ginny cut in.

"Oh, I'm not sure." Her mother looked evasive, which meant she was planning to go with Robin. "Maybe on my own." Which also meant she was planning to go with Robin. What a loser.

For some reason which Ginny couldn't quite fathom, her mother didn't realize that Ginny knew about Robin. She'd been introduced to him, yes, when Lisa and her husband, Mitch, were also around, in that careful way her mother had, as if Ginny might say, *Who the fuck are you?* instead of, *Hello,* thus ruining her mother's credibility forever. Tempting though it was, Ginny had been polite and answered all his predictable questions about college and going to uni without so much as a *Jesus Christ*. She could almost hear her mother's relief at his "What a sweet girl." Idiot.

What her mother wasn't aware of was that Ginny knew when Robin had been there in the afternoon. She knew when they'd gone to bed (Mum's bedroom curtains drawn, two wineglasses in the room), and when they'd done it on the sofa (cushions plumped, coffee table at a different angle), though Ginny didn't dwell on that one.

She'd also worked out that he was married, since they didn't hang out together at normal times and since her mother mostly looked unhappy or had pink spots on her cheeks, which meant she was about to meet him or had just received an illicit phone call. Ginny didn't like Robin, who was too smooth, too conventional, and too married, and she didn't like what he was doing to her mum. But she figured that when her mother wanted her advice, she'd ask for it.

"A party? Cool." Ben twirled the scissors. "I trust you'll be inviting your favorite stylist?"

"Consider it done," said Ginny. Bring it on. She could hardly wait. This could, she realized, be IT. Banish the Ball. Her First Sexual Experience. Way to Go . . .

Ben turned on the hairdryer and began to blow-dry. "Hot enough for you?" He raised one perfectly plucked eyebrow.

He wasn't joking. "Abso-bloody-lutely," said Ginny.

CHAPTER 5

Tess knocked briefly and went straight into Lisa's kitchen.

"Come round for coffee," Lisa had suggested to her on the phone ten minutes ago when Tess started on her news. "It'll be easier to talk. And I'm cooking supper."

Lisa, queen of multitasking, was wearing a green wrap-around pinafore apron decorated with red elephants, over black jeans and a T-shirt. She was dark, petite, and apparently unflappable. Tonight she was stirring the contents of a massive tureen of chili with one hand, directing the proceedings of various children—aged between seven and eleven—with the other. Tess watched and remembered her own experience with Ginny. No husband; an only child. Very different in so many ways.

"Tess." Lisa offered a cheek for a kiss. "Come and sit down."

Lisa's kitchen, with its spicy fragrance of chili, its reassuring lived-in-ness, and the warm glow from its ocher-painted walls, was a haven. When they had moved in next door to Tess's own slightly run-down end-of-row Victorian townhouse and she'd first been drawn into Lisa and Mitch's welcoming circle, Tess had hoped she could absorb and emulate this atmosphere that Lisa seemed to conjure up so effortlessly. An atmosphere of togetherness with Mitch and their children, of family and of home. She couldn't, of course. How could she when she didn't have a Mitch? Should she feel guilty about it? That she could give her daughter only so much; that she couldn't provide a father? But maybe what she had with Ginny—that special one-to-one relationship—was only possible because it was just the two of them against the world.

"I'll be with you in a tick," Lisa told her. "Just got to—" She addressed her offspring. "Get your books off the table now, you lot, if you want supper tonight."

Tess moved aside as three pairs of hands grabbed exercise books, pencil cases, and what have you, chattering all the while. *Have you got my black felt-tip pen? Where's my ruler? That's my eraser, Android. Don't call him Android* (that was Lisa). She shot Tess an apologetic smile. They were like a volcano in full flow. *Volcano* . . . Tess leaned back in her chair. She and Robin could visit Etna. And Palermo. Old temples, cathedrals, deserted sandy bays . . . She felt a brief lurch of self-reproach. Could she just take off for a week and leave her daughter here alone? Should she . . . ?

Ginny's father—a free-thinking, guitar-strumming surfer dude with long limbs and eyes as blue as the swimming pool where he worked as a lifeguard, had stuck around for the first six months of Tess's pregnancy before departing to Australia. He had asked Tess to go with him—he couldn't stand another English winter, he said. But for Tess, the timing was crucial. She was only twelve weeks away from bringing a child into the world. Given the choice of deserting his lover or facing that English winter, David had chosen desertion. It hadn't boded well for the future.

And now her daughter was growing up rather quickly and rather scarily. Because there were, weren't there, so many difficult decisions ahead, so many ways to go wrong. And Ginny was also growing, she supposed, away from her. She watched Lisa's children as they clustered around their mother. *Don't grow too far . . .*

"I'm busy, Freddie," Lisa was saying to her oldest. "Go and do your homework in the other room, or watch a DVD before dinner and we'll do it later."

"You always say that," Freddie grumbled, but he grinned at Tess, claimed an orange from the fruit bowl on the table, and departed cheerfully enough.

"And make sure it's something suitable for the others," Lisa added, shooing her two girls away with him. "I want to talk to Tess."

Tess grinned. She was so hyped up, she could burst. She was a woman of property. In Sicily. And she was going there—with Robin.

Lisa put a glass down in front of her.

"Thanks." Coffee had metamorphosed into red wine, but Tess wasn't complaining.

"I've moved on." Lisa topped up her own glass and chucked another generous measure into the pot of chili. "Cheers." She lifted the bottle. "And congratulations."

"Thanks." Though what had she done? Just belonged to the right family, she supposed.

"Tell me everything," Lisa commanded.

So she did. She had googled the area of Cetaria and discovered that it was perfect for diving. It was close to a national park, now designated a conservation area and blessed with beaches of rock, white sand, and clear, aquamarine water. Volcanic eruption and earthquakes over the years had produced caves with stalactites and freshwater springs, and the marine life was apparently spectacular. Tess couldn't believe her luck. She had always loved the sea. Her parents had bought her first pair of goggles when she was only seven years old. She'd spend hours dipping her head under the waves, squinting to make out the contours of the seabed. Underwater, all colors seemed more vivid, more real; fronds of plants and seaweed danced to the tune of the current; tiny fish slivered across her vision like streaks of oil. Tess was mesmerized by this Other World. Light, fluid, and mysterious.

As she grew up, she'd gone snorkeling on holidays abroad, wanting to go deeper, to see more. Then last year she'd spotted a Professional Association of Diving Instructors open-water course advertised in the surf shop in Pridehaven. It had been a year to the day since she'd started seeing Robin. To celebrate, they'd planned a romantic dinner at a restaurant a safe fifteen miles out of town. (*"I know it's hard, sweetie, but do we really want to cause Helen unnecessary pain?"*) And he had let her down— canceled, with only an hour's notice. It hadn't been the first time, and it wouldn't be the last. "I'll make it up to you, Tess," he'd said. But she had thought then. *I have to do something for me.*

She'd scribbled down the number of the diving course. *You never know . . .*

The course turned out to be just what she needed. It began by making them familiar with the equipment— the wet suit, mask, tank, and weight belt—then taught the safety procedures: how to surface, how to use sign language underwater, and eventually how to transfer these skills to the real-life environment of the sea. Tess was hooked. She had taken more courses, eventually qualifying as an advanced diver.

"What will you do with it, though, sweetie?" Robin had asked her, as if everything in life had to have a practical purpose.

"Enjoy it," she said. "Go on diving holidays alone. Live my life."

He'd shut up then—well, what could he say? He wasn't offering her everything she needed. She had to look elsewhere, and why not? Why should you be dependent on one man for your happiness, your *raison d'être*? She'd learned that lesson when David left for Australia. No one would do that to her again.

But this wasn't a diving holiday. This was a journey for Tess—to see where her mother had grown up, maybe even to find out why she had left and never gone back. Sicily. The Secret Place. To see the house that had somehow miraculously dropped in her lap at what seemed now to be a perfect moment. What would it be like? And what would she do with it?

But leaving Ginny wasn't her only reservation. There was Muma, too, who minded terribly, she knew. What little her mother had said about growing up in Sicily over the years had dropped from her lips in unexplained fragments, tantalizing morsels that were pure temptation for Tess—just like the food in her mother's kitchen. Why hadn't Muma ever wanted to visit the place and people of her childhood? Tess had just about given up trying to find out. Her mother was too stubborn for words.

"And Robin says he'll go with you?" Lisa put in.

"We've booked the flights." Tess was so relieved she could say this,

"Good," said Lisa, sounding worried.

"You don't approve?" Lisa had met Robin for drinks at Tess's on a few occasions, and she had pronounced him charming. To her friend's credit, she didn't judge Tess—at least nowhere near as harshly as Tess judged herself. Tess had never seen herself as the sort of woman to have an affair with another woman's husband. Most of the time she managed not to think about the ghostly Helen, or when she did, she remembered the things Robin said when he complained about her. He only stayed with her for the sake of the children, of course.

"It's not that." Lisa took a slug of her wine.

"What then?"

Lisa threw her a glance over her shoulder and wiped her hands distractedly on the elephant apron. "I just want you to get what you deserve," she said. "A good relationship— with a special man."

"And Robin isn't special enough?" Tess said defensively, although part of her knew what Lisa meant.

"A man who's available," Lisa said. "One who can give you the whole works."

Tess raised an eyebrow. She knew what was coming. And she always tried not to mind.

"Love, security, commitment. You know."

"Yes, I know." The things that Tess tried to pretend— especially when she woke up at four in the morning, alone—that she didn't long for.

"But . . ." Lisa was kind and already trying to backtrack. "At least this time—"

"I can't wait to go away with him," Tess said in a rush. "And to Sicily . . . It means so much to me, Lisa."

"I know, love." Lisa came over, put an arm around Tess's shoulders. "Only . . ." She sighed.

"What?" Lisa was her best friend. But sometimes she didn't want to hear the truth. Sometimes she wished Lisa could . . . well, just lie a little.

"Only why such an about-turn when he's said he can't go away with you before? What's changed?"

Her voice was mild enough, but when Tess looked up, she was surprised to notice her deep frown. Even Lisa, then, couldn't understand. It wasn't that Robin was treating her badly; it really wasn't. It was that basically he was a nice man, and he couldn't bear to hurt them—his children, his wife of twenty years. Who could blame him for that? It wasn't as if he'd intended to fall in love with Tess.

She was about to say some of this, when the back door opened and Mitch came in looking crumpled and weary. "What's this?" He threw his briefcase onto the nearest chair and loosened his tie. "Two beautiful women here to greet me?" He kissed them both. "I hope you're staying to dinner," he said to Tess.

As if in reply, her cell bleeped. "Ginny probably," she said, pulling it out of her bag. "And I'd love to—I've seen what went into the chili. But I can't. I've got a casserole in the slow cooker at home."

But it was a message from Robin, not Ginny. *Sweetie. Can we meet for a quick drink? Your place or the Black Rabbit?*

Tess felt the shiver of anticipation. She really should get back home. But . . . Supper was already prepared and cooking. There was plenty of time. Would a quick drink at the Black Rabbit (ten minutes out of town, the kind of place none of her friends—or, more to the point, Helen and Robin's friends—would go) do any harm?

"Robin?" Lisa must have caught her expression.

Tess nodded. Swiftly, she texted back, *OK, C U at the B R in 15 minutes.*

Lisa was still watching her as Tess tossed the phone back in her bag, pretending a casualness that she didn't feel. "Take care, love," she said.

CHAPTER 6

BACK AT HOME, TESS FOLLOWED THE SOUND OF VAM-pire Weekend to where the music was loudest—Jack's room, so called because an orange-and-yellow-striped giraffe five feet tall and made of raffia, named Jack, was in residence there. Ginny was stretched out full-length on the sofa, studying. Or something.

"I'm just popping out again," Tess shouted. "Be back in an hour, max."

Ginny nodded in time to the music. "Go for it, babycakes."

Tess nodded. She would.

In the car, driving toward the riverside pub, she found herself wondering what Lisa had meant when she said . . . *What's changed?* Nothing had—had it? Unless Robin had finally realized that he had to give something more to their relationship in order to keep it alive.

It was just after seven when she drove into the parking lot and did a rapid inspection of the cars there, just in case. No one she knew—and no Robin. The life of the mistress— you always have to drive yourself, and you do a lot of wait- ing. She sighed. There was an upside—though it was easy to forget this sometimes. Life with Robin was exciting. Sex was exciting. She still had her freedom; she could be as selfish as she wanted to be—most of the time. She didn't have to cook or clean for him. When he saw her, it was because he truly wanted to see her. He was generous, he was kind, and he made her laugh. So . . . ? She checked the mirror and saw the brightness in her eyes, felt the lurch of anticipation in the pit of her stomach. Why did she long for it to change?

"She's arranged a weekend at her parents'," Robin said. "I started to tell her—about going away . . ."He had arrived five minutes after Tess, looking rushed and unhappy. Kissed her, then got straight to the point. Before he spoke, she knew already.

"And?" Tess felt cold inside. Couldn't a weekend with Helen's parents be put off till another time? She wished she'd ordered a large glass. She was driving, but right now she didn't care. What story had he planned to tell Helen, she wondered. A business trip? A jolly with a few well-chosen lads who wouldn't give away his secret?

"She thought it would be a nice surprise." He ran his hands through his hair. He was looking more ruffled than she'd ever seen him.

"So?" He was about to cancel Sicily for a weekend at Hel- en's parents? It didn't make sense.

"She's booked a meal out. Theater tickets. All arranged." He spread his hands and frowned deeply. "It'll mess every- thing up if I'm not there."

And Sicily wouldn't be messed up if he wasn't there? Tess took a breath, realized she was gripping her wineglass so tightly she was in danger of snapping the slender stem. She put it down. "I've booked our flights." God, she sounded calm.

"I know." For the first time, he lowered his gaze. "But I can't get out of this, Tess. It's not only Helen—it's her parents, too."

"Why can't you go some other weekend?" Tess took another gulp of wine. Wondered if some women were born to be mistresses and some to be wives. "Restaurant and theater bookings can be canceled. It's hardly the end of the world." To her own ears she sounded cool. She had begun to separate herself from him, she realized. Already. She was creating distance to decrease hurt, because that was how it worked. And she wouldn't plead. She had told herself from the start that she would not be a demanding, whining mistress, always wanting more (though she did). She would be sexy and fun and take what he was willing to give (which was no longer enough). "Why should it matter when you go?"

He wouldn't look at her. "You don't know Helen's parents."

Tess shrugged. "What? Do they have some sort of power over you or something?"

She'd said it flippantly, bitterly even, but immediately realized she'd hit a raw nerve. He sighed, took a long swallow of his beer—only a half pint, she'd noted; clearly it was indeed a quick drink on his agenda.

"It's not just Helen . . . I mean that's part of it. But it's the money, too," he said.

"Money?" Tess felt the hairs on the back of her neck prickle. They at least knew that she was about to hear something she wouldn't like. "What money?"

"Well, you know they're loaded, sweetie." This time he smoothed his hair down. He was so much the clean-shaven, neat-suited businessman . . . Usually it made her laugh—they were such opposites. But today it just made her sad. Because it was true. They were such opposites. How had she hoped to make them fit?

"No." Why would she? And what did his in-laws' financial status have to do with anything? Tess didn't like the way this was going.

"Well they are. Very much so."

Was she missing something here? Tess fought the urge to scream—loudly. "But . . ." She was confused. "Surely you and Helen are financially independent?" He had a job, didn't he? He had a large house (she'd driven past it several times, couldn't resist seeing where he spent so much of his time without her), a nice car. He wasn't an avaricious man—was he? He wasn't money grabbing. Well, was he?

He laughed without humor. "Who is financially independent these days?"

Tess stared at him. She realized that in their time together they had rarely talked of money, because there was no need. They had no bonding bedrock of joint finances and practical concerns. If they went out to dinner, he always insisted on paying. She cooked for him and gave him drinks at home. Other than that, was else was there? Presents given from one lover to another . . . ? Money had never been an issue. Why would it be? The disappointment was eating into her now. Robin wasn't coming to Sicily. He had let her down again. He would never be around for her when she needed him. Or even when she didn't need him, but simply wanted him.

"You have a mortgage, don't you, sweetie?" he asked. He had never asked her that before.

"A small one, yes." Her parents had helped her get on the property ladder when Ginny was born, and she still owed some on the house. It was a bit run down and not in the best area of town, but it was comfortable, it had character, and it was hers. But for God's sake—why were they talking about mortgages?

"Well, I'm pretty tied into Helen's folks," he said. "She likes to live well. And there's no way I could afford our lifestyle on my salary."

"I see." She was beginning to. This explained why Helen didn't work. And other things besides. "So when they click their fingers, you have to jump."

"It's not quite like that." He grabbed her hand. "But I do have to be careful."

She looked down at his neat white cuffs, at his skin where the dark hair curled from under his shirt. She pulled her hand away. "It's all right," she said. Though it wasn't. "I understand."

"Tess . . ." "I understand your priorities. You've made the whole thing perfectly clear."

"Tess." His voice was low and urgent. Usually she liked it that way, but not now. "Don't you know I'd give anything to come with you? If it was possible—"

"It is." Tess couldn't believe how calm she felt. How detached. "Or at least it was." She stood up. "But you've made your decision." And she had too much pride to try to make him change his mind.

He stood up, too. Took her arm. "When you come back . . . ," he began.

Tess looked at him straight. "No," she said.

"We'll talk."

Tess said nothing.

"I'll make it up to you, sweetie."

Once again, she pulled away. "Good-bye, Robin." Walked out of the pub—not too fast, not too slow. She was worth more than that, wasn't she? She got into the car. Started the engine. She wouldn't cry. Damn him . . . Why should she cry? You cried when you lost something, didn't you? But he'd never been hers to lose, had he? And he sure as hell wasn't now.

CHAPTER 7

FLAVIA DRIED HER HANDS ON THE DISHTOWEL AND walked slowly from her kitchen through the back door into the garden. It was just past midday, and the sun was warm on her bare arms. It would be warmer, though, in Sicily, she thought, pausing by the herb patch, where the mint was already running riot—as it did every year. Every year she meant to uproot it, cage it within the confines of a pot, but every year she couldn't quite bring herself to do it. Nature had destined it to be wild and free—who was she to demand otherwise?

She checked her watch. Tess would be on her way. The plane would be flying over France by now. What would her daughter be thinking as she looked out of the window to the cloud below? Was she excited—or wary of what might lie ahead?

From the pocket of her apron, Flavia drew a notebook and a pen. She untied the apron and slipped it off, folded it neatly, and placed it on the wooden patio table. Lenny had gone out—he was meeting one of his old friends for lunch. So she had the house and garden to herself. She looked around her in satisfaction. Their garden was small—but colorful and well maintained; Lenny saw to that. It was strange that gardens were considered so vital in England, where it was so gray—though she had grown used to the climate over the years, weather being the least of her worries. Still . . . she settled herself into her chair. She missed the dense blue of a Sicilian sky. Missed the sweet summer heat, though she often used to curse it.

"I'll be thinking of you," Flavia had told Tess before she left. And of Sicily.

She sat down and opened the notebook. *You have to tell the story in order to let it go.* Well, she was going to give it a try. She would try to write what she couldn't say. Tell the story about the girl called Flavia who seemed now so distant, so lost. It was time.

My Darling Tess, she wrote. Where to start? From the beginning, she supposed. From that day when it had happened, when it had all begun.

It was July. And hot, very hot. She remembered the heat of the sun on her back, burning into her neck as she stooped, sticking the thin white blouse to her skin. She remembered pushing back her thick hair with the back of her hand, the hand stained from the tomatoes . . .

July 1943

Flavia had woken this morning feeling that something had happened. When she got out of bed and peered out of the window, everything outside was pretending to be just the same. The rose of dawn was already darkening into something sensual and strong. But she knew, just knew. She had woken in the night—just once—and been aware, through the blackness, of sound: a crash not far away. And lights—searchlights maybe—that seemed to rip through the night sky.

Out in the field later that morning she squatted to pick the ripe tomatoes from the next plant in the row. Sweet Madonna, she thought. She had only just started picking, and already her back was aching and her fingers were green. Another July, another harvest: tomatoes and olives, apples and plums. Pick, pick, pick, all day long, so Mama could pulverize and strain, sterilize and bottle, and make her tomato sauce ("the most important domestic task of the year, child"), her jam, her olive oil, her . . . Eugh! Flavia pushed back her hair, which was heavy and thick and making her sweat even more. She wanted to scream . . .

Enough. She straightened. Over the land for as far as she could see, over the green-and-rust mountainous plains beaded with pines and cypress trees, olive groves, vineyards, and the occasional limestone hut hung a haze of heat. It had a color—purple gray—and it had a sound—hummm. She stood hand on hip and called it out loud, back to the land scape. "Hummm." The drone of the insects; a never-ending buzzing; enough to drive you mad.

There was not a cloud in the sky, and all she could smell was the harsh, dry greenness of tomato. There was no sign that anything had changed last night.

"Hey!"

Flavia flinched.

"You are in the land of the daydream," her sister Maria threw across at her. "Again!" She clicked her tongue in that

*superior older-sister way she had perfected over the years and
pointed at Flavia's half-empty basket. "Come on. Hurry!"*

"Come on, hurry," *Flavia muttered under her breath.
Another harvest, another year of working and waiting. And
what was she waiting for? Some young man from the village
to lay claim to her?*

*She moved on to the next plant. Carelessly plucked the fruit
from the bristly stems. Like an old man's beard, she thought.
Like old Luciano, who looked after the goats up on the mountain slopes. The dry, sun-sticky tomato scent had sunk into
her nostrils, her throat, her belly.*

*There weren't more than two or three to choose from. Young
men, that was. Not that she would be allowed to choose. And
who would choose her, Mama demanded, "if you do not learn
to curb your tongue, my daughter." She was too independent,
too headstrong. "Save your fire," Mama said. For after you are
married, she meant. For when—as the matriarch—you take
control. Sweet Jesus . . . Unaware, her fingers gripped the fruit
too tightly and she felt the skin burst, the pulp ooze into her
fingers. She lifted her fingers to her mouth and sucked, threw
the skin to the dusty ground.*

"Tch!" *Maria didn't miss a trick.*

*Flavia pouted back at her, moved to the next plant with
a careless flounce of her shoulders. She knew who her sister
wanted. Leonardo Rossi. She knew because she understood
the language of the eyes—perceptible only to a self-trained
observer like Flavia—which passed between the two of them
in church. Because where else was there? It was the only place
you would see anyone. And even then the gaze must be down-
cast; you must be modest above all things. Pah!*

*She stretched. She was only seventeen; her back and shoul-
ders were still young and supple, but she could see what made*

the old women so gray faced, bent, and worn. Picking toma-
toes for one . . .

She allowed her gaze to rest on the dusky-pink Villa
Sirena, which stood high above the ancient walled square of
the baglio *and the bay—the villa owned by Edward Wester-*
man, the eccentric English poet who also owned the olive trees
that they harvested, the tomato plants that her mother and
father tended, even the stone cottage that they lived in, situ-
ated just behind the villa he had built nine years ago when
he arrived in Sicily. Back then, Flavia was just a child. Back
then, this war was far away, not dreamed of. Now, Palermo—
the most conquered city in the world, some said—had been
entered by Germans and Americans both. It had been "con-
quered," and yet it welcomed its conquerors with open arms
and wholesale prostitution, she had heard. Truth was, Flavia
didn't know what to think. She wasn't even sure whose side
they were on. Once again she pushed the hair from her brow,
not caring about the stains on her hands. What did it matter?
Who would see?

Flavia's family looked after Villa Sirena, the land, and
Signor Westerman as well. It had been that way since 1935,
when, only twenty-one years old himself, he had first turned
up with an inheritance and employed her father to help him
build the villa. Papa had been grateful for the work—he'd
said that often enough—and Signor Westerman, though
young, was a good employer. So much so that Flavia's mother
had applied for the position of cook and housekeeper and
obtained it, too. Along with a full-time job as caretaker for
Papa, who'd had nothing ("nothing, child") before Signor
Westerman came along. Papa, whose children "would have
eaten dirt just like so many others in the village, who might
have died on the streets like them, if not for the kindness of

l'inglese, *Signor Westerman. Madonna be praised." Flavia had heard her father's words so often. "He has saved us. He would not let us starve."*

Indeed, Signor Westerman had always been kind to her, and sometimes, when she was supposed to be helping Mama, he had called her to him, told her stories about England, and read her poetry. He read it out loud in a language unfamiliar to her, but she could hear the way the words danced, and she could close her eyes and let herself dream.

He spoke about England in a mixture of English and Italian that was also hard to understand. But she could understand enough to see that life was different there, so different that it was impossible to imagine. But Flavia did imagine. Where girls went to dances—such dances—and talked freely and walked out alone, or with men even. And lived. Sweet Madonna, *how they lived.*

Maria, she noted, was almost at the end of her row. "Come on, Flavia. You are so slow," *she shouted.*

Flavia's mind wouldn't rest. What had happened last night? What was going on? Why the lights? The noises? Something was afoot. She'd seen Papa meeting with the other men from the village early this morning at Bar Piccolo in the piazza and had noted the earnest faces, shaking heads, serious whispers, and large quantities of espresso being consumed. Despite loitering outside, Flavia had found out nothing—although she suspected it was to do with this war; everything was to do with this war. It did nothing for them, mind (so Papa said). Just took away and killed their young men. Flavia sighed. So there would be even fewer to choose from.

She let her fingertips trail across the tight, swollen skins of the tomatoes. The fruit had absorbed so much sun, it seemed pregnant with it. Now the war had taken away Signor

Westerman, too. It was, everyone said, too dangerous to stay in Sicily; these were turbulent times. Who could predict the actions of Hitler and of Mussolini? And who even knew which were worst—the Fascists or the Nazis? Swiftly, Flavia crossed herself.

The Signor had returned to England—until the war was over. Who knew when he would be able to return to claim his beautiful villa, his land, his olive groves?

And in the meantime . . . Flavia watched Maria: bending, picking, bending, picking . . . there was a smooth rhythm to her sister's movements. Maria was content, she realized, with a jolt of surprise and frustration. How could she be, when so much was uncertain, when Leonardo was God knows where and their family had no livelihood—and perhaps no future—with Signor Westerman away? When they could be killed, victims of a senseless war, at any moment? Was her sister mad?

Maria didn't look mad; rather as if she knew something Flavia did not. Flavia sighed. Perhaps it was the centuries of destruction by earthquake or volcano, or of being conquered by some other marauding tribe, that made Sicilians so sanguine, so content with their lot. Was it a coincidence that in Sicilian, there was no future tense? They were a people who could only look back—never forward with hope.

Flavia turned her face up to the hot sun. No future? It was said that in Palermo there were Fascist slogans in windows— Better a day like a lion than a hundred years like a sheep. But Papa said such words were wasted on Sicilians. They knew about honor—none better. But what did they care about the war? It was not their war. They cared more about survival. Besides, her family liked the English and were loyal to Signor Westerman, who had given them so much. They had hidden all Signor Westerman's things from the house—at least everything of value. Including il tesoro, *which was—she had heard Papa telling Santina's father, when he didn't know she was behind the curtain listening—in a place where no one would ever find it, no one would even dream to look.*

Flavia shrugged. So what? What was it to her—all this intrigue, all the whispering about enemies and valuables that must be kept hidden?

"Let me look." Maria was at her side now, inspecting her basket. What would she do now that her boy had left the village—not to go to war but to hide in the mountains, so people said. Some called them deserters—those men sleeping in local cottages and caves, living off the profit from black-market grain and stolen cattle. Most didn't blame them. But what if he didn't come back?

And when the war ended? What then? Even if you were chosen by any of the young men who had survived the war, what sort of life would be yours? A life like Mama's—if you were lucky. Cooking, cleaning, having babies. Drudgery. Confined to the house forevermore. Apart from church and the market, that was. Eugh . . .

"Your mind is always in another world," Maria scolded. "What is wrong with you? This is our food, our life."

Flavia swung her basket. Our food. Our life. *Was it so wrong to want more . . . ?*

After lunch, Flavia couldn't settle to her siesta. The white light of the early afternoon bore into her eyes and temples as she tossed restlessly on her bed. What was it? Was it just the heat of July? Or . . . ? She got up, splashed cold water on her face, and went downstairs. All was quiet. The world was sleeping, but it was the kind of sleep that came before a storm.

Shielding her eyes from the sun, she stepped past the limp netting and out of the door. The earth of the kitchen garden was dry and hard, but the fava beans, artichokes, and peas were all doing well—Mama made sure of that. While they had land, they would eat. And the harvest would provide seeds for the year to come.

For a moment she hesitated, intending to move toward the sea, where she might step perhaps into the cooling water but drawn instead in the other direction, toward the distant fields and olive groves on the lower mountain slopes. She squinted into the distance. For a moment she thought she saw something—the reflection of light on metal in the field of tawny wheat between the olive groves. She waited, motionless, beads of sweat collecting at the top of her spine and on her brow. Sì. There it was again. A flash, like a signal, a sign.

Flavia spun on her heels, ran back into the kitchen to fetch a flask of water, and in moments was out again. She looked around. There was no one in sight, everyone was inside, trying to escape this oppressive heat. A lizard basked for a moment on the bare white stone rock, then flashed like quicksilver away.

She walked down the path toward the first olive grove. She walked through the trees, shimmering gray and silver in the sun, their gnarled branches now heavy with olives. The earth beneath them, once red, had dried to a pale dusty salmon. The land was throbbing, and mercilessly the cicadas screamed. In the distance the horizon was like liquid violet to her eyes.

At the end of the first grove, Flavia paused under a tree to take a drink from the flask. It tasted like nectar, cool and sweet. She kept looking around her, beyond the field of honey-colored wheat framed by wild poppies and clover that seemed to be vibrating in the heat of the afternoon. There it was again, the flash of light. Just beyond the ridge. Within reach.

Once again Flavia set off across the field and the next olive grove. By the time she got to the ridge, she was gasping for breath and her heart was hammering. She stood for a moment, motionless. The air was heavy and still, so still.

She stepped forward, looked down, and there it was. A plane, half broken, with wreckage all around. "O dio Beddramadre," she said, hand over her mouth. O Holy Mother of God . . . And not twenty meters away, white-faced, holding his leg, and in obvious pain, lay a man; a foreigner. An airman. "O dio Beddramadre . . ."

Flavia put down her pen. She was as exhausted as if she had been through a mangle. And still it felt not enough. She had been mistaken; she could see that now. But there was time to redress the balance, she felt. She could give her daughter something more from her homeland. And then she realized what it must be.

CHAPTER 8

TESS COLLECTED THE RENTAL CAR FROM THE PALermo Airport and drove to Cetaria, all thoughts of Robin boxed at the back of her mind. Right now she was keeping the lid on. She didn't need him. She wouldn't let herself. And Sicily, she could see, would be the ideal distraction. It was hard to tear her gaze from the green-gray mountain slopes, the rusty earth studded by pine and birch trees on one side, and the glimpses of a late sun shimmering over an azure sea to the other. But she had to concentrate on the road. This was Sicily, this was a rental car, and she must remember to drive on the right.

It was early evening and still light when she saw the village an hour later, a cluster of terraced streets huddled below her beside the sea. The road to Cetaria wound down steeply from a belvedere at the top. She drove past a chapel with an apricot stuccoed facade, and before she could get her bearings, the streets had wrapped themselves around her. Tall, shuttered buildings sandwiched the cobbles on either side, and narrow stone steps descended to the level below—occasionally opening out into a piazza or a brief flash-view of the sea. It was a maze.

She parked in a side street, got out, and stretched. It was warm, she felt like a stroll, and it would be far easier to find the house she was looking for on foot. She'd been told to collect the key from a Signora Santina Sciarra who lived in via Dogali, number fifteen, and who was a friend of the family. Which family, she wondered. Hers? Was this someone who had known her mother?

"Is the villa very dilapidated?" she had asked the solicitor dealing with Edward Westerman's will on the phone before she came here. She was determined to be practical. What had promised to be an adventure with Robin might prove daunting when faced with it alone. But he had assured her it was just old, tired, and in need of some TLC. Old and tired, Tess could cope with. Crumbling ceilings and leaking pipes, she could not. She was trying to be strong. But her relationship with Robin had reached a cliff edge. And she wasn't sure whether or not to jump.

Leaving her bags in the car, she walked to the corner. It was dinnertime. She could smell the fragrances of tomatoes, herbs, and roasting meat drifting through open windows, down from balconies and terraces. In the next street, she saw an old woman dressed in black, sweeping her front step, her back bent.

"*Scusi,*" Tess said. Was that right?

The woman peered up at her with black, inscrutable eyes. She did not speak.

"*Sera.* Er . . ." That was most of her Italian used up. And besides, Sicilian was a completely different language—one that her mother hadn't chosen to share with Tess when she was growing up. "Via Dogali?" She showed the woman the slip of paper she'd written the address on. Sicilians were bound to understand Italian; no doubt most of them spoke it to the tourists who regularly invaded their island.

The woman grabbed the slip of paper from her with brown knobbled fingers, peering and clicking her tongue. She was clutching a thick black shawl around her head, despite the warmth of the evening. She let loose a torrent of Sicilian, in which Tess thought she caught the name Santina.

"Yes," Tess said. "Santina. *Sì*." The woman placed a bony hand on Tess's arm and gripped. Hard. She was speaking very fast. Was she asking who Tess was? She thought so.

"I am Flavia's daughter," she said clearly. "Flavia. *Figlia*." Was that right?

Another torrent. The woman turned and beckoned. "*Sì, sì*," she muttered. "Come, come."

She hobbled quickly along the skinny street, her heavy black shoes clomping over the uneven cobbles. Tess scurried behind. How old was this woman? Seventy? Eighty? A hundred? It was impossible to tell. She was bent almost double, and her skin was lined, brown, and weathered by the sun.

They couldn't be far away from Santina's; nothing was far away. And this was where her mother had grown up. Tess felt a thrill of excitement. Had her mother walked down these same streets, smelled these same smells— delicious cooking, yes, but interlaced, she had to admit, with a more dubious smell of stale sewage, or rotting food, perhaps: a scent of decay. The steps of the houses they were passing were clean enough, but the walls were grimy, the paint peeling to reveal the underbellies of the houses themselves—the stone core. Had it been like this back then, she wondered. For Muma? Everyone probably knew everyone in this town. And their business. This woman had, no doubt, lived here all her life. She would know everything that Tess wanted to find out—if Tess could only talk to her . . .

They came to a road that descended steeply toward the sea. Tess caught sight of what looked like a small bay surrounded by rocks, a brightly colored fishing boat pulled up on the quay. But even as she craned to see more, another tall stone building obscured the view. The woman was still muttering to herself, and she caught the name again— Flavia—then *l'inglese*, then Maria and Santina. At one point her unlikely guide even crossed herself. What could her mother have done?

Tess nodded vaguely in response to her words. But her mind was in top gear. She couldn't wait to find out. And maybe Edward Westerman had wanted her to discover her mother's story, which was why he'd made coming here a condition of the bequest. Though . . . How would he know she hadn't been told the story already? She hurried to keep pace with her guide. Still. He wanted her at least to . . . she hesitated . . . *get involved* with the place. For some reason.

The old woman was still nodding and beckoning and scuttling over the cobbles like a black widow spider. Tess nodded back at her and smiled encouragingly—it was all she could do. There must be a puzzle; otherwise why would Muma not talk about those days? The puzzle was a part of her journey. And the past was here—in the gray cobbled streets and high shuttered houses. The past. Sicily, she was beginning to realize, was the kind of place that could haunt you.

They stopped outside a door with a rusty iron grille. Number fifteen. The paint was flaked and green. The woman knocked three times, still muttering.

Tess smiled weakly and waited.

After a few minutes, another old woman—also dressed in black, Tess noted—answered the door, cautiously, peering around first, before opening it a bit more. She nodded to Woman in Black number one, but her eyes widened when she saw Tess.

Tess smiled again and nodded energetically. It probably looked mad, but it seemed to be the way forward.

The two elderly women greeted each other warmly, carrying out a rapid conversation accompanied by much clicking of tongues, shaking of heads, and looking at Tess as if she were an interesting specimen in a zoo. Didn't they have English tourists here? Was Tess different—a homeowner, a potential new neighbor? Or was it because she was Flavia's daughter?

After a few more minutes of this, she began to grow exasperated. She had come so far, and she was so near. Dusk had crept up behind her, and the light was beginning to dim. She wanted to see her house, damn it. She didn't want to be standing here on some stranger's doorstep listening to endless prattle she didn't understand. "Please," she said.

They both looked at her; both stopped talking as if they'd been switched off at the mains.

"Do you have the key?" She addressed this to the second woman. "For Villa Sirena?" She made a gesture of turning a key in an imaginary lock. "Please? *Grazie*."

The second woman gripped her arm in much the same way as the first woman had done earlier. Then the other arm. She pulled Tess forward, and Tess, taken off balance by her surprising strength, was propelled into an unexpected embrace. She felt the woman's bristly chin as she kissed her resoundingly on both cheeks. Goodness.

"Santina," the woman said, pointing at herself.

"You have the key?" Tess asked, not willing to be deflected from the task in hand. The name meant nothing to her—why would it?

At this, Santina practically dragged her over the threshold into a dark, dingy hallway, painted blood red and covered in framed photographs and religious paraphernalia. Santina said her good-byes to Woman in Black number one and, maintaining a firm hold on Tess's arm, led her into the kitchen. This was dominated by an ancient stove, above which various iron cooking implements hung from hooks on the smoke-stained whitewashed wall. There was a small square window with a net curtain and an assortment of wooden chairs placed around a stained, pockmarked table in the center of the room.

"*Espresso*?" Santina demanded. "*Caffè? Biscottu?*"

Much as she was desperate to see the villa, Tess had the feeling that her hostess was not to be deflected from hospitality. And, besides, it had been a long time since lunch at Gatwick, she realized. An espresso might just hit the spot. "*Sì, grazie.*" She sank into the chair Santina had indicated. She was tired. She felt as if she'd been strung out with tension for days—since Robin's announcement that he couldn't come away with her, in fact. How was the weekend with Helen's parents going, she wondered. Where were they now? At dinner? At the theater? Anyway, something in this kitchen had just cut the rope. Her shoulders slumped, and she let herself relax. She was here now. She had made it.

Santina nodded, retreated to the kitchen doorway, and started shouting up the stairs. "Giovanni! Giovanni!"

Who would this be, Tess wondered. An aging husband, perhaps? Another face from Muma's past who would expect Tess to have at least heard of him?

But no. Two minutes later, a Sicilian man—probably in his late thirties, Tess guessed—entered the room. He wasn't tall, but even so, he seemed impressive as he paused in the doorway. Posed almost, she found herself thinking. His thick black brows beetled together when he saw Tess. He rattled out something to Santina, and she rattled back. Like a couple of old-fashioned trains hurtling down a track.

"You are Flavia's daughter?" he asked abruptly in English.

"Yes." It was beginning to sound like a TV series. Tess didn't know whether to be offended by his tone or relieved that here was someone she could communicate with at last. "I'm Tess. Tess Angel." She got up and held out her hand. "And you are . . . ?"

"Giovanni Sciarra." He said the words with some pride. He took her hand and raised it to his lips, eyeing her from under his dark lashes. "At your service."

Hmm. Tess wasn't sure about that. The last thing she needed right now was male attention—of any kind.

Santina poured water from a jug in the white enamel sink and scooped some coffee into a small metal percolator, which she placed on the stove. She hovered by Tess, beaming and nodding, before letting loose a stream of unintelligible words.

Giovanni smiled (a cruel smile, Tess decided, a bit like a
tiger who'd spotted a kill). "I must apologize," he said. "Your
visit—it is *una sorpresa*—a surprise. We thought Flavia's
daughter to be of a greater age."

Tess raised an eyebrow. "Sorry to disappoint you," she
said.

"No, no, you do not disappoint." His eyes twinkled.
"But . . ." He drew up a chair and mounted it by swinging
one muscular leg over, so that—weirdly—he was facing her
over the back slats. Tess tried not to giggle. His new position only fueled the tiger fantasy—only now the tiger was
behind the bars of a cage.

"My great-aunt Santina," he gestured toward the elderly
woman, "and your mother, Flavia, were childhood friends,"
he said. "As you must know."

Tess shook her head. She might as well come clean.
"Sorry," she said. "I didn't know that." She smiled at Santina, who smiled back.

"Ah, yes. She talks about it often," he went on. "They played
together as girls. The families . . . They were very close." He
made a gesture, the little fingers of each hand linked. She
noticed that he wore a gold signet ring initialed *GES*.

"Oh, I see." Hence the effusive greeting. Tess smiled
again at the old woman.

"So . . ." He shrugged. "My father was a good age when he
married my mama."

Ah. "Right . . ." At over forty, her mother had given birth
to Tess late in life—at least by Sicilian standards. Giovanni
would have expected Flavia's daughter to be a bit younger
than his father. But in fact Giovanni and Tess were of a similar age.

Santina was talking again. Giovanni cocked his head to one side as he listened to her, a slight frown on his handsome face. His skin was a dark olive, his eyes brown. Handsome, but maybe a little cold, she guessed.

"My aunt wishes to inquire after the health of Flavia, your mother?" he said, rather formally, when Santina was done.

Tess nodded. "She is well. *Grazie.*"

Santina seemed satisfied. For a moment a faraway look crept into her wrinkled dark eyes, and then she went over to the stove where the coffee was steaming and poured the thick black liquid into a small cream cup. She placed this in front of Tess and stood watching until she felt compelled to take a first sip.

"It's good," she said. And it was. "*Bene. Grazie.*" That had to be all her Italian used up. But at least if she could smile and nod and thank people, she wouldn't be thought impolite, just stupid perhaps.

Giovanni fetched a black jacket from a hook outside the kitchen door and pulled it on. "When you are ready, *Signurina,*" he said. "Or *signura*?" He looked pointedly at her left hand.

"I'm not married," said Tess. They certainly got quickly down to the nitty-gritty around here.

"*Bene,*" he said.

Bene?

"I will take you to Villa Sirena." He held out one hand, palm up, and looked expectantly at his aunt. Santina produced two keys from the pocket of her apron, one big, one small. She placed them reverentially on his palm.

His fingers closed around them, and he nodded. "*Allora, andiamo.*"

"Great." Tess swallowed the last of the coffee and got up. *"Grazie."*

Santina stepped forward to take Tess's hand, holding it as if she wanted to say something or as if she didn't want to let it go. Then Giovanni spoke once more, and she kissed Tess on both cheeks, squeezed her shoulders, and finally released her. But as Tess followed Giovanni Sciarra from the house, she was aware of the tiny woman in black watching them from the doorway. She seemed kind enough, though it was hard to believe her a contemporary of her mother's. Tess sighed. If only Muma had given her some clue about the people in this place. She didn't know who had been her friends, who her enemies. She had no idea whom to trust. But she wasn't in any kind of danger here, was she? She'd only come to look at a house. Her house.

Once alone with Giovanni, she felt a little self-conscious. "Is it far?" she asked. "Only, my bags are back there in the car . . ."

"No." He pointed down some steps, toward a piazza. It was almost dark now, but she could make out a stone archway and some benches. "It is down here, beyond the *baglio*. I will take you there and come back for your things."

Oh. "There's no need . . . ," she began, but he raised a hand to silence her. She followed him meekly down the steps. Here in Sicily, men clearly accepted their right to unquestioned authority. So perhaps she wouldn't challenge it. Not today anyhow.

"The *baglio*," he announced, as they went through the deep archway that sheltered a huge paneled timber door with iron bolts and a high fan window overgrown with vines. Two cacti sentries stood erect either side.

Even in the almost-dark, Tess could sense the beauty of the place, the history embedded in the large cobbles flattened by the tread of centuries, and the weathered, porticoed buildings. The *baglio* was an ancient walled square, part inside, part outside, a sort of courtyard, now lined by little shops, galleries, and a restaurant. An Arabic legacy, she assumed. She had read in her guidebook that Sicily—especially in the west—had many Arab influences.

They crossed the *baglio*, past a tall, elegant eucalyptus tree with dappled bark and past an old stone drinking fountain. Tess wanted to ask more questions, but she also wanted to get to their destination. She was itching to see the villa.

On the far side of the square, they passed some sort of craft studio. Tess stared in fascination: the window was full of glass, gemstones, and mosaics, lit up by tiny firefly lights that skirted the perimeter of the display. "What's this place?"

Giovanni barely glanced round, though his bearing seemed to stiffen. "Tourist stuff," he said dismissively. "How do you say? Crap. Do not bother your head with it."

"Really?" It didn't look like crap to Tess. It looked magical, like another world. And was it a case of miscommunication due to the language barrier, or was Giovanni Sciarra already telling her what to think? But she had no time to dwell on this; she had to practically run to keep up with him.

Beside the workshop, some steps descended toward a rocky beach and the sea. "It's beautiful," she murmured. The sky had darkened to indigo, the sea polished with the sheen of a full moon. Several rocks stood outlined against the sky.

Even Giovanni paused. "The finest view in Europe," he said, as if he were in some way responsible for it. "And it is yours."

For a moment she didn't understand what he meant. Then she looked up to where he was pointing. More steps—a spiral of them—led up to a building crouched on the cliff-top. A villa. 1930s style, as far as she could make out in the semidarkness. "Oh my God," she said. "This isn't . . . ?"

"Villa Sirena." He nodded. "Come."

Tess almost stopped breathing. Could this really belong to her?

She followed him to the top of the steps, where a black wrought iron gate was set into the high stone wall. It was marked *Privato*, and Tess watched as Giovanni unlocked it with the small key. The gate opened with a creak of rusty hinges, and she followed him through, under a swathe of foliage that had grown around it. They were at the side of the house, she realized, as they walked round to a wide expanse of pebbled terrace that led to the front door. Above the door was a fanlight, to the right an old unlit lamp, and above the fanlight and the stucco, she could see a motif built into the external rendering. But she couldn't make out what it was.

Giovanni brushed off a bit of flaky paint, inserted the big key, and opened the door with a flourish. "Villa Sirena," he said again.

But he blocked the doorway, and she detected a slight twist to his mouth.

Envy perhaps? For the first time, she wondered what sort of a welcome she might have in this place. She was after all, a stranger and a foreigner. They might consider she had no right to be here. And then there was her mother's story—whatever that might be . . . She straightened her back and stood tall.

"Did you lock your car?" he asked.

"Well, yes."

He held out his palm in much the same way as he had to his aunt. And like Santina, Tess groped in her pocket for the key and placed it there. She didn't remember the name of the street where she'd parked it, and he didn't ask. He just nodded, brought his heels together as if in a salute and was gone.

Tess took a deep breath. And stepped inside.

CHAPTER 9

TESS SLEPT SO SOUNDLY THAT WHEN SHE AWOKE, SHE didn't know for a moment where she was. Her mind flitted—to Robin, to Ginny, to her mother. And then she heard the silence, and she knew. She was in Villa Sirena, her suitcase opened and abandoned at the foot of the broad chestnut bed frame.

She climbed out, padded over to the big, wide window, where a large square of dimpled muslin fluttered in a faint breeze. The room was warm, the air muffled. She pushed the muslin aside and flung window and shutters open wide.

Wow . . . Giovanni had been right about the view. To her left, rocky crops, olive groves, and tamarisk decorated the mountainside. Small, wispy clouds curled in tendrils around the peaks, delicate and delicious against the pale-blue morning sky. A winding road led from mountains to village, the cluster of houses creating a jigsaw of bright faces, the ancient stone walls and archway of—what had he called it?—the *baglio* they'd walked through last night, and the steps leading down to the bay. And what a bay. In daylight it was even more beautiful.

Nestling in the bay, below the *baglio*, were some derelict buildings and maybe a boathouse with three big arches—because it led to the jetty. Rusty anchors were lined up like soldiers in front of painted and peeling walls the color of pale sand, and there were bars at the windows above stone troughs of white oleander. In front of the building stood a lone fig tree, its branches spread as in welcome.

The finger of the stone jetty stretched into the turquoise water. Tess shielded her eyes from the glare of the sun. Farther out to sea, a sequence of rock formations jutted beige and white, streaked with rusty tears. Not a soul was on the tiny beach; all she could hear was the lonely cry of a distant gull. This was her view, Tess reminded herself. Her view. For a moment, she thought of Robin. She felt a twinge of regret. And then. Dammit. He'd made his choice. She was here, that was what mattered. Alone, but here.

Tess had explored the villa briefly last night after texting Ginny to say she'd arrived safely, but she had been so tired, and the lights so dim, that she'd decided to wait till morning for a proper tour. Now, she realized that the house—her house—was on two floors, and built in a semicircle. The master bedroom, where she had slept, sat on the center of the arc—hence the great views. Tess went from room to room, making straight for the windows every time. From the front three bedrooms she could see the ocean; from the back, the fields and the mountains. There was only one bathroom, but it was a surprisingly modern one. Tess was ravenous, so she soon made her way down the winding staircase with the iron balustrade.

The kitchen was large and untidy, with a flagstone floor and a long oak farmhouse table in the center. Last night she'd noticed a general air of chaos: cupboards left open, their contents scattered around. Not ransacked exactly, more as if someone had been looking for something. Also on the table was a basket of bread and some wine, which she'd assumed to be a welcoming gift for her. But no. According to Giovanni, they'd been left by Santina for the spirits of the house. Right . . .

Giovanni had brought her car round to the front of the house and through the big wrought iron gates.

"You have electricity," he informed her. "And there is an electric water heater." He showed her this and the fuse box before bidding her goodnight.

But this morning she also found coffee, fresh rolls, fruit, and jam. Someone (Giovanni? Santina?) was looking after her—not just the spirits of her house.

She ate her breakfast at a weather-beaten wrought iron table on the terrace overlooking the bay. From here she could see a few people wandering through the *baglio* and the intriguing sight of the mosaicist's shop door flung open to the world.

So much to explore . . . Tess got to her feet and started to wander through the overgrown terraced garden. In the center was a small pond and fountain, while swathes of wild geranium, hot-pink bougainvillea, and lilac jasmine overflowed from big earthenware pots and trailed randomly over walls and steps. She looked back at the gorgeous pink villa. How could her mother ever have left?

Though . . . Tess moved toward the end of the garden, where, beyond, she could see fields of yellow and burnt red shimmering in the distance, and what was left of a stone

cottage on the other side of the wall. Was this the cottage
her mother had grown up in? It was so small . . . But everyone had been poor back then, she supposed, everyone apart
from the Edward Westermans of this world.

She found a broken gate and went through. The cottage was little more than a ruin. Still, she stood there for
a moment, thinking of her mother, the grandparents she'd
never met, her Aunt Maria, who had visited many years ago
but who had kept her distance from her niece, as if Tess
were some alien creature from another planet. Which was
how she must have seemed.

She spun on her heels, retraced her steps, and returned
to the villa. The living room was untidy; its stone fireplace
still held a basket of logs, some strewn on the terra-cotta
tiles of the hearth. There was a big, battered leather sofa
and two armchairs, and a bookcase half full of books, more
dusty volumes piled on the desk beside it. The dining room
looked as if it hadn't been eaten in for decades.

But all in all, things weren't too bad. The electrics
looked a bit questionable—there were wires poking out
of sockets and light fittings—the tap in the kitchen sink
was dripping, some broken shutters were flapping in the
breeze, and she'd spotted plenty of cracks and patches of
damp on ceilings and walls. But the grand villa wasn't as
run down as she'd feared. It needed a face-lift rather than
drastic structural surgery—she hoped. And it certainly
was grand—especially in location and style . . . Squatting
on the clifftop crag above the *baglio* and the bay as it was,
was as superior a creature as she could have dreamed of.
And it belonged to her. If she pinched herself, would she
wake up? She didn't dare.

But the sea was calling, so Tess put on a bikini, T-shirt, and sarong and left by the front door. The rental car was parked in the courtyard on another mosaic of pebbles surrounding a small statue—sculpted by one of Edward Westerman's artistic friends, perhaps, Tess thought with a smile. And in front of the stone wall boundary, a crescent of oleander bushes provided a vibrant border of pink and white.

Outside the front door, Tess looked up at the deep and dusky pink rendering. The motif she had seen last night was of a woman. At least it was a woman's face, a sad face, framed by long hair curling past her shoulders. Her arms were raised at her sides, palms facing in a position of . . . what? Supplication? From the waist her body divided in two and flowed back and around to encircle her. She was covered in stars.

Tess stared at her for a few moments, intrigued. Who was she, and what did the symbol mean? Then she retraced her steps from last night, unlocked the gate, and walked down the spiral stone steps to the bay.

The mosaicist was outside his studio, sorting through trays of jeweled glass and stones. He was about her age, Tess reckoned, dark and kind of brooding. And not friendly. As she came down the steps toward him, his head shot up, his gaze intense and, yes, definitely hostile.

"*Buon giorno,*" she said, with her best accent. She ought to make an effort with the locals.

He grunted what could have been a greeting, or not.

Hmm. What was eating him? How did you say *have you got out of the wrong side of bed this morning, or are you always this grumpy?* in Italian? "Your mosaics are lovely," she said instead, pointing toward the window display in the studio behind him. A lot of them were from the natural world: there was a prancing horse of amber and a green bird, a lizard and a dragon, a dolphin in a churning sea.

He shrugged. *"Grazie."* As if it had been dragged out of him. Well at least he seemed to understand English.

"What materials do you use to make them?" she persevered.

He muttered something unintelligible. If this was an example of the native Cetarian, she wasn't sure she wanted to spend time here, no matter how stunning the landscape. She could even begin to understand why her mother had left.

"Just glass?" Why was she bothering? Tess had no idea. "Or stone?"

"Everything." And just for a moment, his gaze met hers, black as jet. "And anything. If it is right. If it fits."

Goodness. Perhaps, Tess thought, he just didn't do small talk. "Did you find all this on the beach?" She picked up a piece of glass, bright amber speckled as if by salt, its edges rounded and blurred—by the buffeting of the waves perhaps. When she looked closely, she thought she could see the imprints of sand, stone, rock on its pitted surface.

"Sì." His gaze dropped again. "The sea, she is a rich and generous mistress." He let the cloudy teardrops of glass—green, turquoise, brown, and yellow, drift through his long fingers for a moment.

"Tess!"

She swung around. Only a couple of people here knew her name, and sure enough it was Giovanni Sciarra who was striding across the *baglio* toward her, smartly dressed, tapping his watch as if she were late for an appointment somewhere. Was she?

"Hi." She raised a hand and took a few steps toward him. It was quite pleasant to see a friendly face. It almost made her feel as if she might belong.

"You have settled in, I think," he observed.

"Yes." She thought of the provisions in the kitchen. He was a bit macho, but his family had been kind. "Thanks for the bread and fruit and stuff."

He shrugged. *"Di niente.* It is nothing. And now . . ." He made another gesture. "I have come to take you to lunch," he said.

She smiled, though there was something proprietorial in his tone that irritated her. "Is it lunchtime already?" she hedged. She must have got up late, but she'd been looking forward to exploring a bit more. Not to mention going for a swim.

"There is much to discuss. *Andiamo.* Let us go."

"I'll have to get changed." To be honest, she'd rather skip lunch. But . . . She wanted to find out about her mother's family, didn't she? Well, Giovanni would probably know it all. Plus he didn't look like he'd take no for an answer.

"Fine. I will wait for you."

Tess glanced back at the mosaicist, but he seemed oblivious to their conversation and had turned his attention back to his work. They lived in the same village, but Giovanni hadn't even acknowledged his presence. And just at that moment, Mosaic-man raised his dark head to glower at Giovanni with even more animosity than he'd shown toward her. He had a scar on his face, from a long time ago, it looked like. It ran from just below his left eye to just above the corner of his mouth. Tess remembered the offhand—actually quite rude—way in which Giovanni had dismissed the man's mosaics last night. And yet they were so delicate and vibrant, each one formed with precision, creating an image of color and light. Anyone with such creative vision must be . . . What? Interesting? Attractive? Or just think he could be damned unfriendly and get away with it?

"Fine," she said, perversely wanting to annoy Mosaic-man who, after all, hadn't provided her with breakfast. "So, where are you taking me?"

CHAPTER 10

LOOKING BACK, FLAVIA WASN'T SURE WHAT SHE REG-
istered first. The mangled plane, perhaps? It was a miracle
it hadn't burst into flames. The underside of its body had
been ripped clean away—pieces of it were scattered on the
ground, and the smell of torn metal hung in the air like a
broken promise. Or maybe it was the man in an unfamiliar
pilot's uniform, holding his leg at an awkward angle, vulnerable, exhaustion and pain drawn on his face. Or was it
the blood—congealed and sticky in the heat? But she knew,
even now, after all these years, looking back on it at last,
that it wasn't any of these things. It was his eyes.

*His eyes were bluer than the Sicilian sky, bluer than the sea in
summertime. She'd never seen such eyes. O dio Beddramadre
. . . Holy Mother of God.*

*"Please . . ." He seemed to believe she would help him. His
mouth was twisted, his palms open in supplication. "You
have some water? Water? Yes?"*

Flavia understood him. She would have understood him even if she hadn't spent all that time listening to Signor Westerman. And she felt no fear. She didn't think of running away.

She ran lightly down the bank toward him. What should she do? What could she do? She looked wildly around. The land was sultry, unpeopled, and silent apart from the heavy drone of the insects. Something throbbed inside Flavia's head. There was simply earth and sky—and no one.

"Please." He licked parched, cracked lips.

"Sì." She unscrewed the flask, bent toward him, smelled his sweat, the blood, the male heat of him. She put the flask to his lips and gently tipped.

He drank greedily, almost choked, the precious liquid spilling over his chin, then sighed and drank some more, this time with better control.

Flavia squatted on her haunches and waited. How badly hurt was he? She would have to get help. This was more than she could deal with herself. But who . . . ? "Inglese?" she whispered.

He nodded.

She got to her feet and made a stepping motion, one foot in front of the other. She pointed at the man. "Sì?" He shook his head, let out a low, hoarse chuckle. "No. Absolutely no chance, I'm afraid. I've tried."

Flavia screwed back the lid of the flask and put it down next to him. If he couldn't walk . . . ?

"Do you know what happened last night?" he asked, shifting himself awkwardly into a more comfortable position. He gestured toward the sky.

She shook her head. But she remembered the noises she had heard. And the searchlights drowning out the three-quarter moon. How she had hoped for a sign, for something to change. And she remembered the little she had overheard when she'd stood outside the caffé *listening to Papa and the other men of the village this morning. What had it been? An air raid?*

"You understand English, don't you?"

"Sì." She nodded. "A little." But she hardly dared speak it. She hadn't practiced. She would get it wrong, and he would laugh at her.

"There's a bridge near Syracuse . . ." He sighed, seeming unable to say more.

She must do something, say something. She mustn't just stand there like an idiot girl.

"We lost sight of the coast, went badly off course." He spoke with obvious difficulty. "Hadn't had a chance to study the maps of the area. No ground lights to guide us in. Couldn't see a damn thing."

She nodded to show she understood, though she didn't, not really. Could she risk fetching Papa? He was sympathetic to the English; look how loyal he'd been to Signor Westerman. He would guard the villa and its contents with his life, if needed.

"Can you bring food?" the pilot asked. His voice seemed to be getting fainter. "I'd be awfully grateful."

"Sì." But before she did that . . . She pointed. "Your leg?"

He grimaced. "I think it has a pretty bad gash. Some fuselage came down on it—bloody hard."

Flavia frowned. "Broken?" she asked. She made a gesture to clarify her meaning and he winced.

"I don't think so."

So . . . She would need bandages, antiseptic, warm water, at least. And food. But how could she leave him stuck here in the middle of a field in a Sicilian July? It was impossible. He would be roasted alive.

"I go . . . ," she began. "I get help."

A flash of fear crossed his face. "No," he said. "Come back alone. Please. Bring me a hat, some food, bandages, if you can."

Flavia got up.

"Tell no one," he warned her. "They'll kill me. I will die."

Flavia understood. "Wait," she said. Yes, as if he could do otherwise . . .

She flew back in the white light of the afternoon, over the red earth, past the field of wheat that looked soft as a cat's fur in the blurred haze of the heat, through the olive grove where the trees just smiled at her and shimmered, back to the old stone cottage that looked, incredibly, just the same as when she'd left earlier. How could that be—when so much had changed?

She was sweating and breathless by the time she stepped through the net curtain, which was motionless in the still air, and came to the back room, where her father was asleep, snoring gently.

Flavia opened her mouth to speak. But what if she were mistaken? What if Papa told the authorities and they killed the Englishman? She would have his blood on her hands. She . . .

She crept out of the room. In the kitchen, she assembled what she needed. Precious bread, baked by Mama that day with some of her quince jam, oil from their own olives, goat's cheese from Luciano, tomatoes from the vines outside, two wide bandages from Mama's cupboard, a small bottle of iodine. What else? He had asked for a hat. Could she risk taking Papa's? Tweezers perhaps? Some lint and gauze? She filled a canteen with hot water from the stove. Pray Madonna that no one saw her leaving with this lot, or she'd be done for. He'd be done for.

Stealthy as a burglar, she tiptoed around the cottage, out past the limp-netted curtain, across the fields toward the olive grove and the field of yellow wheat. The light was so bright, she was running so fast—her burden clutched in front of her—her heart thudding with the effort and the heat, that she almost felt it wasn't real. That this day wasn't a real day, that she wasn't there, that this wasn't happening, that when she reached the place where the airman and the plane had been, there would be nothing. It would be just a mirage. The land throbbed and burned and seemed to mock her. From somewhere, a bird cried. A mirage.

But he was there.

He opened his eyes, looked fearfully around to check she was on her own, seemed pathetically pleased to see her. And why not? She was bringing what would sustain him. It was nothing to do with her, Flavia. She could be anyone, any girl from the village who had happened on him.

"Thank you," he said. "This is bloody good of you. You're wonderful."

And yet . . . And yet he looked at her as if he meant what he said.

Shyly, she got out the bread, oil, cheese, and tomatoes and watched him as he ate hungrily, chewing the bread; biting, sucking, and swallowing the fruit.

"Eat slowly," she told him, in her native tongue, and he seemed to understand her, for he nodded and ate with less desperation than before.

When he was done, Flavia took the warm water and iodine and bathed the wound in his leg. She could hardly breathe, she was so nervous. He winced at her touch, especially when she took the tweezers and withdrew a fine shard of shrapnel embedded there. Was there more? She couldn't tell. The gash was deep, bloody and swollen; already trying to heal into a crust just below the slashed cloth of his trouser, but there was danger of infection, she knew. Perhaps she had arrived just in time.

"Where . . . ?" she asked him.

He indicated grazes on his arms and shoulder.

Flavia had never touched a man's body before. Carefully she eased back the torn fabric of his shirt. His skin was pale and slightly freckled; she could see the strength in his muscled arms. She bit her lip and concentrated hard. She would be a nurse. She wouldn't think of him as a man, but as a patient.

When she had finished, he touched her hand.

She looked into those eyes. Wondered if she ought to pray— for herself and her deliverance perhaps?

"You are an angel," he said to her. "My ministering angel."

Despite the heat, a strange shiver ran through her. "I must go."

Flavia rested for a while, exhausted by the writing. Food was part of the Sicilian soul, part of her soul. In her time there were few cookbooks. Recipes were handed down from mother to daughter; this was the old way, the best way. She would do the same. She frowned. She would start with *caponata*. This was a concept rather than a dish; every cook has her own recipe. It was best to make it a day or two in advance of eating, in order to give the flavors time to mellow and combine.

So. She began to write. *Cube the melanzane and fry in hot olive oil. Blanch the celery with the olives. Fry the onions. Add the red wine vinegar and the sugar. Heat the tomato paste. Add the vegetables. Cool. Sprinkle on the mint or the basil.*

Sweet and sour. What was Tess doing now? Who had she spoken to? Was she in the villa? Flavia did not want to know, and yet she longed to. Contradictions, thought Flavia. Sweet and sour . . .

CHAPTER 11

"I AM SURPRISED YOU DO NOT KNOW THE STORY," Giovanni said, when they were seated in a restaurant in a nearby village. "Do mothers not talk to daughters in your family?"

Idly, Tess pushed her heavy crystal wineglass across the crisp white damask of the tablecloth. The room held a woody fragrance, due, no doubt, to the ashes in the fireplace and the olive branches in the wood basket—it was the scent of what had been burned the night before. The food was good. They had begun with bruschetta and eggplant slices grilled with garlic, parsley, and caramelized onion.

"About some things, yes." Tess speared a mussel from her second course—*spaghetti con le cozze*—from inside one of the lacquered black shells. She remembered her mother saying that the relationship between a pasta and its sauce was precise and equal. Both tastes should work simultaneously on the palate. And this, she had to say, was good, but not quite as good as Muma's. "But my mother

has always been a bit cagey about Sicily." To say the least.
And Tess had never cooked Sicilian. Perhaps it was a small
act of rebellion—a way of showing her mother that if she
wouldn't tell Tess about Sicily, then Tess wouldn't cook
its food.

"Cagey?" He frowned.

"Wary. Silent. Secretive."

"Ah." He touched his nose. "Secrets, I understand."

Yes, Tess thought. I bet you do. She tried to look past his
easy manner, the practiced smile, and found herself thinking of Robin. It had been a shock to learn that he depended
on his wife's family financially. She supposed it happened
all the time—in some families. And perhaps it was the
romantic idealist in her that thought money shouldn't
come into it; that relationships between men and women
should be based on concepts like love and integrity rather
than the amount of money you had in the bank. Romantic
idealism may not have brought her a life partner to love and
cherish, she thought, tasting a forkful of the intense tomato
sauce, but at least she still had her dreams . . .

"It was like this . . . ," he began.

According to Giovanni, Edward Westerman came to Sicily in 1935, a mere youth with an inheritance (*more money
than was good for him, no?*) and a desire to live in the sun.

"Sounds good to me," said Tess.

"Villa Sirena was very grand when it was first designed
and built," Giovanni said, "using local stone and marble
and a local workforce, too. Now, though . . ." He shrugged.
"It is *moltu malandata,* no?"

"*Moltu . . . ?*" Tess spooned up more tomato sauce. It
contained more than a hint of chili peppers, and she was
reminded once again of her mother. She was beginning to

understand much more about the Sicilian relationship to food.

"How do you say? Run down?"

"Shabby chic?"

"Ah, yes." Giovanni seemed to be watching her carefully—or was that her imagination? "It is a place with many dark corners," he said, in a seemingly casual tone, "places where things can hide."

"Things?"

He shook his head as if he had said too much, but Tess suspected he had been testing the waters; trying to find out how much she knew. Secrets, secrets. What was the matter with them all, she wondered.

Giovanni glanced suspiciously around the restaurant. "Someone is always listening," he said, "in Sicily."

Right . . . And Tess had thought they were just a few ordinary couples and families out to lunch.

Her mind drifted to Ginny. She had called her before they left the villa, but it was obvious that Ginny couldn't wait to get off the phone. "I'm fine, Mum. Honestly," she had said. "You've only been gone a day. Chill." But it was the first time that Tess and her daughter had ever been so far apart geographically. And it felt strange.

"As for the Englishman, Edward Westerman," Giovanni was saying, "it was not only the sun that he craved."

"Oh?" Tess forked up the last of her spaghetti and mussels.

"He had to leave England." He made a gesture. "He was, you know . . . ?"

No, actually. "What?"

"He had parties." Giovanni raised an eyebrow. "Of a certain kind."

Tess was confused. "He was a poet, wasn't he?" She pushed her plate aside.

"But yes. He surrounded himself with artists, writers, people whose minds were broad. People who would not object to . . . you know . . . ?" Another raised eyebrow.

Tess got it. "He was gay?" she said. "Homosexual?"

"Exactly." Giovanni, too, finished the last of his pasta and wiped his lips delicately with his napkin. His expression betrayed that while he might not be homophobic, he certainly did not approve. "In England it was illegal, no? You had your Oscar Wilde, I think?"

Tess laughed. "We did, yes." She sipped her wine—a delicious, faintly honeyed affair from Sicily itself.

"*Sincero*," Giovanni told her. "Pure grape with no chemicals and so no hangover. Simple."

"Great." Tess accepted another glass. "But wasn't homosexuality illegal in Sicily, too?" she asked.

"Ah." Giovanni put his fork on the plate with more force than was necessary. Tomato sauce flew up to decorate the ocher-stippled wall. "You would think so. I would think so." He sighed. "In Sicily we close our eyes to English eccentrics." He closed his eyes as if to demonstrate. But retained a pained expression, she noted.

Eccentrics, Tess thought. From the Latin *ex centro*. Away from the center, resistant to the centralizing process that made everyone the same. It wasn't easy to be eccentric, she concluded. To be brave enough. And she rather thought that she would have liked Edward Westerman.

"They have money, they build a grand *casa*, they give the work to our men and women. Why do we care what they do in their bedrooms, hmm?"

Tess blinked. He didn't sound convinced. But she was glad her own family had been more broad minded. They had clearly shared a bond with Edward Westerman that went well beyond employer and employee loyalty. And he had left Tess his beautiful villa . . .

Outside, the sun was still streaming onto the terrace. Why on earth did Italians so often choose to have lunch indoors? A couple was strolling along the promenade hand in hand. They stopped, as if of one mind, watching the boats moored in the harbor, looking out to sea. He spoke, pointed toward the horizon. She looked, shielded her eyes, nodded, laughed. They kissed. Tess looked away. It was too soon. Too raw.

Giovanni took a deep swallow of his wine. "Sicily was very poor in those days," he said. "There was much hunger. Much discontent."

Tess nodded. She could see how it had been. She tried to imagine her mother a young girl when Edward Westerman had built his 1930s house with its deco sweeping curves, its pink rendering, and stucco decoration. He must have seemed an exotic creature indeed to the young Sicilian girl.

"And your great aunt and my mother were close friends," Tess said.

Giovanni nodded. He indicated the dessert menu, but she shook her head, only accepting coffee. In Sicily, she reckoned, she would have to pace herself. If the two women had been that close, then Santina must know why her mother had left Sicily when she was so young. Why she had broken off almost all contact with her family. Why she had refused to talk about it and never returned here.

Tess scrutinized Giovanni. Did he know? And more to the point, would he tell her the truth? She doubted it.

"Perhaps I could talk to your Aunt Santina sometime?" she suggested. "I'd love to know what my mother was like—as a girl, I mean."

He frowned. "She speaks no English," he said. "Many of that generation speak no English. Why would they?"

"You could translate."

He seemed to consider this. Then his brow cleared. "As you wish," he said. "You can tell us everything. You can trust us."

Tess wasn't sure what she was supposed to be telling them—she'd rather assumed it was the other way around—so she tried another subject. "And the man who makes the mosaics?" she said. "He is not a friend?"

"Amato." He almost spat. "Him you cannot trust. He is not a friend to your family or to mine, of that you may be sure."

Their coffee arrived, and Tess added milk. "Why not?" she asked. Feelings seemed to rise strong in Sicily. Either Sicilians were just naturally overdramatic, or there was an awful lot of interfamily warfare and grudge bearing going on.

Giovanni leaned forward and lowered his voice. "There was a long-term dispute and debt," he said. "And later, a theft. A valuable item. A great loss."

Tess raised her eyebrows in inquiry. Didn't they have courts of law in Sicily?

"The debt was to my family." Giovanni seemed to sit up straighter in his chair. "It was a matter of honor. But the theft . . ."

"Yes?" The more information she could get out of him, the better, Tess decided. All this theft and debt stuff might have nothing to do with why her mother left Sicily, but it was useful background. And anyway, she was intrigued to find out more about the unfriendly Mosaic-man in the *baglio.*

"The theft was from your grandfather," he said. "Something that did not even belong to him. Something . . ." He tailed off.

"Something . . . ?" *The plot thickens* . . . She wondered what her grandfather had been like. Perhaps Santina would be able to throw some light on the subject.

"Alberto Amato was your grandfather's closest friend," Giovanni said. "The theft was a betrayal." His eyes darkened. "A betrayal of the worst kind."

CHAPTER 12

GINNY WAS GETTING THE HOUSE READY FOR THE Party. She fastened up her hair with a clip-comb, tied an apron round her waist, swung assorted cloths over her shoulder, and grabbed the cleaning fluid. Mission . . .

Her mother's bedroom, she decided, would be off-limits (one vodka and cranberry juice stain, and she'd be dead) and used for storing Fragile Objects. Like framed photographs . . . She gathered these up, distracted by one of herself aged five, mid pony ride, wind in her hair, her expression a frozen portrait of fear and delight. Ginny could remember that day, could float down those mental staircases in seconds; smell again that sweet, horsey hay scent; hear the creature whinny and snort; feel the sea breeze whipping her face and the anxiety bubbling in her tummy as the pony broke into a slow trot. And her mother—grinning and waving the camera in triumph. "Hey, Ginny. Look at you!"

Ginny smiled at the memory. When she got off, all she'd wanted was to get straight back on again.

She picked up the only photo of her parents. Her parents—it seemed weird even to think the words, because he wasn't, was he, a parent? You couldn't be a parent if you'd never been there.

She, Ginny's mother, was beautiful, caught like that, off guard. Tall and slender with long, curly blonde-brown hair, and a wide smile. Ginny traced it with her fingertip. She supposed she still was—attractive, that was—men still looked at her, she still got noticed, and she had great legs. But back then . . . Their fingers were interlaced, she was leaning toward Ginny's father and gazing at him with a kind of—*Oh my God, you're hopeless, but I love you*, sort of look.

He was laughing. Tall, gangly, and carefree, just a boy. Her biological father. That had the right kind of distance to it. Ginny frowned. And he'd kept his distance all right. He'd never been in touch—not once.

If Mum knew what was happening here tonight, she'd go *kerazy* . . . Ginny felt the Ball vibrate as it gathered a powdering of guilt. She'd already called and sent two texts from Sicily *"just to check you're okay."* What was she *on* . . . ? Fact was, her mother knew nothing about her, nothing about her life. Why would she? She was her *mother*, wasn't she?

Ginny ducked out of the room and grabbed her iPod from her own room next door. That would take care of it. "Henrietta." The Fratellis at full volume. Her mother, she reminded herself, would never know.

She cleared the living room of all potential breakages with "Chelsea Dagger" in full swing. She heaved the sofa into Jack's room—a chill-out room for the party—and plugged the iPod into her mother's music system. "Got Ma

Nuts from a Hippie" cascaded into the room. She tried out a few thrusts and twirls. Scooped up the rug. *Good God . . .* The wooden floor was perfect for dancing.

A text came through on her phone. She pulled it out of her jeans pocket. It was from Becca. *Wot U doin 4 food*? Ginny texted back: *Potato chips + popcorn.*

In the kitchen, she cleared the surfaces and organized the drinks. There was wine (from her mother's stash; she probably wouldn't even notice); gin (bought by Pops for Christmas Day two years ago, practically untouched); Coke and cranberry juice (Ginny's contribution). People would bring bottles. No problem.

She unlocked the front door and went outside. Lisa was in her tiny front garden, weeding, the two girls playing bat 'n' ball. They shrieked when they saw her. "Ginnyeee! Come and play, Ginnyeee!"

"I can't." Ginny pulled a sorry face. "I'm cleaning the house."

"Really?" Lisa sat back on her heels. "Good girl. Your mum'll be pleased."

Ginny smiled modestly, hooked her fingers into the waistband of her jeans.

"I hope you're taking note, girls!" Lisa called out to her two. "This is what I expect of you in a few years' time . . ."

"Did Mum tell you I'm having a few friends over tonight?" Ginny asked casually.

"Er . . ." Lisa frowned. "No, I don't think she did."

"We'll try not to disturb you." Ginny crossed her fingers behind her back.

Lisa smiled magnanimously and waved her gardening fork in the air. "Don't worry," she said. "We'll just turn up the TV. You have a good time."

"Thanks, Lisa." If things got too raucous, Ginny thought, she could always apologize tomorrow. And, with a bit of luck, Lisa would have forgiven and forgotten by the time Mum got home. Mum. Ginny shivered at the thought. But she couldn't back out now—she'd already invited him.

Before going back inside the house, she snuck round to the side passageway and pulled a packet of cigs from the pocket of her long, gray cardigan. She didn't smoke much—usually just when she was out clubbing—and at home when Mum wasn't around. She inhaled deeply. Would he come to the party? She'd texted him and told him to bring a few friends. He'd texted back that he might just do that. All she could do now was wait. And Ginny wasn't good at waiting.

Back inside and armed with black trash bags, Ginny inspected her own room. She closed her eyes and imagined Ben moving in close, felt his breath warm and sweet on her face, felt his lips searching for hers, felt them fall together onto the bed . . . She was sweating at the thought. If he came in here . . . What would he think? It was a girl's room—full of sweet and cute, pretty and nice. Which was not the impression she wanted to give. No way, José. She opened the first bag. In went all her old makeup—eye shadow and lip gloss, ancient nail polish and glitter dust—into the black hole. Magazines, all the clothes she no longer wore. She was feeling GOOD . . . She began to work more quickly, faster and faster, sweeping through drawers of ancient socks and underwear, pulling dresses from hangers. Books from her childhood (*Lion in the Meadow, Winnie the Pooh*) and soft toys (though White Teddy and Bill the baby owl leaped into the wardrobe for safety). Ginny couldn't stop now. A zoo of animal ornaments, anything that said CHILD, not woman. Fluffy penguin slippers, a poster of a giraffe, a

Miffy calendar. A pen that looked like a peacock, a money box that looked like a grizzly bear, a blanket patterned with zebras. (What was it with her and animals?) Out. Out. Out. The Ball shuddered and rolled.

She put the Fratellis back on. "Creepin Up the Backstairs." The music was inside her head, and her arms were aching. This was it. Exorcism. She could feel it cleansing every pore. But . . .

Would the Ball ever disappear? Would this make the Ball disappear?

By the computer was a whole stack of college work. She'd promised her mother to do some serious studying this week. Ginny took a deep breath and chucked it in. *She didn't want to go to uni* . . . She definitely DID NOT WANT TO GO . . . She wanted to go away, yes, but to travel, to see the world, to be free, to be new. She wanted to be older. She wanted not to be a virgin anymore. She wanted . . . Shit.

She sat down on the bed. She wasn't sure what she wanted. But she wanted something, that was for sure.

CHAPTER 13

A BETRAYAL OF THE WORST KIND . . . TESS DIPPED A foot in the water. It was warm and inviting, the sea shimmering in the distance, the waves curling in fronds around her toes. A betrayal, a theft, and an old family debt, Giovanni had told her. And three Sicilian families involved—the Farros (her mother's family), the Sciarras (Santina and Giovanni's clan) and the Amatos (Mosaic-man's lot). So who had done what to whom? What had been stolen back in the 1940s? Why was it a betrayal, and what—if anything— could it have to do with her mother's leaving Sicily?

Tess waded through the waves, and when the water reached her thighs, she dipped her head, and with one fluid movement slipped into the sea. The initial shock was followed by the moment she loved—when body and liquid merged as if into one. She let out a deep breath. Swimming, diving, just being in the sea felt so good. A way to think—and a way to forget. Closing her eyes against the glare of the late-afternoon sun, she swam with sure strokes into the open sea. Sometimes she wished she could just go on forever.

She was only here for a week. In that week, realistically, she had to decide what to do with Villa Sirena, and she had to find out what had made her mother leave Sicily—and never come back. Tess turned over, floating on her back for a few moments, letting the current take her. Wouldn't it be good if life were like that? If you could just drift on the tide in and out of situations—much as David had drifted, both before and after they met. Or would it? Most people eventually put down roots. And perhaps David had by now; Tess had no idea, he'd never contacted her to say—*Hey, how's my daughter?* or *Here's some money to help out.* No, he'd never been into responsibilities. It didn't suit his lifestyle. So, really, she should have known.

She started a slow breaststroke toward the rock islands. Tess did very little drifting—when she wasn't in the sea. She worked hard; she'd even applied for promotion to supervisor at the water company last week—Janice was retiring, and it had been suggested that Tess was her natural successor. It would mean a good pay rise and more leave. So, the job was okay; she got on well with all her colleagues—with the exception of Malcolm. And if sometimes she thought to herself, *I always wanted more from life than this*, she quashed it immediately and told herself to grow up. She had her health, she had Ginny, Muma, and Dad, and she had a decent job. *Count your blessings, girl...*

Giovanni had touched on the subject of her plans for the villa over coffee. He had leaned back in his chair like the well-fed tiger that he probably was, lit a cigarette, and said, "So, Tess, you will sell the villa, yes? You want to sell it as it is, perhaps, or you want me to organize builders to sort the damp, to repaint, to fix up the place, before you put it on the market?" His expression relaxed, but expectant.

Tess felt blown out with the food and wine and suddenly as if she had been primed for the kill. "I don't know yet," she said. "I've only just arrived, remember."

And after all, Giovanni may have provided her breakfast (and lunch), but what connection did he have with Villa Sirena, and what did she know about him anyway? He had assured her that her mother's family and his family had always been close, but she only had his word for that, didn't she? She couldn't help feeling that he was just a bit too eager to help out. Or was she—heaven forbid—indulging in some sort of Sicilian paranoia syndrome?

Giovanni remained unruffled, sleek as that big cat that kept appearing in her mind's eye. "Of course, of course." He waved his cigarette in the air. "First you must take the holiday, mmm? Explore our wonderful west coast of Sicily. You must take your time. These things, yes, they take the time."

If only she had more time . . .

Now that she was closer to them, Tess could see how fascinating the rock islands were—formations of brown-, white-, and red-streaked granite that must once have been attached to the mainland of Sicily, she guessed. The bits thrusting out of the sea were pitted with cracks and crevices that housed succulent plants and herbs and had also become home to terns and gulls. Maybe she'd hire some diving equipment and find out what was going on under the surface . . .

Tess trod water and chuckled to herself. She hadn't been fooled by Giovanni. He had a vested interest—he was probably hoping to make some money out of it, out of her. And why not? What did she care? He and his family had been kind, hospitable, and helpful. So . . .

There was no one else in the sea. As far as she could see, she was alone in the ocean. How wonderful was that? Robin didn't know what he was missing.

She turned around and began to swim to shore. The villa—her villa—stood imposing on the cliff, its sweeping, curving dusky-pink walls outlined against the azure sky. And yet . . . She did care. Already she felt a pull to the place. This landscape was, in some strange way, familiar. And unnerving. Had Edward Westerman known then how it would be? She closed her eyes again, feeling the tide gently pushing her to the shore. Caressing. Then a sudden sense of darkness. She opened her eyes.

Mosaic-man was standing on the shoreline, arms folded, scowling. If Giovanni was a tiger, Tess thought, then this man was a wild panther. Untamable. He was wearing nothing but a pair of black shorts. Bloody hell. What crime had she committed now?

Tess stood up in the water. Her hair was wet, her mascara must be smudged, and she was feeling at her least elegant. But what could she do? He was clearly waiting for her.

"*Ciao,*" he said, as, predictably, she stumbled on the slippery stones.

He held out a hand. She eyed it cautiously. An artist's hand. Long, tapering fingers, nails cut straight across, a narrow-boned wrist . . . But she grabbed hold anyway, and he escorted her across the pebbles toward the stone wall by the jetty, where she'd left her towel. He was just an inch or so taller than Tess, she estimated. He passed her the towel, grazing her bare shoulder with his hand as he did so.

Had he had a personality transplant? "*Grazie*," she said.

"I wanted to speak with you," he said.

"Oh?" Tess toweled her hair and assumed a look of casual curiosity. Did he also want to sell the villa for her, or organize some builders, perhaps? Or did he want to tell her about a long-past theft or betrayal?

"It is the jellyfish," he said, looking stern. "There are many."

"Jellyfish?"

"Here in the bay." He made a gesture—of a jellyfish scraping trailing tentacles along his arm. He jumped dramatically from the supposed sting.

She laughed. "Ouch."

"Yes, ouch!" He smiled at her. "I work here all the time. I see it."

She nodded. It was quite a smile . . . okay, so maybe he wasn't the enemy after all. At least, not her enemy. "Any other predators I should know about?" she asked.

He waggled an eyebrow. Despite the scar on his face—or maybe because of it—he was, she realized, very attractive, in a dark, brooding sort of way. Autobloodymatically she thought of Robin. Damn it.

"The rest I expect you will find for yourself," he said.

Right. "I expect I will." She smiled.

"You are here alone?" he asked.

"Uh-huh." His skin was that complete nut brown all over—well, everywhere that she could see—that could only happen when you lived year-round in a climate like this one.

"And how long do you stay?" he asked.

Tess wrapped the towel closer around her shoulders. What was with all this sudden friendliness? Or was the scowl his default expression, and he just didn't do mornings . . . ? She wanted to like him, wanted to respond. But . . . Giovanni's warning hung in her head. She was fed up with being taken for a ride. Giovanni had invited her to dinner again tonight, but enough was enough. She needed just her own company—certainly not that of any Sicilian man—no matter how helpful or attractive. God. Anyone would think she'd inherited a millionaire's fortune rather than just a villa, with all these men sniffing around.

"A week," she said, "for now."

The eyebrow was off again. "For now?"

Tess shrugged. What she didn't know herself, she couldn't tell to any handsome stranger. A thought occurred to her. "What were these buildings used for, by the way?" She pointed.

He followed the direction of her gaze. "This was the *tonnara*, the tunnery—a processing plant for tuna." His good mood had already evaporated and his expression darkened.

"Oh, I see." She sensed that it wouldn't be prudent to pursue the subject. "*Ciao*, then. And thanks for the warning about the jellyfish."

She waved him good-bye and headed for the steps up to the villa. She wouldn't phone Ginny again tonight, she decided. She had to show some trust; that kind of thing was important to teenagers. She'd phone her mother instead. She would ask her, she decided, about Santina and the Sciarra family.

But as she ran up the steps, something made her look back over her shoulder toward the ancient *baglio*. Standing by the eucalyptus tree was Giovanni. Body language: pissed off. Well. Tess did a mental shrug. His family feud wasn't her family feud—although he'd suggested it should be. She could speak to whoever she liked, and he couldn't do a thing about it.

CHAPTER 14

THE ALMOND—BROUGHT TO SICILY BY THE ANCIENT Greeks. *The nuts should be plump and rich, oozing with sweet oil.*

Almonds were perfect for *spuntini*—the midmorning snack. There were sugared almonds (white for weddings, green for engagements, pink and blue for births), toasted almonds, and biscotti. The scented blossom of the almond tree was the first to come and the first to go, the petals falling like a late snowdrift in February. The nuts were not picked until late summer; until then they stayed on the trees, deepening in intensity under the protection of their hard shells, warmed from the sun, moistened by their oil. *Mandola . . .*

There was a story . . . Flavia picked up her pen. She would tell her daughter.

In Sicily, the association of the almond tree with love and fidelity is rooted in Greek mythology. Phyllis, a noble maiden, wed Demophon, and waited for him to return from the Trojan War. He never came, and after some years, she died of a broken heart. An almond tree sprang up at her grave. The tree finally bloomed when Demophon eventually appeared and visited the grave of his beloved wife.

Flavia decided to give her daughter the recipe for *taglignozo*—a type of *biscotto*. Tess had loved them when she was a child, still did.

Mix flour, sugar, eggs, butter, cinnamon, and cut almonds. The trick is in the consistency. Use la pazienza, *the patience of the almond tree. Test it with your fingers, with your heart. If it feels too stiff, then add more egg; if too sloppy, more almonds. Then, and only then, will it be perfect.*

Bake in the oven until golden. Wait. Eat cold with a small glass of Marsala . . .

For three days, Flavia returned with water, food, and fresh dressings for his wounds. She visited in siesta in the early afternoon, when most people were sleeping or resting in their beds, and again as evening came and she could fly there under the camouflage of darkness to see him. It was a kind of madness, she knew, as if she were gripped by something only the Devil would understand. But she couldn't stop.

She couldn't not go. In the hours between her visits, she ached to be running across the fields, longed to be there, washing and tending his wounds, listening to his strange speech, looking into the blue waters of his eyes. Had he bewitched her? She didn't consider the consequences of her actions. Nothing else seemed to matter.

On the fourth day, his forehead was hot, too hot, and she knew he had a fever. He ate hardly any of the food she brought, and his smile was so faded that she was afraid. He hardly spoke to her. She felt that he was slipping away. And when she walked back through the olive grove, she sensed that something else had changed.

Back at the house she found them waiting for her—Papa, Mama, Maria—like a deputation.

"Where have you been, daughter?" her father asked. His eyes were black as thunder.

"Just walking," she stammered. But she looked at Maria, and she knew. Had Maria seen her run to him? Had she followed her? Her sister was so self-righteous, so holier-than-thou. Flavia stood straighter. What did she care that there had been no chaperone, that she had risked her honor? His life was at stake. Life, death; they were the real things—the only real things.

"What have you done?" Her mother approached her. "Holy Mother of God, what have you done?"

"Nothing!" Flavia was stung. "I have done nothing wrong. It is just . . ."

And then suddenly it was all too much for her; her fears for his health, her worry that he would not recover, that the fever would worsen and that he would die there in the field, and she would not know until she went there the next afternoon only to find him . . .

Haltingly, she told them about the airman. About how he had sworn her to secrecy and begged him to help her. It was his only chance of survival, she felt.

At this, her father's expression changed. He muttered an obscenity under his breath, and he grabbed his jacket from the hook by the door. "I must tell the others," he said.

Flavia knew he meant his special cronies—Alberto and those who talked with him in the Bar Gaviota. Could they be trusted? She thought of Santina's father, Enzo. Now, him, she did not trust. He had a thin-lipped, dark, and cruel face, and she did not think that he shared her father's sympathy toward the English. He was the sort who thought only of himself and the Sciarras.

"Papa," she called. "You won't hurt him?"

He turned to her. "I cannot decide alone," he said. "We will see. If Alberto agrees, we will bring him here. Help your mother prepare a bed."

"Papa!"

But already he was gone.

Flavia sank to her knees. She would pray for him, the airman who had fallen from the sky and who called her his angel. Pray that he would be safe. Safe . . . She frowned. But even if they brought him here, even if he did not die, now that she had betrayed him, would the airman ever speak to her again?

CHAPTER 15

THE FOLLOWING MORNING, TESS TOOK HER BREAK-
fast out onto the terrace. The house was well equipped.
She'd found linen, crockery, silver, cutlery, anything you
could wish for. And it was fully furnished, although shabby
and untidy. There were faded but gorgeous rugs for the
flagstone floors—with bold patterns in fuchsia, indigo,
maroon—and creamy linen napkins. It was as if Edward
Westerman had just walked out one day, never to return.
Which in a way, he had.

Tess sipped her coffee. She could, she supposed, rent the
villa rather than sell it. This seemed a better idea. She didn't
want to part with it—not yet. It seemed too special a gift.
The disadvantage, of course, was that money needed to be
spent on it—a commodity she wasn't rich in right now. Perhaps she would broach the subject to Giovanni, get some
idea of how many tourists came to Cetaria and how successful such a venture might be.

The wow factor would always be its view . . . She got to her feet and wandered across the terrace to look down at the *baglio* and what she now knew to be the old tunnery in the bay with its army of rusty anchors stationed outside. One of the rock islands out to sea, she noted, was shaped like a ruined castle. And in the misty morning light the stone was almost silver, as if the rocks had been touched with a magic wand, while the sea swept around them, smooth and nonchalant. And inviting, she thought, feeling the familiar twitch of longing to get in there.

In the harbor was a fishing boat, and next to the stone jetty someone was gesticulating wildly and shouting in Italian. Mosaic-man, she realized, letting out a snort of laughter. He certainly had a temper. She shook her head. Perhaps Giovanni was right about the guy after all. He did look a bit manic.

After she'd cleared away, she made her way down to the water for a morning swim. Mosaic-man was stomping in and out of his studio.

"*Ciao.*" His expression was somewhere between scowl and smile. "You go in the sea now—so early?"

"I certainly do." She paused. "Do you work here every day?"

"Work. And eat. And sleep." He nodded inside. "I have rooms at the back."

Tess realized the studio must go farther back than she'd thought. She was intrigued. But did she want to go into the dragon's lair? Probably best not. But, "I heard you this morning," she couldn't resist saying. "You sounded angry."

His eyes flashed fury. "Fools," he said. "They go out to sea, they have nets that are torn, and they throw them overboard. Just like that." He made a motion. "No thought for the danger." He tapped his head. *"Loccu. Stupido."*

Tess nodded. She understood what he meant. Anything could get caught up in a torn fishing net; it was lazy and it was irresponsible. But so far in Sicily she'd very much got the impression that clearing up one's own litter wasn't high on anyone's agenda. It spoiled the landscape. Around every beautifully scenic corner was a pile of someone else's rubbish. Sicily, she was beginning to realize, was a land of contrasts. Beauty with ugliness. Light with darkness. Romance with danger.

And hadn't Mosaic-man overreacted just a little? She regarded him curiously. The scar on his face was an old one—maybe even from childhood, and it lent him a slightly piratical air. But that wasn't all. There was a sadness only half hidden in the shadows around his eyes. It made her want to reach out to him. Something or someone had hurt him. And badly.

"It is not of importance." His look contradicted the words. "It is nothing." He swept whatever it was away with a gesture of his hands. "Take five."

"Take five?" Tess enquired.

"Prendere cinque." He grimaced. "A Sicilian custom. Every day we must take five minutes and let off steam."

Tess smiled. "Sounds like a good idea." She could think of a few people in England whose stress levels might benefit . . .

"Enjoy your swim. *Ciao."* And he was gone.

A sensitive soul, she thought, as she swam across to the rocks. Or something. She could see now why they had appeared so silvery—because of the wild grasses and thyme clinging to their sides.

Her thoughts wandered to last night's conversation with her mother.

"Of course I remember Santina Sciarra," her mother had said in answer to Tess's question. "She was my best friend." Her tone softened. "She's still alive then?"

"Very much so."

"Will you send her . . ." She seemed to hesitate. ". . . my warmest thoughts?"

"Yes, Muma." There was no mistaking the affection in her mother's voice. "What were the rest of the family like?" she asked.

"Her father thought I was a bad influence." She snorted with laughter.

Tess smiled. "Why?" she asked. "What did you—?"

"Enough, Tess." Her mother's voice grew stern. "Let it be."

Reluctantly, Tess stopped probing. But she couldn't let it be. And there was no doubt about it. If Muma had confided in anyone, it would be Giovanni's Aunt Santina. She was the person Tess must talk to. So today she must get hold of Giovanni—if he didn't find her first.

Suddenly, she was aware of some bubbles near her arm, and before she had a chance to snatch it away, she felt the sting of the jellyfish. Damn it. She swam in, her upper arm aching.

Mosaic-man was cleaning and sifting some stones. Beside him was a mosaic about thirty centimeters square on a transparent glass base, half completed in bright greens and golds. She couldn't make out the subject—yet.

Tess put her hand over the telltale red weal on her arm so he wouldn't see.

"They caught you, hmm?" He didn't even look up. "You want coffee?"

"Is that a cure?" She took her hand away. Clearly, he didn't miss a trick.

"Only one cure." He looked up. To her surprise he was grinning. "What do you call it in English?"

"Oh. Ammonia." She grinned back. It might be quite difficult to pee on her own upper arm and she certainly wasn't going to ask him to.

Instead, Tess looked down at his mosaic. "It's lovely. What are the stones?"

He picked up some frosted fragments, wafer thin. "Turquoise, malachite, sea glass," he said.

"You mix the semiprecious stones with glass?" She picked up one of the wafers and ran a fingertip over its fuzzy surface.

He shrugged. "Who decides value? Another man like me, perhaps. The glass from the sea may have been someone else's rubbish once upon a time. But that was then. This is now."

She nodded. Sea glass . . . "Do you wonder where it all came from?"

He smiled. "It is for you to choose." He picked up a frosted peardrop of worn ice. "A shipwreck?" He put his head to one side. Picked up a softened triangle of amber. "A midnight picnic on the beach?"

"And can you tell how old it is?"

"More or less." He delved deep and came up with a bead of green so dark and pitted and rounded it was almost black. "This one, he is ancient as the hills."

"And this?" She selected a clean droplet of primrose yellow.

"As young as springtime," he said. "Translucent. You can see right through."

Tess could see why he liked the sea glass. Each one could tell a story. Each one had a color and a shape unique to itself; each one had come a different way.

"It has been on a long journey before the waves bring it to me," he continued. "It will never break. And it has a light—you see?—coming from within."

He handed her a bubble of green glass, fresh as a cut lime, and yet pearlized, as if lit up by the moon. "Yes." She could see exactly what he meant. "And what else do you use in your mosaics?" she asked.

He shrugged. "I use what I find. Some I buy, yes, if I have a commission, but most are already here in the stone, in the rocks around us, in the sea."

Tess looked around at the rocks from which the *baglio* must have been hewn. The stone was sliced with minerals, she could see. And the cliffs beyond, were . . .

"Marble and limestone," he said. "Coral, too. Amber and agate. Many stones."

Stone was important here. From the bedrock stone of the ancient *baglio*, to the honey-yellow sandstone of the buildings. Tess looked up at the pink villa—imposing on the clifftop. There was so much energy in its very core that at certain times of day and night it seemed positively to vibrate, almost humming with life.

"But what made you do it?" She was curious. "Why did you want to make mosaics from the glass and stone?"

"As a process it is slow, but rewarding," he told her. "It is a soothing activity. Therapeutic." He paused. "And the mosaics—they are part of Sicilian history." He got to his feet, dusted down his hands on his shorts, and headed for the studio. "Sicily itself is a jigsaw."

"In what way?" There was nothing left for her to do but follow. And besides, dragon or not, she was curious.

"The most beautiful mosaics are in the duomo at Monreale," he said. "You should visit. They date from the Byzantine period. Byzantine tesserae are very special, very reflective. The gold and silver leaf is pressed in layers of glass. So." He made a movement with his fingers.

"Really?" Tess looked around the studio. It was small, but light filtered through the narrow windows at the side and flooded in from the front. There was a workbench cluttered with tools, adhesives, sponges, sheets of glass and metal, pots filled with different-colored stone and glass, some already shaped, some unpolished and uncut. In the corner was a small stove, and out the back she could see another room with a bed and a couch.

"The Greek mosaicists—they were famous." He filled a small percolator with water and fixed the filter. "And Palermo's Norman kings, they encouraged the art."

Tess watched as he took the top off a small canister and spooned out coffee. She caught a whiff of its fragrance, like burnt embers: nutty, woody—a scent of darkness. Mosaic-man didn't seem too dangerous now. More like a history teacher really. He fixed the percolator together and put it on the stove.

"But you don't use cut tiles the way most mosaic makers do," she pointed out. His materials came from the natural world; there was no gold leaf here.

He lit the stove, his back to her. "Most mosaicists, they use the *smalti*," he explained. "It is a special intensely colored glass, not a tile. It is cooked in a furnace then cut."

Very different from his method, she thought. Sea glass and natural stone.

He turned to her. "Stones, they have long, slow lives," he said. "They do not die."

Tess wasn't sure how to reply to that. She knew what he meant though—it was uncannily like what she had just been thinking.

He opened a cupboard, took out a small tube of cream and brought it to her. "This may help." He took hold of her arm and massaged in some of the white cream. It was an intimate gesture and took Tess by surprise. But his touch was gentle, just a few strokes and it was done.

"*Grazie*," she said.

"It is nothing." He smiled, and in the dim light she could barely make out the old scar.

But it was something. "What's your name?" she asked him. She couldn't go on thinking of him as Mosaic-man. Giovanni had told her his family name, but . . .

"Tonino." He stretched out his hand. "Tonino Amato."

"Tess," she said. "Tess Angel." He had a strong grip and a dry palm.

"Angel?" He was also holding her hand for much longer than necessary and fixing her with a look that made her feel uncomfortable. As if—like Giovanni—he wanted something from her.

"So where do you get your inspiration, Tonino?" she asked. "For your work, I mean." She could hear the percolator beginning to bubble on the stove, and the air was filling with the smoky and beguiling fragrance of good coffee.

He smiled. "Stories."

"What kind of stories?"

"Sicilian fairy tales, myth, legend, call it what you want." He spread his hands. "We have a history of pillage and rape and poverty, you know this? It is part of the jigsaw I told you of."

Tess nodded. It seemed impossible to have a light conversation with this man. Everything he said or did was imbued with intensity.

"The stories—they are of courage and compassion," he said. "Of oppression, theft, and betrayal."

There it was again. Theft and betrayal. It seemed to be a recurring theme. Could Giovanni Sciarra possibly be right about this man? He had a temper—she'd seen it; but there was also an honesty about him that she liked.

"And the subjects you choose . . . ?" She touched a fish mosaic. The fish was silver gray and yellow, and emerging from a pearly white sea. The fish mosaic had been constructed above a mirror, and above that sat a row of delicate yellow fins. Tess smiled. Ginny would love it. It would be perfect for their bathroom at home. But she didn't want to ask the price, didn't want him to think she was just another tourist, just another customer to flatter. "They are images from the stories?"

"Exactly." He began to pour the coffee into tiny white cups. The coffee was thick and black, the *crema* hazelnut brown.

"So the fish . . . ?" "It is from the story of Ciccu," he said. "He rescues the fish from death and is rewarded when the fish returns a gold ring that he has been commanded to find by the king. Without it, he, too, will die." He put the coffeepot back on the stove. "Courage and compassion are rewarded, you see?"

Tess nodded. Was her family being rewarded—with Villa Sirena? "But they're only stories," she said. "Aren't they?"

"Perhaps." He came to sit beside her, and she was conscious of the warmth of his skin, very close, almost giving her goosebumps. "But the stories give a voice to those that are repressed. The poor, the peasants, those without power . . ."

"I see." Tess thought of what Giovanni had told her about the poverty in Sicily. Her mother's family must have suffered, too—at least until they were employed by Edward Westerman. And she remembered some of the bedtime stories her mother used to tell—about journeys and ogres and wicked princes. Were they, too, derived from Sicilian folklore? Had they been handed down, like recipes, from generation to generation?

"Freud—he believed that old fables and myths were accurate descriptions of the working of the human mind," Tonino said.

Tess stared at him. He was a revelation. "Really?" she said. "Tell me another story, will you?" She let her gaze drift around the mosaics until she came to the green bird. Its head was bent as if it had just spied an insect, its beak bright yellow and parted. The wings were lifted, and the forked tail was upright and poised for flight. Its mosaic feathers glittered and gleamed, jade and emerald in the sunlight flooding through the window. "What about that one?"

"The green bird is really a prince," he said.

Tess sipped her coffee and settled back to listen. Kings and queens and magic spells . . . It was like going back to childhood. She felt safe and sleepy. The coffee was delicious. It was richly roasted, and true to its fragrance, it tasted of charred fires, chestnuts, and nighttime. It caught at the back of her throat, and yet there was a sweetness there, too, that lingered like tobacco.

While they drank their coffee, he continued to work and talk, and Tess listened and watched, half-mesmerized by the movement of his hands as he sorted the stones, as he washed and cut and polished and placed, laying out the pieces and assembling the pattern of his design. He began in one corner and then worked his way out, leaving gaps—for grouting she supposed—constantly changing his mind and replacing stone for stone, his fingers fast and sure.

"And so the princess, she learns that too much humility will work against her," he said. "And that she must defend herself against abuse."

"And the green bird learns that true beauty comes from within," Tess added.

"Exactly."

"Do you think that's true?"

"Do you?"

Silence. She realized that the jigsaw of the pieces he was working on had formed the tail of a serpent. Amber and green. A serpent . . . Good and evil, she thought. Another Sicilian contrast. Temptation.

He looked up at her and suddenly she felt self-conscious. It was as if he had hypnotized her and now the spell was broken. She could still taste the coffee like woodsmoke on her tongue. But now she had to find Giovanni and arrange a meeting with Santina. She got to her feet.

"You must go. Things to do. People to see."

"Well, yes." She wanted to ask him about his family—about the three Sicilian families—but the right time to do so had slipped by.

He turned his attention once more to his design. "And your arm—it is better now, *sì?*"She'd forgotten about it, it was so much better. "Yes. Thank you for putting that cream on it," she said. She paused, but didn't say what she'd half intended to say. Instead, it seemed to hang in the air between them.

He nodded his head. "Though it was not the cream that made it better," he said with a quick grin, gone almost as soon as she saw it appear. "It was the coffee."

She laughed. "I'd better be going."

"Back to the mermaid's villa." He smiled.

"Back to . . . ?"

"Villa Sirena."

Suddenly she got it. *Sirena* was Italian for mermaid. And the motif above the front door—the sad-faced woman with the long curly hair whose body divided and encircled her, covered with stars . . . She was the mermaid in question.

He smiled. "There is a story about her, too," he said. "Maybe one day I will tell you."

CHAPTER 16

AT TWELVE NOON THERE WAS A KNOCK AT THE FRONT door. Ginny opened it in her dressing gown. It was Lisa.

"Just checking you're okay," she said.

"Hi," said Ginny. "Look, I'm sorry if we made a racket last night. We didn't keep you awake or anything, did we?"

"No." Lisa folded her arms. "But it was a hell of a night in with the girls. Who needs men, that's all I can say."

"Yeah. Well." Ginny slouched against the doorframe. Why were your own parties always a letdown? She groaned. "You won't tell Mum, will you?"

"Do I need to?" Lisa was looking serious. But at least she wasn't having a go.

"No," she said. "I'll clear up the house. Mum need never know." She hoped.

"Okay." Lisa paused. "Was there any damage?"

"Damage?" Ginny tried her innocent voice. The Ball shifted—a millimeter, just enough to show its face. What kind of damage was she talking about? Some torn raffia on

Jack's leg when two of the boys had pretended to have sex with him (so gross)? Stains on her mother's cream carpet and sofa? Or her own bruised heart?

"A bit," Ginny admitted. "A few, er, spillages."

"But nothing terminal?"

"Nothing terminal," Ginny confirmed. Though the party had got a bit wild; she had drunk way, way too much; and Jack wasn't the only one to be worse for wear and tear. But no one had died. As for Ben . . .

After Lisa left, Ginny took a closer look at the damage. She shifted the sofa and picked up bottles and glasses. The suspected scorch mark seemed to be mud. Which was what her name would be if Mum got to hear about this—ha ha. There were stains everywhere. But no, nothing terminal.

By three p.m. Ginny had wiped, polished, and scrubbed most signs of the party away. She dragged Henry the Hoover out of semiretirement under the stairs and switched him on. He acted a bit surprised, then rumbled into action and negotiated his way around without regurgitating once. Ginny wondered why people—especially her mother—complained about housework. It was simple. You waited until someone was coming round. Then you cleaned up. Why did people make such a fuss?

Ginny put Henry away and started stacking the dishwasher, since the kitchen was the room her mother would examine first. Becca turned up an hour later as Ginny had guessed she might.

"Yo, Gins," she said. They invariably met up after a night out to discuss and analyze everyone's movements and motives.

"Yo," replied Ginny. Only this time she wasn't sure she felt up to it.

Becca wasn't feeling top dog either. "I have THE most massive hangover from hell," she complained.

"Me too." Ginny tossed her a couple of acetaminophens. "Take some drugs, then."

For about half an hour Becca talked nonstop about Harry, who she'd been making out with all night at the party, barely emerging for air. Frankly, Ginny was surprised she had a face left. Becca had been having URL (UnResolved Lust) for him for weeks, and at the first sign that he reciprocated, Becca had left Ginny to it. (So much for friendship and girl power.) Now Ginny learned that Becca and Harry'd been texting each other all morning. So every word had to be examined, every punctuation mark analyzed, every kiss counted.

"D'you think I should just let it all out?" Becca asked, breasts heaving. "How I feel about him, I mean?"

Ginny was under the impression she'd done that last night. "Dunno." Though even Ginny knew that instant adoration was unlikely to lead to commitment.

Becca sat back in the chair. She had that puppy dog look on her face that she and Ginny always ridiculed when anyone else had it. "He's got a car and everything," she breathed.

"Fabulous." Ginny yawned.

Becca gave her a look. "What 'bout you?"

Ginny sighed. Ben had arrived after midnight with three girls and two guys in tow—not a great start, especially since one of the girls was at least a 38DD, and most of it was on display. He was hammered, and Ginny was so nervous that pretty soon she was, too. The party got louder and louder, and at some point Ben had to break up a fight. Ginny remembered wishing everyone would go home, and she must have said this to Ben, because somehow he'd got rid of them all. Then there was just Ben.

"Did he stay?" Becca asked.

When there was just Ben, Ginny had started to get scared again. She wished her mum was there. She wished she'd never had this party and that her mum had never gone to Sicily. She wished she hadn't drunk so much. And she wished the Ball was the kind of ball you could just bounce away from you or throw into the air for someone else to catch.

"Can I stay?" he'd asked her.

"'Course," she mumbled. She'd wanted him to, hadn't she? Hadn't she planned it? Only now all she could think of was when rather than whether she was going to be sick.

"Yeah." Ginny affected a composure she didn't feel. It had been weird having Ben in her room and in her bed. Because home was just her and Mum, and as for the bed bit . . . Well, she supposed it didn't feel right. Not yet. At the same time . . .

"Don't worry," Ben had said. "I won't come on to you."

Why not? Why in hell not? What was wrong with her? Boys came on to Becca all the time. Ginny had said Ben could stay. What further encouragement did he need?

In the event, after a bit of kissing (he was good—very good) and a bit of fooling around—though they didn't even get to second base, he fell asleep, and after she'd been sick—as quietly as possible in the downstairs bathroom—Ginny did, too. In the morning, despite feeling totally wrecked, she made him a bacon sandwich, and he was up and gone. Ginny decided that she didn't understand boys. Not at all.

"Nothing happened," she told Becca.

"Yeah, right," said Becca and started talking about Harry again. Commitment or not, a lot had happened with Harry—and Becca was happy to describe it in graphic detail . . .

"So are you gonna see him again?" she asked Ginny, as she was leaving.

"'Spect so," said Ginny. She'd been checking her phone every ten minutes all day. And her optimism was plummeting with every hour that passed.

"Stay cool," said Becca.

Ginny nodded. "You, too."

After she'd left, Ginny wasn't sure what to do. The Ball kept knotting up and tipping toward her throat, so she decided to send a text—to her mother. It might stop her feeling so guilty.

Miss u, she wrote. *Hope Sicily is fab. Gxx*

A text came back almost immediately. Ginny smiled. Her mother was getting faster. *Miss u 2, Ginny-pie,* it said. *Will call u lata. Much love Mxx*

Ginny-pie . . . Her mum hadn't called her that for ages. And suddenly, unaccountably, all Ginny wanted to do was cry.

CHAPTER 17

Tess found Giovanni on the other side of the *baglio* talking to a couple of swarthy-looking men. They slunk off when they saw her.

"*Ciao*," she said.

From the look he shot her, he hadn't quite forgiven her for speaking to the enemy. "Tess." He bowed his head.

"I wondered. Could I come and talk to you and your Aunt Santina soon?"

"*Sì*."

"*Sì*." He shrugged. "Come tonight, for *dolce*."

"*Dolce*?"

"Sweetness. Dessert." He made a gesture of kissing his fingers. "A glass of wine, too. Why not?"

"I'd love to. Shall I come to the house?" Though she wasn't convinced she'd find it again. The village beyond the *baglio* was a maze leading up to the main road out of town, and just when you saw one familiar set of stone steps leading up from the piazza on the other side of the stone arch, you spotted another.

This morning, after she'd left Tonino, returned to the villa, and got changed, Tess had wandered around, getting a feel for this place where her mother had spent the early part of her life. On the outskirts of the village there were fields and olive groves to the east and mountains to the west. In the heart of Cetaria itself, the jumble of village houses had been built in stone, now worn and weathered, with faded stucco facades and blue or green shutters, their roofs and guttering made of Mediterranean terracotta. The cobbled streets were narrow and steep, grouped around piazzas with stone benches and old fountains, the occasional tiny *rosario* chapel, and maybe a fig or olive tree. The scent of jasmine and hibiscus filled the air, and views of the bay could be found, almost unexpectedly, around every other corner. The entire village appeared to be bending toward the *baglio* and the sea.

In the mornings, all the women did their washing, cleaning, and shopping. Brightly colored rugs, sheets, and clothes hung out of windows and on lines above balconies, blowing in the wind. The women clustered around food stalls in the main piazza or polished their steps or their windows until they shone, stopping every few minutes for long conversations with other women, mostly old, mostly dressed in black, and mostly bent—with a lifetime of drudgery, Tess supposed. And this was what her own mother would have been like if she had not left for England. So who could blame her?

"I will meet you here," said Giovanni. "At seven." Decisive as ever.

* * *

A few hours later Tess arrived for their meeting, dressed now in a sleeveless white linen dress and thonged sandals.

Giovanni treated her to a long and appraising look. "*Bella,*" he said. "You are looking very lovely tonight, Tess."

"Well, thanks." She was aware that her skin had already acquired a golden tan and her hair was bleached blonder by the sun. And she couldn't stop smiling. Why shouldn't she? She was in an amazing place. She had just had a lovely conversation with her daughter—for once, Ginny had seemed genuinely interested in what Tess was doing, what the villa was like, and what Tess had discovered. Perhaps it was a case of absence making the heart grow fonder. Perhaps her mother had been right, and she and Ginny had turned a corner. So Tess was feeling good—despite everything that had happened with Robin.

He inclined his head.

Tess was curious. "What do you do, Giovanni?" she asked him. "For a living, I mean." He seemed to have a lot of free time for a man of thirty-something who clearly had money.

He shrugged. "This and sometimes that," he said. And then, even more obscurely. "It is difficult, even now, to make a living here in Cetaria."

Some sort of entrepreneur, no doubt, Tess thought, as he strode ahead and she struggled once again to keep up with him. She could imagine that. Not exactly a crook, but then not exactly honest either. A bit of a risk-taker. Ruthless, if necessary. She imagined there were a lot of men like him in Sicily.

There were masses of cars and people about, and she mentioned this.

Giovanni barely broke his stride. "It is the hour of the *passegiata*," he said. "People come out to greet each other. It is tradition." And sure enough, she noticed that as they walked he lifted his hand in greeting to various individuals. A bit like the queen, though Tess decided not to mention this. Sicilian men were very macho. And the cars, she realized, were not driving from A to B but rather in a big circle that encompassed main road and village. Then round and round again. So the purpose was not to reach a destination, but to be out and to be seen. Fair enough. It must be the Sicilian way.

They arrived at Santina's, and the old woman greeted Tess as effusively as before, kissing her on both cheeks so that once again, Tess felt the bristles on the old woman's dark, papery skin. Santina pulled her into the darkness inside the house, along the hall, and into *la cucina*, clearly the pulse of the home.

The kitchen table was laden with pastries. "Cannoli," Giovanni said. "The classic pastry of Sicily. Made by Roberta in the village." There was also a bottle of white wine and three delicate, thin-stemmed glasses.

"Her best things," Giovanni said. "She almost never uses them. You are a special visitor."

"I'm honored." And she was.

Speaking in a torrent of Sicilian, Santina pointed to Tess's eyes.

"What does she say?" Tess asked Giovanni.

"Your eyes are so blue," he said. "Of course, this is unusual in Sicily. She says that your mother must have married a very handsome, blue-eyed man."

Tess thought of her father and laughed. "She did."

More talk.

"She asks if you are married, and I told her no. 'Why not?' she says."

"Perhaps I never met the right man," Tess quipped. She accepted a plate and a small pastry from Santina. The outside crust was crisp as she bit into it, but inside it was rich and creamy.

"Ricotta," Giovanni said, "With honey and candied fruit. The outside is the *scorza*, the pastry casing."

"Mmm." It was heady stuff. Tess didn't want even to imagine the calories. She was used, of course, to the Sicilian pastries. Muma often made *cassate*, cream cakes; *tartufini*, truffles; and *cornetti*, an Italian version of a croissant. But somehow they tasted different here.

She accepted the glass of wine that Giovanni handed to her. "*Salute.*"

He grinned. "Bottoms up. Is that not what you English say?"

She laughed. "Not very often these days."

Santina was still speaking. Giovanni nodded. "Love is for life," she says. "The right man cannot always be there at the right time."

Tess thought of Robin. She really couldn't imagine marrying him. Aside from the indisputable fact that he was married already, she couldn't see them like that—married, together, sharing their lives. And yet—wasn't that what she'd always wanted? The special love of her life, the partner, the soul mate? Wasn't that what everyone wanted, deep down?

"Can you ask your Aunt Santina about my mother?" she said to Giovanni. She turned to the old woman as if she could understand what she was saying. "Muma never talks about Sicily," she said. "About her childhood. I don't understand why. There's so much I want to know." She realized her knuckles were clenched hard.

Santina had a sweet look of understanding on her dark, wrinkled face.

Giovanni spoke to her again, and she nodded, not taking her eyes off Tess.

"Ask her if Flavia had a young man who she loved," Tess said, watching her.

Santina blinked and spoke once more to Giovanni. She gestured toward the ceiling and Giovanni sighed heavily and got to his feet. God, Tess wished she could speak Sicilian—or even Italian.

Giovanni left the room, still talking to them over his shoulder. "There is something she wants you to see," he said. "I will only be a moment."

As soon as he was gone, Santina practically darted across the room. She put her hand on Tess's head, cupping it in her palm. "Your mother was made of fire," she whispered.

Tess gaped at her. "You speak English—"

"Shh." Santina glanced toward the open door. "Giovanni—he does not know."

Tess nodded. She wanted to know why, but now was not the time. The old woman's urgency had created a tension in the air.

"Flavia never did what they want," Santina murmured in her broken English. "Flavia did what Flavia want."

Tess grabbed her hand. "And what did she want, Santina? Can you tell me?"

"Flavia never want the boys from the village. Pah!" Another glance toward the door.

"Who, then?" This was a breakthrough Tess hadn't dreamed of.

"Ah." For a moment Santina looked sad. "She want to be free, my child. Your mother want to be free." She sighed. "In Sicily," she said, "not possible to be free."

Tess squeezed her hand. "And you?" she murmured. "Did you want to be free?" She could only imagine the kind of life her mother and Santina had lived. There was the poverty Giovanni had spoken of, the horrors of the war and fascism. There was the Mafia, for heaven's sake.

Violently, Santina shook her head. "For women, not possible," she said. "We have the home, we given to husband—or we not." She fixed Tess with her inscrutable dark gaze. "This is our life."

But not Flavia's life, Tess thought. "What happened to her?" she whispered. "What happened to Flavia?" All she could think of was her mother—the little firebrand who wanted to be free. She could almost see her playing in the fields with Santina, helping with the chores in the cottage, being read to by Edward Westerman in Villa Sirena. Learning about England—where a woman could be free.

Santina leaned so close that Tess could feel the dryness of her skin and smell her warm breath. "She find the Englishman," Santina whispered. "She find him, child. Sì." She nodded energetically.

Tess heard Giovanni's heavy tread on the stairs. "What Englishman?" And what did she mean—she found him?

Santina stroked her hair, touched her cheek, and moved back to the other side of the room. She began to hum, softly.

Giovanni entered the room. He handed his aunt a piece of embroidery, an old sampler.

She smiled and brought it over to Tess, speaking once more in Sicilian.

Giovanni translated, looking bored now. "She says that she made this with Flavia. It was a sort of, how do you say, friendship thing." He shrugged.

Tess touched the fabric, a kind of thin natural linen. The stitches had faded with time, but she could make out the cross-stitch pattern, the interlocking diamonds. "It's beautiful," she said, looking straight at Santina.

She inclined her head.

Tess gave it back and took a sip of her wine, which was sweet and thick. *Dolce* indeed. She didn't know now what to ask—or how much to say.

Santina began to speak once more. "Something happened," Giovanni said darkly. "During the war. My aunt was no longer welcome at your mother's house. The Farro family had a secret. She did not know what it was. Flavia did not say. And she never found out."

Tess frowned. Another secret? She accepted another *dolce*. They were so good. But something told her that there might be more than one version of the past. Santina didn't want Giovanni to know she understood English. Maybe she also didn't want him to know the truth?

Santina smiled and nodded.

"She likes to see people eat," Giovanni remarked. "She used to make all the *dolci* herself, but they take forever, and these days she gets tired."

Santina listened as he translated and then replied. "She says that you need *la pazienza*—patience as well as energy," he told Tess. "You cannot hurry *dolci*."

Tess nodded solemnly. Was she just talking about *dolci*? Tonino, too, had mentioned patience, but she only had a week to find out what she needed to know, to decide what to do with her inheritance. Did she have the time to be patient? "And then my mother left for England?" she asked.

Giovanni passed this on. "Not then," he said, after Santina had replied. "Flavia left a few years later. By then the Farro and the Sciarra families were once more *simpatico* and close." He gestured with his hands as he had done once before. "Flavia was sad, my aunt says. She never told her why, but she thinks it was a matter of love."

Isn't it always, Tess thought.

But half an hour later, as she left to follow Giovanni out of the house, Santina gripped her upper arm. "I cannot say more," she muttered under her breath, before kissing her on both cheeks. "*Ciao, ciao.*"

Cannot say more . . . An interesting way of putting it, Tess thought. *Cannot* because she didn't know the full story—or *cannot* because Giovanni Sciarra was in the room? She wasn't entirely sure. One thing she did know, though—she had to get Santina on her own somehow; only then might she get the uncensored version of her mother's story . . .

It was just after nine. The *passegiata* had long finished, and the streets were almost empty. Tess wanted to dawdle across the *baglio*, take in the fragrances and shadows of nighttime alone. But Giovanni was striding ahead again, clearly determined to escort her right to the front door. But no farther, she decided.

"Have you thought about it?" he asked, as they passed the huge eucalyptus tree. "What you will do with the villa?"

"Yes, but I haven't made a decision." She could smell the faint blue menthol of the leaves as they brushed against

her shoulders, mingling with the salt air and the damp-
ness of the stone. "I might even rent it out—to vacationers
perhaps."

"Ah." He turned. "You do not want to sell?" In the darkness she couldn't see his expression.

"No. At least not yet."

He shook his head. "We should discuss this matter."

"Should we?" As they passed Tonino's place, she saw that
the door was firmly shut. And in the window, almost complete, was the serpent mosaic. The bright greens seemed to
glitter in the lights surrounding the display like the sun on
the sea; the black markings of slate like tiny arrows. Yellow
glass eyes shone from the flatness of the head. It was both
beautiful—and evil. She shivered. Couldn't imagine anyone buying it, actually.

"But yes." He held out the crook of his arm as they
reached the bottom of the steps, and after a moment's hesitation, she took it. "I will take you for dinner tomorrow.
Somewhere special, yes?"

"You really don't have to—" Tess demurred. He was very
kind, but she couldn't help worrying that there might be a
price to pay.

He cut her off, one finger on his lips. "I insist." His voice
was stern. "In Cetaria we take our responsibilities seriously.
And I must tell you more about the Villa Sirena."

"Tell me what?" Tess was intrigued. More secrets? And
why should he feel responsible for her? At the top of the
steps she unlocked the gate, and they walked round to
the front of the villa.

"And perhaps you will tell me something in return." He
was close now, almost whispering in her ear.

"If I can." Tess moved fractionally away. What now?

"Your mother—she gave you some message perhaps?" By now they were under the lamp by the big old front door, and she saw the irritation spark in his dark eyes. "Something in the house?" he went on. "Something to look for? Some special object whose whereabouts she knows of, yes?"

Tess frowned. She had no idea what he was talking about, but he also clearly had no idea of how silent her mother could be on the subject of Sicily.

"That is why you have come all this way, *no*?" he asked. "To locate it?"

"No," she said. "She told me nothing."

"Nothing?" Marginally, his shoulders slumped.

"Nothing."

"*Va bene.*" He shrugged in that Sicilian way and held out his hand, presumably for her key.

"I'm tired, Giovanni," she said. "I must say goodnight." You obviously had to be firm with these men. Give them an inch and . . .

"As you wish." He gave a curt nod. "Goodnight, then."

"Till tomorrow?" She reached forward to kiss his cheek.

"*Sì. Dumani.*" He turned and went out the front way, opening the gates and signaling to her to close and lock them after him. In seconds, he was swallowed by the night.

Tess opened the front door and walked straight out through the hall and the kitchen to the back terrace, only pausing to throw her bag on the kitchen chair. She stood for a moment, looking down at the bay. The darkening sky was still blushed with pink.

She had hoped to find some answers tonight, but now there were more questions than ever. During the war the Farro family had kept a secret—what was it? She sensed that Santina knew. Her mother—the little firebrand; she chuckled; this so summed her up. Muma was still a little firebrand—none of her family dared cross her. And her mother had found an Englishman? This could be, she realized, Santina's broken English. Maybe Muma had *met* an Englishman . . . ? Then there was the debt, the theft, and the betrayal . . . And now it seemed that there was a mysterious something hidden in the villa. Tess shook her head in confusion. And why on earth shouldn't Giovanni know that his Aunt Santina had learned to speak English?

There was a man standing at the water's edge looking out to the rippling ebony sea. It had to be Tonino. He looked restless. Sad, too.

What was his secret, she wondered. After all, it seemed that in Sicily, everyone must have one.

CHAPTER 18

They brought him under cover of darkness.

So he was not dead, Madonna be praised. Not dead, but barely breathing, his chest rattling with the effort of staying alive.

Her father and Alberto—they had done this alone, God knows how—wore grave faces and spoke sotto voce, adaciu, as if someone who might betray them was hidden in the very stone core of the cottage itself. Mama fetched towels, warm water, and bandages, moving swiftly and silently through the house. Maria just shook her head in despair. Anyone would think that she was one of them—an adult—instead of just a girl, only a few years older than Flavia herself.

"Pray for him, daughter," said Mama, as if Flavia—who was no longer sure that God could be trusted to answer her prayers—wasn't doing just that, every hour of every day. Pray to Madonna. Pray for forgiveness. Pray that he lives.

"And tell no one," added Papa. "Not even Santina."

She knew then that he had not told Enzo. This would have been Alberto's decision, she guessed. It was common knowledge that there was bad blood between the two families, a seam of distrust that stretched back through generations of Amatos and Sciarras—a dispute over some land, she had heard, a squabble that had grown more bitter over the years— fed by gossip and mistrust, by underhand dealings and dangerous alliances. Her father had always been stuck in the middle of the two.

She stole into the room they had prepared for the airman, the tiny bedroom where Mama's sister slept when she came to stay. He lay in the bed, still as a statue. His forehead was white and pearled with sweat.

Gently she placed a cold wet cloth on his brow. Then . . . Dare she? Brushed her fingertip across his cheek, just to see. His skin felt cold and clammy.

He opened his eyes. She blinked at the unexpectedness of it, at the alien blue stare, at the pale light of him. Had he forgiven her?

"I am sorry," she murmured.

"My angel." His mouth curved into a crooked, painful smile.

Flavia was flooded with sweet relief.

"My angel," he said again. Then closed his eyes and slept.

"Sogni d'oru," she murmured. Sweet dreams . . . Golden dreams . . .

Flavia put the book away for another afternoon. It was tiring her. Not so much the writing of it. What was exhausting was reliving the emotions. How could she help it? As she wrote about him, she remembered—the look of him, his paleness, the blue of his eyes; the scent of him, of illness to begin with, that faint smell of medicine fighting decay. And the way he spoke. *My angel* . . .

The irony was not lost on Flavia. Flavia Farro had become Flavia Angel. But she was getting ahead of herself. There was still much more to tell, so much more that Tess would need to know . . .

Street food, market food; bloody and raw, vibrant and fresh— the true guts of Sicily. Tightly packed stalls in a network of narrow alleyways. Oxen and goat, cheeses and breads, offal and fish, fruit and vegetables. Arancini—*little rice balls with meat or cheese.* Panelle . . . *Chickpea fritters, bought in the street, eaten with the fingers in a soft roll. Or as an antipasto—to undress the appetite. Hot and satisfying, crisp and succulent. A deep-fried Arab legacy.*

Bring the water to boil, add the chickpea flour gradually, stirring in the same direction. Flavia underlined *"the same direction." Add chopped parsley and black pepper. Cook to a paste that pulls away from the side of the pan. Turn out onto an oiled surface. Smooth. Cool. Cut into oblongs. Fry until golden. Add lemon juice. It is complete.*

CHAPTER 19

THEY HAD DRIVEN ALONG THE COAST TO A SMALL family-run restaurant. And Giovanni clearly knew the family; the signora and various signorinas kept dashing out of the kitchen red faced and eager to check that he was happy and all was well.

"The villa you have inherited. I must tell you. It is not a good place," Giovanni said, as their antipasto arrived. It was *caponata*, a sweet-and-sour vegetable stew made with eggplant, celery, onions, and olives, a dish Tess's mother often prepared, though hers was very different.

"Not good in what way?" she asked. "In a bad state of repair or bad history?"

"Both," he said. "It is true that much needs to be done for the place to regain its former glory. And . . ." He touched his nose. "Bad things have happened there. It has a dark story."

Hmm. "No chance, I suppose, of you telling me what bad things?"

Giovanni hemmed and hawed and waved away another waitress/signorina. "It is not for delicate ears," he said.

Should Tess tell him that her ears were far from delicate . . . ? Presumably it was all to do with the famous debt, theft, and betrayal he kept going on about. And the mysterious "it." Not to mention the war, of course. And the fact that Edward Westerman had been gay.

"Sicily has a legacy of darkness," he said, mopping up the last of his *caponata* with a chunk of sweet yellow Sicilian bread.

Yes, she was beginning to get that.

"It is therefore in your interest to sell."

Tess had always been a rebel. She realized now that she must have got this from her mother. She sipped the wine that Giovanni had ordered, a Nero d'Avola, rich and black curranty, with, yes, just a hint of pepper. When someone tried to tell her what to do, she always wanted to do the opposite. "I'm going to keep the villa," she said. "For now."

Giovanni let out a deep sigh. "You are stubborn, *no?*"

Tess put down her glass. "Perhaps. But I like the place. I hear what you say. And I'm grateful to you for trying to help." She crossed her fingers under the table. "But I don't get any bad vibes from Villa Sirena. So I don't want to sell it—not yet."

Giovanni shook his head. He looked like the harbinger of doom. "And your mother?" he asked gloomily. "What does she say?"

Tess hadn't told her. But she could guess the reaction. "She won't like it," she admitted. "She'll want me to put in on the market and get back to the UK. *Pronto.*"

Giovanni waved a languid finger in the general direction of *la cucina*, and one of the girls appeared to whisk the plates away. "*Sì, sì, beni.* Yes, it was good," he told the anxious face. He turned his attention back to Tess and nodded sagely. "Your mother is a wise woman," he said. "Perhaps she knows more than she says?"

Probably. She didn't say very much, after all. Tess leaned forward. "So what is it?" she asked.

"It?" He frowned.

"What is the thing you thought she might have asked me to look for? Something special? Something secret? Something valuable?"

Giovanni glanced swiftly from side to side and then fixed his gaze somewhere over her left shoulder. "*No capisco*," he muttered. "I do not understand you, Tess. It is of no importance."

She wasn't convinced. It had certainly seemed important the last time he mentioned it.

Their pasta arrived with a flourish. *Spaghetti con le fave*—with wild fennel, broad beans, and olive oil. Giovanni had informed her, on checking with the *signora* when they first arrived, that it was today's best pasta and that therefore they both must order it.

"And if you do not sell," he continued, when the waitress had disappeared. "What will you do with the place? You mentioned vacationers, I think." He managed to imbue the word with so much distaste that Tess had to smile.

She speared a broad bean. This must be their season; she thought she'd spotted some growing by the roadside on the way here. "I'm not sure yet," she said. Because however would she find the money to do it up? Tess thought of the *pazienza* both Santina and Tonino had mentioned. She hadn't yet thought of an excuse to visit Santina again (or a way of finding out when Giovanni might not be at home). And she hadn't yet had a chance to quiz Tonino about the famous family feud. But she had a few days left. She just had to be patient.

CHAPTER 20

DURING THE NEXT TWO DAYS IT WAS AS MUCH AS Ginny could put up with—no word from Ben, and listening to Becca drooling incessantly on about Harry this and Harry that and Harry was the boy she'd been waiting for all her life. All her life. At seventeen. Honest to God. Sometimes Becca just did her head in.

Pictures were appearing on Facebook with alarming rapidity. Harry and Becca in a bar having a drink on their first "anniversary" (one day after they got together), Harry and Becca on the beach kissing. Yuk! Why would anyone want to see that? Status: *Becca is in a relationship*. No . . . Whoever would've guessed?

Finally, when Ginny had reached the depths of despair because Ben hadn't messaged or texted her, he called.

"Hi, babe," he said. "Feel like meeting up for drinks?"

Did she? Oh yes, yes, yes.

She got ready in a flurry of nerves and anticipation, phoning Becca twice to check her outfit was okay and then changing her mind and opting for the jeans she'd been wearing to start with.

She was forty-five minutes late and was practically peeing herself with terror at walking into the pub on her own. Even before her eighteenth birthday last month she'd had fake ID for ages—everyone did. But she wasn't used to pubs. And . . .

He was with five of his friends. There was a pub quiz. It was awful.

Ginny clammed up. The Ball had so many knots and tangles, she couldn't speak. She felt a complete idiot—even more so because the one answer she knew was the name of one of the characters in *EastEnders*. What a loser!

At the end of the evening, though, Ben clamped his arm round her shoulder (which was difficult as she was so tall) and said, "D'you wanna come back to mine?" Like they were going out or something.

Ginny shrugged and tried to look as if she'd been expecting this development. "Okay," she said, in her couldn't-care-less-really sort of voice. But it meant something. It had to mean something. Didn't it? She began to breathe more easily.

On the way back to his, they talked about families.

"What's your dad like, then?" Ben asked. He had a flap of dark straightened hair that hung over his right eyebrow—sexy and dangerous.

"My dad? No idea," she said. This had been her stock response for the last few years when asked about her father. To start off with, when she was a kid, she hadn't thought too much about it. There was Mum, there was Nonna, and there was Pops. It seemed enough.

Then she realized that for her friends it was different. They all had fathers. Fathers who they talked about at school, fathers who took them out on the weekend, who drove nice cars and came to parents' evenings and shows. She realized, too, that Pops was trying awfully hard to fill this gap; that he—if not her mother—acknowledged that there was a gap. But whatever he did, however hard he tried, it wasn't quite the same.

"You've never known him, then?" asked Ben.

"Never met the guy." Ginny had accumulated as many facts about her absent father as she could. His name was David; he was what her mother referred to as "a bit of an old hippie, I'm afraid." And there was the photo of the two of them—Mum and David; he with the careless smile, the casual arm around her, the faraway eyes . . . She wondered where his eyes had been that day of the photo. Where his head had been.

To give Mum her due, she had never criticized David. "You were unexpected," she had told Ginny one day when she was about five or six years old. "A wonderful gift."

An accident, she meant. An unplanned pregnancy. Ginny knew that now. But she liked the way Mum put it—as if Ginny had been a nice surprise waiting on the doorstep one morning.

"And David?" She could never say "my father," and her mum never tried to make her.

"He was never really cut out for fatherhood," her mother said.

Ginny had tried to analyze her tone. She had always been interested in personalities and working out what made some people tick and some people tock. This was the reason she'd first started studying psychology at A-level and why she had applied to do a psychology degree at uni in September, too.

Ginny shuddered at the thought of this, felt the Ball perform a half somersault. And it wasn't anticipation—it was hideous terror. Everyone was supposed to want to go to uni—unless they weren't clever enough, of course. No one was supposed to dread it.

But psychology—the science of people and their minds and behavior that had promised so much—had turned out to be little more than a bunch of theories and statistics. That Ginny, frankly, couldn't get her head around. Similarly photography, which had seemed promising enough to start with, consisted more of studying other photographers' methods than taking your own photos. And General Studies just meant having a good argument. (Which was why it was her best subject, she supposed.) College, Ginny had decided, was a con.

She staggered a bit—not from the drink, she'd taken it easy tonight, but 'cause it was hard to walk when a boy who was shorter than you had his arm round your shoulder. She was walking hunched forward, her hip level with his waist. Really, she should have her arm around him.

Her mother's tone when she spoke about David and fatherhood (and why wasn't he cut out for it? Everyone else seemed to do it. Wasn't it something you took on regardless rather than something you were or weren't suited for?) wasn't wistful or loving or regretful—it was just kind of accepting.

"Did you love him?" Ginny had asked once, when she was about ten or eleven and needed to know these things.

"Oh, yes," said her mother. "I loved him."

That was good. "And now?"

"Now?"

"Do you love him now?" Sometimes her mother could be remarkably dense.

"Not in the way you mean," her mother said (though in truth Ginny didn't mean in any special way, she just meant love). "Not anymore. It's all too long ago."

That of course, was in the days pre-Robin, in the days when there wasn't a man in her mother's life—or at least only the occasional, unimportant, unremarkable date. It was in the innocent days, the days when Ginny laughed a lot and everything seemed simple. It was also of course Before the Ball.

"Did he just bugger off somewhere then?" Ben asked.

"Yeah. To Australia."

"Why didn't you go, too, and have me there?" Ginny had asked her mother. She quite liked Australia. Her life would have been very different.

"I thought about it," her mother said. "But there wasn't long to go. And there was Nonna and Pops . . ."

Even at ten or eleven Ginny knew what she was saying. Her grandparents could be relied on. David could not.

She didn't say this to Ben—it was too private. She just churned it around in her head, as she often did. And she and Ben walked on and up the hill toward where he lived.

"Mine left about ten years ago," Ben volunteered after a while. "He lives in Bristol with his new wife. She's a right old dog."

Ginny wondered what it would be like to know that your father had a new wife—old dog or no. Because it was all very well for parents to rant on about how they, too, had a life to live and how they shouldn't/couldn't/wouldn't live through their child/ren (her mother did this a lot; it was her Me-Time rant). But they had brought them into the world, hadn't they? So they *were* responsible, and your child should be your first consideration, surely, way before enjoying yourself or taking off on holidays or marrying a new wife or whatever.

"Mine went off to live in a hippie colony," Ginny told him. At least it was interesting. Better to be absent and interesting than around but boring, bald, and with visible nose hair.

At the age of fourteen she had missed him fiercely and considered trying to contact him via the Internet. At fifteen she changed her mind and hated him with equal ferocity. He had never tried to contact her, had he? Why should she bother to try and get in touch with him? Maybe she'd just turn up in Australia one day when she was hugely success-ful (at what, she wasn't sure) and show him what he had missed out on when he walked away. *What had he missed out on?* asked the Ball. Ginny ignored it.

At sixteen she began to blame her mother for letting him go. Obviously she hadn't tried hard enough to keep him.

But now, well, she had learned to use his absence to her advantage. She had seen how strict her friends' fathers could be. One lone parent was far easier to manipulate. Her mother wasn't a pushover—she could be one tough cookie. But she was susceptible to emotional blackmail. And Ginny had become expert at applying it.

Back at Ben's he suggested a movie, popcorn, and beer. When the movie finished, Ben put on another one, and Ginny fell asleep.

At some point in the night they transferred themselves to the bed, though they kept most of their clothes on. Ben could take hers off later, Ginny thought—partly in hope and partly in terror. She cuddled in close to him, and they kissed—hot kisses getting steamier by the second. He was touching her, in all the right places, too, sending sweet streaks of desire right through her. But just as she thought, *this is it, this is it,* he stopped, grunted, "Sorry. Better get some sleep, then, I s'pose." And turned around. Huh? By then Ginny had woken up—in more ways than one.

In the morning, Ben's mother made her a bacon sandwich and she went home to analyze what had happened.

He hadn't seemed up for it—not really. Could it be possible that after all, Ben was gay? It seemed unlikely. Did he just want someone to watch movies with or sleep with? Maybe. Did he not desire her? His kissing suggested that he did. Or did he desire her and also respect her? Er . . . Was he waiting—for a sign that Ginny didn't know about—or to get to know her better, or until a decent period of time had elapsed? Studying psychology was—as she'd suspected—absolutely useless. Because Ginny had no idea.

CHAPTER 21

IT WAS ALMOST THE END OF HER WEEK, AND TESS woke on Tuesday morning with a sense of sadness. Tomorrow she'd be driving to Palermo and flying back to the UK. Time had gone too fast. She was looking forward to seeing her family. But Robin . . . She stretched out in the big chestnut bed. He'd sent her several texts and tried to call a few times, but she hadn't replied or picked up. Cowardly, maybe, but she'd face him in due course. It was unresolved between them—she knew that—and they had to talk. But it would be in her own time and on her terms.

And she was no further in her quest for information. She had gone round to Santina and Giovanni's house twice yesterday, knocked on the door as if she were "just passing." Once there was no answer, once Santina had answered but Giovanni was around and they hadn't had a chance to talk. It was all very well being patient, but Tess was beginning to feel as if this were a nonstarter.

As usual, Tess breakfasted on the terrace, where the air was still and warm. And as usual, she could see Tonino in the bay, standing on the white rock by the lookout post, his face as rugged as the stone he worked in, his dark hair outlined like a raven's wing against the pale blue of the morning sky, his body—he was dressed in black jeans and white T-shirt today—in clear relief against the navy ocean.

Looking out to sea. The man was always looking out to sea, but she hadn't yet seen him go in it. Well. She cleared her breakfast things and took them into the kitchen. Inside, the villa was cool and yet welcoming—completely contradicting what Giovanni had told her at dinner the other night. So . . . Was Giovanni Sciarra being straight with her—or did he have another agenda?

Tonino was in his studio when she got down to the bay. Since the morning he'd made her coffee, his replies to her questions had been mostly monosyllabic, his expression neither friendly nor hostile. Indifference—and it was infuriating. She had no idea what he thought of her, and for some reason that she didn't want to acknowledge, she felt rattled by this.

She paused by the window of his studio. The serpent was glittering demonically at the center of his display. She wanted to ask him about the story it came from, but Tonino was wearing a face mask and cutting some stone, particles of dust and grit flying in the air around him, so she walked on by.

Next time she came here, she thought, walking down to the water's edge and letting the tiny waves at the shoreline lap around her toes, she would bring her diving equipment and explore properly. Which for her meant underwater. And she would get to talk with Santina. Alone.

Tess closed her eyes. She would miss the tranquility of this place, not to mention the warmth. In England it would still be chilly; here, Sicily's springtime was opening up into summertime. Already the sky was becoming listless and hazy with heat. She lingered for a while, simply enjoying the feel of the sun on her skin.

"*Ciao.*"

She swung around. Tonino stood there regarding her intently. He had changed into shorts and his usual flip-flops and was still wearing the white T-shirt, open at the neck.

"*Ciao. Bong . . .*" She felt herself stumbling over the words of greeting. Why, oh why, she thought for the umpteenth time, had her mother not spoken Sicilian—or even Italian—to her as a child? By now she would be fluent—bilingual even. But she knew the answer to that question. Sicily was off-limits. It was okay to eat its food—even Muma hadn't been able to wean herself away from that. But everything else was *no grata.* "I was just absorbing the peace."

He nodded. "It is peaceful here, yes. You like our village, I see that."

"Do you think you will always live here?" Tess swirled her foot in the water. She imagined he and his family had been here forever.

"It has everything I need." And yet, even as he said this, he stared out to sea again, and Tess saw it once more—that sadness. He loved the place, he loved the sea. But it was more complicated than that. He was more complicated than that.

"And your family?" she asked. "What about them?"

He blinked and turned back to her. "My grandfather was Alberto Amato," he said.

Tess raised an eyebrow as if she'd never heard the name before.

"He was a spear fisherman. A legend. He could hold his breath for over four minutes when he was free-diving, and he could dive down to sixty meters."

She nodded. That was pretty impressive. "And your father?"

"He was a fisherman, too. He went out in his boat. In May and June he took part in the *mattanza*. They all did."

"*Mattanza*?"

"The ritual of the blue-fin tuna fishing." He pointed to the buildings that stood back from the bay, the warehouse with three big arches, and the faded processing plant itself, now disused and abandoned. "They worked in a team. Many men in small boats."

"What was it like?" she wondered aloud.

"It was once a thriving business," he said. "But a blood-thirsty one. Another word for *mattanza* is massacre. But . . ." He shrugged. "They say Cetaria owes its name to the plenty of fish in the sea. Literally, it means 'earth of the tunnys' in Greek." He shook his head sadly. "Still, the tuna slaughter—it was not pretty to watch. And it was hard for the men who had to do it."

Tess shivered. She understood how hard it must have been to make a living. But she was glad that tuna was no longer caught and killed that way.

"They kept the boats in there." He pointed to the ware-houses. "They say that the boathouses still echo to the 'Cialoma.'"

Tess listened. She couldn't hear anything, unless it was an echo of emptiness. "Which is what, exactly?"

"A song," he said. The fishermen sang it to find strength to haul in the nets.

"And yet now it seems so tranquil." The buildings were at rest; for them, time had stood still. The fig tree and the oleander stood in front of the rusting anchors as if to symbolize their newfound repose.

He shrugged. "If you wish for complete tranquility," he said, "you must visit Segesta."

"Segesta?" She had seen it on the map. But sightseeing had not been her priority when she came here. She had preferred to explore her mother's village, look for information, and chill out in the villa and in the sea. She had needed to think—what should she do about Villa Sirena, and what should she do about Robin?

He rubbed at the scar on his cheek. "But of course. You cannot come to Cetaria and not visit Segesta."

Tess smiled. "I'd like to. But I'm going back tomorrow."

He lifted an eyebrow. "You have today."

"I suppose." She was reluctant. She had half-thought that she would try Santina again—only she didn't want Giovanni to get any wrong ideas. "What is there to see there?"

He brushed back his hair with the back of his hand. There was a faint dust—from the stones, she supposed—coating the skin of his face; almost a glitter. "A temple," he said. "An amphitheater."

"Really?" It sounded impressive, she had to admit. You didn't get to see temples and amphitheaters every day of the week. Especially in Pridehaven.

"I could take you." He was staring at her as if he could see out the other side.

"But your work . . ."

"It will wait. Unless . . ." He bent his little finger. "You have other plans?"

"No." She spoke quickly. No doubt he had seen her with Giovanni. She didn't want him to think that she and Giovanni . . . Because it wasn't true, and it would only annoy him if he disliked the Sciarras as much as Giovanni disliked him. "I'd love to come." She looked around the *baglio*. "Do you have a car? Because . . ." She was about to say that she could drive them in her rental car—she hadn't made much use of it so far.

He grinned. "Better than that," he said.

"Oh?"

"Meet me here in an hour." There was a spark—maybe of danger—in his dark eyes.

Tess didn't hesitate. "I'll be here," she said.

When Tess came down the stone steps an hour later, he was waiting for her.

"*Ciao*." He handed her a crash helmet. Right. Lucky she'd opted for the blue linen shorts then rather than the short denim skirt. His scooter, a Lambretta, which looked stylish rather than powerful, was parked by the entrance to the *baglio*.

She climbed on behind him. "Hold on tight!" he yelled, and they were off.

They drove out of the village and along a road lined by bamboo, cacti, and olive trees, heading toward the soft green slopes of the mountains, whose high granite croptops were half-hidden today by wispy clouds. Tess felt the exhilaration race through her as she clung to his waist.

Well, there was nowhere else to hold on to . . . at any rate, no place she felt safe. Not that they were going fast—they couldn't; the scooter didn't have the power. But the wind in her hair and on her face felt good. She felt good. She couldn't remember feeling this good for a long time.

The noise of a shot rang out, echoing around the hills. Jesus . . . "Mafia?" yelled Tess.

He just laughed.

They rode under a viaduct past tall cypress trees, between vineyards to their left and eucalyptus trees to their right. Beyond lay silver olive groves and fields of yellow wheat and grassland interlaced with scarlet poppies, white daisies, and spiny yellow thistle. They slowed at a crossing, and Tess saw a lizard dart across a rock by the roadside. Green with orange markings. She thought of Tonino's serpent and the fish. About her mother's girlhood. And about a life here that was so different from the one she knew in England.

It was a bumpy road, pitted with holes and deep ruts that had Tess bouncing on the scooter's passenger seat.

Tonino slowed down. "Segesta," he announced.

An old man was standing by a tourist bus collecting tickets from a line of people. Tess waited for Tonino to stop so that they could park and join the line, but instead he sped past the old man with a cheery wave, and they rode on up the winding road. It was steep, though, and the Lambretta began to slow down until it was barely chugging along.

At the bend, Tonino stopped and pointed back the way they'd come. "The Hellenic temple," he said.

Tess turned. The honey-colored temple stood serene, dominating the landscape, and she could see this was the perfect way to first view it. It looked as if it had been deposited there by some beatific God above.

They got off the scooter. The air was perfectly still and heavy. All Tess could hear was the occasional birdsong and the hum of insects—crickets or cicadas, maybe.

Tonino looked up. "The swallows are back from North Africa," he said.

Surrounding the lonely temple were the green and red plains and the mountain thicketed with oak and laurel. At the bottom of the slopes was a dried-up riverbed, a deep gorge. It was hypnotic, Tess thought. The land seemed to throb like some giant magnet. The power of the temple or the power of the land? Or both?

Some minutes elapsed before Tonino motioned for her to get back on the scooter behind him and they rode slowly up to the amphitheater, at the very top of the hill.

They must have been between busloads of people, for they were alone.

"It's amazing," she murmured, almost afraid to speak too loudly. The ancient theater was huge and deep, the semicircle of rugged white stone rows dropping down toward the area of the stage. Behind the stage, she could see trees, mountains, valleys, and in the distance, the glint of the sea.

"Come." Tonino led her down the cobbled steps into the front of the theater, where she sat on the pitted stone ledge—rounded and worn over the centuries.

He walked to the center of the stage, grinned, flung out his arms to the sky, and to her utter amazement, began to sing—in Italian, in a beautiful rich tenor. Tess was transfixed. She vaguely recognized the aria—from some Italian opera, by Puccini maybe. But she had never heard it like this before—in a Greek stone amphitheater, under a

Sicilian sky, sung by the most enigmatic man she had met in her life.

When the last note had echoed and died, he bowed low, and she clapped. "Amazing!"

"Can you imagine . . . ?" He sat beside her on the white stone. "What it must have been like here in Greek times? The stage of mud and rock, the stars above you?"

"Mmm." Tess hugged her knees. She was beginning to.

"A hot, still night. The mountains. A darkening sky . . ."

He was quite a poet. She smiled.

"At festival times, the place is floodlit," he said. "People come in the evenings with a bottle of Prosecco and a cushion."

"It must be magical." She couldn't help the note of wistfulness that crept into her voice. Once again, she thought, *I don't want to leave this place* . . . She felt as if the gift that Edward Westerman had bestowed on her was about to be snatched away.

"And sometimes they come to watch sunrise." He was doing that intense looking thing again, as if he were gauging her reaction, testing her in some way.

Tess nodded. She was unwilling to say anything to break the spell.

"They stay for breakfast, and someone comes in a van to sell Sicilian sausages and buns."

She had to laugh at the incongruity of this.

"What?"

"A hot dog van always gets to the unspoiled locations sooner or later."

"Hot dog?" He frowned.

"Sausage in a bun." And no, she didn't know why they were called hot dogs either.

A busload of people had arrived in the car park below them and was now moving in convoy toward the theater where they sat. "Time to go," said Tonino.

They jumped onto the scooter and rode down the winding road toward the solitary temple. They parked the Lambretta, climbed a path bordered by agave and myrtle trees. And there it was. Even bigger than she'd realized. Even older and even more beautiful. The honeycombed stone was weathered and wildflowers were growing in the nooks and crannies of the giant pillars.

"The swallows nest here now," Tonino said. As he spoke, some goat bells chimed in the distance.

"How old is it?" she asked him.

"Fifth century BC. They say it was never desecrated because it was never finished. It is still waiting for its roof, you see?"

"Mmm." She could see. And now it would have to wait forever . . .

He smiled at her. "It is peaceful, yes?" he said.

"Yes," she agreed. "Thank you."

"For bringing you?" He shrugged. "It was nothing. When you live in a place . . . It is good to remind yourself of what is there sometimes."

"For not letting me miss it," she said.

He acknowledged this with a small nod and gestured her toward a wooden bench by a fig tree.

She sat. It was a sheltered spot, but she was still surprised to see him pluck two plump green figs from the tree.

He passed one to her. "An early crop," he said. "It has been a good spring. This is San Pietro. Normally she must be ready for the feast day at the end of June."

She bit into the velvet skin, felt the red pulp inside—grainy, sweet, and indiscreet on her tongue.

"Still, the first of the season, I think," he said.

Tess thought of how different these two men were—Tonino Amato and Giovanni Sciarra. Giovanni a business-man, Tonino an artist. Giovanni taking her to restaurants where he could be assured of the best food and service; Tonino bringing her to a ruined temple, singing to her, and feeding her ripe figs fresh from the tree. Very different . . .

"Why does Giovanni Sciarra hate you so much?" she asked, before she could stop herself.

His expression changed, a deep frown furrowing his brow. He muttered something that sounded like "*bastardo*. . ." "It is an old quarrel," he said, his fingertips just touching his scar. "And we are not the first. Why do you concern your-self with it, Tess?" His voice was cold. "What is it to you?"

She got to her feet to stand beside him. "I'm just curi-ous." And she still was . . . How could she know who to trust when she hadn't even heard his side of the story? "Giovanni told me some of it . . ."

Again he swore under his breath. "Long ago they took our land. They knew who to serve and who to punish. That is one thing. But murder," he growled, "that is another."

"Murder?" Tess stared at him. "Not Giovanni . . . ?"

"No, not him." He turned away from her. "His family, the Sciarras. They caused my uncle's death. They have no scruples. They will stop at nothing." Again, he traced the line of his scar with his forefinger.

"But what happened?" Tess couldn't leave it there. "What about the police? Wasn't there an inquiry? Why would they—"

She stopped short because Tonino was laughing, harshly, without humor. "This is Sicily, Tess," he said. "We are talking about the Sciarras."

"But—"

She got no further. He had taken a step closer and held her by the shoulders. "Leave it, Tess."

She turned her face and his mouth seemed to brush against her hair. There was something about the curve of his jaw that was familiar to her. It reminded her of something—or someone. He smelled of wild mint and lemons. Tess touched the scar on his face and felt him flinch. "This scar . . . ," she said. Suddenly she knew.

"Yes." He bent his head. "When we were teenagers. We always fought. It was in our blood; our forefathers were the same."

She traced the length of it. Giovanni. But why had this uncle been murdered, and how had the Sciarras got away with it? Who did they serve, and who did they punish? It was all too confusing. A debt, a theft, a betrayal—and now this. Murder . . . ?

She let her hand move to his shoulder. She wanted to put it on the nape of his neck where the dark hair curled enticing and warm. But . . . It was this place, she supposed. It must be this place.

"You haven't yet," she reminded him softly, "told me the story of the mermaid."

Their faces were only inches apart. "But I will do," he said. He bent slightly and she felt just the briefest touch of his lips on hers. He tasted sweet, of ripe figs and musk. "You will come back to Sicily, I think," he said. "You will come back here to Cetaria, yes?"

"Yes." The nape of his neck was as warm as she had expected it to be. For a moment, she didn't think of Robin, Ginny, or Muma and Dad. She thought of nothing, not the Sciarras, the Amatos, and the Farros of Sicily; not Villa Sirena nor the secrets it held. She didn't even think about her mother's story. She didn't know when, but, "I'll come back," she said. "I promise."

CHAPTER 22

A table without bread, they say, is a day without sunshine. Bread, the Sicilian staple. Fresh and golden, thick and chewy on the tongue. Religion and ritual. Plaited loaves, crossed loaves, upside-down loaves; black bread, nutty bread, unleavened bread, seed bread. Cooked in brick ovens fired by olive wood.

As far as Flavia knew, the tradition of decorative "votive" bread had been popular in Sicily for centuries. Paschal (Easter) bread and other religious feasts gave Sicily's more creative bakers a chance to reveal their sculpturing talent. There was the *ferro di cavallo*, or horseshoe; the *pesce*, or fish; and the *mafalda*, twisted in form.

It is not simple . . . The right amount of yeast must be used to make the bread expand perfectly while baking.

Would Tess ever bake her own bread? Probably not, Flavia had to admit. Nevertheless the art would not be forgotten, not while she had breath in her body and strength in her hands. Flavia began to write down the recipe; her recipe, handed down from Mama and from her mother before her.

Bread, the symbol of all that continues. Bread, the staff of life . . .

Tending to the airman brought a sense of purpose to Flavia's existence. She became more disciplined, more selfless. She no longer tried to avoid chores or daydreamed the hours away. She worked hard in the house and in the fields, so that she could run back to nurse him. She knew that she surprised them—Mama, Papa, and Maria—with her vigilance. But, after all, he had fallen from the sky, and she had found him.

So she laid claim to him. To touch him, to bathe his wounds, to feed him, to help him sit up and, later, to support him as he stood for the first time, unsure, like a kid goat—this brought her satisfaction. For the first time in her life, someone needed her.

He was surprised that a Sicilian family should care for him. "Why?" he asked her through parched lips on one of those early days, once the worst was over and they knew he would live. "Why do you care? I'm awfully grateful. But why have you helped me?"

Flavia wiped his face gently with the washcloth. His cheekbones were high and prominent, his brow wide, his skin stretched and white. And his mouth—the bottom lip was full and sensuous, the upper lip slightly crooked, slightly off-center. It was that imperfection that caught at her, that made her want to stare at him for hours.

"My family—we like the English," she told him. "We work for Englishman." And haltingly, she told him about Signor Westerman, about the grand villa, and the poetry he had read to her, when, as a girl, she had flown around his casa with her cloths and her polishes.

"So where is he?" The airman looked around as if he expected Signor Westerman to materialize from the stone walls.

"He returned to England," Flavia told him. "It was too dangerous here."

At that he nodded, his gaze drifting away from her. She knew he was thinking about the raid that he had been part of. The raid that had brought him here. *"Bloody war,"* he said. *"It'll have us all, you know."*

He was a good listener—he had nowhere else to go, did he? So at other times, Flavia talked—in whispers if need be—about her family and her life. She told him things she had only ever said before to her best friend, Santina. *"I do not belong here,"* she said. *"I never have."*

"Where do you belong?" he teased.

But she didn't want him to laugh at her. *"I belong where I can live,"* she told him. *"Where I can breathe. Where I can be me."*

He nodded then in understanding. *"You're a wonderful girl, Flavia,"* he said. *"I hope you get everything that you want, I really do."*

"I will—if I fight for it," she said, braver with him now than before. He had told her his name—Peter—and sometimes she whispered it to herself, at night, when there was no one to hear.

"Still," he said, *"your people are good people. They saved my life. You all did, dammit. And maybe when you're all grown up you'll feel differently."*

"*I am not a child.*" *Flavia drew herself more upright.* "*I am seventeen.*"

"*Seventeen, eh?*" *But he only looked at her and smiled.*

Seventeen, Flavia realized, was not enough.

"*Maybe, Flavia,*" *he said to her one day,* "*this other life, the one that you long for, is not as good as you expect it to be.*" *He was watching her with a strange intensity in his blue eyes.* "*Our dreams always seem so perfect. But maybe the other man's grass is no greener.*"

Flavia listened to the words. The other man's grass . . . ?

"*Still, I would like to see it,*" *she said. She could only imagine the kind of life where there was choice, where your pathway was not mapped out for you by another. But how could he understand? He knew so little of how things were in Sicily.*

Gradually, she relaxed even more with her airman. They began to laugh together. He always seemed to be waiting for her, and his expression had changed when he watched her moving around the room, tidying his things or bringing fresh water to his bedside. He began to tease her, to tell her stories, to talk about England. And when he spoke of England, there was a longing in his eyes that made her jealous.

Then one day she darted into the room in a hot fury— Maria had made her clean out the brazier, even though she had done it already and it was perfectly clean. Just out of spite. Just to stop her . . . coming to see him, she almost said.

He was sitting up in bed, and she sat down beside him.

He smiled. Patted her hand. "*Perhaps I should take you back to dear old Blighty,*" *he said.* "*Show you what it's really like.*" *And his expression darkened.* "*When this damned war is over.*"

She didn't realize he was joking. "Would you?" she pleaded. There was a long pause. He stared at her and said nothing. "Would you take me?" She lifted her face to his, and he let out a small groan. Bent his head closer.

When he kissed her, it was like nothing she had dreamed of. His touch, the graze of his lips on hers . . . She felt something inside her turn to liquid, a hot liquid that burned her.

When he pulled away, she wanted him to take her back, to kiss her again, to hold her—so close that nothing could ever pry them apart . . .

But he wouldn't even look at her. "Go, Flavia," he said. "Please go."

Flavia put down her pen. She needed to rest. She needed to think. She was old, and the memories were almost too vibrant and alive for her to deal with. She had half expected the story to be dry as dust in the telling. But she hadn't expected this, this . . . torrent of sadness.

When did she fall in love with him? Who could tell? Was it the moment she found him in the valley, torn and bleeding and lying amid the shrapnel of his plane? Was it when he almost died and she thought she had lost him? Or was it perhaps when he kissed her?

Once more, Flavia lifted the pen. She must keep the writing—if not the emotions—under control. She must remember for whom she wrote: Tess. Her beautiful daughter, Tess, who needed to hear this story. And yet . . . not just Tess.

"What is it?" she asked him the next day. "What have I done?" Again, he wouldn't look at her.

"Nothing," he said. He looked sad. Gently, he brushed her hair from her face, his fingertips smooth on her cheek.

Flavia closed her eyes. How good it was—the touch of this man.

"It was wrong of me," he said, "to kiss you. A chap shouldn't take advantage of a girl like that."

"You did not." And this time, she moved forward to kiss him. This time she held his face and she parted her lips and she felt his taste on her tongue like nectar. Flavia was not afraid to show her passion. All she wanted was to be held in his arms. All she wanted was to kiss him. Again and again. She would drown in him if she could.

But she was getting ahead of herself now.

Flavia closed her eyes for a moment. It was too painful. Which was why . . .

It was so far away, Lenny said, and of course this was true. But distance—whether in time or in geography—didn't always lessen the pain. And she could feel it now, after all these years, deep in her gut, just as she could feel his soft lips on hers that first time.

She could see now that she had been vulnerable, even ripe for the picking, some might say. Although it hadn't been that way. It really hadn't been that way.

She had been almost the same age as her granddaughter Ginny was now, she realized with a start, although Ginny had celebrated her birthday in early spring and Flavia would not have been eighteen until wintertime. And yet . . . there were worlds between that young Sicilian girl and her English granddaughter, whole worlds.

Help me find the words, she whispered. She had to tell honestly how it had been.

She had helped him heal, her airman, and then she had given him her heart. It had been so easy, so natural. She had loved him. Sometimes she thought she would always love him. That he'd haunt her till her dying day. That she'd never be free.

Mama must have sensed the danger. Or Maria told her. She spoke to Papa, and they stopped her from spending time with him alone. But it was too late by then. Much, much too late.

CHAPTER 23

TESS WAS RESTLESS NOW THAT SHE WAS BACK IN Pridehaven. She wasn't looking forward to going back to work, it was raining, and the house looked suspiciously tidy. "Anything happen while I was away?" she asked Ginny, who had been studiously avoiding her eye since Tess's return.

"Happen?" she echoed. "Not really. Why?"

"Everything looks cleaner," Tess said, regarding her daughter's reflection in the art deco mirror above the fireplace. Ginny was on her laptop—studying or Facebook? Who could tell? Personally, she didn't understand why it was necessary to tell dozens of acquaintances the minutiae of one's life—with illustrations; she worried that the real world was in danger of disappearing completely. But she knew she was in a minority.

"We didn't make that much of a mess." Ginny sounded defensive. "I just cleared up a bit afterwards, that's all."

Ah, yes, the pizza and movie night in with the girls. "Great," said Tess. *Once upon a time you used to tell me everything,* she wanted to whisper. "Great." Only for some reason, she didn't feel it.

At work, Simon Wheeler, her boss, called her into his office, known as the Goldfish Bowl, for obvious reasons—it was small, all glass, and had no privacy.

"About this job . . . ," he said.

"Yes?" Tess was glad she was wearing heels, her cerise silk blouse, black jacket, and pencil skirt. As supervisor, she'd have to look smart—for at least the illusion of control.

"I'm afraid you were unlucky this time, Tess," he said.

"Sorry?" Had she misheard? And what did luck have to do with it? She had been given the impression that the job was hers.

"We've given the position to Malcolm."

"Malcolm?" She hadn't been aware that Malcolm was even in the running. She leaned forward. "But he's only been here five minutes."

"Five months, actually," Simon said smoothly. He tapped his pen on the desktop—an irritating habit that betrayed his discomfort. "And that isn't the point, Tess. He's had supervisory experience elsewhere. I'm sorry."

She said nothing. There wasn't much point. Simon and Malcolm went to the pub together sometimes, and she was pretty sure Simon and his wife, Marjorie, had had Malcolm and Sheila round for dinner. Also, of course, not that she thought she'd ever have to say it—not in this day and age—but Malcolm was a man.

"We gave you fair consideration." Simon straightened his tie. More discomfort. "You were an excellent candidate."

"Except that Malcolm was better," Tess said. Who would have thought it—the all-boys-together network operating at a West Dorset water company, for God's sake?

"He showed more commitment," Simon said. "More ambition." He frowned. "I hope, Tess, that you won't feel bitter about this."

Commitment? Ambition? Tess got to her feet. "I'll try not to," she said. Bitter . . . ? Bitter . . . ? She felt bloody angry, that's what she felt. She felt passed over. Betrayed, even. "But I do think that I deserved the post, Simon."

Simon sighed. "It's not easy managing a team, Tess," he said. "People skills are paramount. Handling people is not a breeze."

"I know that." It wasn't fair. She had worked hard for this company, and until Malcolm had appeared . . .

She looked out of the Bowl. A couple of the girls were laughing and joking with Malcolm. People skills, she thought. Janice shot her a sympathetic look. They all knew, she realized.

"I'd like to hand in my notice," she heard herself say. It sounded childish. But how could she stay here now? Everyone would be smirking behind her back, feeling sorry for her or sucking up to Malcolm. And Malcolm would be her immediate boss.

"Now, Tess." Simon, too, got to his feet. "I want you to mull this over. Decisions made in the heat of the moment—"

"Are instinctive ones," she cut in, "and therefore probably sound."

There was a pause. It wasn't a friendly one.

Simon came over and put a slug-like hand on her shoulder. Tess wanted to brush it off, but she managed to restrain herself.

"Give it more thought," he said. "Until you hand it to me in writing, I don't know a thing about it, okay?"

Patronizing ass . . . Tess couldn't bring herself to reply. She opened the door of the Goldfish Bowl and left his office, heading straight for the coffee machine. Damn it. The person she most wanted to tell was Robin. She wanted to hear his voice—calm and measured—hear his sympathy, and absorb his righteous indignation. *Obviously, you're the best person for the job, Tess*, he would say. *If he can't see it, then he's a fool.*

And yet . . . Robin didn't think she was the best, did he? Tess fumbled with the polystyrene cup. Chose espresso, on a whim. To Robin she was also second best—because he wasn't with her. He was with his number one—his wife.

And now she wanted to cry. Fuck. Espresso in hand, she headed for the bathrooms, hoping they'd be empty. She couldn't face gossip or bitchy sympathy. Commitment? Bloody hell. How could you be committed to water?

In the Ladies, she gulped her coffee, which made her feel worse because it was so unlike the espresso Tonino had made for her in Sicily. In fact, it was so unlike it that it didn't deserve to be called coffee at all.

Sicily . . . She couldn't get it out of her head. She couldn't stop thinking about Segesta and the taste of ripe figs. She was beginning to wish Edward Westerman hadn't even left her Villa Sirena; it had unsettled her, turned her life upside down, changed everything.

Back at her desk, she typed a letter of resignation. *I feel that my skills and experience have not been fully appreciated*, she wrote. *And it is with some regret* . . . Yeah. Like hell.

She waited until four, when she saw Simon go out to talk to Malcolm, and then she put it on Simon's desk. She got her things together, picked up her bag, and left the office. So, she had chucked in her job. On principle. What now?

She had only been back from work a few minutes when Lisa rang.

"I was looking out for you," she said. "But you went rushing inside like a mad thing. Are you okay?"

No, thought Tess. "Yes, of course," she said. She would tell Lisa—she told Lisa everything eventually, but just for now she wanted to curl up with it alone.

"I wanted a word about Saturday night," Lisa said.

Saturday was Lisa's fortieth, and she was throwing a big party. Quite frankly, it was the last thing Tess was up for in her current mood, but as she'd told Lisa yesterday afternoon over coffee and caramel biscuits, she wouldn't miss it for the world. "Yes? I can get round by four to give you a hand," she said.

"Lovely, sweetie, but I forgot to say . . ." Lisa hesitated. "You're welcome to bring Robin, okay?"

Tess sighed. Robin had tried to ring her three times today. And she hadn't picked up. "I'm not really seeing Robin anymore. Not after Sicily." What would have happened, she wondered, if she had gone to Cetaria with Robin? Well, Tonino wouldn't have happened, that was for sure. Not that anything *had* happened. And if Giovanni was to be believed, nothing *should* happen . . . But if she was still in love with Robin . . . She thought about it. The way she'd felt . . . Tonino's almost kiss . . . She wouldn't have responded— would she? She had to accept it—she and Robin were over.

Lisa laughed. "It's not over till the fat lady sings, Tess. You haven't actually finished with him yet, have you?" Tess heard Lisa put her hand over the phone and hold a brief muttered conversation with one of her children. *I told you, it's in the understairs cupboard . . .*

"No." What she needed, Tess decided, was a stiff drink. And then perhaps another.

"What are you afraid of, Tess?"

Good question. What was she afraid of? That Robin would talk her round? That he'd persuade her, the way he'd always persuaded her before, that she should go on seeing him, that things would change, that he'd leave Helen, that pigs might learn how to scuba dive . . . "I'll do it," she said. Lisa was right. Tess had to sort it out properly. It was the only way forward.

"Okay." Lisa sounded pleased. "Good girl."

At seven p.m. Tess left Ginny and the latest *X Factor* boy band on full volume, got into her Fiat, and drove toward the other side of town, where Robin lived. She'd done this several times since they'd been together. Fortunately, he'd never spotted her (at least so she assumed), and she'd never seen him. She wasn't even sure why she did it. To get a glimpse of his other life, perhaps? Because she could? Or to see her—the fragile Helen who had to be fussed over and protected in a way that Tess had never been.

Not that she wanted to be, she reminded herself, indicating right and waiting for a gap in the traffic. But it might be nice for someone to want to.

She turned into his road. Robin probably bought his Sunday paper from that newsstand on the corner. Perhaps she wasn't the sort of woman that men wanted to protect? She changed into third gear but continued to drive slowly. After all, she'd given birth to her child (alone) and brought her up (alone). Often, she didn't bother with lipstick. Her favorite clothes were jeans and a sloppy T-shirt (though she could clean up as well as the next woman, she liked to think, and even Ginny thought she had great legs), and she cherished her independence. What room then for fussing over, for protection?

When she saw Robin, she was so shocked that she almost lost control of the car. He was strolling along the pavement looking perfectly at home (well, he did live here). By his side was a woman.

Tess clenched her hands more tightly around the steering wheel. Whatever she did, she must not draw attention to herself. Ha. The woman was tall, blonde, and willowy and looked about as much in need of protection as a rhinoceros. Not that she looked like a rhinoceros—unfortunately. She was sleek and attractive, she was smiling, and she must be Helen.

Tess slowed as much as she dared. Robin had his arm round the waist of the non-fragile-looking Helen, as if he quite wanted it to be there. And just as she passed them, teeth gritted, mind in neutral, *you can do it, girl* . . . she saw from a quick sideways glance that he was laughing. Laughing! He was happy; they were both happy, Tess realized. How dare he be so happy . . . ? She felt numb with shock. And if he was so happy with his wife, then . . . Why?

CHAPTER 24

"IT'S QUITE A MILESTONE, DON'T YOU THINK?"

Tess turned to see who was addressing her. Male and forty-something—fair hair, red faced, faint stubble. Shorter than Tess, overweight. Drinking beer. She took all this in before she even replied.

"Forty?" she said. "Yes, I reckon so."

"Not that you'd know." He looked her up and down with clear approval. "You haven't reached it yet. Obviously."

And you have—obviously. Tess made her smile vague. "Excuse me." And drifted toward the food table.

Mitch was piling a plate high with chicken, potato chips, and coleslaw. "Thought your luck was in, then, Tessie," he joked.

"Save me." He was such a type. The type you found at parties alone, when you went to parties alone. Like she did. And for how long, she wondered. For how long would she be the single unattached woman at parties? What was the *matter* with her, for God's sake? She helped herself to food—more for a distraction than because she was hungry. It was high time she did something about it.

"Okay," said Mitch. "Only it's my wife's birthday party, so I won't be available all night, I'm afraid." He waggled a bottle of cava at her, and Tess held out her glass for a refill.

"What's wrong with me, Mitch?" she asked. And that was another thing. These days she tended to get maudlin at parties.

"Nothing that I can see." He patted her shoulder.

Was she too fussy? Did she want something that didn't exist? Or was she stuck in a cyclical pattern—attracting the wrong kind of man and then regretting it later? Like Robin. That hadn't sunk in either. It was still hovering on the edge of things as if Tess wasn't quite sure what to feel. But one thing she did know. The second she saw him with his not-so-fragile Helen, it was over. Really over. Even more over than it had been when she'd known it was . . . over. She just hadn't told him yet.

"Great party," she told Mitch. "Who are all these people?" Lisa had introduced her to the first arrivals, and Ginny had been here, too, for a while, but after that the party had swept ahead on its own impetus as more people arrived and joined in the melee, Lisa—as hostess and birthday girl—at the center. Mitch had laid out tables for food in the living room, and people were sitting on sofas and various chairs, or milling around with glasses and plates of nibbles doing party small talk. Ginny—predictably—had left to meet up with a friend.

"Oh, who knows?" He shrugged. "Friends, work colleagues, parents of the kids' friends, relatives, the odd neighbor or two, you know." He winked. "Do you think it's time for the cake?"

Tess spied Lisa on the other side of the room talking to the forty-something guy. She caught Tess's eye and made a frantic signal. It looked like "help!"

"Yes," Tess told him. "ASAP, I'd say."

She squeezed through the throng. He was right about one thing, though—forty was a milestone, and it would be Tess's turn soon. Lisa at least had Mitch and a proper family. Tess's life was so unsettled. No man, no job, daughter about to fly off into the World Outside and growing further away from her with every day that passed. Oh, yes, and a house in Sicily. A smile crept onto her face.

When she got to Lisa's side, she grabbed her friend's arm and propelled her away. "Sorry," she said to him. "I have to steal her. Come on, birthday girl."

"Thank you," breathed Lisa, who, Tess had to say, was looking stunning in a simple black minidress with a scooped neck and the white-gold jewelry her husband had bought her for her birthday.

"You're welcome."

And then Mitch came through the door, kids in tow, holding the cake between them—lemon drizzle with lots of silver balls and candles. Tess, Ginny, and the kids (until Ginny left to meet up with a friend. Who were all these friends anyway? And when had Ginny stopped telling her everything—was there a precise moment?) had made it last night at Tess's, while Mitch whisked Lisa off for a romantic birthday meal.

"Oh!" Lisa flushed, put a hand to her mouth and said, "However did you . . . ?"

And then one of the young guys started playing "Happy Birthday" on his guitar, and they all sang, and Mitch produced more cava and filled up lots of glasses, and they proposed toasts, and Lisa cut the cake and wished . . .

Tess laughed and clapped and sang with the rest of them. She looked around at the cheerful faces, and she danced—first with Lisa, then with the kids, then with Mitch, and even with the forty-something man. But her heart had gone AWOL. She didn't want to be here any longer. She wanted to be gone.

"Maybe we should go out sometime," the man, who was called Mark and who was a colleague of Mitch's, said after their dance.

You see, Tess told herself. There's nothing wrong with you. You're just selective. "I probably won't be around much," she told him. She wouldn't do that anymore, she decided. Accept dates with strangers she didn't even want to get to know. Life was too short, time was too precious. Every minute could count.

"Oh?" He seemed disappointed. "Going away?"

"Yes," she said. She didn't know when. It depended on Ginny as much as anyone. She had thought—when she still had a job—that it would be in six months or so, depending on when she could wangle the leave. But now . . . It was a clear and defining moment. She knew the way forward.

What was it? Her mother's secret past that she longed to uncover? The lure of the villa, or the turquoise bay? A promise made to a man at an ancient Greek temple? Whatever. The pull of Sicily was strong. And she didn't even want to resist.

*   *   *

Tess had only been back home for half an hour when Robin rang. She almost didn't pick up, then she thought of the party and what it felt like always to be on her own.

"Got you," he said. "At last. Don't ring off. I know you're avoiding me." He sounded out of breath, as if he'd dashed out of the house on the pretense of emptying the garbage or something.

"You usually call when I'm at work," she said primly. Though not for much longer . . . She was working out her notice. Robin could say what he liked, and it would make no difference. The future was uncertain, but hey, couldn't that be exciting?

"Tess, I was an idiot," Robin said. As it had always done, his voice slid through her defenses like hot butter.

She decided not to disagree.

"I should have come to Sicily with you. I shouldn't have let Helen pressure me. I got cold feet. I was scared. I can understand why you must hate me."

"I don't hate you," she said. Which was strangely true. She was just irritated. It was all the same old stuff. The same old Robin. Nothing would ever change.

"I'll make it up to you," he said. "How about dinner tomorrow night? You can tell me all about it. The house. And everything."

"I don't think so." Tess was almost surprised at her own resolve. Before, she would have given in; she just couldn't help herself. But now . . . From somewhere she could feel the pull of Sicily, and it was pulling against Robin. It was on the other side. And winning.

"Tess. Tess, darling . . ." Practically a purr. He still thought he had her. "You're upset. I can understand that. But if you just give me one more chance . . . It'll be different this time."

"I've always wanted more of you, Robin," she said. "And now I realize that I can't have it." She really didn't know why it had taken her so long.

"That's where you're wrong," Robin said. "You can have more of me, because—"

"I can't," Tess said. "Because you're married. And now . . . I don't want even the little bit that's left. Not anymore." She had always thought he was special. But there was nothing special about a man who sucked up to his in-laws because they had money. And there was nothing special about a man who kept you on the sidelines of his life. Lisa was right. She deserved to be a bigger priority.

"But Tess . . ."

"Good-bye, Robin," she said. "Please don't call again." She clicked off her cell, straightened her shoulders, and imagined she could feel Robin's weight just slipping off. Nice.

She thought of Ginny and the exams that had already begun. A week on her own in the house, and her daughter seemed more stressed out than ever; avoiding Tess's eyes and sneaking off to meet up with this mysterious friend. Her daughter, she realized, was slipping away from her. Images skated through her mind: Ginny's first tentative steps—arms up for Tess to rescue her and swing her round in a dizzy circle; Ginny's first day at school—serious dark eyes in a pale face, navy cardigan, and gray pleated skirt; the first time Ginny looked at Tess appraisingly and said, *That color suits you, Mum* . . . And they began clothes shopping together. Singing along to Oasis—*Don't look back in anger* . . . Tess blinked back the tears.

And then she had an idea. Of course. She wondered why she hadn't thought of it before. She had been given a chance to make it come right. She just had to take it . . .

CHAPTER 25

GINNY WAS MARCHING TO BEN'S. SHE WAS MARCHING because she was angry and trying not to cry. And she was trying not to cry because she'd just had a row with her mother. Rows with her mother left Ginny feeling resentful, upset, and not wanting to admit that her mother could—under any circumstance—be right.

The row had been mainly about Ben, although like most rows, it had turned into a different animal from the one it was to start with. It had run along the lines of:

"What are you doing tonight, darling?" (Mum)

"Going to Ben's." (Ginny)

"Oh." (Mum)

"Oh?" (Ginny) "What d'you mean, oh?"

"Nothing." (Mum). "So is he a boyfriend?"

"No, just someone I see." (Ginny)

"But you're seeing rather a lot of him, aren't you, love?" (Mum)

"I like him." (Ginny)

"Fine." (Mum)

"Is it?" (Ginny)

"Is it what?" (Mum)

"Is it fine?" (Ginny)

"Well, yes, I suppose." Pause. "But are you studying as much as you should be? You're spending so much time with this . . . Ben, that—"

It was the "this Ben" that annoyed Ginny the most. She knew her mother wanted to meet him, but she was (a) reluctant to put Ben through this ordeal and (b) pretty sure that when her mother did meet him she would do her utmost to discourage the relationship. So it wasn't a hot idea.

Ginny tried to make her shoulders relax. She steadied her breathing. The Ball just loved it when she got uptight; this made It glow and grow.

Her mother had already asked the usual parent-type questions like: *How old is he?* (Subtext: Is he *much* older than you?) *Where does he live?* (Subtext: Is it the *right* side of town?) *What do his parents do?* (Subtext: Are they *professional* people?) And *Has he always wanted to be a hairdresser?* (Subtext: Is this the *limit* of his ambition?)

"They're divorced," Ginny had told her. "His mum works in the Hare and Hounds."

"In the pub? Really?" She had seemed surprised, though why she would think that everyone's parents worked in banks or offices Ginny had no idea. And then: "Well, bring him round. I'd like to see what takes you out of the house every night." (Subtext: *You used to stay home with me, and now you go out gallivanting and leave me on my own.*)

"I will." But she hadn't. Apart from (a) and (b), there was just too much subtext.

The trouble with Mum was that she never knew when to stop asking questions.

Ginny turned left at the end of the street and dug into her bag for a cigarette. She'd give up after the exams, she decided.

"It's my life!" Ginny had shouted at her mother in answer to the time/studying/Ben question. She had shocked herself. Maybe she was feeling guilty about the whole exam thing. Maybe it was because the Ball was turning, turning, as if it might spin out of control.

Her mother took a step away from her at this apparently unprovoked attack. That was the other thing about Mum—she didn't fight back.

Ginny knew she didn't have to go in for the kill. But she did. "So why don't you just butt out and let me live it my way?" *Butt out* was a good touch—she'd heard it on *Friends*.

Her mother stayed calm but poured herself a glass of red wine—which showed that Ginny was getting to her. "Parental responsibility," she said. "That's why I don't 'butt out' as you put it. You're only just eighteen. And how well you do in your exams could affect your entire life."

Fuck. "You're just jealous," she informed her mother.

"Of Ben?" She looked confused.

"Of the fact that I have a boyfriend." Talk about kicking someone when they're down. And no one had been more relieved than Ginny when Robin dripped off the scene. At least she supposed he had; she sensed something was different, and Mum wasn't showing any of the Signs. But doing battle was about searching for your enemy's weak spots, and then pressing the raw nerve.

Her mother, however, was made of stern stuff. "So he *is* a boyfriend," she said, with a small smile of triumph.

Ginny felt tricked. "Oh for Chrissake, Mum," she said.

That was when the row became something entirely different. "It's just that I was wondering if—after the exams—you'd like to come to Sicily with me," her mother said. "For a holiday." She was beaming. Ear-to-ear stuff. "It would give us a chance to . . ."

Ginny jerked to attention. Sicily? What was she talking about? "You've only just come back," she pointed out. Did she want to go to Sicily? Well, no. And especially not with her mother. It wasn't at all what she had in mind.

"I'm going there again," her mother said.

Ginny wondered if the first visit had perhaps unhinged her mother's brain. She'd come back in a weird mood; no sooner returned than she'd quit her job; no sooner quit her job than she'd apparently broken off with Randy Robin. And now she wanted to return to Sicily. And with Ginny. For why . . . ?

"I need to decide what to do with the villa," her mother said. "I need to think about things." She'd got that look on her face again. That odd look. On hold . . .

Ginny stared at her blankly. Why would her mother need to think about things? And where exactly did her thinking leave Ginny? She swallowed hard, to push the Ball from her throat. "I might do a gap year," she ventured. "I might not go to uni in September." And not any other time either, she added silently.

She heard her mother draw breath. Sensed her counting to ten. "You could take a gap year," she said. "I suppose. Only . . ."

"Only what?"

"Sometimes it's harder to go to university when you've had a gap year. Harder to . . . I don't know, get into studying again."

Yeah, thought Ginny. Because a gap year gave you the time and opportunity to realize it wasn't what you wanted to do in the first place. After all, there were graduates flying around all over the place all too overqualified to get ordinary jobs and too inexperienced to get decent jobs. And they were loaded with debt. She knew all this from General Studies. In fact, in a strange kind of way you could say that General Studies was responsible for her not wanting to go to uni, which was also ironic. In fact, quite a lot of stuff was. Ironic.

"I was thinking of doing some traveling." Ginny waited. Traveling would probably teach you far more than uni would—about life anyway. And if she went off traveling, wasn't it just possible that the Ball would stay behind?

"Or you could come to Sicily with me," her mother said, looking excited again.

"For Chrissake, Mum!" Ginny's hand holding her mug of tea jerked back, and she spilt some on the table.

Predictably, before she had a chance to react, her mother was on her feet getting a cloth. Ginny sighed. "Sorry."

"Well, what's wrong with Sicily?" her mother asked.

"Mum, a gap year is about getting away from stuff." How could she not understand? "It's not something you do with your parents."

"No." Her mother tossed the cloth back in the sink. "I suppose not. But you wouldn't go traveling on your own, would you, love? I wouldn't feel happy about you—"

"Dunno," she said. Though she would—if necessary.

"But where would you go?" her mother asked.

"I dunno. I just want to get away." Rather to her own surprise, this emerged with rising bitterness, a bit like a snake spitting venom. Did she hate Pridehaven so much? Did she hate her friends and her life at home? Did she hate everything?

"Is it because of this . . . Ben?" her mother said, though she looked sad rather than angry.

"No, Mum! You're not listening. It's because of me!" And she'd walked out and slammed the door.

Ginny arrived at Ben's house and banged on the door. Why could parents (or mothers in her case) never understand?

The following morning Ginny woke up with an odd feeling of dislocation. Then she realized where she was. Oh, shit. She was in Ben's bed at Ben's mother's house, and he was sleeping beside her. And she hadn't told her mother she wasn't coming home.

Also beside her were six empty bottles of beer; two plates with the greasy remains of hamburgers, french fries, and beans stuck to them; and two DVDs. Her clothes and Ben's clothes were strewn lifelessly around the room as if they'd gone to an all-night party while their owners were asleep and had collapsed midjive with all the body knocked out of them.

This was a bit how Ginny felt. Everything had changed, and yet nothing had changed. Should she get up? She considered her options. She had to go to college this afternoon, so she could head home to "study" for this afternoon's exam. Not that she would. Not now.

She slipped out of the bed without waking Ben and went to the bathroom to pee. On the landing she paused and listened, but it seemed Ben's mom was out of the house. Good. She didn't want to stay here any longer than necessary—not even for a bacon sandwich.

Ginny returned to Ben's bedroom and began locating her clothes. She dressed quietly, one eye on the lumpen frame in the bed that was Ben. Still comatose; he would be for another hour, she guessed.

She hadn't stayed at Ben's since her mother's return from Sicily, but last night she didn't text her mother, and she switched off her phone. That would show her. Sometimes Ginny wondered if it was the Ball that made her behave so badly. Sometimes she wondered if it was her bad behavior that had created the Ball in the first place. Sometimes all she wanted to do was hug her mother and burst into tears. But the Ball (or something) stopped her.

When she was dressed, Ginny went over to the bed and stared down at Ben's face. Even when he was asleep, he was great eye candy. But she had come to a conclusion during the night.

Ginny left the room and crept down the stairs. She let herself out of the front door, feeling different from the way she'd felt when she'd come into the house last night. Everything had changed, and yet nothing had changed. She was still the same person, wasn't she? But she would never be the same again.

The row with her mother had been the catalyst. Why should she play games? Why shouldn't she say what she felt? This reminded her a bit of the conversation she'd had with Becca the day after the gathering that had turned into a party, and this in turn made her sad, because Becca was hardly ever around anymore. She was superglued into her relationship with Harry. Still, Becca had said what she thought.

So Ginny had done the same.

"I like you, Ben," she said when they'd gone—as usual—up to his room. "I like you a lot."

He stared at her. "Yeah, well, I like you, too." He laughed. "Obviously." He slumped onto the bed. "Siddown."

She stayed standing. "It isn't," she said.

"Huh?"

"Obvious."

"Oh."

He looked down then, and that's when it hit her. Power. It surged through her. Because she realized the truth. Amazingly unbelievable as it seemed, he hadn't properly come on to her because he was scared. Not because he didn't desire her or he wanted more time or any of that other shit. He was just scared.

So she got down on the bed beside him and showed him he didn't need to be. Scared.

And now? As Ginny walked back home she thought about her nighttime conclusion. It was that sex was hugely overrated. And she felt the glow of relief, liberation . . . And regret.

CHAPTER 26

"So, tell me, love. How was your week in Sicily?"
Her father gave her a hug, and deep in his arms, held fast,
Tess felt as though she was relaxing for the first time since
she'd got back. Already Sicily seemed a lifetime ago; since
then, there had been Work, Robin, and Ginny.

She smelled the comforting, familiar smell of her father
and his cardigan. Shaving cream and old wool. And bur-
rowed a bit deeper. When she was young, it was her mother's
attention she craved. Dashing to and fro from the apartment above to the restaurant, always preparing food and
cooking, washing and ironing, pausing to advise or to scold,
her mother had been a hurricane. And in her eye was the
same sort of fiery temper . . . How could anyone get close?

Her dad, though . . . In his late seventies, he was still a fit
and wiry man. He had energy. He could make Muma laugh
and cry. He would tease her, comfort her, dance with her.
He was the calm after the storm. A rock. He was as reliable
as Muma was unpredictable. As Tess grew older, she had

come to appreciate what before had always been there. And right now, a rock was about what she needed.

"Interesting," she said, catching her breath and reluctantly allowing herself to let go of him.

Her mother shot her a sharp look over her shoulder. They had spoken on the phone when Tess arrived back home, but briefly, both of them giving nothing away, Tess thought now.

"You never told me it was such a stunning location." Tess went over to kiss her mother on both cheeks. She was looking tired and kind of tense, but that was Muma's modus operandi. And when she was tired or tense, she simply did more cooking.

"You make it sound like a film set," her mother said. "It is just a place." She gripped hold of Tess's arm with a bony hand, reminding her fleetingly of Santina Sciarra.

"A beautiful place." Tess grinned at her father, who was shaking his head behind Muma's back. Why did he let her get away with so much, Tess wondered. Didn't he want to see the village where his wife had grown up? Didn't he feel shut out sometimes by her secrecy?

Her mother let go and shook a zucchini at her. She was making something complicated in layers with fish and tomatoes and zucchinis. No doubt it would be delicious. "Beauty is only skin deep," she said darkly. "Beware it doesn't charm and trap you."

Tess laughed. "Is that what happened to you, Dad?" she teased. "Did Muma charm and trap you?"

"Of course." He began to lay the table. Forks, napkins, a small dish of *parmigiano*. "She used all her powers. And by God, she was a beauty. Dark, flashing eyes, black curly hair..."

Flavia whipped at his arm with her dishtowel. Tess laughed. Her mother's hair was still thick and wavy, but white as cotton wool these days, and always pinned back and up so it wasn't in the way of the cooking.

"Your mother could be pretty persuasive, you know, love," he added.

"Ha." Flavia turned her back on him, but Tess caught her smile.

Her father had always been tall and lean with very dark blue eyes—the eyes that Tess had inherited and which had so fascinated Santina. When she was a child and he used to put her on his shoulders on the beach on summer Sundays, she used to dream for a moment she'd bang her head on the sky. And now? She didn't want either of her parents to get older; she couldn't bear to think of losing them.

"What about you, love?" He twinkled at her. "Did you meet anyone nice in Sicily?"

"Humph." Her mother snorted and muttered something unintelligible into the dishtowel now draped across her shoulder.

"Actually," Tess said, ignoring her, "I met two very personable men."

"Single?" quizzed her father.

"Definitely."

"Sicilian, I suppose," said her mother disparagingly. "Sicilian men are like bees round a honey pot when they see an attractive woman. Not to mention a woman who has property. And trust me; they are all the same—they expect too much, and they live in the past."

"Not necessarily." Tess helped herself to a slice of tomato. Though, thinking about the longstanding Sciarra and Amato feud now inherited by Giovanni and Tonino, perhaps Muma had a point.

"Be off with you." But her mother laughed. It was a family tradition to pinch her ingredients before they made it to the pot.

Tess chewed the tomato slowly round the edge. She knew that her mother would have to ask.

"Tell me, then."

"What?"

Her mother clicked her tongue. "What were their names?"

Tess hid her small triumph. "Giovanni Sciarra. That's your old friend Santina's great nephew. And . . ." She hesitated. "Tonino Amato."

"Hmph." Her mother snorted again.

"I suppose you know Tonino's family, too?" Tess kept her voice casual.

Her mother opened the oven door, transferred her main course from table to middle shelf in one fluid movement. "I do," she said. "Alberto Amato was my father's closest friend."

Tess tried to hide her excitement. Muma was talking about Sicily. "Wasn't Alberto a fisherman?" she asked. A spear fisherman, Tonino had said. She recalled the pride in his voice as he'd spoken of him.

"Yes, he was." Her mother sat down heavily, and Tess saw her father throw her a concerned glance.

"He was Tonino's grandfather." Tess poured out the wine she had brought into three glasses. Her parents always insisted they didn't drink and then knocked it back anyway. "Tonino's father was a fisherman, too. He worked for the tunnery at Cetaria."

Flavia nodded again. Her dark eyes were faded and milky with age, but still alert. She was, Tess reminded herself, a remarkable woman. "I remember him," she said. "He was not much more than a child when . . ."

"When . . . ?" Tess tried not to look too eager.

"When I left."

This was the most her mother had ever talked about Sicily and the people she'd known there. Tess was almost afraid to breathe in case it broke the spell.

"Alberto and Papa used to spend hours in the village bar drinking grappa and putting the world to rights." She chuckled at the memory. "And I often used to loiter outside and eavesdrop. Until . . . until . . ." The dreaminess in her voice seemed to snap. "Things change," she said.

Tess's father went to her side and patted her hand. The skin was wrinkled and marked with liver spots. It was a hand that had always worked, even now when she suffered from arthritis in the joints of her fingers.

And you? Tess wanted to shout. *What did you do?* But she didn't. It would only make Muma clam up completely. "The two families seem to hate each other," Tess said, trying to sound casual. "The Amatos and the Sciarras." Perhaps her mother could tell her more. Perhaps she would know about the theft and betrayal, the debt and the murder—or the secret "it" that Giovanni seemed to be looking for.

"They always did," Flavia said. "Their fathers, too, and their grandfathers before that." She turned to Tess almost accusingly. "That is what it is like in Sicily," she said. "Who would wish to be involved in that sort of life?" She got to her feet again and started busying herself with putting the cooking pans in hot water to soak.

Oh dear, Tess thought. Another No Entry sign.

"And what of the house, love?" her father asked diplomatically. "This villa—your unexpected inheritance. Did you like it?"

"Oh, yes." Tess sipped her wine. She had liked it all right. "I've taken lots of photos." She watched for her mother's reaction. "I'll bring them round when I've downloaded them."

Her mother shot a dismissive glance across at her. "You have placed it with an agent?" she said. "It is quiet there, but pretty enough for tourists, I suppose."

Tess ran her finger along the rim of the glass. "Actually . . . ," she said.

"Tess!" Her mother sat down again—more abruptly this time.

In a second, her father was once more at her side. "Flavia? Sweetheart?"

She waved him away. "I am fine," she said. She glared at Tess.

"I thought I'd keep the villa for a while." Honestly. Why was she letting them make her feel guilty? What was wrong with her? What was wrong with her family? Tess got up, switched on the faucet, and began to run water to wash up the cooking pots. The last thing she wanted was to upset her mother. But the house had been left to her for a reason—there was some purpose to all this; there had to be.

"What for?" her mother asked bleakly. "What would you keep it for?"

"Holidays?" Tess didn't dare say what she'd hoped—that she, Ginny, and her parents could all go there together. Happy families, she thought bleakly. Some hope. Especially after last night. She squirted dish soap into the bowl and let the water fill it with soapsuds.

Her father was clearly struggling. "That's an idea, love," he said.

"A bad idea," said her mother. She got to her feet. "I knew no good would come of it," she muttered.

Tess and her father shrugged at each other.

The phone rang, and with unmistakable relief he moved toward the door to answer it. "That'll be Joe," he said to nobody in particular as he left the room.

"He hopes . . . ," said Flavia, with a conciliatory smile.

"He certainly does." Tess smiled back and piled the pans into the dishpan. Truce. She thought of the trip to Segesta, the shot she had heard. "Did you know anyone in Sicily, Muma," she said, "who was involved with the Mafia?"

Her mother was opening cupboard doors to get out the plates for supper and slamming them again with rather more force than necessary. She snorted with exasperation. "Involved with the Mafia?" she repeated. "Oh, Tess. Many people paid protection money." She took plates and dishes over to the table. "It is the way things were in Sicily. It was a system that worked. People paid it like a tax. They would be looked after. Many people did not see it as a bad thing."

Tess frowned. "But did the system carry on like that during the war?" Her mother was only a teenager back then, but knowing Muma, she would have had a good idea of what was going on—even if she wouldn't say.

Flavia shrugged. "Some. The Mafia as an organization was driven underground by Mussolini. But they got their power back toward the end of the war." She sighed as she placed plates in position on the table. "Rest assured, Tess, they will always retain their power."

And now? Tess scrubbed the frying pan clean. Did they still have power now?

Her mother was moving around the kitchen, picking up a teacup here, a cloth there. It was as if she couldn't be still. "Naturally they regained power when the Fascist government fell," she said.

"How come?"

"Because the Allied forces handed over administrative control of Sicily to local men who they knew to be anti-Fascist." She laughed.

"And these men were . . . ?" Tess was hoping for names.

"Mafia who had been lying low under Mussolini," her mother replied. "Many of them considered men of honor." She straightened up, but did not look her daughter in the eye.

Tess was skeptical. Surely her mother didn't believe all that she was saying? "Who were they, Muma?" she asked. "Were there any particular families in Cetaria?" She wiped her hands on a dishtowel and began to dry the pots and pans.

"Hush now." Her mother shook her head. "It is better not to know these things." She busied herself with tidying the kitchen counter, but Tess couldn't accept that the subject was closed.

"Isn't that a bit head in the sand?" One by one, she put the pots away. In her mother's kitchen, everything had a precise home.

"Sometimes the sand is the safest place for the head to be," her mother replied.

"But—"

She whirled round pretty fast for an old lady. "Don't involve yourself, Tess," she said. "Not with Sicily and not with those kinds of thoughts either. Sicily is a dark place for me—and for others, too. But it is the past. I broke free long ago. I am here. This is my life. I no longer need to look back."

Tess took a deep breath. "But perhaps I do."

"It is nothing to you." The words seemed to whip out of her.

"But, Muma," Tess said, thinking of what had happened at the party, how she had felt. That clear and defining moment. "It is. And I need to go back there."

"Need?" Her mother's eyes were dark and unreadable.

"Want. And need." Tess crossed the room and held her mother's hands. They felt so thin and fragile. "I don't want to upset you," she told her. "I really don't. But I've been thinking about it. And I have to go back there."

"Why?"

Tess had expected anger or tears. But Muma just looked sad. "I just feel it." She shrugged. "I think it's why Edward Westerman left me the villa. And I am half Sicilian, after all. Perhaps Sicily is in my blood, too."

Her mother hadn't broken away from her hold. But she stared into space, and Tess hated that defeated look more than anything.

"Tell me, Muma," she pleaded.

Her mother shook her head. "You have to find your own way," she murmured. "No one can find it for you, my darling Tess."

But she could help, Tess thought. If she wanted to, she could illuminate the path a little.

"When will you go?" she asked. "What about work?"

"I gave my notice on Thursday." It still seemed a bit unreal, as if it might have happened to someone else after all. Perhaps it hadn't sunk in yet.

Her mother's eyes widened. "Because of this?"

"Because they were unfair."

They sat down together at the table, and Tess explained what had happened. "And also maybe because of this," she admitted. The whole scenario had a sense of synchronicity. As if it were meant to be.

"And Robin?" Her mother curled her tongue around his name as if she could hardly bring herself to say it.

"It's over," Tess said. "Definitely over." She wondered how many times she would have to say it before she and everyone else believed her.

"So you are decided?" Something in her mother's expression had changed. "You are determined to return to Sicily?"

"Yes." Tess knew she had to. "With or without your support," she said. "Though I'd much rather you told me you understood."

Her mother nodded. She seemed to hesitate and then come to a decision. "Wait here," she said conspiratorially, getting up and looking over her shoulder as if the Thought Police might suddenly appear to arrest her.

"What . . . ?"

Two minutes later, she was back. She grabbed Tess's hand and opened her palm, shoving something inside.

Tess looked down. It was money: a roll of notes. She didn't know how much money, but it looked like a lot. "What's this?"

"It's mine," her mother said defensively. "Not your father's. I was saving it."

"What for?" Tess stared at her.

"For something like this," her mother said. "Take it. It's yours. And I will try to understand."

"But I couldn't . . ." So many thoughts were scrambling through her head. Like this would help her go back to Sicily and even stay there for a while—but why the turnaround? And was she doing the right thing? What about Ginny . . . ?

"Ginny . . . ," she said.

Her mother raised an eyebrow. "Something is not right," she suggested, as if she already knew.

Tess told her the gist of the row. It had left her shaking. Where, she wondered, had she gone wrong? Her fun-loving daughter had somehow metamorphosed into a truculent teenager. But the worst thing was knowing that her favorite companion for as long as Ginny had been able to form words no longer wanted to spend time with her. And she definitely did not want to come to Sicily.

Tess felt herself wrapped in her mother's arms—something that didn't happen very often. She was almost afraid to breathe in case Muma let her go. "It will pass," her mother said. "It is natural, and it will pass." She stroked Tess's hair as if she were a child again. "Let Ginny stay with me for a few weeks. Go to Sicily if you must. Maybe it would do you both good to have some time apart."

Tess swallowed back the tears. She'd felt so many new emotions over the past few weeks, she was in turmoil. The woman inside her was desperate to return to Sicily. Not just to solve the puzzle, but to have an adventure, to enjoy her villa, to live a little. But now that she'd been given permission from her mother, now that she had the means to do it, the mother in *her* was holding her back. She had taken the responsibility of bringing Ginny up alone, and she should see it through.

She sighed. It wasn't so unusual for Ginny to have stayed out (though she was banned from doing so during exams). Teenagers seemed to sleep willy-nilly at each other's houses; it didn't mean they were all indulging in rampant sex, just that they couldn't be bothered to come home. And even if she was having rampant sex, Tess told herself, Ginny was eighteen. So long as she was using condoms, did it really matter? (Yes, actually. Of course it mattered.) But she always sent Tess a text to let her know where she was—that was the rule.

And when Tess had finally got hold of her on the home phone this morning, Ginny hadn't even said she was sorry. Tess knew it was no use getting angry—and getting angry wasn't her style. But at times like this she wished that David had not been such an absent parent. She didn't know what to do.

Perhaps Muma was right, perhaps it would do both Ginny and Tess good to have a time apart. Ginny loved and respected her grandparents; there was no way she would misbehave with them. Perhaps Tess couldn't do it alone after all. She thought of the money her mother had given her. It would certainly be enough to live on for several weeks while she made up her mind what to do next. What to do . . . ? It was a big question. But . . . She didn't want Ginny and herself to grow any further apart. "I'm still not sure I'm doing the right thing," she confessed.

"Do not misunderstand me, Tess." Her mother was looking her straight in the eye. "I do not want you to go. But I see that you have to." She nodded. "And I see that you need a break." She put a hand on Tess's shoulder. "You are not Wonder Woman, my darling. You have brought that child up alone and you always, always have worked too hard. Now you have no job and a villa in Cetaria. So you can go away and think about it. Whatever *it* is."

For the second time that evening, Tess considered how remarkable her mother was. Strong, unselfish, and understanding. She felt as if she should still be protesting. But on the other hand . . .

"Do not worry," her mother said. "Just go, sort out your thoughts, and then it is finished." She opened the door of the oven, where their dinner was bubbling nicely. "Now," she said, with her first smile of the evening. "Call your father, and let's eat."

CHAPTER 27

SO THERE IT WAS, FLAVIA THOUGHT. TESS WANTED to return to Sicily. She needed to return to Sicily. Perhaps it was her destiny.

Flavia sat in the room where she liked to do her writing, because it had a view of the garden and because the afternoon June sun streamed in and warmed her. She watched Lenny in the garden, clipping haphazardly at the hedge. She had known from the first moment she heard the news of Edward Westerman's death and his bequest to her daughter that this was only the beginning. She was an old woman—how could she fight the pull of Sicily?

So . . . She had let her go. And she had made it easier for her. Why? Well, because Tess was her daughter and because she was so stubborn, she would never stop until the thing was resolved. Very well, then. So be it. She would try to understand.

She picked up her pen, stretched out her aching fingers. And she would do her part. A little every day. She would get there.

Sicilian cheese: *il frutto*—the fruit of the milk. This was something Flavia had missed, at first, more than most things Sicilian. She remembered the local shepherd from the mountainside, his craggy face and the wooden staff he carried, his strong thick-soled boots.

Pecorino, the cheese from the sheep, *caciocavallo* from the cow, goat's cheese. And ricotta—made from the whey of other cheeses; not a cheese, not really; simply ricotta.

She used to watch the ricotta making in the village, stand with Mama in the hut with the blackened walls while the cauldron of milk was stirred and stirred, growing hotter and hotter until it began to separate. She could still smell the sweet creamy fragrance of the wet curds, the pungent olive wood smoking and sparking beneath the pot.

There were many recipes with ricotta that Flavia could include. Ricotta complemented the *dolce*, spinach, red peppers . . . It could be cubed and served with olives, sun-dried tomatoes, and salad leaves. It could be drizzled with olive oil and sprinkled with parsley or mint or black pepper. Most of all, it was a taste of the mountainside, a taste of history, a taste of everyone's beginning. She wanted to give that to Tess.

Flavia heard him cry out—as if even in sleep her ears were attuned to him.

Soft, like a cat, she slid out of bed, wrapped her robe around her, and ran light footed over the flagstones into his room.

"Hush. Hush," she murmured to soothe him.

"It's so damned hot," he muttered. "I'm burning up."

Yes, he was sweating. She fetched a cold flannel. Laid it on his brow.

He put his hands over his eyes. "It's the lights. They're blind-ing me . . ."

Sometimes it was the lights, sometimes the noise, often both. Flavia laid a cover over the lamp by the bed. They left it on, because darkness, too, was a problem. She knew that he was dreaming. He had had this dream many times since he had been with them. It was a dream—a flashback—of the moments before his plane had crashed; she recognized the signs.

"You are safe," she murmured in English, as she always did, so that he would understand. "You are here, in the house in Cetaria, with me." It was still dark, and apart from her whis-pers, the house was silent.

Over the past weeks he had taught her more English, and she had taught him snippets from her mother tongue so that he could converse a little with her father. This seemed important.

He began to spend time outside—always close to the house. And as he walked around the terraces and the orti, his walk-ing began to improve, and his leg grew stronger.

Her father came in to see him every evening before din-ner, bringing a glass of wine, asking how he was and looking grave.

"Bene," Peter would say to him. "Grazie, Signor."

"But still very weak," Flavia would add. Of course, she wanted him to get better, but she did not want him to leave. His wound had healed, and the shrapnel had all been removed. He was making good progress. But he was not ready to go, and she was not ready to see him go. She could not bear the thought of parting.

From his dreams and from what he'd told her, Flavia knew that the English airman's objectives last July—the aim of the

*gliders' mission—had been to seize a bridge outside Siracusa
and hold it until troops arrived by sea to capture the town.
She knew that he had been carrying a gun and much ammu-
nition (and assumed that Papa and his cronies had taken
this—in Sicily, you never knew when such things would be
useful). She knew that he had flown that night from Mascara
in the Atlas Mountains and that he had been unable to hold
his flight position, that he had been blinded by the searchlights and lost sight of the coast.*

"Steady on, old man," he muttered now, his voice rising.
"We're going too fast. We're going to—"

*She held his hand. She knew what was coming. Crash.
Blackness. Oblivion.*

"Peter," she whispered.

He gripped her hand. Squeezed it hard. She didn't flinch.

"Flavia."

*A different voice intruded from the doorway. "Go to bed,
Flavia." Her father.*

*"But, Papa . . ." No one else could calm him like she could.
No one else could feel what he felt.*

*"Go." Her father had the look on his face that meant he
must be obeyed.*

*So although she could hardly bear to leave him, Flavia
took one last look at Peter and ran back to her room.*

*Their voices continued rising and falling way into the
night. Once, Flavia crept back and stood outside the door to
listen.*

*"You will leave the house," she heard her father say in Sicil-
ian tongue.*

*She flinched. Clutched at the stone wall for support. But
there was no comfort there. Soon it would be winter. She had*

known it was coming. But . . . She didn't even know if Peter understood.

"I will give you assistance," said her father. "But I will not give you my daughter."

Hot tears ran down Flavia's face. She wanted to fling open the door and shake her fists and scream at them, but she didn't dare. She could not be forbidden from seeing him completely. She could not be locked up like an animal that could not be trusted.

"I love her," she heard Peter say. "I love Flavia."

Her heart almost stopped beating. He loved her.

"No," said Papa.

All her life she had heard this. Papa's "no," which brooked no argument.

Back in her room, Flavia cried tears of frustration. Before Peter, her life had been nothing. Nothing to look forward to, nothing to long for, no hope for change. All she could see, the most she could expect for her future, was to find a man who was kind, who would look after her. She would be in his bed, have his children, be tied to la cucina. *Like Mama. He would go out with his friends—to Bar Gaviota to drink grappa, to the* corso *to see the dancing. She would be stuck inside. Entrapped. Church, market,* la casa. *She would rather die.*

What else was there?

"What else is there?" She would demand of Santina. But Santina would do what her family required of her. She could not give Flavia an answer.

And then Peter.

Flavia lay flat on her back and stared up at the ceiling. There was a sliver of white-pink light creeping through the half-closed shutters. Dawn. Peter had fallen into her life—literally—like a star from the sky, and everything—everything—had changed.

She drew her knees up to her chest and flung her arms out wide. Peter loved her.

It wasn't that he was alien, unknown, exciting—though he was. It wasn't that he could take her to another place, a new place, one that she'd already been told about by Signor Westerman, where she knew her life could be different. Though that was part of it, too. It was Peter himself. The touch of his skin, the beat of his pulse. Flavia loved him. She loved him with all her heart.

CHAPTER 28

GINNY LET HERSELF INTO THE HOUSE WITH A FLIP OF relief. Her last exam finished. The farce was over. Zippedy zebras . . .

"Darling?" Her mother was in the kitchen. What Ginny didn't understand was why her mother hadn't been looking for another job. What was she going to do? Parents had to work, didn't they—otherwise, where would all the money come from?

"Hi." Things hadn't quite got back to normal since the argument between them. It was difficult to know how to be afterwards. Did you pretend nothing had happened? Did you say you were sorry? Or did you sulk for a while to make a point? Sometimes Ginny was just so desperate to reach out to her mother—it had always been so easy before, but now the Ball seemed to pull her back just as she wanted to go forward.

"How did it go?" Her mother had opted not to discuss their row at all. She was sitting at the kitchen table. Spread in front of her was a map.

"Okay." Actually, Ginny had hardly written a thing. The only way, she thought, of avoiding uni and psychology was not to compete. And it had been surprisingly simple to just sit there, doodling, letting that part of her brain switch right off. It was surreal—almost otherworldly. As if she were somewhere quite different. What did any of it matter? Inside her, the Ball rumbled agreement. *What did any of it matter?*

"Want a cup of tea?" Her mother got to her feet.

"Okay."

As well as not discussing their row, her mother was doing something else lately—this hovering thing, like Ginny was too delicate to touch, too volatile to speak to, on the edge. Ginny hated it. It made her want to jump right off.

"So—out celebrating tonight, then?" her mother said in a false cheery tone. "End of exams . . . Free at last!"

"Maybe." Ginny didn't know if she could be bothered, though it was true that quite a few of them would be out and about. Becca would be there for a start. But Becca would be with Harry and Ginny knew how she would be.

She couldn't deny it, she felt totally derailed by Becca's obsession with Harry. One minute she had a best friend around all the time, and the next she was never available. As for the Ball . . . Flunking her exams had not made any difference to the size of It. If anything, it had grown more confident, taxiing round inside her at all hours of the day like a Thing Possessed. (Which was also ironic, when you came to think about it.)

Her mother put a mug of tea on the table in front of her. "How's Ben?" she asked carefully.

Oh, shit. "All right." And that was another thing . . .

Why were relationships all about the balance of power?

Take Ben. In the beginning, he'd had it. Ginny hadn't known what to do. Then they'd had sex, and she knew—just knew—she was in charge. He wanted her—all the time. It was great, exhilarating—not the sex, but being so wanted. Even the Ball kept quiet during sex; it was afterwards it would start screaming.

"Now that your exams have finished," her mother was saying in that bright voice, "you'll have to think about what to do next."

Ginny scowled at her. "You mean, like today?"

Her mother took a deep breath. "No . . . But soon."

Ginny sat down abruptly. "I told you. I want to go traveling."

"Then you'll need money." Her mother's voice was also kind of brisker than normal. Like she'd decided to stop being nice.

Ginny groaned.

"You'll have to get a job."

Ginny pulled a face. Why were parents always so negative? They could never bring themselves to simply say— enjoy . . . ! "I know that," she said. "I'm not stupid." Work would be better than studying psychology. It had to be.

"And you're sure you won't change your mind about coming to Sicily?" Her mother jabbed a finger at the map on the table. "We'd have such a lovely time."

Ginny wouldn't even give her the satisfaction of looking. "No way, José."

"Okay." Her mother shrugged and folded up the map. "I'm only going for a few weeks," she added. "A month at the most. Or two."

"A month or two?" Ginny stared at her. So she could afford to take off to Sicily for a whole month—or two— and yet here she was going on about Ginny needing a job. Honestly. And what about Ginny? What was she supposed to do while her mother was in Sicily? Again. She swallowed.

Her mother put out a tentative hand. "Is everything all right, darling?" she said. "Ben . . . ?"

Ben was no longer scared. And although he still wanted her—they had sex all the time—it had lost its urgency, and Ginny had lost the power. Just like that. In fact she'd go as far as to say that he took her for granted. And worse, she'd realized that not only was she derailed—because of Becca and the whole exams/uni/psychology thing—she was also bored. Bored out of her mind. And hating just about everything—including herself.

"Fine," she said. "Everything's fine."

"If you don't want me to go," her mother said, "I won't."

But clearly she wanted to. "Go to Sicily," Ginny said. "I'll be all right."

She felt deserted. Left in limbo. Bereft. *What about me?* she wanted to wail. She swallowed again. It was painful.

"Nonna wants you to stay with her and Pops," her mother said brightly. "It would be a bit like a holiday."

Ginny snorted. They only lived three streets away. But . . . "Okay," she said. And then she got up to go to her room, because suddenly the Ball was making her head ache and she wanted to cry—again.

Upstairs, she put on her iPod and scrunched up her eyes. She saw a birthday cake with candles, and she could hear people laughing. It was her thirteenth birthday party; just the four of them—Ginny, her mum, Nonna, and Pops. Her family.

Nonna had made the cake—as usual—but the night before, Mum had iced it, complete with the chocolate buttons and sprinkles Ginny asked for every year.

Pops produced a bottle of champagne from the fridge. "Da-daa!" He grinned and shook it up a bit.

Mum and Nonna backed away, shrieking in unison, and Ginny giggled. Pops eased off the cork. Mum, Ginny, and Nonna clutched each other by the arm, waiting for the explosion.

Whack! The cork cannoned out in a rush of air and ricocheted from the ceiling. Mum and Nonna shrieked again.

"Glasses!" shouted Pops, as the liquid frothed from the lip of the bottle.

Mum grabbed them and held them steady so he could pour. She raised an eyebrow at Ginny. *Happy birthday*, she mouthed.

"Thirteen," Pops mused. "Now your life really begins, my lovely."

Ginny watched the champagne fizz up the glass like a promise.

"To Ginny." Her mother handed Ginny a glass and raised her own.

"To Ginny," they echoed. Family.

"You're a teenager now." Mum's hair was as tousled as ever, but she was wearing a new pink lipstick. She moved around the table lighting the thin, waxy candles—blue, pink, white, and yellow—until the chocolate cake with cream-frosted icing was a beacon of flames.

Ginny looked at the chocolate buttons and the sprinkles and the thirteen candles burning. She felt a weird dip inside. She thought about her life ahead—school, university, career, and the biggie—True Love. It was exciting—but scary. She looked from one to the other of them. Pops beaming, Nonna smiling her encouragement, Mum's face flushed and proud. And she thought of what she was leaving behind—childhood, she supposed. Safety. Ginny gulped the champagne, which tasted dry and unfamiliar on her tongue.

"Now, the world is your lobster," Nonna pronounced.

Ginny glanced at her mother. Her lips were twitching. Ginny felt the giggles rising up in her like the bubbles of champagne. She caught her mother's eye. They spluttered with laughter, bending double, Mum practically in tears and having to put her glass down on the table.

"And what is so funny?" Nonna's hands were on her hips, her eyes fierce and her tone indignant.

"Nothing, Muma," said Tess.

"Nothing, Nonna," said Ginny.

But they both started laughing again anyhow. Until Nonna sighed loudly and Pops said, "Oyster, my lovely. The world is your oyster."

And by now Ginny wasn't even sure what was so funny, but it was anyway.

"Group hug," said her mother, drawing them into a circle and clearly struggling for control. "Time to sing." The candles were burning down and spluttering wax onto the frosted icing.

"Happy birthday to you. Happy birthday to you." Their voices rose: Nonna melodious and throaty, Pops a deep tenor, Mum clear and confident. *"Happy birthday, darling Ginny..."*

Mum was holding her hand now. "Blow out the candles, sweetheart," she said. "Make a wish."

Ginny took a deep breath and blew. She wished that she would soon know what it was all about—Life. And she wished that nothing would change.

Everyone clapped and cheered. Nonna produced the knife to cut the cake, Pops poured more champagne, Mum touched her hair, very lightly.

All that mattered was family...

And that was what she had lost, Ginny thought now. She flicked to the next track on the iPod shuffle, and she thought of Nonna and Pops, of the food Nonna cooked and how the house was always warm and homey and made her feel safe. Perhaps it wouldn't be so bad. And besides... It would be far, far easier to avoid the whole work and university issue—not to mention what happened when the results came through... if her mother wasn't actually here.

CHAPTER 29

BY THE TIME TESS GOT BACK TO CETARIA, THE SEAson had already taken off in Sicily. The hotels seemed full, bars and restaurants were overflowing, and tourist traffic streamed down the *strada*.

But Cetaria was sufficiently off the beaten track to escape mass tourism, and the *baglio* and bay seemed unchanged to Tess as she drove the rental car into the village early Wednesday evening. The sun was low, but still warm, casting its honey glow onto the rippling water in the bay. And in the distance, on the hills, a different, pinkish light was filtering between the tapering spires of the cypress trees.

Tess drove toward via Margherita, the side street that led to Villa Sirena, winding down the car window to sniff the scents of evening cooking wafting through the narrow streets: sweet caramelized onions and tomatoes; fragrant herbs—oregano and basil; roasting meat. Aware of the rush of anticipation inside her.

She drew level to the black wrought iron gates, jumped out to open them wide, got back in, and did a sharp right turn between an ancient Piaggo Ape Car and a blue-and-yellow Fiat Panda.

Behind the oleanders and the old stone wall, the villa stood waiting for her, dusky pink and glowing faintly in the sunshine, the mermaid motif above the door seeming to smile gently as she inserted the key and opened the front door. Tess didn't much like the idea of renting out her villa. But it was better than selling out completely . . . If she rented it out for vacation stays then it would still be here for her when she was able to get away.

So . . . All she had to do was find the money to do it up a bit (well, a lot) and . . . Geronimo. She would have her very own vacation home in Sicily.

Tess went back to get her stuff from the car. Who wouldn't want to spend as much time as possible in this seductive place? She could smell the jasmine that grew around the side of the villa. The scent was heady and yet familiar. She felt as if she'd hardly been away.

And that's why she was back here. Because it was a place she wanted to be. Villa Sirena was her link with Sicily and the girl her mother used to be. How could she let it go?

She hadn't traveled light—this time she'd brought her diving equipment—so she had to return to the car three times before she was done. An old woman was walking past the gates. She looked in.

"*Buona sera,*" Tess called out cheerfully. Listen to her . . .

A grin stretched across the old woman's brown, leathered face. "*Sera,*" she said in reply.

Tess shut the front door and went straight out back. She leaned on the rail by the terrace and looked down into the *baglio*. Tonino's door was not open, and he wasn't outside his studio. She smiled. No need then for her stomach to churn. Even though it felt as if she'd come home.

The following morning she threw open the shutters, ate a hurried breakfast, and took her diving equipment down to the bay. She was wearing her wet suit and had been organized enough to stop on the way from the airport at a diving center near Palermo, where she'd rented a scuba tank. Everything ready to go.

The *baglio* was quiet—just a few people wandering around and drinking espressos in the bar; Tess could smell the rich fragrance of freshly roasted coffee mingling with the sweetness of breakfast *cornetti*. It was still morning, and the *baglio* had a white and expectant feel. Tonino's studio door was propped open now, but there was no sign of him.

The serpent, she noted, was still in the studio window, its green scales smooth and shining, its yellow crown flat against the head. Hang on. She paused. Crown? Yes, it was unmistakable now she looked more closely; at the points of the yellow-glass coronet were pearls of amber, and along the base were threads of brown. She did a double take. And the thing had a face. Green eyes, curly eyebrows, a 'stache, and a beard—in pearly-white glass this time. With a serpent's tongue, a forked flash of jet. Right . . .

But there was no evidence of whatever Tonino might be working on now. And he was nowhere to be seen. Tess shrugged away her disappointment and lugged her gear over to the water's edge. The rock formation fascinated her. The coastline itself was jagged cliff, but these rocks were like granite towers thrusting through the water. She reached the stone jetty. She couldn't wait to get in to explore. She wanted to know what lay beneath, what was at the core, at the bottom of the sea.

"Hey!"

She recognized his voice before she even turned around. The tone was belligerent, but . . . She gave a small wave. "Hi!"

He was striding toward her. But his face when he reached her was dark and angry. "What do you think you are doing?" He gesticulated toward her gear—the air tank, the weight belt, the face mask.

"Diving?" She shrugged. Nice to see you again, too, she thought. That moment in Segesta, that almost-kiss, it seemed suddenly like years ago.

"Alone?" He was practically breathing fire.

Tess took an exaggerated look around the bay. There was a couple sitting on the wall a little way away, watching the confrontation with some curiosity, and an older man on the rocks over the other side. But she didn't seem to be with anyone that she could see. "Why not?" she said. "I'm not going very far." Yes, she knew that one of the rules of diving was that you didn't dive alone. You didn't dive alone in case you got into difficulties. If you got into difficulties, you might need a buddy to help you out. But of course Tess wouldn't do anything foolish or take any risks. She knew what she was doing, damn it. But she wanted to explore, and where was she supposed to get a diving buddy from, for crying out loud?

"It does not matter." He glared at her, hands on hips. He was wearing the black shorts again and a blue T-shirt the color of the Sicilian sea. His skin seemed even browner than before, his eyes darker. "It can be dangerous. You should never dive alone."

Tess rose to her full height though she had to admit she felt a tad self-conscious in her close-fitting wet suit. You had to buy a size too small because it stretched out in the water in order to fit you like a second skin. "I know that," she said. "I am a qualified diver." And why did everyone keep trying to tell her what to do around here? She didn't need anyone to control her life—she could do it for herself—probably.

"Then you should know better," he snarled.

Tess's eyes widened. She had been very, very wrong about this man. She should have listened to Giovanni Sciarra. Tonino was getting this way out of proportion. She remembered how angry he'd been about the fishermen's nets. Perhaps he was some sort of maniac—creative but seriously deranged?

"Is it any of your business, do you think?" She adjusted her mask and made all the final checks. As she dangled a foot into the water, it frilled tantalizingly around her toes. She pulled on her fins. She hadn't bothered with diving gloves; it wasn't cold. This was just an initial exploratory, for God's sake.

Once again, he folded his arms. "It is irresponsible. It is not good practice." And he didn't walk away.

So . . . What? Was he going to stand there at the water's edge until she got back? And, she realized, he seemed to know a lot about diving regulations. She turned back to him. "Do you dive?" she asked.

For a moment it seemed as if he wasn't going to reply. Then, "No," he said. "Not anymore."

Not anymore . . . Nothing, Tess felt, could stop her diving. It was her passion. "If you're that worried about it," she threw back at him, "come with me."

Very slowly, he shook his head.

Tess shrugged. "Okay, then, I'm going in." She put in the mouthpiece and waved a hand.

He gave her a long, hard look, turned, and walked away.

What, she wondered, was his problem?

CHAPTER 30

ONCE THE WAVES PASSED HER KNEES, TESS BENT AND slid into the water on her belly. It got deep very quickly, and she felt the coolness slip into her wet suit, where it would warm from her body heat and keep her from growing chilly. She ducked her head under for a moment. The seabed was rock and gravelly sand with a coarse stubble of sea grass. There were no jellyfish in evidence, but she did identify a shoal of pale and stripy salps. What a bunch of smoothies they were—cool, elegant, almost iridescent.

She swam toward the double-headed rock; she could see its reflection in the water ahead—rippled and broken by the tide. The past weeks, the in-between weeks, that strange conversation with her mother, the ongoing battle with Ginny (I don't understand teenagers, she thought), the split-up with Robin . . . all seemed to pale into insignificance now that she was back here in Cetaria.

Under the surface, sunlight was filtering in strands through the water, the color of which moved from the palest blue to a bright peacock green and all the shades in between. She moved slowly, getting into a relaxed, gliding rhythm.

What was she hoping to achieve by coming back here? What was she looking for? Was it something to do with the villa, Cetaria itself—its bay and *baglio*—or maybe the two men that she'd met here? Or was it her mother's past that she was searching for? Maybe all these things were intertwined . . . Maybe she just had to look a little harder to find that elusive something . . .

She dived down deeper as she reached the first big rock formation, running her hand along its rough, cratered edges. This was rock that had been eaten and eroded by the sea for centuries, creating a unique overhang. Bubbles of carbon dioxide left her respirator and floated like mercury mushrooms up to the surface. The rock might seem immovable, she thought, and yet she could see already that these rock islands had deep fissures and cracks underwater as well as above the surface, where the sea swallows nested and cacti grew. Different sections of the rock came from different places and had been here for different lengths of time.

Closer to the seabed, spiky pink sea urchins and layers of thin bright-orange sponge rested among the mauve rockweeds. Tess wasn't a geologist, but she knew a bit about the earth, stone, and erosion. This rock formation was in fact a living and moving thing. Sicily of course, was prone to volcanoes and earthquakes—the earth did literally move. And now that she could get the underwater picture, she saw that there was a whole host of rock islands here with carved inlets and tiny sea caves. Lots and lots to explore.

She swam slowly around the boulders. Like here. Two pillars of gray rock and a similar one acting as a lintel just behind the second tower that peaked from the water. Maybe it had been another underwater cave—once. She floated in closer. A different, darker, less eroded and pitted rock was wedged between the pillars. A thread of iron ran through it. She played her fingers along its edges. Almost as if some great godlike Neptune figure had rolled it into place. Or perhaps there had been a fall. The fissures between it and the original rock were quite deep and wide in places; in others they had molded almost into one.

Placing one hand on top of the other, she dropped farther, right down to the gravelly seabed. She was out of her depth, of course, but not exactly in dangerous waters. So what was Tonino's problem? She had intended to try to find out more about these feuding Sicilian families, but now she wasn't sure she even wanted to talk to the man. So much then for Segesta and the taste of ripe figs . . . Some girls, she told herself sternly, just never learn.

Under the small boulders on the seabed she uncovered a dark-red starfish, flapping swiftly into another rocky fissure, and a regally decorated scorpion fish that swam sedately away. She plucked a shell from the sand; inside, it was perfect mother-of-pearl, and she tucked it into her zip pocket. The sea fans—yellow and red gorgonians— were waving their downy foliage in tune with an underwater current that was becoming part of Tess's own rhythm the longer she stayed down here. She swam on to the next monolithic rock tower.

She would also have to use this time in Sicily to think about how she was going to make a living now that she was no longer working at the water company. Perhaps she'd make a list of possibilities when she got back to the villa. And she'd get hold of Giovanni, she decided, talk to him about builders. Try to see Santina, too—she wasn't going to forget about that part of her mission. She'd get organized. Never mind Tonino. She didn't need *him*.

The second rock was deeply mossed and was older and paler than the first. She examined it with interest and then drifted over boulders and thick sea grass to get to the rock cluster on the other side. Here she spotted some yellow sea daisies and a large sad-faced conger eel. One part of her mind continued to record what she saw; another part was mulling over recent events. You had to concentrate when you were diving. Focus was the thing. Lucky she was female and good at multitasking . . . Because this, for Tess, was still one of the pleasures of diving. Uninterrupted thinking time.

A shoal of anchovies hovered around her as, twenty minutes later, she eventually rose up to the surface by the jetty in the bay. She waded in to shore and took off her mask and fins.

Tonino was working outside the studio, and she had to pass him to get to the steps up to the villa. She intended to walk straight on by, but something about the way he sat, something about the set of his jaw as he glanced up at her and nodded, made her pause.

She looked down at the mosaic he was putting together. "What are you working on now?"

He took an age to reply. "Have you heard the legend of Colapesce?" he asked at last.

Tess shook her head. It sounded random, but then he was a random sort of guy.

Tonino picked up a piece of green stone—malachite, perhaps—and held it up to the sun. "Colapesce spent days underwater exploring the seabed," he said. "He reported that Sicily was supported by three huge pillars, but there was a problem."

"Which was?" Already Tess was fascinated. It wasn't what he said. It was his voice. His stillness.

"One of the pillars was broken," Tonino said solemnly.

She waited. What did that mean? That Sicily had some fatal flaw in its very foundations?

"But the king wasn't interested. He just wanted to know how deep Colapesce could dive. So he asked him to bring up a cannonball shot from the lighthouse."

"And did he?"

His voice was hypnotic, he used the stones as he spoke, passing them from hand to hand, polishing, holding them to the light, making a selection.

"He tried." Tonino paused. He wasn't afraid of silences. "But when he reached the cannonball, he looked up, and the sea above him was hard and still and closed like marble." Tonino's eyes snapped shut, then open again like a lizard's.

"So what did he do?"

"Nothing. He was trapped there forever." Tonino clicked his fingers, and abruptly the spell was broken.

"Oh." Tess flinched. What was that supposed to mean? Don't go farther than you know you can? Your passion can be the death of you? The danger of high expectations . . . ? What? She had the feeling that he wasn't going to tell her.

"Why did you mind so much?" she asked him. "About the diving?"

He looked beyond her, out to sea. "The ocean is beautiful," he said. "But also, she is cruel."

Tess toweled her hair and slung the towel over her shoulders. He hadn't really answered her question. "You're right," she said. "But I wasn't taking any risks. I just went to have a closer look at the rocks."

"What are you searching for when you dive?" he asked, not looking up.

"Oh, you know, the usual . . . Marine life. Plants and corals." She laughed. "Maybe a pearl."

"A pearl . . ." He inserted a piece into his mosaic. "I had a friend," he said, "a close friend. Another scuba diver. We dived together for sport, and one day we began to dive the wrecks. Also looking for pearls, you might say."

"The wrecks?" He helped her off with her air tank, and Tess sat down on the wall beside him.

"Salvage." He returned to his mosaic pieces, sifting and sorting. "A diver can earn good money from salvage—brass, silverware, who knows what."

Tess nodded. She had already learned that in this country you had to earn money where you could. She unzipped the top of her wet suit; she was beginning to feel a bit clammy.

"There is a wreck out to the west, completely submerged. We arranged to dive together. I had . . ." He seemed embarrassed. "A prior engagement. He did not wait." He paused. "My friend, he died out there."

Tess stared at him. God. Death and destruction. Darkness. Sicily seemed positively ingrained with it. "When?" she whispered.

"Two years ago."

Despite the heat of the sun, Tess shivered. "What happened?"

"It seems almost certain that he got caught up in some old fishermen's nets. He was found with some netting still tangled around his wet suit." His eyes were darker than ever. He wouldn't look at her. "What else could have happened? He was an experienced diver, and the fishermen—they throw their nets into the sea sometimes when they are torn. They do not care."

"And you think that he couldn't break free?" she asked him.

Tonino shook his head. "He must have untangled himself enough to get to the surface eventually, but not enough air was left, I guess. There would have been no time for decompressing. He must have died in the boat alone."

Tess was silent. She knew what he was saying. Decompression sickness. The bends. It could happen when the gases in your blood had not had enough time to adjust to the change in pressure and bubbles formed. That was why when you dived more deeply you had to organize your time to allow for decompression stops on the way back to the surface.

Fishermen's nets. Divers scuba diving alone. Now she understood his anger with the fishermen that morning. And she understood his guilt—for not being there for his buddy the only time that it mattered.

"I'm so sorry," she said.

"I had the knife that would have cut him free—just like that." He made the gesture of a knife slicing through the air.

"But you can't blame yourself," Tess said quickly. "It was his decision to go alone." She was about to add that these things happened. But it would sound trite, and, anyway, he wouldn't agree.

He looked at her and shook his head. "They say it is a bad place."

"Cetaria?" She gazed around her. Her mother had said much the same, and yet to Tess it seemed like paradise. The ancient stone *baglio* with its piazza, stone fountain, and gnarled and silvery eucalyptus tree. The turquoise bay with *i faraglioni*—the rock tower crags jutting from the sea. The maze of narrow streets and pastel stuccoed houses. Villa Sirena. The underwater grotto of the natural reserve. Not to mention the sunshine. How could it be a bad place? Bad things could happen anywhere.

He nodded. "It is lovely, yes," he said. "But it is not always a happy place."

"No." She felt that. There was some sorrow—almost secreted in the very stone. She looked up toward his studio. "And what about the serpent?" she asked.

"The serpent?"

She gestured toward the studio. "The one wearing the crown."

"Ah. Prince Scursini," he said.

"Probably." Tess wriggled the wet suit down a bit farther. The sun was warm on her face and arms. She'd go back and get changed in a bit.

"A queen longs for a son," he said, "even if he should be born a *scursini*."

"Which is what exactly?" She watched him. It was as if he could slide into another world, a bit how she felt when she was diving. It was a good way to forget.

"A serpent," he said. "In Sicilian folklore a serpent is dangerous. If you look into his eyes, you will be paralyzed."

He glanced up at her, and Tess promptly looked away. She wasn't taking any chances.

"Sure enough, the son is born a *scursini*," he said. "By day he is a prince, by night a serpent. And in time the serpent wants a wife. He rejects and destroys two women of low birth who are brought to him."

"Like you do," murmured Tess.

"But the third woman uses her wits as well as her beauty. She releases him from the spell and gets her just reward."

"Let me guess," she said. "Marriage to the prince? Happy ever after?"

"Of course," he said.

Tess frowned. "But don't you find it a little, well, archaic? For this day and age, I mean?"

He gave her a sly glance. "You do not think the beast/bridegroom story can be applied to these days—*no*?"

"We . . . ll." She laughed.

"And you do not think that woman is the healer . . . ? And can have brains as well as beauty?"

He seemed to have all the answers. "Okay, I'll give you that one, too." This man was still a mystery. And she wasn't sure whether to trust him—or not.

"So." He shrugged. "The stories are symbols."

She nodded. "I see what you mean." Powerful symbols, too. She got to her feet. "I must get out of these wet things," she said.

"You should, yes." And again there was one of those odd moments between them. Nothing and yet not nothing, she thought. Seeming to mean more than it did. A bit like his stories really.

CHAPTER 31

GINNY WAS STRETCHED OUT, HANDS FOLDED BEHIND her head, staring at the ceiling. In this position she could make the Ball lie low, almost float out of sight, and pretend—for a while—that it wasn't there.

This ceiling was different from the dirty-white ceiling in her bedroom at home, which had deep, decorative cornicing, the odd cobweb (housework was not Mum's number one priority), and a stained glass lampshade. She and her mother had bought it at Pridehaven Market ages ago. Mum had spotted it first, alerted Ginny, and then they'd circumnavigated the table, pretending to be interested in other stuff so that they could seem more casual when Mum began to barter.

When had they stopped doing stuff like that together? Ginny stared at the lampshade in her memory's eye, as if it could answer this question. It wasn't as if she'd chosen not to, not really. Reds, blues, yellows . . . She could—and had—stared at it for hours when she was in her room studying.

This ceiling at Nonna and Pops's was different. Stark, staring, stippled bright white. And no spider would dare spin a web for fear of the orange feather duster that Nonna whisked around ceilings and walls every day—more as a warning, Ginny thought, than to dislodge any dust that might have settled there during the previous twenty-four hours.

This lampshade was chocolate brown and exactly matched the curtains; the carpet was what Nonna called "oatmeal"—the type that didn't show the dirt. Not that there ever was any. And for some odd reason—because Ginny had never cared about housework either—this was reassuring.

When her mother had left for Sicily this second time, Ginny's sense of derailment had increased. To prevent this, she had divided her life into manageable compartments. There was college—over as far as Ginny was concerned, leaving more of a gap than she had expected. She closed her eyes. Murky gray with orange highlights—a top-dog discussion in the refectory between a random group of friends, a band called Prickly Pairs playing in the gym, a club night in Dorchester in the Christmas holidays. All things, she realized, that had zilch zebras to do with studying. What she missed about college was the social life.

In an adjoining compartment were Becca and other friends, some of whom had gone off to Ibiza on a post-exam trip and most of whom she didn't feel she could relate to anymore. They all seemed to know where they were going—uni—and what was expected of them there—to meet people and get a degree. Meantime, they were preparing to launch into Stage Two of their lives without question, without a hiccup, without ever seeming to wonder . . .

Why? What the hell am I doing? Where the hell am I going? Or even, Who the hell am I? (Questions that plagued Ginny daily.) These friendships were silver blue. The ones that had already half disappeared were almost opaque, and Becca was royal. Ginny opened her eyes to see a fly dare to land on the ceiling. Nonna would have a fit . . .

Becca was the only one of her friends who was on Ginny's wavelength. Which was why—Ginny supposed—they had got so close this year. Which was why . . . She screwed her hand into a fist. It was so *rancid* now that Becca had Harry. Not the fact that she had Harry, but that she was *obsessed* by Harry.

Becca had understood about the uni thing, perhaps because she had never expected to do it herself. "You don't have to go," she had said. "They can't make you." This faceless "they" featured in a lot of their conversations. It could refer to Ginny's mother, Becca's parents, friends and relatives over thirty, tutors and other staff at college, shop assistants, anyone in authority, or any mixture of the above.

Becca had also said, "What's the point? We might as well just start working and get some cash together. Do you want to be saddled with a twenty-grand debt at twenty-three?" And other such reassurances that had fueled Ginny's resolve to flunk her exams and thus avoid the whole uni rigmarole altogether.

She fidgeted into a more comfortable position in the bed. Only now she had flunked her exams, she was more terrified than ever. Like, what would her mother and Nonna and Pops say when the results came through? How would she deal with the fact that she'd disappointed all the people in her family who mattered to her? And what exactly would she *do*?

She sighed. And that wasn't all. You weren't supposed to be jealous when your girlfriend got a boyfriend. But she was. She couldn't help it. Royal blue was growing green overtones.

As for Ben . . . His compartment was red and unsettling. She didn't want to keep seeing him, but she had to. She had to because she wanted it to be different, him to be different, her to be different, even. She wanted to be confident, to be clever, to be funny. She wanted to be loved; or at least looked up to and desired like crazy. But somehow—it wasn't working out that way.

Compartment four was home life. Even as it drifted into her mind, a calming coverlet of pale lilac (with her mother it had always been yellow), she heard her grandmother calling up the stairs.

"Time to get up, Ginny dear, it's eight o'clock."

Ginny smiled. Nonna was a well-oiled machine. She said the same thing every morning, like a mantra.

"Okay, Nonna," she called and pushed back the bedcovers.

The home compartment had become tranquil, rather than edgy and bitter. Now she was no longer perched on a lemon precipice, she was lying on a heathery plain.

She went into the bathroom for a shower. It was white. White wall tiles, white washbasin, white bath, white toilet. White ceiling and white floor. It was like being in an igloo. She pulled back the—white—shower curtain. For Nonna, white meant clean. And clean was the way she liked it.

The thing about living here, Ginny thought, as the hot water rained on her shoulders, was that Nonna believed in structure. So she would get up at eight, she would help with the chores and she would come home by eleven at night.

Nonna and Pops's day was one of routine. They did chores till coffee time (eleven a.m.) and then Nonna prepared food until lunch (one p.m.). After lunch, Pops had his rest, and Nonna secreted herself in her "quiet room" to read. She always took a book in there with her. She wasn't reading, though. Ginny had wandered past the window and had seen her writing in a notebook, writing in a fast and fevered un-Nonna-like way that seemed to be making her exhausted. Riveting. Whatever could it be . . . ?

At three they had tea and then went shopping or for a walk or into town. At five they returned for coffee and a sit-down, and at six Nonna began preparing dinner, which was served at seven. At nine they settled down in armchairs in front of the TV, and at ten thirty it was hot cocoa and then bed.

Ginny soaped her body all over. She had thought the routine would drive her crazy. But in fact you could rely on it. Structure provided boundaries. And within boundaries you could be safe. You could get back on the rails. Maybe.

When she had rinsed all the lather from her body, Ginny stepped out of the shower and enveloped herself in one of Nonna's fluffy white towels. She liked feeling safe, especially when all the other compartments felt wobbly and precarious and were losing definition somehow. She worried that one day the Ball would start rolling and eventually all the colors would merge into a sludgy, unrecognizable mess.

Downstairs, Nonna was doing dishes, wrinkled hands deep in suds. "Now, my girl," she said, when Ginny appeared. "What are you going to do today?"

Ginny wasn't sure. She had intended to wander round to Ben's, as she usually did. But she had the feeling that Nonna might have decided otherwise.

"Dunno." She helped herself to cereal. (*"What do you mean you don't eat breakfast; how can you start the day without breakfast? Whatever is your mother thinking of? Tsk. Tsk."*)

"A gap year," Nonna said, out of nowhere, speaking slowly and carefully, as if this was a language that was foreign to her (which in a way, it was, of course), "is a good idea."

Ginny was relieved. "Yes," she said. "It gives you time to decide what you want to do with your life." It was fluent and well rehearsed, but from the expression in Nonna's dark eyes as she turned to look at her, it failed to convince.

"Experience of other cultures is important, I agree," Nonna said. "And it is very pleasant to have a long holiday, without committing yourself to living there."

Ginny eyed her curiously. Was she being sarcastic? Or . . . "Is that what you would have chosen to do, Nonna?" she asked. "When you left Sicily to come to England?" If gap years had been invented, she meant.

Her grandmother paused in the act of rinsing a plate. She paused for so long that Ginny began to wonder if she had heard her.

"No," she said at last. "I wanted to commit. I wanted it more than anything."

She turned her attention back to the dishwashing, and Ginny shook in a few more Rice Krispies. More than anything . . . ? That was an awful lot.

"But," her grandmother went on, "a gap year is also a luxury that has to be paid for."

Uh-oh, thought Ginny. She sensed something unpleasant approaching. And with Nonna, the unpleasant couldn't be avoided with emotional blackmail the way it could with her mother.

Her grandmother dried her hands on her apron and turned to face Ginny. "You must find a job," she said decisively.

"What kind of job?" Suddenly the Rice Krispies were difficult to swallow. The Ball was in the way. Of course she had looked for a job, but it wasn't easy in Pridehaven.

"Any job," said Nonna. Her face was kind but stern. "And I think you should find it today."

CHAPTER 32

AFTER TESS HAD DRIED OUT FROM HER DIVE, SHE had a *cornetto* with *crema* and a *caffè latte* in the piazza of the *baglio*. Delicious. Tonino was nowhere to be seen. Like most Sicilians she'd met so far, he seemed to make up his own hours of business on a whim. She bit into the soft *cornetto* covered with icing sugar, her teeth and tongue meeting the sweet, thick vanilla *crema*. She thought of Ginny. There were some things about Cetaria that her daughter would have loved.

From the other side of the stone archway, she could hear the hustle and bustle of the market and the buzz of voices; Sicilians often sounded angry, or at least on a volatile edge, when they were probably just having a normal conversation about the weather. Beyond the *baglio* she kept getting glimpses, too, of the colors, while the smells—of fresh fish, spices, and fruit—were wafting through. There was nothing like a market. She amended this as she stepped through the archway right into the middle of it. There was nothing like a Sicilian market.

Market day was apparently a social occasion, as men and women stood around in clusters chatting, the men smoking and drinking espressos from mobile coffee vans, the women armed with shopping bags and determined expressions. And at the stalls, vendors held out loaves of *pane* or a purple cauliflower for inspection, while the women frowned and questioned, argued and haggled before eventually deciding on whether and how they should part with their money. *Carciofi freschi . . . Funghi belli . . . Tutti economici . . .* The calls rang out, the market traders vying for custom.

At the fish stall there was a line (of sorts), though in Sicily, Tess noted, this meant pushing your way to the front while apologizing profusely and trying to catch the fishmonger's attention before the woman next to you did, by talking to him very loudly. This was followed by the performance of more gracious apology and discussion about who might have been first, with everyone insisting that the other be served before they were. Or at least that's how it seemed to Tess. Ah, well, she thought. Social etiquette was very rarely rooted in logic. She lingered to enjoy the show and to gaze at the white, flaccid squid (she wouldn't know what to do with it), plump speckled cuttlefish (ditto), and great slabs of tuna laid out on marble loaded with ice.

She had decided to visit Santina and Giovanni today to (a) try to get the old lady alone and (b) ask Giovanni's advice about getting estimates for restoring the villa. It was common sense—she needed someone who spoke both Sicilian and English fluently. He was a businessman, seemed to have time on his hands, and had already been given the responsibility of key holder of the villa. He was the obvious choice. But she would make it plain that she was in control and that she would not be harangued into selling. If he could live with that, then she would be grateful for his help.

She paused by the stall selling herbs and spices, inhaled the fragrance of dusty, drying clumps of oregano, thyme, and wild fennel. Behind the stall were sacks of chickpeas and lentils with metal scoops and an ancient pair of scales for weighing. In some ways—in the traditions of the ordinary folk—Sicily was probably still much as her mother had lived it. Cetaria certainly hadn't entered the new millennium, let alone the twenty-teens.

Tess ducked to avoid the bruised purple garlic, plaited and hanging in ropes from the canopy of the stall. And came to the fruit and vegetables . . . zucchini with golden flowers, shiny peppers of flame and yellow, lacquered red chilies and fuzzy yellow peaches. She picked up a *melanzane* and stroked the slick skin with her thumb—the eggplant was sleek, dark, and yet luminescent—the color of Sicily, perhaps, she thought with a smile.

She would eat in tonight, Tess decided on impulse, and she bought half a watermelon whose juice was practically bursting out of the wrapping, some fruity cheese, a small loaf of delicious yellow Sicilian bread, some tomatoes, and black olives. A feast.

As she paid for the olives, she saw a woman on the other side of the market stall smiling at her. Tess instinctively smiled back. The woman was small and had a pixie face framed by dark hair cut in a perfect bob. She was wearing bold, deep-red lipstick and somehow didn't look Italian. Had they met before? Tess was just wondering whether or not to approach her, when she saw a familiar face only a few meters away.

She maneuvered a path through the people around the stall. "Santina?" What a piece of luck. But she might have guessed Santina would be here on market day.

The old lady turned, muttered something in Sicilian, and glanced quickly around her. She grabbed Tess's arm and pulled her to one side, where they were half-hidden behind a canvas canopy.

Once there the old woman reached up to take Tess's face in her hands. "You are back," she said, her toothless grin revealing her pleasure.

Tess smiled back at her. "I couldn't stay away," she confided. "I wanted to find out more—about my mother and why she left Sicily." She leaned closer. "Do you know? Can you tell me?"

Once again, Santina got that faraway look in her dark eyes. "Why, she fall in love," she said in her thick accent. "Flavia, she fall, quick, like this." And she feigned a swoon.

Tess grinned. "Really?"

"Ah, yes." Santina nodded energetically. "She was . . ." She counted on her bony fingers. Fixed Tess with an intense gaze. "Seventeen."

"Only seventeen?" That was younger than Ginny. "Was it a Sicilian man?" she asked. "What did her father say?" Though she could imagine. Santina had already hinted at what life was like for women in Sicily when her mother was young. She couldn't see it going down well.

But Santina shook her head. "Englishman," she hissed.

"Englishman?" Of course, she had mentioned an Englishman before. "She met an Englishman here in Cetaria when she was seventeen?"

Santina shot another look from side to side and Tess looked, too. But what were they looking for—and why on earth would anyone else be interested all these years

later? "Flavia find an airman," Santina said, rolling her
r's and flinging her arms in the air. "She find him and
she take him home. She save his life. Yes. They fall in
love. He promise her the world." She clutched her breast
dramatically.

Tess could only stare at her. She was already filling in
the details, making sense of Santina's broken English. An
English pilot—injured presumably—discovered by a Sicilian girl—a girl who was already rebelling against the life
that had been planned for her, a girl who wanted to see
the world, who wanted to be free; she could work out the
dates . . . It didn't take a genius. "What happened?" she
whispered. Around them the jostle and hum of the market dimmed to nothing, and Tess was back there with her
mother in wartime Cetaria when Flavia fell in love.

"Flavia's father—he send him away," Santina told her
in hushed tones. "He have other plans for his daughter,
another man . . ." She crossed herself. "In Sicily we marry to
make friendships strong. You understand?"

Tess nodded. She understood. Family alliances. Power.
"Who was she supposed to marry?"

Santina chuckled. "My cousin Rodrigo Sciarra," she
said. "My father—he always want alliance with your family. He need Flavia's father's help against his enemies, sì?"

"And isn't your cousin Rodrigo—?"

"Giovanni's father, sì."

Tess's mind went into overdrive. The plot thickened.
And the enemies Santina spoke of no doubt included the
Amatos.

"Ah, but it was not to be." Santina looked sad.

"And Flavia . . . ?" Tess asked.

"Flavia—she has a broken heart. Yes, this is true. I think
she has a broken heart forever."

CHAPTER 33

Two days later, Peter left for the hills.

Flavia had begged her father not to send him away. "I love him, Papa," she said. "If you care for me at all, you will show some pity . . ."

"What do we know of him, my daughter?" her father replied. "Nothing. Your place is here, understand that. Your place is not with him. And this . . . this feeling you imagine you have . . . It will pass. Believe me."

Nothing she said, no amount of tears could move him.

As he left, Peter took Flavia's hands in his. She was trying very hard not to cry.

"I will write to you," he said. "And you have my family's address, don't you?"

She nodded. Written on a piece of paper and branded on her heart.

"I will come back for you, my dearest," he said. "Will you wait for me?" He was standing by the door, bathed in the

warm evening light. But behind him, never far, were the shadows of nighttime.

"Sì." She nodded.

"Even if it takes me a long, long time?" He studied her face.

"Even if it takes forever," she said.

In the doorway, she saw Papa with his stern expression. She didn't care. They would find a way. "Forever," she repeated. "I will wait forever."

There were many bandit gangs in the hills, dealing in contraband grain and other commodities, and Flavia feared for Peter's safety.

Papa had kept his word and given him supplies and a contact in Palermo, where he would be safe until he could undertake the next stage of his journey. They heard that he had made it to the city. But she remained anxious. Although there were men like her father who had sympathy for the English, for many others—since 1940 when Mussolini had got off the fence and supported Germany—England had become their country's enemy. There were informers everywhere. How could a man know whom to trust? Separatists . . . Fascists . . . Mafia . . . Flavia was not political, but she listened to the men's talk when she could; she always had. It was the only way you could find out anything about what was going on. No one would tell you.

Now, Flavia sighed as she reread the words she had written this afternoon. Had she captured any of it at all? The fear? The desperation? The longing? The love?

Once again, she picked up her pen. If she had known how hard it would be, she might never have begun.

But—she had waited for Peter, hadn't she?

The war ended. Signor Westerman returned to Cetaria in 1946—just after Enzo's brother Ettore disappeared, and after the awful falling out between Papa and Alberto Amato. This had rocked the village and torn the two families apart. "I cannot believe it," Papa had cried, close to tears. "That he would do such a thing to me." And yet he had believed it.

Flavia waited. There had been no letters, and they said the post was still unreliable. But surely Peter would come for her now?

Months passed, and life after the war resumed some semblance of normality. Maria and Leonardo were reunited. But Flavia refused any suitors her parents presented for her. She heard nothing, and yet she waited. She listened to her father— ranting and cursing—and waited. She wrote to him, and still she waited.

Most people remained very poor—but the Farros were better off than most, with the patronage of Signor Westerman and the contacts of Santina's father, Enzo. Flavia had never liked or trusted Enzo, and he made no secret of the fact that he disapproved of Flavia—disobedient daughter that she was—and of any influence she might have over his daughter Santina. But Enzo had become increasingly important to Papa—Flavia saw that—even before the falling out between Papa and Alberto. And now Enzo was smug. One day she saw him and Alberto in the village square, shouting, almost coming to blows there in front of a watching crowd. She heard people talking—about how the families had always fought; over their land, over a woman, even over their family positions in the local cemetery . . . It took the roadsweeper Nico to break them up this time. Flavia shrugged and went on her way. She was sorry that Alberto no longer came to their house, but it was not her concern.

Flavia also learned to cook. In la cucina, *pounding and mixing, kneading and rolling, she found solace for her grief; a way of finding the patience required, even a deep sense of comfort. She watched Maria marry and become the woman she, Flavia, would not be. And she waited.*

Until—at last—she could wait no longer.

There is both humor and poignancy built into Sicilian cuisine, she wrote. And so it is in life. Like *pasta du maltempu.* Bad-weather pasta—originating from those times when the fishermen were unable to go out in their boats. It was sad, but it could make you smile. Bittersweet . . .

Always, there was the pasta. In Sicily it was made from semolina flour from the yellow durum wheat, but here in England, often not. Flavia was proud of the fact that she still made her own fresh pasta, even now. Dried pasta, naturally, was not the same.

Make a heap of flour with a hole in the middle, like a volcano. Pour in the lava of the eggs and mix in with your fingers. When it is the right consistency, knead the dough with your fingers and the balls of your hands. Tess had watched her mother do this often enough . . . she should know.

Aim for a quiet rhythm. Let the rest of your body be still while the hands work. Fold, knead, and twist the dough into a supple, elastic ball. Now put your back into it. Throw the dough onto the counter to release the tension. Flavia chuckled. Could be the tension of the pasta or the tension of the cook.

Repeat this process for at least fifteen minutes. Let the dough rest. The rest is as important as the work. Roll into sheets, flipping and flouring to prevent it from stick-ing. Roll and stretch and roll until it is as thin as daylight in winter. Dry and cut. Boil for two or three minutes in a large pot with lots of water. The pasta needs to swim in the pan . . . Remove when it is al dente *to the taste. Introduce it to tomatoes . . .*

CHAPTER 34

Broken heart forever . . . ?

But before Tess could question her further, Santina glanced behind Tess, and she saw a sudden flicker of fear in her eyes. Furtively, she touched Tess's arm before scuttling away.

Frustrated, Tess turned around to see what had spooked her. She saw the woman with the pixie face. And felt a hand on her shoulder.

"Tess."

She gave a small start and turned back. "Hello, Giovanni." Didn't he have a habit of turning up unexpectedly . . . ?

They kissed on both cheeks. He smelled of limes, she thought. Clean and crisp with a bit of a zing. He was dressed smartly—in a dark suit, but didn't seem in the least overheated. He must be cold blooded, she thought. Or just accustomed to Sicilian weather?

"I heard you were back," he said, steering her away from the market and the woman with the dark hair and pixie face. How, she wondered? It seemed that nothing got past Giovanni.

"I was on my way to see you," she told him, trying not to mind his guiding hand on her arm. He was deferential, though, she noted, to the matrons of the town, weaving a pathway through the women and market stalls with a *"Prego, Signora"* here and a *"Grazie, Signora"* there. Santina was nowhere to be seen.

"Ah, good. Coffee?" he asked smoothly, and before she knew it, they had left the market and emerged into another piazza she hadn't seen before. Or *piazzetta*, perhaps, as it was so tiny. There was a church, too, a little chapel with an iron bell and an old wooden door; in front of it stood an olive tree and a stone bench.

"Okay. Why not?" She could always use more coffee.

He stopped at a bar and led the way inside. In contrast to the church and *piazzetta*, it was all chrome and mirrors and abstract art. Tess blinked. A sudden intrusion of modern Sicily—how bizarre.

They sat down at a table by the door, and Giovanni ordered two espressos with a tiny jugful of hot milk. "So," he said. "You cannot stay apart from us, *no*?"

Tess stirred a little of the milk into her coffee. "Cetaria is a beautiful place," she said.

He raised an eyebrow. "This is true. And you talked with your mother when you went home?"

Tess sighed. "I think I told you, Giovanni, that my mother doesn't like to talk about Sicily. So if there is something hidden somewhere, I can assure you that I know nothing about it." And she didn't want to know. There were enough mysteries here already.

Giovanni shrugged, not looking in the least convinced.

Irritated, Tess leaned forward. "Tonino Amato told me the reason for your family feud," she said. "No wonder you're such enemies."

Giovanni sipped his coffee. He didn't seem remotely concerned. "And that reason is?" he inquired.

Tess took a deep breath. It was too late to back down now. She'd wanted to ruffle his feathers, hadn't she? "Your family murdered his uncle." It sounded like quite a reason to her.

"Luigi Amato?" He looked furious now. He loosened his collar. Well and truly ruffled. "You should get your facts right, Tess. That man died of a heart attack. And he got what was coming to him. He was a coward, a thief, and he did not pay his debts. The feud . . ." He almost spat. ". . . you speak of began long before Luigi's death."

What could she say to that? She had no idea which of these two men to believe. "Does it really matter now?" she asked him. "It's all in the past. Isn't it about time your families put all this history behind them?"

Giovanni laughed. "This is Sicily, Tess. And everything matters."

Right. How often had she heard that already?

Giovanni had composed himself pretty quickly. "But what of the villa?" he asked. "Have you decided what you will do?"

Tess hesitated. "I'm still reluctant to sell."

"I understand." He nodded.

Good. She was relieved. She wondered if she'd misjudged him. "So I was wondering if you knew of a reliable building company," she said. "Someone I can trust." She laid emphasis on the last word.

"Of course." Giovanni looked affronted. "I can take care of the whole affair for you." He clicked his fingers. "You only have to ask, my dear Tess."

"Yes, but—" Tess wished she could get him to be a bit less all-encompassing. "I want to deal with it myself," she said firmly. "And I need an estimate first."

He raised an eyebrow. "For what?"

Tess sipped the coffee. It was good. Nutty, but not as subtle as Tonino's coffee. It did, however, have the advantage of being prepared in a pretty hot espresso machine—a pile of gleaming chrome behind the counter. "Enough basic building work to make it sound," she said. "New electrics, probably. Decorating throughout. I'm not sure what else." She needed to decide exactly what she was going to do with it. "I want some advice from someone who knows his stuff," she went on. "Someone who can speak a bit of English so that we can communicate at least."

"Of course, of course, *no preoccuparti*. Don't worry." He waved his hand airily, and she noticed again his gold signet ring. "*Allora*. We can get advice, we can make the plans, the work can go ahead, I can oversee the builders . . ."

"Whoa, Giovanni." Tess put up a hand. "I also need to keep a grip on the costs."

"Costs?" His lip turned up slightly. As if costs, she thought, were rather beneath him.

"I'll have a budget," she explained patiently. "But I don't even have that until I get a mortgage—or a bank loan perhaps."

"You need a loan?" Giovanni downed his coffee in one, breathed out, and wiped his lips with the white paper napkin. He was perfectly clean shaven. Even his eyebrows formed an exact semicircle—not a hair out of place. And his hands, as he crumpled the napkin onto the tabletop, were smooth, the nails neatly manicured; hands that were unused to practical work, she could tell.

"Mmm." She needed money from somewhere, that was for sure.

"That will not be a problem," he said.

"No?" Tess was confused. "Do you think I could get a loan for the project from a Sicilian bank, then?" This was one aspect that had been bothering her. She was a single parent with no job and no obvious assets. She still had a small mortgage on the house in Pridehaven that her parents had helped her to buy eighteen years ago when she was pregnant with Ginny. Even to continue repaying that would be a struggle. It would be quite a while before Villa Sirena started recouping anything she spent on it. So how could she hope to manage another mortgage or loan?

"A bank?" He laughed out loud. Put his fingers close to her mouth. "Shh. We will keep things more personal, yes?"

What was he suggesting? But before Tess could reply, he glanced up, his fingers moved to her cheek, and he was caressing her face, his thumb touching her lips, like a lover.

She flinched. "Giovanni . . . ?" What was he doing? She blinked as a shadow crossed the table between them and she glanced up instinctively to see through the open doorway into the narrow street bordering the *piazzetta* the unmistakable form of Tonino passing by.

Tess made her way slowly back to the *baglio*. Giovanni had offered to accompany her, but she reckoned he'd done enough damage for one day. She couldn't rid herself of the feeling that it had all been staged. Not Giovanni's offer of help, if that was what it had been, but that caress on her lips, her cheek.

She touched her face with her fingers. She certainly hadn't invited it—had she? Or wanted it. Giovanni Sciarra was an attractive man, she couldn't deny that. But Giovanni had never given her any indication that he . . . that he . . .

The market was breaking up now, all the vans and Apes (little three-wheeled delivery trucks) had been loaded up and driven off, chugging back to wherever, exhausts smoking, leaving a pile of debris—mostly rotting vegetable leaves—behind.

Could Giovanni have seen Tonino coming down the street? Did he know (because he seemed to know everything) that she and Tonino had spent time together? He hated Tonino and would probably do anything to make him angry. But *would* it make him angry? Giovanni's touch had certainly been intimate enough to make Tonino think that she and Giovanni had some sort of special relationship. And she hadn't done anything to dispel that. But . . . She shrugged. What was their feud to her, anyway? It wasn't her business. She'd had just about enough of both of them.

On the other side of the market square in a side street she hadn't walked down before, Tess noticed a hotel. Hotel Faraglione. Hotel of the Rock. It was quite small, pale mauve and stuccoed with mint-green shutters at the windows. Sweet. And yes, from the balconies you'd get a good view of the rocks.

The garden looked pretty, with a palm tree and bougain-villea in deep purple and orange flower, so Tess wandered closer to take a look, still swinging her carrier bag containing her market purchases from her hand.

What did it matter if Tonino had seen them? But—he would have, some voice whispered. And, it did.

The front door of the hotel was wide open, white muslin blowing at the windows, and inside someone was sitting at a reception desk writing busily. The woman from the market. Pixie face. Friendly smile. Red lipstick.

Tess watched her for a moment. She'd guessed she'd turn up again—Cetaria was too small for her not to.

As she lingered, drinking in the scents from the garden and suddenly realizing that she was starving and should get herself some food as it was way past lunchtime, the woman looked up.

Surprise registered briefly on her face, and then she gave a half wave, turned to speak to someone behind her, stood up, and came to the doorway.

"Tess, isn't it?" she asked in perfect English.

"Er . . . Yes." The place was obviously even smaller than she'd thought. Everyone knew everyone who as much as set foot in the village. "You're English?" She walked toward her.

"I am. A Londoner originally. Nowadays trying my best to be Sicilian, of course." She laughed. "I'm Millie. Millie Zambito. My husband, Pierro, and I run this hotel."

"He's Sicilian?" Tess shook her hand, which was tiny and small boned, her fingernails also painted bright red, she noticed. Tess relaxed. It was such a relief to speak to someone English here in Cetaria. Giovanni and Tonino spoke the language well enough, but it wasn't the same. And there were complications. Wasn't it always the way . . . ?

"Yes, he is." Millie looked back toward the reception desk. "Would you like a glass of wine or some juice? Most people are having their siesta around now. I can take a break."

And before Tess knew it, she was sitting in Millie's private garden in a canvas deck chair, eating fruit and wafer-thin biscuits drizzled with olive oil. Millie had put her carrier bag in the hotel kitchen larder and had already regaled her with the story of how she and Pierro had met at a party in London when he tripped over her as she was sitting on a cushion on the floor, apologized profusely, and ended up taking her out to dinner.

"Typical Sicilian," Millie remarked, lighting a cigarette. "An apology is never enough. They always go OTT."

Tess laughed. "I shouldn't say this," she said—Millie's husband was Sicilian after all, and so was her own mother— "but I do find them difficult to understand at times."

Millie shot her a searching gaze. "You've met Tonino Amato," she said. "The guy who does the mosaics in the *baglio*?"

Tess nodded. "He's a bit . . . well, dark." And that was putting it mildly.

Millie smiled an enigmatic smile and drew in deeply on her cigarette. "That's the Sicilian inheritance," she said. "Dark, grim, but very interesting . . ."

Well, he was certainly that.

"Do you like him?" Millie leaned forward, a curious glimmer in her eye, but Tess was hesitant. She didn't know her quite well enough—yet. And besides, it wasn't easy to explain. Feelings never were.

"I'd like to know more about him," she compromised.

Millie's lips compressed. "Wouldn't we all," she said. She sipped her juice. "And you've met Giovanni Sciarra?"

"Uh-huh." Millie seemed to be waiting for more, but once again she didn't elaborate. It was a pretty effective grapevine they had going in their village—she didn't want to fuel it more than necessary.

"He hasn't made a pass at you, has he?" Millie poured more juice. "Some people think he's a bit of a troublemaker."

Tess decided not to go there. "His family were holding the key to my villa," she told her. "I don't know him well, but he's been very helpful."

Millie laughed. "I'm sure he has," she said. "And you're wise to be diplomatic. Giovanni's family has lived in Cetaria forever. So has Tonino's, of course. Pierro's new in town—only twenty years." She rolled her eyes. "And of course I'm way too foreign to be accepted. But . . ." She gave Tess another look. "When you learn the language and when you live here, you start to realize—gradually—what they're all about." She stubbed the cigarette out in an ashtray.

"Where does Pierro come from originally?" Tess asked, devouring another savory biscuit. She reckoned it would take her a whole lifetime to find out what they were all about.

"Catania." Millie stretched out in her chair. She was small, almost doll-like in her figure; her legs were bare, and she had kicked off her shoes. She looked as if she were on holiday herself rather than running her own hotel. "Sicily's been taken over so many times," she said. "You'll find in the east there's more of a Greek influence—democracy and harmony—while here they're more kind of sultry and brooding."

"Mmm." Tess thought of Tonino. Sultry and brooding indeed.

"They say it's the shadow of Africa." Millie plucked a grape from the plate.

Sun and shadow. Oppression. Tess thought of the *baglio*. "The place is very Arabic," she said. "Moorish." Yes, in more ways than one.

"Exactly." Millie crossed her legs. "And the Arabs didn't bring only couscous and citrus fruit to Sicily," she said. "They even brought spaghetti." She laughed. "Before that, they all ate potato dumplings!"

"Really?" So many times Tess had watched her mother, tipping flour into a heap on the kitchen table, adding the eggs, olive oil, and water, and mixing with her fingers into a smooth paste. She never measured the ingredients—she just knew the right amounts by feel.

There were, she realized, so many memories of Muma in their kitchen at home that were integral to her childhood. Perhaps that was why every fragrance of this place seemed familiar to her. It was the dough, the tomatoes, the herbs and spices she'd grown up with, ingrained into her senses just as surely as they were ingrained into Muma's. They might as well, she thought, have grown up in Sicily—they had certainly taken its food with them. And she wished she had taken more notice, learned more from her mother in the kitchen.

"This village was where my mother grew up," she told Millie and found herself explaining Muma's reticence about Sicily, about how they'd never been back. She decided not to mention Santina Sciarra.

"And she never told you anything about those times?" Millie looked skeptical. "But why ever not?"

Tess shook her head. "I have no idea." Even when her Sicilian grandparents died—Tess was twelve—her grandmother outliving her grandfather by only six months, her mother had not gone back. She remembered the pacing of the kitchen, the weeping, the row between her parents. Her father saying, "You'll always regret it if you don't go." Her mother's voice rising in desperation. "I will not go back, Lenny. I cannot." Her father retreating to the shed to smoke his pipe, before at last he emerged and took Muma in his arms and held her. "There, my pet. There . . . Don't you worry now."

And gradually things had drifted back to normal. Muma's eyes became less red as every day went by.

Tess rarely thought of her grandparents. She'd never known them after all. And there were so many other things to think about—like swimming and music and boys . . .

"Come to dinner with us on Friday," Millie said, when she'd finished the story. "Pierro would love to meet you. And it's such a relief to speak English for a change." She glanced at her watch, and Tess took the hint.

"That would be lovely," she said. "Thank you."

And she walked back to the villa with her carrier bag full of market produce, feeling almost light headed. Millie was self-confident, glamorous, and fun. A friend—maybe. Why not? The idea of finding a friend in Cetaria gave her a good feeling.

She walked through the *baglio*. But what about her mother? What about Santina's story about the injured pilot and her mother's broken heart? Tess stared out toward the navy ocean she loved so much. She had wanted to find out her mother's story, but was she ready to hear it?

CHAPTER 35

It was the end of a summer that had continued into Octo-
ber with an outrageous white heat that left Flavia sapped to
the bones.

They had made the traditional salsa—*to eat in win-*
ter to remember the summer, as Mama used to say—and
half the village had come to the terraces surrounding Villa
Sirena to eat and dance into the night. It had been a good
year for tomatoes—especially the pizzutelli, *the dark-red,*
thick-skinned cherry tomatoes that made the best sauce. The
cauldron of salsa had cooked continuously for two days, bub-
bling red lava, the tomatoes and basil stirred and squashed
by neighbors and family alike, decanted after hours of sim-
mering into sterilized empty beer bottles. And now? They all
longed for rain to break the unbearable pressure.

One morning Papa and Mama were whispering together,
but they stopped abruptly when Flavia entered la cucina.

"What?" she asked.

"We are planning a lunch," Papa said, "for All Souls' Day. You will cook, sì?"

"For how many?"

Flavia didn't mind. She enjoyed preparing food, and the more she was catering for, the better she liked it. Planning the menu— with their limited resources—distracted her, while the washing and peeling and chopping of vegetables and the rhythmic rolling of the dough for pasta sent her into a hypnotic state that allowed her to dream. She liked to dream.

Flavia put more coffee on the stove. She still dreamed of Peter. Something told her that he would still come for her— even though it was almost six years since his promise, and she had heard nothing. She sensed that he was her only hope of escape. And since he had not come, then she was sure there must be a very good reason. But how could she find out what the reason might be? How could she decide the next step?

"There will be five of us," Papa said. There was a strange glint in his eye.

"Just five?" Flavia was disappointed. All Souls' Day, or the Feast of the Dead, was important to Sicilians. Il giorno dei morti. Traditionally, it was a day of celebration, one on which to pray, go to the cemetery, and remember family and friends who had passed away. But there was only one man Flavia would be remembering. She would never forget him.

"And we want something special," Papa went on.

Flavia's ears pricked. *"Who is coming?"* She was already planning. Perhaps they would start with melanzane *and* peppers—she had a special way of preparing these with a dash of balsamic and olive oil that was rich and would lift the melanzane. *And at summer's end they had a glut of both vegetables; Flavia's mother's thriftiness had worked its way down to her—it had to, times had remained hard, and much food remained unavailable.*

"Enzo," Papa said. "With his nephew Rodrigo. Ettore's boy."

"Enzo?" Flavia was surprised. She fetched the small white cups for espresso. Enzo wasn't special. Papa saw Enzo most days. Since the big falling out between Papa and Alberto Amato, Enzo Sciarra had become his closest crony, but Flavia still didn't like or trust him. As for the drama concerning Alberto . . . The village had never recovered from the shock. And poor Alberto—well, Flavia couldn't believe that he had done what they accused him of. He had always been kind and gentle with her. Enzo though . . . He rarely came to the house. He and Flavia would always be awkward with each other, despite her friendship with Santina.

Mama nodded. "We have much to thank Enzo for," she said.

"Oh?" But Flavia understood. Every family must have their alliances. Every family must be protected. Flavia worried over it, but Papa was only looking after his own. "And is Santina not coming for the lunch?"

Papa looked shifty. "Santina has other family business to attend to," he said. "Sadly she cannot join us."

That was a shame. Flavia still loved her childhood friend. It was just that Santina was content with the old ways; Flavia was not.

Perhaps they would follow with pasta con le sarde *with pine nuts and raisins, a sweet-sour taste of the sea. Sardines were always plentiful. And only yesterday Papa had been given a parcel by one of his contacts, containing lots of good things for the kitchen—dried fruit, chickpeas, lentils, and nuts. Had Papa had to give anything in exchange? Flavia hoped not.*

There would be olives, too, already being harvested from trees heavy with fruit.

For dolce, *perhaps* cassata—*dense with candied fruit, the lightest ricotta. And on the terrace were some ripe* zibibbo *grapes—palest green and sweet as honey. She would serve them with coffee and some of Papa's liqueur. It was traditional too to make* biscotti, *flavored with cloves and called the bones of the dead. Children would receive such goodies—prepared for them by* i morti *during the night. Flavia smiled to herself. An unpretentious lunch. But special enough. She nodded to herself. Special enough.*

At the market Flavia bought herself a lemon ice from the ice man to quench her thirst. She'd come to buy ingredients, and these days there was more food available; the scent of suckling goat and chickpea fritters frying hung greasily in the air. Big-eyed cats wound their tails around table legs as they hung around hoping for scraps. She finished up the last of the yellow ice chips from the paper cup. It was still warm, but soon it would be winter. Another winter.

She nodded at the fishmonger loudly proclaiming the freshness of his swordfish, red mullet, and octopus and chose from the blue sardines laid out on a marble slab. She smiled and greeted her acquaintances—the women hunched in their black dresses and shawls, the men in black berets and baggy trousers. Everyone was thin after the war. Everyone looked weary still.

As Flavia prepared the lunch, she began to formulate a plan. For some time now, she had been doing tasks for Signor Westerman—mostly secretarial jobs like writing and posting letters, but also fetching shopping and often cooking for him when he had visitors. He always paid her well, and she had been saving this money.

"For your bottom drawer," Mama said. But Flavia had other ideas. If Peter Rutherford would not come to her, then she, Flavia Farro, would go to him.

She could still picture Peter's face—and especially how he looked that day when she had found him in the valley, his glider crashed into pieces around him, bits of fabric stuck on the jagged metal and billowing in the faint breeze coming from the mountains. His white face, the way he bit his lip. And his eyes . . . She could still see his eyes. In her head. In her heart. Always.

She sliced the eggplant, getting into a good rhythm with her favorite knife. Its serrated edge dealt neatly with the glossy purple skin and carved through the spongy center of the vegetable without mess.

As she worked, she let her thoughts drift to what Peter had told her about his life in England. For Flavia it had become a litany—a way of remembering; she would not lose these nuggets of Peter, no matter what happened and no matter how much time passed.

Peter had told her about the place his family lived—Exeter, in the southwest of England. It sounded pretty—there was a river and a cathedral, trees and small thatched cottages, and it was close to the sea.

She turned her attention to the red peppers. His family probably had less money than Signor Westerman, but they were not poor; she knew this. Flavia was certain that England could not be as poor as Sicily. And they had won the war. So why shouldn't Flavia leave Sicily and go to get a job

*there, in England? She could read and write—English, too.
She could cook—"like an angel," Signor Westerman said, and
she was quick witted—too clever for her own good, Papa often
remarked. Flavia assembled ingredients and began to make
the vinegar.*

*Peter's father worked in a bank, he had said, which
sounded grand, and his mother looked after the house. No, he
had told her with a laugh, they didn't have servants, just a
daily woman who came to do the cleaning. Well, that was a
servant, wasn't it? Peter had one sister, who was called Lynette,
and one brother called William. He was the youngest, the baby
of the family.*

*Flavia cleaned her knife and washed her hands. So far,
so good.*

It was surprising, Flavia thought now, that these memories of a distant past could be so clear in the mind—clearer
sometimes than what had happened yesterday. She put
down her pen for a moment and sighed. When she emerged
from her writing, she was almost surprised to see them—
Lenny and Ginny, chatting together or poring over the
computer. It took her a moment to adjust, to come back to
the present. To remember who they were—and who Flavia was, too. It was as if her young life had been so rich, so
vibrant, that it was ingrained in her very soul. And the food
of her country echoed this.

The picking and preserving of tomatoes had colored
and punctuated Flavia's childhood and adolescence. The
pungent scent of fresh tomatoes in the sun, the cauldron
of bubbling fruit to make the bottled salsa . . . But could she
transfer it to paper and make it live . . . ?

In Sicily after the salsa, *there is the* strattu—*the paste that is laid out on wooden boards to harden and darken like blood under the burning sun. It is a concentration, an aftermath of the salsa, a purée that becomes like putty before it is kneaded and packed into glass jars and covered with olive oil.*

It is no coincidence that red is the color of blood and also the color of passion. In Sicily, it is also the color of the earth, and it is the color of the setting sun. Salsa is the lifeblood of Sicily.

For the salsa, *you need ripe tomatoes, fresh basil, and sunshine. Warm the bottles in the sun. Wash the tomatoes and leave to dry outside. Start up the cauldron. Remove the seeds and cook the tomato pulp, stirring and mashing as you go. Remember the warmth and the passion. Add the basil and cook to thicken. Fill the bottles and leave in the sun under a blanket to cook some more. Add family and neighbors, music, dancing, and a feast of food and wine.*

This is the base for every tomato sauce. Add garlic and onion cooked in oil and a pinch of sugar to make the sauce still sweeter.

The pranzo, *the lunch, was more successful than Flavia had expected. She had no doubts concerning the food—it was the company she'd been worried about. However, Enzo was more pleasant to her than usual, complimenting her several times on her appearance and the lunch dishes. "This spread reminds me," he said "of my poor wife. God rest her soul."*

Flavia remembered his wife, Santina's mother, who had died several years before. She was a thin, scraggy woman, old and bent before her time, worn out by Enzo's cruel treatment and constant demands.

Enzo's nephew was from a neighboring village, but Flavia had often seen him around. His father, Ettore, Enzo's brother, had spent much time in Cetaria with Enzo—they were as thick as thieves—until he mysteriously disappeared some years ago. As far as Flavia was aware, no one knew now if he was alive or dead. Enzo never followed it up—so maybe he knew more? Anyway, since Ettore's disappearance, Enzo had more or less taken over his brother's paternal role, and Rodrigo now seemed to spend much of his time in Cetaria, too. He also—in Flavia's opinion—had something of his uncle Enzo's arrogance. Most Sicilian men were arrogant as peacocks, but those with certain connections were more so than most. They had too much power for their own good. They would not be denied.

The talk meandered between the men and was of politics, as usual. They referred to an article published in the news-paper, Sicilia del Popolo. *There was a sense of postwar dis-illusion and discontent, it said, and there had been some demonstrations in and around Palermo; peasants and young Communists, a brass band, the cry of "land for the workers!"*

"Idiots!" Enzo, she gathered, disapproved. "They do not know what is good for them."

Her father nodded his agreement. There were bandits and gangs in the countryside, he informed them; many people were challenging the old ways of the landowners; many peo-ple wanted to make their voices heard.

Flavia cast a glance toward Rodrigo Sciarra. Did he want his voice to be heard? Or was his voice simply the echo of his powerful uncle's?

Over dolce, *Flavia noticed that Rodrigo Sciarra was pay-ing her more attention than strictly necessary. He was praising her culinary skills to the heavens, while Papa sat back strok-ing his beard, with a contented look on his face, as if he alone had been responsible for tutoring his daughter in this area of her expertise. And at one point, when Rodrigo poured her some sweet dessert wine, he placed three fingers of his hand on her wrist in a gesture of intimacy that set alarm bells pealing.*

Papa, she saw, had noticed the gesture. And was smiling. No . . . She scraped her chair back and began to clear plates.

"Stay where you are. I will do it," Mama fussed, taking Fla-via by the shoulders and pushing her none too gently back into her chair.

Flavia cast a look of hopeless desperation her mother's way, but her mother took no notice. It had been decided, then. She could do nothing.

Papa and Enzo got slowly to their feet on pretense of fetch-ing liqueurs. And Mama disappeared into la cucina—*to make the coffee, she said.*

"Flavia." Rodrigo grasped her hand. He smelled of cologne.

"Please do not say more," she begged.

"But for so long I have watched you from afar," said Rodrigo.

Flavia sighed. She was sure this wasn't true. This was something cooked up by Enzo and Papa. Clearly they wanted the two families to unite—this would be the final rift in Papa's friendship with Alberto Amato, and it would show everyone where their loyalties lay. Hence the obvious: Rodrigo and Fla-via. This, then, was why Santina and Rodrigo's mother, Fran-cesca, had not been invited to the lunch; it was not a family lunch at all. It was a conspiracy.

"No," she said.

"Admired you," Rodrigo said.

"No."

"Dared to hope."

"Please do not." Flavia tried to extract her hand, but his grip was of steel.

"I can offer you a good life."

Flavia looked into his dark eyes. Perhaps he could. Yes, perhaps he could. But it wasn't the life she wanted.

"I have not encouraged you," she said carefully. *"I have given you no reason to think that I hold you in special regard."*

"Nevertheless," Rodrigo persisted. *"I think you could grow to love me—no?"*

Flavia didn't want to hurt his feelings. "It is not so simple," she began.

"Our families—they are close," he said. *"They are simpaticu. Why should we not get on—you and I? It is natural. It will cement the union."*

All very well, Flavia thought. But what about love?

Rodrigo was now stroking her arm. He was very persistent.

"There is someone else," she said quickly. *"My father should have told you."*

"Someone else?" Rodrigo stared at her. *"Veramenti? Is this true?"* He seemed to be mentally reviewing the eligible men of the neighborhood.

It wouldn't take him long, she thought ruefully. "Veru. It is true," she said.

"Surely not?" He frowned.

"My father should have told you," Flavia repeated. *"He had no right . . ."*

"Ah." Rodrigo looked triumphant, as if he had just solved a difficult equation. *"You are thinking of the Englishman, yes? Your father said he had been a problem."*

"A problem?" Flavia bridled. *"The only problem,"* she said, *"is that I love him."*

Rodrigo drew back, clearly affronted. "But you have not . . . ? With this Englishman, you have not . . . ?"

"No!" Flavia felt herself blush, felt the heat reach to the roots of her hair. Though she would have. If he'd wanted it, she would have. What did she care for her reputation?

"Ah." He wagged a finger. "You are a foolish girl. But you are a Sicilian girl. And you must marry a Sicilian man." He drew himself up to his full height. "Rodrigo Sciarra can make you forget him."

Flavia heard throats being cleared and coughs from outside in the passage. All Souls' Day was a day for engagements and new beginnings, too. She should have known. "I am sorry, Rodrigo—but my answer is no," she said quickly. "Please do not press me further."

The others reentered, Mama armed with a coffeepot and the biscotti of the dead, looking expectant and hopeful, Papa with a bottle of grappa and raising an eyebrow at the mournful Rodrigo, who shook his head sadly. Enzo's expression changed from geniality to thunder in a second.

Flavia didn't stay for the aftermath. She excused herself and took refuge in la cucina until the last biscuit had been eaten and the visitors had gone.

The row with Papa went on for the rest of the afternoon and well into the evening. Flavia had never seen him so angry. He raged, cursed, called her every name under the sun.

"For the love of God . . . What use is it to have an ungrateful daughter?" he had eventually demanded of Mama. "What good is she—if she cannot make a man happy, if she cannot form a bond with the family of his closest friend?"

Flavia listened to him and knew it was not just a case of friendship. Her father was walking a delicate tightrope with *a precarious edge. Why shouldn't he sacrifice his daughter? They didn't call it La Piovra—the octopus—for nothing. The Mafia had tentacles that could reach far and wide. If the Mafiosi wanted you, there was nowhere to hide.*

At one point, Flavia dared to mention Peter's name. "I still love him," she said. "I made a promise to him. I am not free to marry another man."

"That scoundrel!" her father yelled.

"You helped him," Flavia reminded him. "You saved his life."

"Would that I had not bothered." His face was twisted in anger. "And where is he now—this boy you say you love, this boy who has not come back for you? Promises? Pah! The promise of that English boy means less than nothing. You are a fool if you cannot see this."

Flavia flinched.

"The war is long ended." He looked around him. "Where is he? Why has he not come? Why has he not written you one word? Can you tell me that?" He reached for his stick as if he would beat her, and it was at this point, as Mama put a hand on his arm to restrain him, that Flavia ran.

She ran into the balmy, cobalt darkness and across the fields she knew so well, over to the valley, where she stayed for what seemed like hours, thinking about what had happened. The night air was heavy as a quilt around her and she felt as if she could not breathe. But she knew what she must do.

When she came back, she went straight to Villa Sirena. She glanced briefly at the motif above the front door. Flavia knew the story. She, too, had been trapped. She understood. She let herself in with only a light knock at the door. L'inglese would still be up; he never retired before midnight.

And sure enough, Edward Westerman was seated in his customary place, a glass of red wine on a table by his side. As usual, he was wearing a crumpled linen suit, and his old Panama hat was balanced on the arm of the chair. He was, perhaps, less than fifteen years older than her, and yet for all that, Flavia knew that he was a man of the world, an experienced man. Even before the war, when she was a child, Signor Westerman had never seemed young. He would know what to do.

"Flavia," he said, as she entered the room. He didn't seem particularly surprised to see her.

"I need to go to England," she blurted.

"Is that so?" He picked up his glass and took a sip. "Now, why would that be, I wonder?"

"I need to get away." Haltingly, she told him about Peter, about her father, about Rodrigo.

Her father had worked for Signor Westerman for a long time, and she didn't want to be disloyal. But she needed his help. "I need to live my life," she said. "My way."

He nodded. Of course he would understand. He, too, had had to live life his way—and had come to Sicily to do it. "How can I help, my dear?" he asked.

"I have saved some money." She told him the amount.

"It is a long journey. Two days by train."

"I can do it," she declared. "I only need to borrow a little more money. I will send it back to you. I promise."

Edward Westerman seemed thoughtful. "I have an idea," he said. "If you are determined to go to England, then I might have an errand for you. I have a package—a manuscript of mine—that must be conveyed safely to my older sister, Beatrice, who lives in London. It would be a considerable service to me."

"A package?" she inquired. London. She could hardly conceive the thought.

He looked down modestly. "Some of my own poetic works. I hope Bea will act as a go-between for me and my publishers. But . . ." He sighed. "Times are hard. We will see. Perhaps I am wasting my time even churning out the stuff."

"Oh, no, Signor," Flavia protested. She loved his poetry. It deserved to be published. He was a good man. He should be successful. And if she could help in any small way . . .

"You're very kind." He smiled.

"And I will certainly take the work to London for you," she said.

"Very good." He took another sip of wine. "I don't trust this damned postal system." He patted her hand. "But I trust you, my dear. And Bea will help you when you get to England. I will see to it."

"I am grateful," Flavia said proudly.

"And naturally, I will pay you for doing it." He nodded. "That will enable you to complete your journey, I think." He stared into his wineglass. "You must be prepared for disappointment though, my dear. People, I have found, have a habit of not living up to our expectations."

She looked down at her hands. "I know."

"But . . ." He gripped her wrist—quite hard, and for a moment she flinched. "You only have one life, Flavia, and you must live it. In a new place a person can be whomsoever he or she desires."

"Papa—" she began, though in a way she sensed that he was talking about himself just as much as he was talking about her. He had left England, left friends and family; reinvented himself. It was a similar story. He had felt an outcast in his own country, and so did she.

"Your papa has his method of doing things," he said. "Don't you fret. I'll make things right with your papa."

She bowed her head. "Thank you."

"Come back tomorrow," he said. "And we will make our plan."

Outside, she heard the rain come. A huge torrent washing down on the roof and streaming over the terrace, as if the sky itself had fallen to the ground. The sound of the downpour seemed to clatter through the hills and valleys as the water sluiced the parched red earth. Some thread of tension in the air was released, and something in Flavia, too. And she was glad.

CHAPTER 36

GINNY WASN'T SURE WHAT MADE HER GO IN. THE Bull and Bear was a bit of a sleazy pub, and she'd never wanted to work behind a bar. To be a barmaid, like a character from *EastEnders* or *Corrie* . . . But it was a job.

After Nonna's breakfast bombshell, she had typed up a résumé on the computer—Pops had always kept up with technology . . . he'd even talked about getting an iPod, though when Ginny's mind conjured up a vision of Pops with earphones, it didn't quite work somehow. And after lunch she'd trailed around shops and restaurants in Pridehaven, thrusting copies into the startled faces of shopgirls and waiters. *This is me. This is what I have done with my life . . .*

Not a lot, they probably thought. A paper route, babysitting, college. A girl without direction. A drifter. That's what they called it in some of her mum's old hippie songs . . . That's what her father had been.

It was pretty hopeless. No one seemed interested. And perhaps she only went into the Bull and Bear because it was six p.m. and she didn't want to go back to Nonna and Pops's and tell them she'd failed. With her mother, she could rise to this sort of challenge (angry and defensive always worked well), but with Nonna, expectations were high. Ginny hated to disappoint her; her diminutive, white-haired grand-mother had a quiet dignity that Ginny envied.

"I was wondering," she said to the guy behind the bar—in his late thirties she'd guess—"if you had any vacancies for bar staff?"

"Who's asking?" he said.

Well, that was bleeding obvious. "I am," she said.

He grinned. "Yeah, but what's your name, love?"

"Ginny Angel."

"Over eighteen?"

"Yeah."

"Previous experience?"

"No."

He seemed surprised. "Why d'you want to work behind a bar?" he asked.

Ginny racked her brains. Why would anyone? "I like people," she said. Which was a lie. "And I'm an evenings sort of person." Which was another.

He raised his eyebrows.

Dumb dog, she thought. The place was probably open all day. "I'm quick," she said. "I can learn."

"Okay," he said.

"Okay?"

"I'll give you a try," he said. "The last girl walked out a week ago, and I haven't got round to advertising for a replacement yet. Start tomorrow at six?"

"Er . . . Great," said Ginny.

"Aren't you going to ask how much I pay?" he asked. "Or what hours I'll be wanting you to work?"

"Okay." She waited, but he said nothing. "How much do you pay?"

He told her. It wasn't that much, but it was a lot more than nothing.

"Okay," she said.

"The hours are negotiable," he went on. "We'll talk about that tomorrow."

As soon as she left the pub, she sent a text to her mother. *Guess wot? I got a job!*

Her mother phoned her right back. "Well done, darling," she said. "I worked in a bar once." She sounded quite nostalgic.

"At least I'll be earning some dough." Ginny wished her mother's voice didn't make her feel quite so sad. It reminded her how much she missed her. "So I can start saving," she added. "To go away." The Ball made her twist the knife.

"Yes." Her mother's voice was small and slightly hurt. "Is everything all right at home?"

"Fine and dandy." Ginny turned into Nonna and Pops's road, a cul-de-sac that was going nowhere; Bramble Close, Pridehaven—what sort of an address was that? Safe houses in safe streets in a town that had lost its edge . . . A dead end, a going nowhere sort of town.

"And Nonna? And Pops?"

"They're cool." Ginny wondered what her mother was doing right now, why it had been so important to drop everything and go back to Sicily. Maybe it was some sort of midlife crisis—an early menopause or something. Maybe . . .

"So . . . ?"

"Gotta run, Mum," she said.

"Okay, darling. I'll—"

"Bye," And Ginny clicked to end the call before she could say more. It was one of those want and don't want situations; love and hate; bittersweet. The way these things were.

Nonna didn't seem at all surprised that Ginny had found herself a job so quickly. "Good girl," she said, and dished up cannelloni with meat and white sauce *parmigiano* and nutmeg for supper. Yum.

"I think I'll go round to Ben's," Ginny said when they'd finished. "After I've washed up."

Nonna started clearing plates. "Are you doing something nice?" she asked. "Something special?"

Probably not, Ginny thought. "Dunno," she said.

"Well," said Nonna. "Just so long as you enjoy yourself, my dear." But she gave Ginny a look. It was a strange look. As if she was wondering why someone like Ginny was even bothering with someone like Ben. And this made Ginny think. Why was she bothering with Ben?

At Ben's, they watched a movie, and then a couple of his friends came round, and they all went out for a drink. (This was what nearly always happened when she went round to Ben's.)

They talked about stuff Ginny wasn't remotely interested in (bikes, cars, football) and made (sexist) jokes she didn't find funny. At ten thirty she thought about Nonna's look and got up to go home. The Ball tried to stop her, but she surprised herself by finding the strength from somewhere the Ball couldn't go.

She walked home alone. It wasn't that she no longer had feelings for Ben—she did. But . . . She wasn't enjoying herself, was she? Ginny thought of Nonna's look. It was simple. She wasn't doing anything special. So why was she there?

The streets were well lit, and she wasn't scared. Just a little sad—because of Ben. And a little anxious—tomorrow night she would be starting her new job. The question was—would the Ball come too . . . ?

At Nonna and Pops's there was a lamp on in the bedroom and a porch light left on for Ginny's benefit. "Make sure you switch it off when you come in," Nonna always said. And Ginny always did, even though at home she'd developed a habit of announcing her presence by leaving all lights blazing in her wake.

Now Ginny let herself in with her key, switched off the porch light, and crept upstairs, even though they weren't asleep. She could hear the murmuring of their voices as she slipped into the bathroom.

"Well, she must do what she thinks is best." (That was Pops.) "It's her life."

"Yes," said Nonna. "It is her life. But she is also stepping into mine."

And Ginny knew they were talking about her mother and the mysterious house in Sicily. And again she wondered—why had that old man left it to her? What would she do with the place? And why did Nonna mind so much?

She fell asleep that night thinking of her mother, who in her dreams had mellowed from acid lemon and acquired much more of a honey glow. Tomorrow morning she would wake up, and she was beginning to think there might be no Ben. The Ball might start getting a bit too big for Its boots. But . . .

There would be a new job, and if she started saving, maybe a sort-of direction. It was as if she had started getting the faintest, merest glimmer of where she wanted to go . . .

CHAPTER 37

TWO DAYS LATER, TESS WAS SCRAMBLING OVER THE hillside behind Cetaria—according to the guidebook she'd bought in Palermo, this was supposed to be a rocky trail, but there was an awful lot of rock and not much trail—when she saw Tonino Amato. He was working on some stone in a little glade just ahead of her. She had only seen him from a distance these past few days—the day before yesterday she'd spent in Palermo, and yesterday she'd been busy in the villa. Edward Westerman's belongings would have to be given away or sold; some of the furniture was redeemable, some definitely not; and other household effects needed to be sorted into what she was keeping and what she was not.

Tonino's head was bent in concentration, and he was using a small hammer and a kind of metal chisel to tap into the rock.

"*Ciao,*" she said, half wanting to turn and run—in the opposite direction.

He didn't even look up. "*Ciao.*"

"For Colapesce?" she asked.

"Perhaps." He continued hammering.

Okay . . . She could see now that he was extracting thin slivers of slate—presumably to use as a backing for some of his mosaic collages; she'd seen them in the studio. She sat down under an olive tree on a rock near to the one he was working on and stretched out her legs. It was very warm and very still, and the thin grass was scattered with wild clover. She could hear the buzz of insects and the occasional goat bell from farther up the trail. And Tonino's *tap, tap, tap*. What should she say—do you come here often? Might as well come straight to the point, she thought. "You wouldn't be avoiding me, I suppose?" she asked.

Finally he looked up. His gaze was searching but brief. "Why would I?" He didn't seem to require an answer.

Why indeed? He was, she thought, perfectly self-contained in this place, with his stones and mosaics, with the sea and his sadness. It was terrible to lose a friend. But shouldn't everyone move on—sooner or later? She thought of what her new friend Millie had said about shadows. This man was all shadow—and yet the work he produced screamed for the light. Didn't mosaics always work best in sunlight?

"I'm not involved with Giovanni Sciarra," she said, hugging her knees. Just in case that was his problem.

"None of my business." *Tap, tap, tap.*

"Maybe. But I'm not. I wanted you to know that."

"I've seen him hanging around Villa Sirena." Tonino's lip curled. "You should be careful."

Once again, Tess was exasperated. "He's been very helpful, actually," she said. "The villa was left to me by Edward Westerman, and . . ."

Tonino shrugged.

"And he's been advising me what to do with it."

"What will you do with it?" He glanced up at her again.

"I don't know yet. But the point is . . ." She sighed. "I'm not romantically involved with Giovanni, okay?"

Tonino shrugged again.

Well, she had tried. Tess got to her feet and felt the soft, silvery leaves of the olive tree brush against her hair.

It was true that Giovanni had come round yesterday. He had offered her a personal loan—an investment, he called it. The terms sounded fair—ideal even, since she'd have nothing to pay back for the first nine months, which would give her time to get things going in the villa. After that, there would be interest to pay, of course, but not at an unfeasibly high rate. He had brought her some papers to look at—wanted her to sign on the dotted line there and then, but Tess was a little wary.

"I'll think about it," she'd told him. She'd talk to her father first. Maybe even get some legal advice from England.

She started to walk away.

"Why did you come back to Cetaria?" Tonino asked abruptly.

She stopped walking. He seemed to have forgotten their conversation at Segesta, that almost-kiss. Of course it would have been simpler not to have come back—to have got an estate agent to put the villa straight on the market, or even to let Giovanni supervise its refurbishment without interference from her. But there was more—her mother's story for a start. She had been thinking about what Santina had told her, imagining her mother's desperation to be free, picturing the young Flavia in love with an English pilot who was a million miles away from what her family wanted for her—Rodrigo Sciarra, for heaven's sake. What else could she have done at seventeen in a country at war? She couldn't have followed her pilot back to England—not then, anyway. Tess looked down beyond the dwarf palms, olive trees, and terraced vineyards crisscrossing the slopes. There was a good view of the village, the mountains beyond, and the open sea. This afternoon the water was glazed as if with steel. And even her mother's story wasn't the half of it, she thought. "Something in this place . . . ," she said.

"But you have a life in England," he said. "A family?"

She had her parents. And that was another thing. She had always thought of Muma and Dad as being *the* love story. Unquestionably. So where did this English pilot come into the equation? "I'm not married." She had thought he would realize this since she didn't wear a ring. "But I have a daughter."

He raised his head and looked at her. Dark, dark eyes.

"She's eighteen. She's staying with my parents at the moment." She thought of Ginny. How could you be prepared for the moment when your child walked out of the life you'd created for her and entered the rest of the world—the scary world, the world you had no control over? How could you prepare yourself for how you'd feel? Tess had the notion that she ought to at least start making a stab at it. Because it might not be long coming. Ginny had a job, and she wanted to save enough money to go away, for who knew how long. They had been so close. And yet now Tess doubted that Ginny even missed her. She certainly didn't show it. When Tess called, she couldn't wait to get off the phone.

"I was never married to her father," Tess told Tonino, who seemed to be waiting for her to continue. "He left before she was born. He wasn't the marrying kind."

Tonino nodded. He didn't seem shocked—or even surprised. "Since then," he said, "you have been in love, yes?"

"Yes." Tess sat down on the rock again and fished her water bottle out of her bag. She took a deep drink and then passed it to Tonino, who nodded his thanks and did the same. Yes, she had been in love, but not often, for a woman in her late thirties. The occasional fling, the occasional more than fling, the times when she had thought—yes, this one, perhaps. And then Robin. She eyed Tonino squarely. "And you?"

He offered a half smile. "Not married, no," he said. "There have been women from time to time, of course."

Of course.

"And, once, I loved someone."

She watched him and waited. How much would he tell her? How much did he trust her? "It didn't work out?" she asked.

"She was with someone else," he said. "Someone who . . ." He trailed off.

Instinctively, Tess knew who he was talking about. "Was it your friend?" she asked. One look at his face told her she was right. "The one who died?"

"Yes." He put down his tools. "All the time they were together—it was impossible."

Tess traced a pattern in the dusty earth with the tip of her walking boot. "But she knew how you felt?"

"Of course." He pried apart a piece of slate and shot her another look. "Women always do."

Tess wasn't so sure, but she'd let that one go. "And after he died . . . ?" Though she could guess.

"It was even more impossible." He sounded angry. "Helena—she did not think so. But, yes, still impossible."

He began filling the canvas knapsack at his feet with his tools and some stone and slate.

Tess guessed that people weren't supposed to randomly collect bits of rock from places that were probably protected conservation areas, but men like Tonino wouldn't care about those sorts of rules. To them, the land and the sea were there to help man make a living. They used what it offered and took care not to fuck it up for themselves.

Tonino got to his feet, slung the bulging bag over one shoulder and held out a hand to her.

Tess took it. "So she left Sicily?"

"Yes, she left." He paused as if he wanted to say more. "The day my friend died . . ." He tailed off.

"What happened?" Though from his expression she could hazard a guess.

"I was having coffee with Helena." He met her gaze then looked out into the distance over the hills. "It was not what you think."

Tess shook her head. "What then?"

"We were talking about us. About how it could not be. About how we could not hurt him. That is what we were doing." He clenched his fist until the knuckles showed white. "At the time when he . . . When he . . ."

He was unable to go on. Tess put a hand on his shoulder. "It still wasn't your fault," she said. "You were doing the right thing."

"Helena—she never got it," he said. "She never saw why afterwards we could not be together."

"No." Tess could imagine how it had been. Helena, heartbroken, turning to the other man who loved her, the one who was supposed to understand—because he had loved his friend, too. And Tonino's guilt. He must have felt as if he'd killed his friend in order to have her. Some men, she knew, would have grasped the opportunity and the girl, but not Tonino. He was far too intense a personality to shrug off the guilt. He'd be swamped by it; it would make him unhappy for the rest of his life. "And since then?" She echoed his question.

His hand closed more tightly around hers. "Women," he said. "But not love."

When he kissed her this time, it was quite different. Before, it had been no more than an exploratory brush of the lips, almost accidental. But as he turned, as he held her face in his hands, as he bent his head toward her, as his lips pressed against hers, she knew that he meant it. And as the sun warmed her face, she gave herself up to the feeling and kissed him back unreservedly. She wanted to. She had to. Giovanni Sciarra might be right about him, but just for that moment, Tess simply didn't care.

Back at the villa that evening, Tess was churning with the unexpected emotions of the afternoon. She hadn't thought that after Robin, she would leap into another relationship. And yet here she was. Leaping? Well, yes. Maybe.

She decided to make herself some pasta with a simple Gorgonzola sauce and some salad for dinner. She wasn't sure that she could eat at all. And she would have an early night, she decided. She needed to think—and maybe even allow herself to look forward to tomorrow.

After the kiss—and she almost dissolved when she hit the playback button—they had walked for maybe an hour in the olive grove.

Tonino had a great respect for the olive, he told her, touching the gnarled, twisted bark in a way that made her curl up with something that felt like a cross between jealousy and desire. "It is hardy," he said. "And yet responsive."

"Responsive?" Her voice caught in her throat. Good God . . .

"To water. To food. To love."

He'd better stop right there, Tess thought, before she hit the boiling point.

"It has a remarkable grain when carved and oiled," he said. "It burns quickly, and the fragrance . . ."

"Yes." She knew that scent; she'd smelled it the first time she came to Cetaria.

"The olive—she is wise. And the olive grove—it is a still and tranquil place." Tonino splayed his fingers across Tess's head, almost as if she were a statue he was working on, she thought, his fingertips lingering on the base of her skull, on her neck.

Tess closed her eyes as she recalled the sensation. How could anyone put so much sensuality into a touch? Even someone who was a craftsman, who used his hands to create every day.

She crumbled some cheese onto a plate and began to prepare the sauce. Butter and flour first, mixed into a paste, then hot milk, added gradually.

As they walked, he had told her much more about his family and background. About his father, the tunny fisherman, and his mother, small and fierce and endlessly loyal. They had both died young: his father from a heart attack— Tonino blamed the type of work he did, out in all weathers, desperately trying to put food on the family table.

Tess remembered what Giovanni had told her about Tonino's uncle Luigi dying from a heart attack. She didn't want to think that Tonino had lied to her—but she wouldn't bring it up now. It wasn't the right time—or place. "And your mother?" she asked gently. "How did she die?"

"He was the love of her life," he said. "When he died, she had nothing left to live for."

"She had you," Tess reminded him. Again, she heard the echo of Santina's words. *Flavia has broken heart forever . . .*

He laughed—but the laughter barely reached his mouth, let alone his eyes. "I was not around most of the time," he said. "I went away. I studied in Palermo and I went to the mainland for a while—to Naples. That is where I began to dive."

Tess was surprised. She'd seen him as being always fixed in Cetaria; he'd seemed so rooted here. "What did you study?"

"History," he said.

She thought of the folk myths and fairy tales, his obsession with the past. History. That made sense.

"Also I did some carpentry and some sculpting." He shrugged. "I became interested in the mosaics and returned here to Cetaria when my father died."

In order to look after his mother, she supposed.

"When I got back here, I began the salvage work on the wrecks. And after she died . . ." His words dried up.

"You stayed," she said.

"*Sì.*" There was money in the family—from an inheritance—and he had used this to start up the mosaic business in the *baglio*, he told her. Pretty soon he was making an adequate living. "I need quality in my life," he said. "But it does not have to be the kind of quality that comes from material things."

But was he really happy here—working in the *baglio* and spending hours staring out to sea? Tess doubted it somehow.

She stirred the sauce and added more milk until it was the right consistency, then switched off the heat and added seasonings and the pungent blue cheese. She drained the pasta and tossed it with the sauce. She'd certainly found out a lot more about Tonino this afternoon. And what would she find out tomorrow?

When, eventually, they had scrambled down the mountainside trail from the olive grove and strolled back into the village, Tonino had not let go of her hand. It was an odd feeling. But a good one.

Tess took her pasta and salad with a glass of chilled white wine out onto the terrace. It was almost dark, but still warm, and she lit a candle and placed it in the center of the wrought iron tabletop. She didn't feel lonely. She felt at peace with the world. Was that what an afternoon with an attractive man could do for you?

They had walked into the main piazza, past the Hotel Faraglione—and Tess thought she saw someone at an upstairs window, looking out, half-hidden behind a muslin curtain. She probably had. But it was Sicilian paranoia syndrome again to imagine that everyone in the village was looking at them. Wasn't it?

Tonino certainly didn't seem to care. He continued chatting as they made their way across the ancient *baglio* past the stone fountain and the eucalyptus tree. As far as the bottom of the steps that led up to the villa. She waited for a hint that he wanted to come in, not sure yet what she'd say. But, "I must do some work now," he said. It was very quiet; the air seemed to pulse slowly around them. "But I can see you tomorrow, yes?"

"Yes." Tess didn't know whether to be relieved or disappointed.

"In the afternoon?"

She nodded.

"We could go out in the boat." He nodded toward a small yellow fishing boat that was moored by the stone jetty. "To the reserve. It is very beautiful."

"Okay. Sounds good."

"We can swim there," he said. "And have a late lunch."

He let go of her hand. He didn't kiss her. He just held her gaze, and she felt as if he was telling her something, making some sort of promise.

Tess finished her meal, drank the wine, and watched the sky darken and shift into nighttime. The stars were clearly defined against the backdrop of the night sky, and the moon was almost full and surrounded by a shimmering halo of cloud. She thought of Tonino down in the *baglio* in his studio—so near, but still so far. She almost thought that he had given her this time, this thinking time, on purpose, so that she was sure she knew what she wanted. What did she want? An uncomplicated life, a return to England, and a job that bored her? Or an adventure that might end up in financial suicide and a broken heart?

Tess stood on the terrace and looked out at the ghostly silhouettes of the rocks in the bay, the dark sea oily in the light of the moon, the canopy of an indigo sky. Ginny no longer seemed to need her. So it was a bit of a no-brainer, really.

CHAPTER 38

On the bumpy ride to Castellammare along the dusty coastal road in the horse and cart Signor Westerman had procured for her, Flavia tried to prepare herself for the journey ahead. "It will be long and hard," Edward Westerman had said—he had done the same journey on several occasions in his life, once in wartime. That must have been arduous indeed. But how much harder for a young girl from Sicily—a girl who knew nothing about where she was headed, a girl who was quite alone.

Apart from Peter. She must remember that. She must hold on to the faith that somehow, somewhere, he would be there for her. Waiting.

It was a misty dawn and would be a dry and breezy day, she guessed. On one side of the road the reddish mountains rose, studded with rocks and greenery, serene in the pale morning light. On the other, she caught tantalizing glimpses of the sea. This was her landscape—and she was leaving it behind. How long would it be before she saw again the island on which she had grown up, the only home she had ever known?

And her family . . . For the first time, Flavia felt the pang of homesickness, a premonition perhaps of what was to come. Maria—annoying, yes, in an older-sisterish kind of way, but still familiar and much loved. Mama, with her quiet, dark energy, the love for her children held back, lassoed, in order to tend with total dedication to their father. And Papa. Papa who wanted to control her life, who would not listen to what Flavia felt, or desired or needed; Papa who was stuck in the old way. They were her blood, but she could not stay with them. Not now.

Bumpity, bump . . . Flavia bounced around in her seat as the cart negotiated the ruts in the road. The driver whistled, and the horse snorted as if in reply. The road was deserted, but it was still early. So early that no one yet would even know that she was gone.

Flavia held on to the side of the cart. Papa had not been so bad, she thought, when Alberto Amato was his closest friend, when Enzo Sciarra was just another crony in Bar Gaviota—to drink grappa with, to talk to, to play dominoes. In those days, she was sure, he had gone his own way. Look at how Papa had responded when she found Peter . . . For a moment, Flavia closed her eyes, recalled that moment when she first saw him. O dio Beddramadre . . . The heat of that day . . . His blue eyes burning into her like cold fire . . .

The horse and cart trundled on. The man who was driving asked no questions; no doubt he had been told to do so. In Sicily this was not unusual.

Papa had been pro-English during the war. He had supported the underdog, too, fiercely hated what the war was doing to his beloved island. He had done what he believed in— he wouldn't have taken Peter into his home otherwise. But over the years . . . Papa had changed, no doubt. All that business with Alberto had changed him; Enzo's growing influence had changed him. And now—he was blood, yes, but she could not stay. She dared not. It was Rodrigo Sciarra now, but who would he want to marry her off to next? Flavia shuddered, although she was not cold in her coat and woolen blanket. Signor Westerman had told her to wear lots of clothes. "Wrap up warm, my dear," he had said. "It will be cold in England." England . . .

If she stayed, Mama would try to use reason to get Flavia to change her mind about marrying Rodrigo. She would not understand. "He will treat you well," she would say. "It could be so much worse." That was the Sicilian women's philosophy, Flavia thought, their curse. This was why they did not fight for change. "Do you want to live your life an old maid? Do you?"

No! Something inside Flavia shrieked the word. Of course, she did not. But neither did she want to marry a man she did not love. She did not want that man to touch her and caress her; she did not want to look after his house or have his children. It was no way to live. She had said that to Santina so many times. "It is no way to live."

Dear Santina had looked at her so sadly and whispered, "But Flavia, there is no other way."

She was wrong. Flavia blinked the tears out of her eyes. There was another way.

As they overtook an ancient cart laden with vegetables on its way to market, Flavia saw they were approaching Castellammare. The road wound down to the wide bay and the sea, to the railway station where she would be catching the train to Palermo, and then on to Messina. This was the first—and shortest—leg of her journey. And it was almost over.

Flavia knew that Santina was wrong—that she had to be wrong, because now she knew there was so much more. She had seen a glimpse of it, heard a whisper of it. More than a whisper. Now there was Peter, and she could not let that go.

Flavia had never been on a train before. She had tried to prepare herself for it, but the size of this clanking, spluttering monster was utterly overwhelming. She counted ten coaches. Mamma mia . . . Signor Westerman had told her that the train would take her to Messina, and from there it would be rolled onto a gigantic barge and taken across the straits to Italy. This, too, was mindboggling. "So we will book you a sleeper," he had said. "You will need it."

Flavia finished the brioche she had bought herself for breakfast. Courage. She took a deep breath, grabbed the battered travel bag Signor Westerman had given her—it held so little and yet everything she now owned—and jumped aboard. It was like leaping into the jaws of a lion.

The hissing, clattering train wound its way around the island to Palermo. Flavia peered out of the window. They said the city center was a ruin—piles of rubble and open-roofed palaces little more than shells. But all she could see was the busy station platform, more people boarding and alighting—and then doors slamming, whistles blowing, and it was on to Messina. The train was a force to be reckoned with, Flavia thought. A mighty creature. She could feel its power, its energy, its rhythm, as it drove them relentlessly onward.

And then—just as Signor Westerman had predicted—the train was sucked noisily onto a huge ship (or so it seemed to Flavia as she hurriedly crossed herself) and taken across the water. It wasn't far—about five miles—and took only thirty minutes, but she was able to leave her compartment and go out on deck to get some much-needed fresh air. This was so bizarre—to travel on both a ship and a train at the same time.

But perhaps just one bizarre experience of the many that were to come, Flavia thought.

She looked down at the white and foaming water as the train ferry churned its way forward. She breathed the sea air, deep into her lungs. The wind razed her skin, and her dark curls flew out behind her as she stood at the rail. It was as if her life, her old life was simply being blown away.

The train ferry was called Scilla. *She was an impressive sight, indeed, to Flavia as the boat chugged majestically across the Straits of Messina, and Flavia felt privileged that she had been given the chance to sail in her. Thanks to Signor Westerman. She could not have done this without him. Papa would rant and rage when he discovered she had gone (maybe he knew already? Maybe even now he was hammering at the door of La Sirena to find out if the Signor knew her whereabouts?) But she was not worried. Signor Westerman was a man who could calm Papa with just a few words—he had that gift.*

Of course she felt guilty—marriage to Rodrigo Sciarra would have improved Papa's standing in the village; he would have gained more privileges, more food and help for his family. Life was not easy in postwar Sicily, God knows. Every man needed all the help he could get. But Flavia Farro would not prostitute herself for that. She could not. "Sorry, Papa," she whispered. Though perhaps he would not blame her for grasping this opportunity—just as he had when offered a way out of poverty by the very same man.

Nevertheless, she looked back at the coast of Sicily, her island, and she touched her heart. "Arrivederci," she whispered. "Good-bye."

* * *

As they approached land, they were summoned back to their seats.

They had arrived at Villa San Giovanni. A man on the train (she had allowed herself to talk to him, as he was accompanied by his son, a boy of twelve years old or thereabouts, who could not take his eyes off Flavia) told her it was the busiest passenger port in Italy. Flavia looked around her at the hustle and bustle, at the people scurrying that way and this. The place was a heaving hubbub of activity—people talking and shouting, running, hugging, waving, crying; important-looking men in naval uniform striding here and there; dockers loading cargo; cranes lifting goods from the ships; horns blaring. And in the air she smelled anticipation and excitement; a sense of journey and change.

The maritime station itself showed little sign of wartime or neglect. Her traveling companion proved to be a fount of knowledge ("It is built in the Fascist style, and in the departure hall a magnificent Cascella mural showing the great man, Mussolini, il Duce, lifted aloft by farm workers . . . You must see it, my dear; everyone must see it"), but although Flavia tried to show interest, in her heart she was done with caring about politics. She was scared of what was happening in Sicily—not the poverty, but the oppression, the corruption, the darkness. People are people, she thought, the world over. Some good, some bad.

Flavia couldn't believe that this one clattering train could take her all the way to Rome. But it did. And so the journey continued. It seemed interminable. Then there was the sleeper train from Rome to Paris; the entire journey was a blur of sleeping and waking, of the train blundering and crashing down an everlasting track. Of looking out of the grimy train window—first in daylight, then in darkness—onto a changing landscape of fields, hills, villages, towns. Whistles blowing, doors slamming, people saying good-bye. No one was saying good-bye to Flavia, and she had never felt more alone. Porters with trolleys carrying baggage. Railway station after railway station, platforms stretching long fingers toward the future. Her future . . .

Flavia was exhausted. Who would have thought traveling could be so tiring? She had brought food rations—chunks of yellow Sicilian bread—Mama's bread, she thought with a lump in her throat, some late grapes from the vine, and goat's cheese, and these she had nibbled at when the hunger pangs reminded her. And a flask of water, from which she took regular sips when her throat was dry.

At the Gare du Bercy in Paris, they transferred to the Gare du Nord. Another day had begun. Paris . . . Flavia could not believe she was in Paris. Not in the city, of course, but even so . . . She shivered. It seemed so much colder here.

She hurried along the platform. And people looked so different. The women were smarter, more colorful. There were still hints of wartime drabness, but these women looked as if they were going somewhere. As if they had some life, some purpose other than the home. She thought of her mother and the other women in the village, the black dresses and shawls, the darkness. Already she had entered into a different world.

And now she was going somewhere. She steadied her breathing, quelled the anxiety that kept rising despite all her good intentions. She mustn't think about the bad things; she must focus on the positive. She must think about love. This was why she had come on this journey. For love. Because she would never find another love like this, she knew. It was a once in a lifetime thing. It was worth the anxiety, the fear, this whole exhausting journey. It was her destiny.

And now she was heading for England. London, Victoria. There would be another ferry—but this time she would travel as a foot passenger; only first-class passengers would get a sleeper. Flavia didn't care. Now, she just wanted to reach her destination. England . . .

CHAPTER 39

"WHAT DO YOU RECKON?" ASKED BRIAN, THE MAN-
ager of the pub. "You're young."

Ginny narrowed her eyes and scrutinized the guitarist
more closely. "He's a bit old," she said. At least forty. And
he wore thick glasses and a permanent silly grin. Charisma
was not the word that immediately sprang to mind.

"He can play," said Brian, tapping his fingers on the bar.
"And sing."

"Mmm." Ginny was noncommittal. She hadn't realized
the job would require auditioning skills. The Ball was being
a bit jumpy. It knew there was something bothering her.

"But . . . ?" inquired Brian.

The guitarist had moved seamlessly from "It's Not
Unusual" to "Leaving on a Jet Plane." "And I'll soon be leaving, too," he said into the mike. "Not in a jet plane, but in a
worn-out old Volvo . . . Ha, ha."

Perishing pelicans, thought Ginny. "I can't see him
appealing to anyone under forty," she said. "Does he do
anything else apart from ancient covers?"

Brian chuckled. "You're a harsh critic," he said. "But you're right."

"I want a younger crowd," he had told her when she came in to work at six. "I want this place vibrant and exciting. The place to be. The brightest nightspot in town."

"Right." Perhaps Ginny had come along at a good time. Though she couldn't help thinking that Brian was being a bit ambitious.

"I've got three acts in tonight to play a few numbers. You can help me decide who to book."

It seemed like a lot of responsibility to Ginny. "But I don't even know how to pull a pint yet," she told him.

"Don't worry," he said. "We'll deal with that later."

"Okay, Ryan," he said now to the old guy, who on second thoughts could be fifty or even sixty, since he had a medallion nestling in the gray chest hair poking out of the top of his shirt. "Thanks, but no thanks. I'm more interested in hiring a band."

Act number two hadn't turned up.

While act number three (a band, a young band) was setting up, Brian showed Ginny how the till worked. "The days are gone when you have to add up." He laughed loudly. "All you have to remember is what you just served 'em with. The till does the rest." He lit a cigarette even though there was a clear NO SMOKING sign over the door. "Think you can manage that?"

"Uh-huh." Smart ass . . .

"Okay, boys. Hit us with it."

Hit us with it . . . ? Someone should remind him, Ginny thought, that he was over thirty.

They were good. Not great, not professional, not slick, but good. They were also loud, and they were raw. They rocked. Even the Ball kept a low profile.

"Well?" Brian asked, after the first song—a cover of that Kings of Leon number. "Sex on Fire . . ."

"Fab," said Ginny.

Brian nodded. "I thought you might say that."

They played a few covers—from the eighties and nineties as well as the noughties—and a few originals. Brian and Ginny both approved of the mix. There were four of them—a tall, skinny guy on keyboards with tattoos and a shaven head; a front man with floppy blond hair, blue eyes, and looks to die for; a lead guitarist with broad shoulders and spiky hair; and a dark, bemused-looking guy on bass. He looked kind of interesting in a moody sort of way, and when he caught her eye during the third number, she felt herself blush.

"I'm off men," she had told Nonna and Pops this morning at breakfast. "I've become an anti-man zone. They don't fulfill any need. I'm going to studiously avoid the male species for a while. I'm a mean, man-hating machine."

"Charming," said Pops.

"'Cept you," Ginny reassured him.

But since then, she'd had three texts from Ben, ranging from "Hey, where did you go?" to "What's with the disappearing act, baby?" to "Still on the planet—or what?"

She struggled to interpret these. Did they mean he cared? Ginny fingered the cell in her pocket. She was glad he'd bothered. But *I've gone to look for something special,* she texted back. *See you.*

He could take that how he wanted. She was going to find another hairdresser.

"Any reason?" Nonna had inquired, following Ginny's dismissal of the male species.

"They prefer their friends to their girlfriends," Ginny told her. "They're boring. They don't know how to have fun."

Her grandmother smiled.

"It's one rule for boys and another for girls," Ginny went on. "It isn't fair."

"It never was, my darling," said her grandmother. "It never was."

"All right, boys, you're booked," said Brian, when the applause from the half a dozen customers in the bar had died down. "Every other Saturday night do you?"

Ginny looked up. Just as Dark and Bemused gave her a particularly bewitching smile . . .

CHAPTER 40

THEY TOOK THE BOAT INTO THE TURQUOISE WATERS of the nature reserve, and once the motor was switched off, the silence was broken only by the lap of the water and the occasional cry of a seabird. It was two thirty, and the sun shimmered over sea and mountains with a white light that was almost blinding in its intensity.

Lazily, Tess trailed her hand in the cool water. It was so clear, she could see a shoal of small bream swimming in formation just below the surface and the flat, broad rock and pebbles of the seabed below. Already, she felt, she was getting to know this place—above sea level and below.

Tonino seemed at peace for almost the first time since she'd known him. He had lost his perpetual half frown; his mouth was not set, but easy and relaxed, his eyes lightened by the sun when he pushed his sunglasses onto his head.

He looked across at her, smiled, and let his hand rest lightly on hers. His palm was dry and the pressure firm; she could sense rather than feel the strength in him. There was something of the stone he worked in about this man. As if he were part of the Sicilian landscape, embedded in the rock itself. Then the water touched their hands in a slippery caress, and his skin softened, her hand slotting more surely into his.

"Here is the cove," he said.

Tess followed his gaze. He had allowed the boat to drift around the headland, and in front of them now curved a semicircle of fine white sand dotted with red-and-cream rocks and bands of sea grass washed upon the shore. As she watched, a solitary butterfly—a Red Admiral—flapped its gorgeous wings and skimmed the shallow aquamarine water.

Tess realized she'd been holding her breath. "It's a very special place," she said. But what she really meant was . . . This is special, this moment, this experience with you in this boat, in this bay. Whatever he was—and she still wasn't sure—she only knew that she was drawn to him like an insect to honey. It might be impossible to resist—even if she wanted to.

He stripped off his T-shirt, stood up in the boat and dived in an arc into the water. The boat rocked and she held on to the sides and laughed. She watched his dark head go under first, the rest of his body following in one fluid movement. Like a seal, she thought. Please, not a shark. She thought of Robin. But less and less, she realized. Less and less.

A small pink jellyfish floated across the rippling circle where Tonino had dived in. She smiled. And as she watched, he emerged crisp and wet and grinning.

Tess laughed once again. She wanted to be in there, too. She was wearing a bikini and a sarong, which she untied without further ado, so that she was ready.

He pulled the boat farther in and moored it, tying the rope to a crag of rock. The boat gave a small sigh and a scrape against the pebbles and then was still. Tonino offered her his hand.

"Grazie." She smiled.

"Prego." He bowed playfully and hand in hand they waded through the water, out toward the open sea rather than to dry land.

"Shall we?"

She nodded, reached out her arms and slid into a slow breaststroke. The water was cool on her hot skin, silky and intoxicating. She turned over and floated on her back, the sun burning against her closed eyelids, sending a kaleidoscope of red and golden images into her vision, into her head. These were the colors of Sicily, she thought. Red earth, golden sun . . . Red tomatoes, yellow durum wheat . . .

"This is like paradise," she called across to him. Worlds away from family feuds, thefts, betrayals, and murder . . . Not to mention the Mafia.

"Correction." The water was dripping from his black hair. He stood up and ran his hand through it. "It *is* paradise."

She squinted toward the mountain, outlined against a cloudless azure sky. "Can you get to this bay by the path in the nature reserve?" She could just make it out in the distance, a band of red earth winding through palm trees, tamarisks, and prickly pears.

He shook his head. "It is only accessible by boat." Once again he grinned. "Lucky us, do you not think?"

"Lucky us." But the water—or something—was making Tess shiver so she waded out of the water and onto the beach, dropping onto the white sand. The red mountains rose around the pocket of the cove, their lower slopes

scattered with rock roses, wild spikes of rosemary, and
sweet yellow broom.

He joined her a few minutes later. He had brought the
knapsack from the boat and a huge blue towel. He spread
this out, and she sat up as he unpacked the knapsack. Fizzy
water and—mmm—Prosecco, both bottles wrapped in
cool bags, Serrano ham, ricotta cheese, tomato salad, thick
yellow Sicilian bread, and oranges.

"It looks delicious," she said.

And it was. They ate hungrily, drank Prosecco from the
glasses he had also brought along. "Never drink good wine
from plastic glasses," he said. "No, no, it is not the thing."

Slowly, he peeled an orange, letting the rind fall into a
spiral around his brown fingers. He took a segment and
offered it to Tess.

She took a bite. "Sweet and warm," she said. "Like the
sun."

He nodded. "The orange is a daytime fruit," he said.
"The lemon, she is of the moon."

"Lunar," said Tess. The color of moonshine. And the
scent of nighttime.

Finally, replete, they lay on the towel, Tess almost dozing.

"You are very different," he murmured, after some minutes had passed. "To what I imagined."

Oh yes? She became attentive. "And what did you imagine, exactly?" She propped herself up, looking down at his
tanned body, at the dark tendrils of hair that curled over his
flat stomach. She didn't dare look farther.

He didn't open his eyes. "Another tourist." But she heard
the contempt in his voice and tried not to be hurt. After all,
she wasn't another tourist—she was half-Sicilian herself.
And why shouldn't he resent the tourists that came and

plundered the beaches and towns and temples of Sicily with their brashness, their noise, their mountains of rubbish? Well, because the tourists gave him the food on his table, for starters, she thought. If not for the Germans, the English, the wealthy Italians from the north who bought his glittering mosaic tableware, his inlaid furniture, his mirrors and tiles, then how would people like Tonino make a living?

But . . . Vanity won out. "How am I different?" she persisted. She couldn't believe how much she wanted to touch the hollow in his neck under his Adam's apple. How much she wanted to trace a path with her fingertip past his sternum and his rib cage, down to his navel. And down . . . Her gaze was drawn to the waistband of his close-fitting black trunks, which fitted him like a second skin. And . . .

"You are a beautiful woman." His voice was husky, and she realized that now his eyes were open and he was watching her watching him.

Tess felt the heat on her shoulders and in her breasts. But she had a feeling it was coming from inside rather than from the sun this time.

"Lots of tourists are beautiful women," she pointed out though somewhat shakily. This was dangerous ground. She had seen them posing in white bikinis on the decks of ostentatious yachts and sailboats, all with improbably dark golden tans and blonder-than-blonde hair. Much younger than her, too, she thought, looking down at her stomach and legs—which were, okay, well toned, thanks to all the swimming and diving she did, but perhaps not as trim as they'd been when she was twenty—or even thirty.

"Your hair . . ." He trailed a hand through it; twisted a tendril between thumb and forefinger. "It is like a weed of the sea."

Tess laughed. She'd had smoother compliments. Still . . . "Seaweed?"

He nodded. "Like a mermaid," he said. "Yellow and brown and red and amber. Like jasper."

She had seen those mottled stones in his studio. They looked like the stones you often saw on the bottom of the ocean; dappled by sand and moss. "You still haven't told me the mermaid story," she teased. "The story of Villa Sirena."

"You must be patient," he said. "I will tell you when it is time."

Right. But when would it be time?

"Your eyes are blue violet," he went on. "Very rare in Sicily. Very rare in sea glass."

"Sea glass?" She had been propped up on one elbow, now she collapsed down on the sand again next to him. He certainly had some inventive pick-up lines.

He hadn't stopped touching her hair. "The green, the amber, the brown—they are common enough. But to find the perfect sea-buffed blue violet . . ." He shook his head sadly.

"Lucky for you to have it in the flesh, then," she said.

He smiled. "You are also provocative." He leaned closer. "And interesting. Funny. And infuriating."

"Oh, I see." She laughed. An irresistible combination, was it? "Well you're not so bad yourself."

"And . . ." His dark gaze was smoldering into her now.

Like molten lava, she thought. Like black liquid oil. Oh, God. "And?" Her voice wavered. What was the matter with her? Anyone would think she'd never been on the edge of paradise with a gorgeous and sexy man before. Exactly.

He put a finger on her lips. "And I want to kiss you. Again."

Tess didn't really have time to consider how she felt about this prospect—*yes please; oh yes please*—before his lips were on hers and he tasted like honey and ricotta and Prosecco all mixed into one and it was so good, too good, and then his body was closer, closer, and he was touching her shoulders and her thighs, and he was kissing her throat, her neck, her breasts, and . . .

She was sinking. Sinking and lost and abandoned and loving every sensual, blissful second of it.

Minutes later, as he was nuzzling into her neck, and attempting to remove her bikini bottoms with his free hand, she felt him stop, his hand resting on her thigh, as he raised his head and looked over her shoulder out to sea. He swore softly.

"What is it?" Tess struggled to sit up.

"The sea, she grows angry," he murmured.

Tess ran her fingertip down the length of the scar on his face, feeling the contours of his cheekbone, letting her fingertip rest on his lips. But she had lost his attention. She followed the direction of his gaze and tried to breathe more normally. In the distance, she could see the waves being whipped into white horses. "It does look a bit choppy out there," she agreed. Closer to shore, the water was wrinkled, no longer calm and unruffled, as it had been only an hour before.

He was on his feet in seconds. "It is a very strong wind," he said. "We must get the boat back to harbor. Or we will be stranded here. Come." He took her hand and she got to her feet.

Would that be so bad, thought Tess? But she didn't waste time. She threw the picnic things back in the hamper, grabbed her towel, and ran down the beach toward the boat. Suddenly the wind felt chill around her bare shoulders.

"How long?" she asked him.

He helped her in. "Ten, fifteen minutes." Already he was unmooring the boat. He pushed it out and jumped in. Started the motor, and they were away, the engine on full throttle, the boat pitching and crashing through the waves, speeding back toward Cetaria Bay.

Racing the wind, thought Tess, pushing her hair from her face, trying not to look at him. She wasn't worried. Exhilarated, more like. He had said ten minutes, and in ten minutes they would be safe. The sea was rolling, and the little boat was being tossed about a bit. But they would make it. She was sure they would make it.

He reached for her hand. "*Mi dispiace*, Tess, sorry."

She smiled and shook her head. Better to be so close to the sea that you could sense these sorts of changes, than blind to it. Still . . . Inside, she was conscious of a warm ache of desire. It would have happened. Maybe it should have happened. But it hadn't. Not yet.

They got into harbor with the wind right on their tail and howling. Behind them, the waves were climbing high, and the open sea had changed dramatically from turquoise into murky gray. Tess had pulled on a sweater but was still shivering, her hair matted with salt water and tangled from the wind. The change had been fast—she had never realized that the Mediterranean Sea could be so wild.

"Just in time," said Tonino, bringing in the small craft and helping Tess out of the boat.

He'd just finished mooring it securely into position, when his cell bleeped with a text message. With an apologetic glance at Tess, he checked his phone and read it. He frowned.

"Problem?" Tess was wondering whether or not to invite him in for coffee. It wasn't the most original line in the book, and his coffee was an awful lot better than hers, but she didn't want the afternoon to end. Not yet.

His eyes flickered. "There is someone I must see," he said. "They sent a message. They say it cannot wait."

"Okay." The disappointment hit her like a fist. They had, what you might call, unfinished business. But on the other hand, it was all moving so fast; maybe it was a good idea to slow things down. "That's fine," she said brightly. "Go ahead. I'll see you—"

"Later," he said. Gently, he touched her face. "At seven?"

"At seven." She knew what he was saying. There would be no going back.

CHAPTER 41

No, Tess didn't want the afternoon to end. So instead of staying inside the villa, she grabbed her raincoat from the peg in the hall and descended the steps back into the *baglio*. She'd visit Santina.

She ran through the puddles of the *baglio*, collar up, ducking into doorways with each heavy burst of rain. Even so, she was soaked by the time she got to number fifteen and knocked on the door with the flaking green paint and rusty grille. She leaned in as far as she could get out of the rain and crossed her fingers that Giovanni wasn't at home.

Santina opened the door a fraction and then flung it wide. "Tess!" She broke into a torrent of Sicilian and pulled Tess into the dingy blood-red hallway. "Come in, come in, my child," she said.

Thank goodness. Giovanni must be out.

Tess was propelled along the narrow hallway lined with photographs, certificates, and religious paraphernalia into the kitchen, where Santina had obviously been preparing vegetables. Spinach and beans were laid out with a small, sharp knife on a wooden board by the enamel sink, and more vegetables had been piled into a metal colander. "Sorry to disturb you—" she began.

"*No*, no, no . . ." Santina made gestures to indicate Tess should get out of her wet things.

She was glad to oblige.

The old woman took her coat and hung it on a hook by the stove, clicking her tongue and shaking her head throughout. "Some coffee?" she suggested, pointing to her little percolator. "Some *dolce*?"

"Lovely." Tess nodded. She was itching to launch into her questions. "Giovanni?" she asked.

Santina shrugged. "Who know?" she replied. "The Sciarra men—they always have go their own way."

Tess was fascinated by this. "But you're a Sciarra," she said. "You're family." And she knew how families stuck together in Sicily.

Santina touched her forehead. "I different," she said. She shook her head violently. "I different."

It was one thing, Tess supposed, to disagree with one's family and their way of life, quite another to discard it completely. "You never married?" she asked.

Santina was filling the percolator with water at the sink, and so she had her back to Tess. "It never happen," she said. "Mostly I look after the family men." She turned, a strange look of defiance in her dark eyes. "I too have the fire in my belly." She patted her stomach. "I do what I can."

Tess nodded. Like her mother, she thought. She watched Santina take the percolator to the stove and fill it with coffee from a small canister. "How did you know?" she asked her. "About my mother's broken heart?"

Santina lit the stove and placed the percolator on the flame to boil. "We write letters," she said. "Years go by. We write letters, Flavia and me."

Tess had wondered about that. "And now?" she asked.

"*No*." Santina shook her head vehemently. "Now, *no*. Not for many years."

No matter how much she cared for her old friend, her mother wouldn't have wanted the contact with Sicily—Tess knew that. She would have had to let her go. "But why?" Tess asked. "Why did she hate Sicily so much, Santina?" Surely it couldn't have been just because her father wanted her to marry Rodrigo Sciarra?

Santina shook her head. "She not say, not to me."

And Tess had done the sums—why had it taken her mother so long to go to England? It couldn't have been just because of the war. "My mother was twenty-three years old when she left Sicily and traveled to England," she said. "That's six years after she met this English airman you told me about. A long time."

Santina was fetching the tiny white cups and saucers and plates from behind the fabric that curtained the kitchen cupboard. She shrugged. "She wait," she said.

She was very patient then, thought Tess. She must have loved him an awful lot. "And he helped her when she arrived in England?" She could imagine how scary it must have been to a young, sheltered Sicilian girl to arrive in England alone. Her mother was very brave.

Santina shook her head. "*No, no*," she said. "Signor Westerman from Villa Sirena. He help her. His sister in London help her. She cook, yes!" She laughed.

"Ah." It was all becoming clearer now. Tess accepted the tiny cup of coffee and pastry from Santina. "*Grazie*." So her mother had waited for him in Sicily—but he hadn't come. So what had she done? Well, she'd gone to England to find him, of course. And Edward Westerman had helped her do it—just as he had helped Tess come to Sicily. She sipped the coffee. The jigsaw was gradually slotting into place.

"So I suppose she tried to find the English airman, and it was like looking for a needle in a haystack," she suggested to Santina.

"Needle . . . ?" Santina frowned.

"She couldn't find him?" Tess said. "So she gave up her search and eventually forgot all about him." Another sip of coffee—it was rich and warming. And a bite of *cornetti*, the icing sugar sticking to her lips. "And then she met my father?"

"Ah, no," said Santina. Her expression was one of compassion. "She find him, my child. She never forget that man."

"But—?" Before Tess could say more, she heard the door opening and a stream of Sicilian that signaled the arrival of Giovanni.

He stopped short when he saw Tess sitting in the kitchen. "You," he said.

"What?" Tess was confused. Giovanni was looking very angry.

He said something else in Sicilian and she caught Tonino's name. Santina was looking from one to the other of them, twisting her apron between her fingers. What was going on? Had Giovanni somehow found out about Tess and Tonino? Not that there was too much to find out—yet.

"What?" she repeated.

Giovanni turned on her. "I warned you, Tess," he said. "I told you to keep away from Tonino Amato."

But how did he know? There was only one way, Tess realized. Tonino must have told him. "It's your quarrel, Giovanni." She tried to keep her voice level. "Not mine."

He came closer. Gripped her arm just a bit too tightly. His mouth was set and angry and his eyes seemed to burn into hers. "That is where you are wrong, Tess," he said. "Your family has as much reason to hate Amato as mine."

"Oh, don't be ridiculous." But she felt a flutter of fear in her stomach. How well did she know Tonino—really?

"*Il tesoro*," Giovanni muttered. "The treasure."

Ah, thought Tess. The mysterious "it." Now they were getting somewhere.

"Your grandfather—he had the responsibility for *il tesoro*," Giovanni said sternly. "And Amato's grandfather—he stole it. He was your grandfather's best friend. So. Not only a theft. But a betrayal, too. You see?"

Should she believe him? Tess looked down at his hand, still gripping her arm.

"Sorry, Tess." Giovanni let go of her. He seemed to be recovering his cool.

"Anyway," she said, aware that she was desperately trying to find excuses. "That was Tonino's grandfather, not Tonino himself." And unlike the Sicilians, she didn't hold people responsible for the behavior of other members of their family.

"They are all the same," growled Giovanni. "They are Amatos. And that man, he tricks so many women . . ."

Hang on a minute. "So many women?"

Giovanni shrugged. "You will find out, Tess," he said.

She had heard enough. All the pleasure of the afternoon was in danger of evaporating completely. "I must go." She got to her feet. She would ask Tonino to tell her his version of what had happened. She wouldn't judge him—not yet.

Giovanni nodded gravely. "Take care, Tess," he said.

It had stopped raining and the sun had reemerged as Tess made her way back toward Villa Sirena. Should she drop in on Millie on the way home? Why not? She might be able to shed some light on the situation. Tess did a detour past the Hotel Faraglione and went to the reception desk.

"Is Millie around?" she asked the girl there.

"Sorry." The girl spoke perfect English. but with a strong accent. "She is with someone. She cannot be disturbed."

"No problem." As she left, Tess thought she saw her friend with someone at an upstairs window. The silhouette looked familiar. But . . . Oh, she was probably imagining it. Anyway, she had a lot to think about. Her family, Tonino's family, *il tesoro* . . . Not to mention her mother's story. Her mother, who had not forgotten her English pilot, who had come to England, and who had found him.

CHAPTER 42

AND SO FLAVIA HAD COME TO ENGLAND. *GOD BE THANKED* . . .
Her life in Sicily was at an end.

*Flavia stood shivering on the platform at Victoria station,
Signor Westerman's old travel bag crouched at her feet, damp
and heavy as a stone. London in November. Flavia's first
impression was of gray. Unremitting gray. Wet, too. And cold.*

*Around her, people huddled in groups with bags and cases,
faces blank as if they were frightened to even acknowledge
where they were or where they had come from. Others strode
along the platform, some of them running as if to an emergency. Flavia heard the scream of the whistles, the mighty rush
and the blow of the steam engines. She had to move. She had
to get . . . somewhere.*

*In a blur, she followed the stream of bodies, some of whom,
at least, seemed to know where they were heading. Out of the
station they went. Flavia stopped. Holy Madonna. A cold,
damp wind slapped her face. She flinched and pulled the*

collar of her coat higher around her neck. Tall red buses, big black cabs, people, people, people . . . What next? She clutched her travel bag to her like a comfort blanket; it was all she had.

Move, girl. She stepped forward. She should board an omnibus, ask someone the way—the money that she had would have to last her at least until she found Peter, possibly even until she found work. But how could she speak to any of these strange people? So this was London—and everyone was clearly in a terrible hurry. Even as she stood there, undecided, the mist seemed to thicken around her, dank, acrid, and suffocating.

Flavia became flustered. No one was smiling. Most didn't even glance her way. And who could blame them for looking unfriendly when it was foggy and cold and wet underfoot— Flavia's thin shoes were leaking terribly—when it was a struggle to even see a field's length in front of you.

"Get a black cab from the station," Signor Westerman had told her. "No messing about, my girl, d'you hear me?"

She had nodded.

"Give them Beatrice's address. And give Bea this letter." He had pressed a thick white envelope into her hand along with the poetry manuscript that she had promised to deliver to his sister. His sister's address was written black and clear on both.

"Sì, I will," Flavia had promised. Thinking, I will do it my way. This was her adventure, after all.

But Signor Westerman had been right. London was too much for her—especially in the cold and the fog. And she was exhausted from the journey, her knuckles white and clenched, her eyes raw. Pretending a confidence she did not feel, she raised an arm to hail a black cab. Rather to her surprise, it stopped. Flavia showed the driver the address.

She hugged her bag close to her chest as she sat in the back of the cab and breathed out in relief. Her journey to England was over, although in a way her journey had also only just begun. She peered out of the window. So many of the buildings were derelict or in ruins—following the bombings, she supposed. Elsewhere, new buildings were being erected; she could see that the skyline was changing. London had suffered in the war, she knew. But the extent of the destruction shocked her.

She could make out brightly lit shops and cafés, hairdressing salons, and huge cinemas. Gigantic advertising lights shone out of the gloom. She strained to read them; she must practice her English now. *Jacob's* cream crackers, **Swallow** raincoats, **Brylcreem** for your hair. Goodness. How strange it all was. She felt a streak of excitement run through her. This was liberation. This was another world.

Progress was slow. The roads were sardined with traffic—black cars and red buses, trolleybuses and horses and carts, too—and the pavements thronged with people: men in belted raincoats and hats, smart-looking women in woolen coats—their scarves an occasional splash of color in the murk. A man in a helmet and white armband—a policeman, she realized—held up a hand to halt their passage, and at his signal, men and women strode across the road, clearly on some important mission. The city was a riot of activity. And yet its voice seemed muffled in the limp mist that surrounded everything. London. It was new, and it scared her half to death. But Madonna save her, how she wanted it . . .

They drew up outside a grand, three-storied house in an elegant road of large brick houses with bay windows. This must be West Dulwich. Flavia looked up and along the road in wonderment. The fog seemed to be lifting and there were *trees here, their leaves dripping rainwater into puddles on the pavement; it would really be very lovely, she thought, if the sun started shining.*

"C'mon then, Missy." The taxi driver seemed in a hurry to be gone. Why was everyone in a rush?

She fumbled in her purse for money. He had dumped her bag on the wet pavement. In Sicily, she thought, the driver would at least take your bag to the door. But you're not in Sicily now, she chided herself. That was what she was escaping from. Remember? She thought with another spear of guilt of Mama and Papa. Would they be angry, upset? She had left a note of explanation, but it was brief, and she was relying on Signor Westerman to make it right with them, to make them see. Of course she would have told them if she could. But Papa would have stopped her from coming, she knew it.

She'd had no choice. And choice was something that she wanted and needed. It was, Signor Westerman had told her, her human right.

"Thank you so much," she said clearly to the driver. "Goodday to you."

He stared at her. "Yer welcome." He laughed, shook his head, and was off.

Flavia checked the number on the piece of paper and then up at the house. This was Thurlow Park Road, and this house was the one. She walked up the steps. But it seemed so grand. Supposing Signor Westerman had made a mistake? Supposing Beatrice Westerman didn't live here or had gone away . . . ?

Courage. She squared her shoulders and rang the bell.

In such a grand establishment, she was expecting a servant, but the woman who came to the door didn't look like a servant. She was tall and thin, and her fair hair was frizzy. She wore metal spectacles, looked quite a few years older than

Signor Westerman, and seemed much taken aback when she saw Flavia standing there with her suitcase.

"Hello," she said politely. "Can I help you?"

"Miss Beatrice Westerman?" Flavia asked in her best accent. For there was a definite resemblance to Signor Westerman in the shape of the woman's nose and chin.

The woman nodded. "I am she."

"I have a letter from your brother, Edward." Flavia dug the thick envelope out of the outside pocket of her bag. It was a little crumpled and damp from the journey, but otherwise intact. "And I have package in my suitcase," she added for good measure. "Of his poetry."

"From Edward?" Beatrice's eyes lit up. She took the envelope and turned it around in her hands. "You've come all the way from Sicily?" she asked Flavia.

"Yes. On a train," Flavia confirmed.

Beatrice Westerman put her head to one side like a bird. "Indeed? And you can understand what I say to you?"

"Yes." Flavia nodded. "I speak English a little. Your brother . . ." She hesitated, "and others, they teach me."

Beatrice smiled. "I see." Though she still looked confused, Flavia supposed it wasn't every day that some strange, foreign girl appeared on your doorstep with a message from the brother you hadn't seen for years.

Flavia wanted to tell her to read the letter, and she wanted very much to go inside the house, where it might be warm and hopefully comforting, but it would be impolite to say any of these things, so she hovered on the doorstep while Beatrice stared at her and turned the letter over and around in her hands.

"My family—they work for your brother," she explained. "In Cetaria."

"Ah, yes." Beatrice seemed to recover herself. "Do come in. I am so sorry. Come inside and we shall have some tea." She beckoned Flavia through the door. "Or coffee," she amended. "Though I only have instant, I'm afraid."

Flavia had no idea what instant might be, but it didn't matter. She was in the warm.

Bea Westerman made tea and produced dainty cucumber sandwiches with the crusts cut off, limp lettuce hearts, and washed-out tomatoes. She extracted a cube of pink, fleshy ham in jelly from a tin with a wind-up key, which she proceeded to slice thinly with a sharp knife. A tin of red salmon. Red salmon . . . ? And synthetic-looking cakes with a stiff cream that she laid out on a lace tablecloth on a small side table.

"It isn't much," Bea Westerman said apologetically. "We have more tinned food now, of course, but not as much tea or ham as I would like." She shook her head sadly. "Rationing, you know."

Flavia was surprised. She knew about rationing, of course. She knew about having no food, about having to scrimp and forage. But she had thought that would all be over by now in England . . .

They sat in upholstered chairs in a room that was painted pale blue with a cream ceiling. Apart from the chairs and the table, there was a bookcase, which reminded Flavia of Signor Westerman, a glass-fronted cabinet full of china, a rather grand marble fireplace, and paintings on the walls of, Flavia supposed, the English countryside. It looked very green and watery, and as Peter had said, there were fields and trees and hedgerows.

She watched Signor Westerman's sister read the letter through twice. When they had finished eating, she settled herself with her hands on her lap and regarded Flavia solemnly.

"You will stay here tonight, my dear," she said. It didn't sound like a question.

"Thank you," said Flavia. She wasn't sure she would have been up to searching for alternative accommodation in London on this wet November afternoon.

"And for as long as you wish," Bea added. "Your family in Sicily have been good to Edward. It is now the turn of those of us here in England to help you."

Flavia felt a tear come to her eye at this kindness, and she quashed it with some resolution. It was ridiculous—this was not the time for weakness. She would need all her strength to settle into this alien place, all her strength for what was to come.

"My brother tells me that you will be looking for a job. And he informs me that you are a wonderful cook."

Flavia tried to look modest, but she knew a wide smile had spread across her face.

"So I suggest that until you find alternative employment, you work for me," Bea said briskly. "You can do the cooking and occasionally help Mrs. Saunders with some of her cleaning duties—she's getting rather old and can't bend like she used to—and I shall ask you to do a few small errands for me. In return, you will have your keep."

Flavia tried to follow her meaning, tried not to look blank.

"Your food and your bed," Bea explained. "And a little pocket money." She paused. "What do you think?"

Flavia thought she understood what was being offered. "Yes," she said. "Thank you. But . . ." But there was something much more important she had to do first.

"Ah yes, your mission." Bea nodded. "Edward mentions this in his letter. But he doesn't offer too many details." She smiled encouragingly. "Do tell me all about it, my dear."

So Flavia, who had kept Peter a secret for so long from so many, told her the whole story. About how she had first found him with the wreckage of his glider. (And this time she was surprised to see Bea Westerman's eyes fill with tears.) About how she had nursed him and how he had almost died. How they had fallen in love and how she had written to him. So many letters . . . So much love.

"So I must find him," she said in conclusion. "I must find him and discover what has happened to him."

Bea nodded gravely. She seemed to be considering her words carefully. "It has been an awfully long time," she said at last. "In six years . . ."

"I know." Flavia didn't have the words to explain. Yes, in six years Peter could have died—he might never have made it back to England. But she felt in her heart that he was alive. There was a light in her heart, and she knew that when he died, it would be extinguished.

"His situation," Bea said, "might have changed."

"Perhaps." Flavia knew this, too. "But we made a vow. A promise. I do not think he would break it."

"Maybe not," Bea said. "But wartime . . ." She sighed and then rose to her feet. "It changes us all."

Flavia wondered how Bea had been changed by wartime. Had she perhaps had a sweetheart who had gone to war? She wasn't too old, was she, though she was older than Edward, and somewhat more serious.

"I will assist you in your quest," said Bea. "We will talk again tomorrow. But in the meantime Mrs. Saunders will be here in a jiffy, and she'll show you your room and where you can have a wash. You will want to rest. You can start work tomorrow. What do you think, my dear?"

Flavia nodded. "Thank you," she said. She must unpack the manuscript, which she had laid at the bottom of her suitcase, and give Bea Westerman her brother's poems. It had gone very well, she felt. Bea was friendly, and Flavia was more than happy to work for her for a while. Better than that, she had promised to help her find Peter. Peter . . . She suddenly felt overcome by exhaustion. She was in England and already a step closer to the man she loved. Now her journey had really begun.

Biancolilla . . . Cerasuola . . . Nocellara del Belice . . . *The versatile Sicilian olive: wise, ancient, beautiful, bitter . . . Used for medicine, soap, cooking, lighting, eating . . . Its wood the most fragrant, its oil steeped in tradition and ritual. The tree provides shade from the hot summer sun, wood for warm winter fires. An essential of life.*

Flavia remembered Papa and the other men taking the brown sacks full of olives down to the press in the village square. Checking the weights on the scales, following their progress around the big barn as they traveled from machine to machine until the cloudy green oil was poured into jugs ready for sealing. Then back at the house eating Mama's freshly baked bread with the new oil.

Roast peppers, she decided, *with rice, pine nuts, lemon juice. and chopped green olives. Served with a fresh young salad, the leaves to be found by the roadside or in the fields.*

CHAPTER 43

Tess was lingering in the shower, trying to regain the sense of euphoria she'd felt on the beach with Tonino. Once she emerged, reality would intrude, she knew it.

The bathroom was one part of the villa that left nothing to be desired. The tiles were blue and white, the sink and bidet were wide and solid, the power shower did what it said on the tin. The claw-toothed tub in one corner and the decorative mirror above the sink—which looked distinctly Venetian to Tess's uneducated eye—not only added a touch of decadence but also reminded her where she was—in her beautiful 1930s villa in Sicily. She'd remember that when she did the place up, she told herself, reluctantly switching off the jet of hot water. A place like this needed touches of class; it was born to be glamorous.

She wrapped herself in one of the giant black towels she'd found in Edward Westerman's airing cupboard when she first arrived and regarded her steamy reflection in the mirror. She wiped the glass. She was flushed—and not just with the heat of the shower. She looked like a woman who wanted to be made love to, for God's sake. She'd better wake up and quick. This was Sicily. She was English (more or less). The last thing she needed was a fling with a Sicilian man who had Family History and was Bad News. So don't get carried away, she told herself firmly.

But the problem was—she knew she wanted him. Lying on that sandy beach in the cove this afternoon she had experienced it—that *fuck it* moment when logic jumps out of the window and unbridled lust takes over.

She checked her watch, which was on the glass shelf. It was six now. She wouldn't have long to wait. She had time to call Ginny first. Ginny . . . What would her daughter be doing now, in England? she wondered. And Muma? They all seemed a whole world away from Sicily and what was happening to her here. She thought of Ginny's face when she'd told her she was coming back here—the sudden vulnerability almost shattering Tess's resolve. Did she really see vulnerability? Sometimes it was hard to believe. Ginny seemed so confident, so independent, so resentful of Tess and everything she stood for. She sighed. No one prepared you for these things when you decided to have a baby. Or when— like Tess—you were propelled into motherhood without really thinking about it at all. No one warned you that your daughter would one day change into another being—an adolescent—whom you would irritate beyond belief every time you so much as opened your mouth. Tess smiled. But it would pass. Muma had promised her that it would pass.

For supper she would make some pasta and grill some sardines. She had white wine *frizzante*, fresh nectarines, some crackers, and pecorino cheese. That would have to do. Tonino . . . She wasn't sure what she was going to say to him, but . . .

She spent forty-five minutes blow-drying her hair, applying her makeup, and deciding what to wear (loose white linen trousers and a honey-cream silk top). She called Ginny, who was not in a communicative mood—nothing new there. Then she started preparing food. There was almost too much to think about now. She didn't know where to start.

At seven fifteen she reminded herself that Sicilians were never on time. At seven thirty she opened the wine, and at eight she cooked the spaghetti. At eight thirty she looked down from the terrace onto the *baglio*, but his studio was in darkness.

Okay, so she was having second thoughts, too, but at least she'd wanted to talk to him first. By nine she'd drunk the whole bottle of wine, eaten the spaghetti and sardines, and didn't really care if he turned up or not. Men were—as she'd always known—a complete waste of time, space, and energy. And Giovanni Sciarra—damn his socks—was obviously right.

By ten thirty, when she heard the knock on the door, Tess had also drunk five shots of *limoncello*—which was the only other alcohol she had in the house—just for the hell of it and was practically asleep on Edward Westerman's worn brown leather sofa. Should she answer it? She didn't want to, but . . .

Tess opened the door. He looked wild, disheveled, and drunk. And he was glaring at her (again) as if he were angry (again). Hang on a minute—shouldn't she be the one who was pissed off?

"What happened?" she asked.

He leaned heavily on the doorpost. "You own this villa, yes?"

"Yes, I told you." This hardly seemed the time or place for a discussion on property ownership.

"But you are not a relative of Signor Westerman, no?"

"No." Tess was beginning to see where this was going. Maybe she wasn't the only one who had been warned off. Maybe his family hated her family as much as her family (according to Giovanni) should hate his.

"Are you going to come in?" He didn't look dangerous, but he did look as if he might fall over any second.

"I am not sober," he said, fixing her with an uneven look.

"I guessed," said Tess, moving to one side so he could lurch past her. "And as matter of fact, neither am I. I drank our bottle of wine." And the rest.

Tonino hung on to the doorframe of the living room, took a deep breath, and made his way inside as if he were walking a tightrope.

Tess shook her head in despair. She'd better make coffee. She waved him toward the leather sofa and headed for the kitchen.

"So . . . ," said Tonino, seeming to lose the thread.

"So?"

"So. You do not even know the man, Westerman, is that right?"

"I never met him," Tess agreed from the doorway. "What does that have to do with anything?"

Tonino was sprawled on the sofa. "I assumed . . ." He spoke slowly and carefully, hardly slurring. And in another language, Tess noted with admiration. "You were a relative of his."

"No." In the kitchen she put on some coffee and took stock—which would have been a lot easier if hadn't she drunk all that wine. After being warned off, Tonino had clearly headed for the nearest bar.

She took the coffee into the living room. "Tell me what happened," she repeated, putting the tray on the table.

Tonino was now sitting with his head in his hands. She resisted the urge to hug him. "Who are you?" he whispered.

So—she'd been right. "I'm Flavia Farro's daughter," she said. "My mother lived here in Cetaria. Her family worked for Edward Westerman. That's why he left me the villa. But . . ." She glanced at him. His eyes were glazed now, but whether from alcohol or from what she was saying, she couldn't tell. "But you know that, don't you?"

"You lied to me," he said.

"I did not." Tess was indignant. "I told you my name. I told you I owned the villa. Everyone else in the village seemed to know who I was before I even arrived."

"You tricked me," he said.

"Rubbish." Tess sat down next to him. She was angry, too, she realized. After all, she was the one who'd been kept waiting, who had cooked for him, who had been stood up— well almost. And she was the one who was supposed to hate *him*. "I never tricked you. It's not my fault you assumed I was related to Edward Westerman. That's after you'd decided I wasn't just another bloody tourist."

He looked up at her sadly. "But you never put me right. What about honesty, Tess? What about trust? I thought . . ."

"So did I." Suddenly Tess wanted to cry. It was true—she could have told him who she was, only she didn't want to get embroiled in some old and ridiculous family feud that meant nothing to her. And how could it matter after all this time? But she was kidding herself. It did matter—to people like Tonino Amato and Giovanni Sciarra. They could bear a grudge forever, it seemed. And that was probably why she hadn't told him. She had wanted him to like her for who she was, not dislike her for who she was descended from.

"Do you know what happened between our families?" he asked her. He seemed suddenly to have sobered up.

She shook her head. "Not exactly." Only Giovanni's and Santina's versions anyway, and there were still a lot of gaps.

"But you knew there was a quarrel?"

She nodded. God, she felt miserable. What a come-down after all that chemistry that had been zinging between them.

He grabbed her hands. "Why didn't you tell me yourself? Why did you let me find out from . . . ?" He tailed off.

"Who?" His grip was so fierce he was hurting her. It was like Giovanni Sciarra all over again. "Who told you?" She shook her hands free.

"It does not matter."

And she supposed it didn't. It could, after all, be anyone. If Tonino had been at all sociable, he would have known along with the rest of them. And it was probably Giovanni. Giovanni would have enjoyed putting the boot in.

"Okay," she said. She poured out the coffee. Black, she decided for both of them. "I'm sorry I didn't tell you before. I should have. But let's get this into perspective . . ." He said nothing. A sense of perspective clearly didn't come easy in Sicily.

"Our grandfathers had a row," she said. "In 1940 or whenever it was."

"1945," he said. "September 5th."

"Right." His precision with the date didn't bode well.

This time Tess took hold of his hands. "But what does it have to do with us? That was . . ." She tried to work out the sum, but in her present state of mind, it defeated her. "Over half a century ago," she said. "And remember—my grandfather and yours were best friends once."

Rather unsteadily, and clearly concentrating hard, he took the coffee she'd poured for him. "You, Tess," he said, "are more English than Sicilian. Otherwise you would understand."

"Perhaps," Tess suggested, "you could explain it to me?"

"You mean tell you the story?" He gulped back the hot black liquid. "So you really do not know?"

It was probably best not to mention the theft and betrayal. "I really don't know," she said. Because she wanted to hear his side of the story. "So tell me."

CHAPTER 44

Tonino took a deep breath. "So . . . ," he began.

Always, Tess thought. Always, he was telling her stories.

"There is the treasure, *il tesoro*, which belongs to the Englishman, Edward Westerman, yes?"

"Yes." She nodded. So far, so clear. "But what is it?"

"Ah." He sighed. "No one seems to know. Only that it was very valuable."

Another mystery. Now there was a surprise.

Tonino leaned forward in the chair. "Your benefactor," he looked around the room—with curiosity rather than bitterness, she felt, "was forced to return to England for the duration of the war."

Tess nodded, although the mention of the war made her think of her mother and the English pilot whose life she had saved. She closed her eyes and tried to imagine this house, Villa Sirena, shut up and empty during those wartime years. What a waste.

Tonino's voice cut into her thoughts. "And your grandfather made sure Villa Sirena was empty of anything valuable—in case it was looted."

"Who would it be looted by?" Tonino seemed much more sober now he'd drunk the coffee. And she was, too. But Tess wasn't getting the impression he'd changed his mind.

Tonino shrugged. "Germans, I suppose. Or Mafia. In Sicily, war or no war, there have always been unscrupulous men."

And not just in Sicily, Tess couldn't help thinking.

"So he asked my grandfather, Alberto Amato," Tess heard the pride in his voice, "his most trusted friend, to help him hide one of Edward Westerman's most precious possessions. *Il tesoro.*"

"Why?" Was it so big he couldn't carry it? The mind boggled.

Tonino bowed his head. "I do not know."

"And where did it come from in the first place?"

"I do not know that either." He spread his hands. "Perhaps Edward Westerman's builders found it when the foundations for the villa were being dug. Who knows?"

Giovanni might know, she thought, since he appeared to know everything. But would he tell her? Probably not. Her mother might even know—though it was unlikely she would have been privy to her father's secrets. Santina? It was possible. But it sounded as if it might be something of historical value. The equivalent of finding a Roman urn in a field in England.

"Which would mean that it did not legally belong to him," Tonino said.

"Right." That made sense. If it was a Greek or Roman artifact he had found, it wouldn't matter that it was his land.

What would matter was that it was important historically and should be declared to the authorities, she supposed.

"It is not unusual," Tonino said, "for such things to be found here. And it is common practice when building work is being carried out, for Mafioso to keep an eye on progress—with binoculars . . ." Here he put an imaginary pair of binoculars to his eyes.

"Really?" Tess blinked.

"But yes," he said. "Large sums of money could be at stake."

"And no one knows what it is," she murmured, "or where it is."

He gazed at her. With regret, she wondered? "Sometimes," he said darkly. "It is best not to know."

Honestly . . . This man and Muma would get on like a house on fire.

"It was assumed that *il tesoro* remained in its hiding place till after the war," Tonino said. "And the trouble only began when my grandfather was sent to fetch it. The war was over. Soon Signor Westerman would return to Sicily."

"What happened?" Tess asked, though she guessed what was coming. A theft and a betrayal, Giovanni had said.

"My grandfather, he could not locate it," Tonino said. For the first time he seemed ill at ease, as though this was an aspect of the story he was not comfortable with. "There was a problem."

"A problem?" Tess asked. "You mean it wasn't where he'd left it?"

Tonino shrugged. "Something like that," he agreed.

Tess stared at him. "So someone else got to it first?"

"No. I mean, yes. Or maybe no," he said.

Clear as mud.

"I do not know," he admitted. "Because I do not know where he hid it. He told me only that it was as well hidden as the very foundations of Sicily. But the important thing was what happened next."

"Which was . . . ?"

"People—they spoke to your grandfather. Especially the Sciarra family. Enzo had wormed his way in closer to your grandfather. No doubt he, too, knew of *il tesoro*. They hated my family. They were suspicious. In Sicily . . ."

"Yes," she said. "They're always suspicious."

"They said that my grandfather had . . . what do you say, sold out."

"Sold out? As in sold *il tesoro*?" Why would he? Everyone would know what he'd done. But then again, if *il tesoro* was worth a lot of money, who knows? Greed was a powerful thing. For a Sicilian in the 1940s, that sort of money could transform lives. And presumably if Edward Westerman wasn't supposed to own it in the first place, he couldn't say much about it disappearing . . . What with the war and general looting and what have you . . . It would be easy for *il tesoro* to slip the net. It must have been a temptation.

But Tess realized that none of this would go down well with Tonino, who was clearly convinced of his grandfather's innocence.

"Sold, yes," said Tonino with a sigh. "Or sold the information of where it was hidden. I do not know." He looked so dejected. Tess realized her own anger with him had dissolved. She wanted to make it all right, but she didn't know how.

"And my grandfather believed Enzo and the others, I suppose?" she said. "He thought your grandfather must be guilty?"

Tonino nodded. "Enzo Sciarra was an evil man," he said. "Not content with causing the death of my Uncle Luigi, now he accused my grandfather, Alberto Amato, of disloyalty and theft." He sat up straighter.

Theft and betrayal, Tess thought. Oh, dear. "How did Enzo Sciarra cause Luigi's death, Tonino?" she asked him.

"Torture." His dark eyes when he looked across at her were blank of emotion. He rubbed at the scar on his face and it seemed to become more raised, red, and livid at his touch. "The Sciarras demanded protection money," he said. "A lot of it. For my uncle's new business venture—a restaurant and bar." He continued to stare at her.

Tess could hardly breathe for the tension in the room. "Protection money?"

"When he couldn't—or wouldn't—pay up, Enzo made him a visit. That is the way it would work. Maybe he went further than he intended—I do not know. Maybe he wanted just to frighten him. But after the visit . . ." His voice almost failed.

"Luigi died," whispered Tess.

Tonino nodded. "A heart attack, they said. Many things can cause heart failure, Tess, you know?"

She knew. And she was just getting a glimpse of how dangerous some of these men could be. Muma hadn't been joking when she said that Sicily was a dark place. Beautiful, yes. But with a dark, dark shadow.

Tonino got to his feet. "The Sciarras have a lot to answer for," he said quietly.

"And have they always hated one another—the Amatos and the Sciarras?" Tess asked. She didn't want him to leave, not now, not like this.

"They were neighbors once." He paused. "Many generations ago. They shared the land and the harvests; they were friends, they depended on one another." He hesitated. "But the Sciarras became connected by marriage to another local landowner—richer, more powerful. They became greedy; they wanted more." He shrugged. "In Sicily, this happens."

"So they argued over the land they originally shared?" Tess wanted all the facts; the whole picture.

"*Sì*." He eyed her sadly. "They fought, and the Sciarras won; they took everything—all the Amato land and living. By then the Sciarras were enmeshed in the tentacles and had powerful friends. *La Piovra*, Tess. You understand?"

She understood.

"What happened to your grandfather?" Tess got to her feet and went to him. She put a hand on his arm, but he didn't respond.

"Being accused of disloyalty and theft, being mistrusted by his dearest friend . . ." He paused. "It destroyed him," he said. "Alberto Amato was never the same man again." He took a step away from her, his eyes cold. "And that is what I cannot forgive your family for," he said grandly. "The lack of trust, Tess. The dishonor of our family name."

"I see." It had nothing to do with her, and yet she knew that this wasn't the point for Tonino. She felt as if she should apologize on behalf of the grandfather she'd never known, the grandfather who had believed what they all told him, who had not trusted his closest friend.

"So . . ." Tonino made a gesture with his hand. Now you understand, it said. Now you know the whole story.

Tess took a deep breath. She drew closer to him once more. "But do you think it's right," she said, "for you to hold a grudge against my family for so long? Especially a member of the family—me—who wasn't even there at the time?"

"You will not comprehend it," he said. "But our families were like this." He linked his little fingers together. Tess remembered this gesture as the one that Giovanni too had used. "That is why it is unforgivable." He turned away.

Unless of course, she wanted to say, what they all believed was true. Unless Tonino's grandfather really had succumbed to temptation . . . Unless her grandfather and all the others were right all along. But that wasn't the best plan.

Because he was walking toward the door. Walking out of her life, she realized.

He turned at the doorway. "I knew my grandfather," he said. "He was a good man."

Tess felt humbled. There was nothing more she could say.

"Now do you see why love is impossible between us?" he asked her. He opened the door. He wasn't waiting for an answer.

Love, she thought. Love? Only four letters. But a big, big word.

Who'd said anything about love . . . ?

CHAPTER 45

THE BAND ARRIVED TO SET UP AT SEVEN THIRTY. THEY were due to play from eight fifteen till nine thirty, then after a short break, on till eleven. Brian had put up posters, and already there were a dozen people in the bar. While they were doing the sound check, Dark and Bemused glanced over toward Ginny, and she smiled. Despite the Ball's best efforts at being a wet blanket, she had been looking forward to tonight. She couldn't help it.

"Looks promising," said Brian, rubbing his hands together. "Bring it on."

Magic Fingers, the band was called. Yes, bring it on, thought Ginny.

By eight fifteen, the number of people in the bar had doubled, and by nine the place was humming. Brian's girlfriend Chantal was also working behind the bar. She had a high-pitched laugh, a retro blonde beehive, and talked a lot, but seemed kind and capable. "I've been working behind a bar for fifteen years, love," she told Ginny. "What I don't know now, I never will."

Ginny was busy—distracted only by an occasional shy glance from Dark and Bemused on bass—so she didn't have too much of a chance to think about The Thing that was bothering her. The Ball had been having a field day with it all week, but tonight she'd decided to bury her head in the sand. Shame she couldn't bury the Ball at the same time . . .

Magic Fingers segued smoothly from a song called "Blue"—"written by Albie," the blond lead singer said; it took Ginny a few seconds to realize that Albie was Dark and Bemused on bass. *Albie* . . . It was a good song. Soulful. Ginny would like to hear it again—without the accompaniment of a list of orders from some guy at the bar and the rattle of loose change and Brian yelling "Speak up, love," by her left shoulder.

They segued into "Yellow" by Coldplay. *Look at the stars* . . . Ginny shivered, even though it was getting hot in here. Shit, she thought. It would be such bad luck.

At nine thirty in their break, the boys ordered beers, which, Brian said, were on the house. The success of the evening had made him unusually generous, Ginny thought. And it was true that the band had transformed the Bull and Bear. The place was buzzing. And Ginny—once she'd mastered the drinks and the till and the pumps—was loving it. As she'd told Brian in her interview, she was quick, and it turned out she was good at the chat, the banter, the not letting them get too close or too clever.

"Hey, gorgeous, what d'you reckon to our sound, then?" The blond lead singer was coming on to her. "I'm Matt. Hi." He had a sexy grin and she guessed that he came on to most girls and probably had a 99 percent success rate. She'd be one of the other 1 percent she decided. He wasn't her type.

"You sound pretty good," she said, and then flashed a special smile at Dark and Bemused. "I loved your song," she said. "Blue. Great lyrics."

"The quiet ones always get the hottest chicks," grumbled Matt. But he didn't have long to wait. In minutes he was surrounded by a sea of girls lining up to talk to him, flashing painted eyes and deep cleavages his way.

"Thanks," said Dark and Bemused. "What's your name, by the way?"

"Ginny." They touched hands over the bar.

"Three pints of lager, love," yelled someone.

"Two mojitos on crushed ice . . ." (Blimey, that was a bit upmarket for the Bull and Bear, thought Ginny, seeing Brian's glazed expression as he struggled with the rum.)

"Vodka and cranberry and a pint of bitter . . ."

Suffering snakes. "Sorry," she said to D & B. "Got to—"

"Maybe later," he mouthed, and she nodded.

Ginny turned and found herself face-to-face with Becca.

"Hey!" Becca's grin was huge. "What're you doing here, Gins?"

Ginny felt ridiculously pleased to see her. "My new job," she said. "Where's Harry?"

Becca pointed. He was with one of his friends, both drinking pints as if they were water, beer splashing down their clothes and onto the floor.

Becca rolled her eyes. "Some sort of drinking marathon," she said. "It's pathetic."

"Take a break for ten minutes, love." Brian was breathing down her neck. "Go and talk to your friend."

The band was back on, and the people at the bar had thinned. Ginny slipped round to the front and hugged Becca. She wanted to say, *I've missed you*, but held back. Becca was the one who had dropped her when she took up with Harry. Becca was the one who couldn't be bothered to answer texts or hang out anymore.

"I've missed you," said Becca. "Sorry I've been preoccupied." She looked toward Harry, as if trying to work out why.

Infatuated, more like, thought Ginny. "S'all right," she said.

"How're things?"

"Okay. I'm staying at Nonna's at the min. Mum's in Sicily." She pulled a face. You'd hardly know she wasn't around though; she called or sent texts every night. Ginny reckoned they were communicating more than before she left.

"And how's Ben?" Becca shouted in her ear.

God, but this band was LOUD . . . "We finished," Ginny shouted back. "It wasn't going anywhere."

Becca nodded in agreement. She'd always understood. Though where, Ginny wondered, had she wanted it to go? She hadn't much enjoyed where it was in the first place. It wasn't like she'd required any kind of declaration or commitment from Ben. She supposed she'd just wanted some sign that she wasn't wasting her time. Because at the end of the day, she realized, although he had been her first, she had invested the virginity thing with a significance it didn't really have. At the end of the day Ben had the right kind of looks, but he wasn't very interesting.

She told Becca this.

Becca laughed and nodded. "Girlfriends are much more fun." She nudged Ginny in the ribs, and Ginny felt a slight twinge. She must have winced because Becca moved closer. "What's up?"

"Nothing—bit of a stomachache."

"What's up—honest answer?"

That's exactly what they used to say to each other. And suddenly Ginny wanted to confide in someone.

"I'm a few weeks late," she said. "That's all." That's all—like it might not be the end of the world if she were pregnant. She felt the pressure from the Ball release slightly. But she did have a stomachache—like she had constipation or something. Was that what being pregnant felt like?

"What?"

Ginny repeated the information, yelling into Becca's ear this time. *Tell the entire pub, why don't I*, she thought.

"Shit," said Becca. "I need a fag. Let's go outside."

"Five." Brian signaled to Ginny. She nodded.

"Have you done a test?" Becca, always the practical one, asked as soon as they were outside. It was dark and cool after the high body-heat in the pub, and her ears were ringing. Ginny hugged her arms around herself.

"Nope." She hadn't dared. The thought occurred to her—what would her mother say? She'd go ballistic. "But I've got this feeling," she told Becca. "I don't feel right. It feels like I might be." She groped in the pocket of her jeans and fished out a cigarette, though she didn't really feel like smoking it.

"Crap," said Becca. It was this way with words she had that had made her such a great friend. "You've got to do a test. There's no point just sitting around being negative . . ."

Ha. "Hope it is," said Ginny, and they both giggled. It was mad, but she couldn't help it.

Becca nudged her. "You've got to be positive," she said.

"I hope not," said Ginny, and they giggled again. Ginny had to hold on to the wall, she was laughing so much—it must be hysteria.

She glanced at her watch. "Gotta go back in," she said reluctantly. She stamped the cigarette out under her foot.

It was amazing, she thought, as she pushed her way through the crowd, how even the possibility of being pregnant—which was so bad, so impossible to contemplate— could become funny with Becca. And how having a good laugh could diminish the Ball's power somehow, as if it thrived on misery.

After the band had done an encore and Brian had gone down to the cellar to change the barrels one last time, they started packing up, and the customers finished their drinks and began drifting away. Ginny cleared and wiped tables and loaded glasses onto the bar.

"You went down a storm, boys," said Brian, handing over their cash. "Cheers."

"See you in two weeks then, guv," said Matt, winking at Ginny.

Two weeks, she thought. That was a long time.

"What's wrong with next Saturday?" said Brian. "You saw 'em. They couldn't get enough. You could be our resident band."

"Well, okay, cool." They all grinned at each other. Deal done.

Dark and Bemused came up to Ginny to say good-bye. "Maybe we can have a coffee sometime," he said.

"Yeah," said Ginny. That was—if she wasn't carrying another man's child . . . Could she get into another relationship before she knew? Coffee was only coffee. But . . . She didn't think so. So when he asked for her number, she didn't immediately whip out her cell.

Becca and Harry were two of the last to leave. "I'll call you tomorrow," Becca said and mouthed "Do the Test" in such a scary, eyes-wide way that Ginny took a step backwards and collided with Brian, who was stacking glasses.

"Careful, love," he said, but when he handed over her money, he gave her an extra tenner, so she knew he was in a good mood. She pocketed it. That would pay for the pregnancy test . . .

She looked up in time to see Dark and Bemused about to walk out the door. Shit. It gave her a bad feeling. The Ball said *no*, but what the hell.

She hotfooted it across the room to give him her number. 'Cause he might not ask again.

Chapter 46

Ginny went into Boots three times the next day before she plucked up courage to buy the pregnancy kit. Even then, terrified she'd see someone she knew, she took the precaution of hiding the blue-and-white packet under a red washcloth in the basket.

How stupid was she? She thought back to when this—if there was a *this*—had happened.

"When were you last on?" Ben had asked one of the last times when they were still together. He'd run out of condoms and had apparently only remembered this fact just as they reached a fairly crucial moment.

Ginny could hardly breathe. Sex had got better since that first time. A bit. She would discuss it with Becca, she decided. Perhaps there was something else she should be doing. Perhaps it was the Ball holding her back. Or perhaps, well, that was it—all there would ever be.

She tried to think back. "Er, two weeks ago," she told him. He didn't even break rhythm. "Approximately."

He exhaled loudly. And came. "That's all right then," he said into her ear. "No worries."

Yeah. Her own fault. Women had to take care of that sort of stuff. They were the ones who'd suffer the consequences. How could you rely on a bloke?

She thought of her mother in Sicily. She'd phoned again last night before work, done the usual parent small talk. "So . . . Tell me all the news. What have you been up to? How's everything?"

Impossible questions. She wasn't a newscaster with a teleprompter—she wasn't going to tell her mother what she'd been *up to* (Oh, yes, and I might have got myself pregnant . . . not sure yet . . . I'll let you know when I've done the test)—and *everything* was too big a subject to even contemplate.

Ginny had wanted to ask about the villa—she really had. She'd wanted to ask her mum how she was, and she'd even wanted to tell her she missed her. But she didn't say any of these things. And when the call ended, she wanted to cry. Because everything was going wrong. Well, one thing in particular.

She walked back to Nonna and Pops's, the blue-and-white packet stashed safely in her bag. It was raining now; some summer this was turning out to be. Bet it wasn't raining in Sicily . . .

Nonna was making dough in the kitchen; the scent of it—sweet, oily, and mellow—filled the whole house with well-being. Yum. Ginny stopped to grab an almond biscuit on her way upstairs. Did being pregnant make you eat more? Well, you were eating for two . . . Shit.

She had half an hour before she was due at the Bull and Bear to help with lunches. Time enough.

In her bedroom she pulled the instructions out of the packet, read them once without digesting a word and then another twice to make sure she understood. Then she took the thing into the bathroom to pee over.

Now she just had to wait.

That was the hardest part. She washed her hands and examined her face in the mirror. No spots for a change— that was good. Though on the other hand, wasn't clear skin another sign of pregnancy?

The doorbell went. She heard Nonna go to answer it. She could hear conversation. Surprise in Nonna's voice, and another voice—a soft, lazy drawl. Something didn't sound quite right. She looked at her watch and resisted checking the electronic panel on the tester. Please, don't be a line . . .

She poked her breasts experimentally. They didn't seem especially tender or swollen. That was a good sign, wasn't it?

"I suppose you'd better come in," she heard Nonna say. "She's upstairs."

Uh-oh. The Ball shimmered inside her. But who would it be? Becca? Ben?

"Ginny, dear," Nonna called up the stairs.

"Yes, Nonna?" she called back, glancing at the blue panel, stalling for time.

"Could you come down?"

Right. Brilliant. Spot on. "In a sec," she called back. "Can you just hang on while I—" What? See if I'm pregnant . . . ?

She checked her watch again. One more minute. It seemed to take an eternity to pass. She grimaced at herself in the mirror, tried to touch her nose with the tip of her tongue. How did people do that? *Why* would people do that?

Finally, she took a deep breath and looked at the little panel . . .

"Ginny?"

Shit. "Coming."

She took the steps two at a time and stood in the doorway of the lounge. Inside the room, a man of about forty was sitting in Nonna's best armchair with the printed roses and lace antimacassars. He looked completely out of place. His hair was sun bleached, untidy, and graying, and in one ear was a tiny silver-hooped earring. He was wearing faded jeans and a T-shirt with a picture of a goat on it. He looked vaguely familiar.

"G'day," he said. He stood up. "So you're Ginny?"

"Yes." She looked at her grandmother.

"My dear." Nonna looked very serious. "This will be a shock for you. It was a shock for me. You see . . ."

The man stepped forward. "Thing is, I'm your dad," he said. "Pleased to meet you at last, Ginny."

CHAPTER 47

IN ALL THE TIMES GINNY HAD THOUGHT ABOUT HER father—during the love and the hate, the longing and the resentment, the desperation and the grief—she had never once imagined him turning up in Pridehaven. When she'd pictured them meeting—and she had, oh, yes, she had—it had always been Ginny who found *him*, visited him in Australia, took him by surprise, made him regret—deeply regret—what he'd once thrown away. Not to be melodramatic . . . But: her childhood, her life, her love. So now she was pretty much dumbstruck. And "Bloody hell" was all she could say.

Her grandmother tutted. "It is the shock." She glared at him. "Turning up here like this, out of the sky . . ."

"Sorry." He addressed this to Ginny. "I had the other address. Tess's address. That is, your mum's address."

"How?" asked Nonna.

"She sent it to me a long time back, care of my sister in Newcastle." He smiled. "So I went to the house. I spoke to the woman next door."

"Lisa," said Ginny.

"Lisa," he agreed.

"And she gave you this address?" Nonna sounded surprised. Ginny was surprised, too—Lisa was normally very protective.

"She did." He shrugged. "Although I might have misled her a bit."

Nonna's hands were on her hips. "What did you tell her—exactly?"

"That I was an old friend." He caught Ginny's eye, and despite the fact that she was still in shock, she had to smile.

"You could have called us," she said.

He spread his hands. They were brown and kind of weathered. They seemed like the sort of hands that were used to hard work, outdoor work. "If I'd phoned, you might have told me where to go."

Ginny nodded. "I might." But no. Curiosity would have won out. She couldn't help wanting to know more about him. Like her, he was tall and slim; like her, his cheekbones were prominent in his face. Like her, he had a wide mouth, and his hair was blond. It gave her a weird feeling, to see this man and to know . . .

"Could I take you out to lunch?" He was giving her a searching look, too. She guessed that he was absorbing stuff about her just like she was about him. "I just want to talk. After that, you can still tell me where to go."

Ginny thought about it. She liked the way he spoke, the way he wasn't putting pressure on her. She glanced at her grandmother, who was giving nothing away. She guessed that if she told him to get lost, he'd just shrug and go on his way. But she didn't want him to—not yet. She wanted to hear what he had to say.

"I've got to work," she said.

"Can I give you a lift?"

Ginny hesitated. A lift meant close proximity, and she wasn't sure she was ready. She felt her grandmother take a step toward her and knew that she would support whatever decision Ginny made.

Then he grinned. "I bought something pretty gorgeous on the way over," he said. "Take a look."

"What is it?" She followed him to the window.

He twitched open Nonna's net curtain. Nonna just kept her arms folded and suspicion on her face. Outside the house a bright orange VW camper van was parked—a classic.

"Wow." Ginny couldn't help it. He was right. It was gorgeous. "You're on." She glanced at her grandmother once more. "All right, Nonna?"

Her grandmother nodded. "All right, my dear. If that's what you want."

He drove the van with an easy confidence. She could see why her mother had fallen for him.

"Can I pick you up after work?" he asked, when they got to the Bull and Bear. He had scored more brownie points for not commenting on the fact that she worked in a pub and for not mentioning college or the fact that her mother was in Sicily. "Maybe we can go for a coffee or something, yeah?"

"Okay," she said. She slid open the door and jumped down. "Cool. I finish at three," she told him. "And thanks for the lift."

In the bathroom at work, she sent Becca a text: *Negative, thank Buddha. My dad turned up 2day. Weird or wot?*

CHAPTER 48

TESS'S CELL RANG JUST AS SHE WAS ABOUT TO GO FOR a dive. The best cure for a hangover was a swim. A dive—well, maybe not, but Tess had already made up her mind to explore the rock islands and marine life west of Cetaria Bay a little further.

It was her mother. She picked up. "Hello, Muma."

"Tess." Her mother's voice sounded shakier than usual.

"Is everything all right?" She had spoken to Ginny only last night, but she felt the usual flutter of panic. She supposed for mothers it never quite went away.

"Fine, fine." Her mother was quick to reassure. "But something has happened, my dear. Or perhaps I should say someone."

Tess frowned. "You're not making any sense. Is it something to do with Ginny? Is she okay?"

She could almost hear her mother taking deep breaths. "I don't know quite how to tell you this, my dear," she said. "It is David."

"David?"

"Yes. He turned up here this lunchtime. He's come to see Ginny."

David. Ginny. Eighteen years ago, and yet it could have been yesterday . . .

When Tess had imagined this moment during her pregnancy, it had always been David who had handed her their baby.

But it wasn't. It was her mother. She handed Tess her baby, and she said. "It is a girl, my darling. It is a girl."

Tess looked down at the tiny wrinkled face, shrouded and swathed in white cotton; felt the soft down of her hair, saw the unfocused eyes of her daughter.

"She is beautiful," her mother said.

Tess held her to her breast, felt the first pull somewhere deep inside her as the baby rooted for the nipple. She had imagined it, yes, but she had never dreamed of what this moment would really be like. She wanted to hold her daughter to her breast forever, she wanted to protect her with her own life; she knew she would always love her, no matter what.

"Yes." Tess looked up at her own mother and saw that her eyes were filled with tears. She had known it, too, this moment. Of course, she had known it, too.

Tess reached for her mother's hand and held it in her own. Hands and gazes locked in mutual recognition: mother and daughter. This was what it was all about, she thought. "Thanks, Muma," said Tess.

After her mother rang off, Tess tried calling Ginny—okay, she knew she was at work, but she had to try. And then she decided to go for that dive anyway. She needed to think. Why on earth would David turn up after all these years? What did he want from her? And more to the point—what did he want with Ginny?

According to her dive map of the area, the natural reserve began just west of the beach, right here. She had been farther into the reserve before, of course, with Tonino in the boat. But one perfect afternoon, which had now gone horribly wrong, was not going to stop her going that way again. This was her life, and she was in control of it. She was not going to let the Robins, the Davids, or the Toninos of this world fuck it up. Whatever the reason. She would go for this dive, and then she would speak with Ginny. And then . . . ? She would see.

As she got her stuff together, she thought of Tonino's reaction if he saw her going into the water to dive again alone. Should she forego the beach dive and maybe drive along the coast a bit, hire a boat? And then she thought— dammit. It was his problem. She wanted to do a beach dive from here. It was safer anyway and less hassle than going out in a boat alone. He could rant and rave all he liked—her welfare was not his concern.

It was another sunny day, and there were a few tourists in the *baglio* when Tess made her way down to the bay; one family clustered around Tonino as he bent over the mosaicked surface of a round table outside his studio, using a sponge to press grout between some tiles. They were admiring the mosaics, including some candleholders made of slate and sea glass and two more tables with mosaicked surfaces that Tonino had brought outside.

They were asking him about one of the tables, and he was giving them his full attention. At least it meant she didn't have to speak to him. *Love*, she thought. Had he really said that?

Tess trudged by in her wet suit, scuba tank on her back, fins in hand. He gave her a long, hard look and then turned back to the German tourists.

What did she expect? He had told her what had happened to his friend; he had told her what had happened to the girl he loved and also to his parents. And now he had told her what had occurred between their grandparents. It was a lot of baggage for one man to carry.

And now there was David . . .

The sea felt warmer than yesterday. Tess went in a little way, adjusted the mask, pulled on her fins, and did the usual checks. There were a couple of swimmers out by the rocks today. She wondered if Tonino had warned them about the jellyfish.

She swam toward the rocks, floating down smoothly when the water got deep, staying relaxed, using the minimum of energy to conserve her air supply. By the rocks, she could see some anthias feeding. The other swimmers had gone in now, and Tess let herself enjoy the sensation of being alone in the ocean, with only the fish for company.

She let her mind wander as she poked around the crevices of the rock, lifting boulders to reveal sea urchins and starfish and even some brightly colored red mullet. It was so peaceful down here, so still.

So . . . David—for whatever reason—had turned up in Pridehaven. He had got hold of her mother's address, spinning some yarn to Lisa—and Ginny had agreed to see him.

Well, she couldn't blame her. He was her father, whether he'd always been there or not. She wasn't a child—though hardly yet an adult, Tess had to admit. She could make her own choices. Still . . .

The water in places was a bright luminous green, the plant life and sponges varying shades of orange and purple. Tess let some weeds trail through her fingers. Neptune grass. It was magical down here. An underwater wonderland. Down here everything seemed so simple. Problems like Tonino and age-old family rivalry and all the other family stuff just didn't exist. And that was part of the attraction.

Tess kicked herself gently through a wide gap in the rock islands. On the other side, the difference was noticeable, the water lighter and greener, the sponges more vibrantly colored, the fish more plentiful.

She continued to explore, gradually letting all the anxieties drift away with the current. "Don't do anything silly," her mother had told her. "There's nothing to worry about."

But as Tess checked her gauges and began to make her way back to shore, decompressing slowly and naturally as the water grew shallower, she knew she had to return to England. Her first instinct was to protect her child—that was what motherhood was all about. Even if it was from Ginny's own father.

CHAPTER 49

FLAVIA SPOKE TO LENNY ABOUT DAVID WHEN HE came home from doing some gardening for one of their neighbors. Edna was fit as a sparrow; privately, Flavia thought her neighbor just liked having a man around—which was fine; Flavia was more than happy for Lenny to be out of the house for an hour or two every now and then.

"You shouldn't have invited him in," Lenny growled. "I wouldn't have."

"Whatever he has done, he is still her father." Flavia sat down on the chair on the patio and watched Lenny. The man still had so much energy. Now he was digging over a flower bed. Always digging, that man. She had never quite understood the English and their gardens. If you were growing fruit and vegetables, then fine, that all went into the pot. But they went to an awful lot of trouble for their spring and summer planting. Still, she had to admit that the garden looked glorious for it—there were asters, snapdragons, purple trailing lobelia . . .

"He's never been her father." Lenny lined up the spade and made his first slit in the moist brown earth.

"Biologically, he is." Flavia knew what it was. David had left Tess when she was expecting Ginny, and Lenny had never forgiven him for leaving his daughter high and dry, a single mother with a baby to care for.

"Biologically, bollocks," said Lenny. He put his boot hard down on the top of the spade, and it sliced through the earth like butter. He kicked it up with the blade, made a chopping motion. He'd go round the whole flower bed like that, then again with a fork to crumble up the heavy chunks. He didn't seem to find it hard work, either.

Flavia felt weary just watching him. "I know," she said. "I know how you feel." She sighed. "But Ginny is eighteen and the girl knows her own mind. Have you considered that she might need him?"

"What the blazes for?" Lenny retorted.

Of course, he'd tried his best to be father and grandfather to Tess's girl, but no one could be everything. "Recognition?" Flavia suggested. "A sense of identity? To be acknowledged?"

Lenny snorted. "Sounds like a load of claptrap to me," he said.

Well, as far as Tess and David were concerned, he had a blind spot. But Flavia had often wondered how it might have affected Ginny—having a father who had never given her the time of day.

"Up to Ginny, even so," she said firmly. "Not up to us." She would not take anyone's right to choose away from them—this, after all, was what her father had done to her.

Lenny met her steady gaze. "Better tell Tessie, though," he said.

"Oh, I have done."

"And what did she have to say?"

"Not much—yet." Flavia knew her daughter. She was shell shocked. And God alone knew what else was happening over there. She could hear all of Cetaria in Tess's voice, it seemed. The sadnesses and the beauty; the past.

"Is she coming back home?" Lenny looked excited at this prospect. Bless him, he was a simple soul. Flavia, too, would like to haul her daughter back to England. But there were two reasons why she held back. One was that Tess clearly hadn't resolved whatever she needed to resolve. And number two was Ginny.

"I'm not sure," she said. It might be a good idea to give David a chance. He wasn't a bad person, just irresponsible. And he was a lot older now. She had a feeling that, for her granddaughter, he wouldn't be a bad thing.

Flavia turned to the back of her book. It could be said that Sicilian recipes were imprecise. They rarely bothered with exact weights, and Flavia was used to thinking in terms of "a few (*alcuni*)," "a touch of (*un tocco di*)" or "a lot (*assai*)." It was a matter of instinct. And yet, in typical contradictory nature, precision—for example, in the use of basil or oil or the relationship between a pasta and its sauce—was what could transform the ordinary into the special.

She carefully wrote out the next recipe—*melanzane alla parmigiana*; her granddaughter's favorite—hers, too, when she was young. And so . . .

* * *

Flavia remembered the journey to Exeter very well. She got herself comfortable in the chair and stared out into the garden, unseeing, reliving every detail. She turned

to the beginning of her notebook and found her place. She
picked up the pen . . .

*A week later, hurtling to Exeter on the train, sitting rigid and
erect with nerves, Peter's address written on the piece of paper
clutched in her hand—memorized in her heart—Flavia
reflected back on the past eventful week.*

*Compared with home in Sicily, her duties were light and
easily fulfilled. As there, it was a question of ritual. First, she
must light the fires to warm the house. Her instructions were
precise. She must build each one in the grate in layers: first,
thinly chopped wood, then crushed paper doused in kerosene,
then pieces of coal on top. It was not difficult. The fire caught
easily. And the smell of coal smoke was always there in your
nostrils—from early morning to last thing at night. Not dry,
sweet, and fragrant like olive wood, but itchy and sulfurous,
seeming to permeate your very skin. There was cleaning to do,
too, but mostly food preparation, and it was this duty that
Flavia enjoyed the most—though the ingredients left much to
be desired. She was accustomed to making do with little—but
it was the procuring of the freshest ingredients that was the
hardest part.*

*She had time off, too—time in which to talk to Signorina
Westerman ("Please, please call me Bea.") and learn about
England, and time in which to walk around London, get her
bearings, "become accustomed to this country," as Bea put it.*

*There was much to learn. Flavia stared out of the train's
grimy window onto equally grimy terraces of cottages with
squares of garden and oblong allotments of vegetables, onto
roads and rivers, trees and fields of green. English people, she
concluded, were very fond of putting things into compartments. And English people were so different. It wasn't just the*

language and the currency that were hard to come to grips with. It was the customs—what to say to who, how to behave.

She sat back in her seat, and a puff of dust rose into the air. She was also learning how to be free. Because, yes, here you could wander around without restrictions. But Bea had told her: "There are places you don't go, that are unsuitable for a young girl; there are people you don't talk to" (most people, according to Bea). "There are still—even in England—rules that must be obeyed." So . . . so far, Flavia had not ventured very far from West Dulwich. But she had already seen the Rag and Bone man and heard his strange cry; she had spoken to the butcher's boy, who rode a bicycle with a small wheel at the front to accommodate his tray of meat; and she was accustomed already to being awakened each morning by the comforting clippety-clop of horse's hooves and the chink of glass as the milk was delivered to the houses of the neighborhood. This seemed very grand indeed.

Flavia shivered and swayed to the rhythm of the train. The window was closed, but the train was drafty. It hissed and rolled, smelled of steam, coal, and hot oil; despite all this, for Flavia, this train was a carriage from paradise—taking her where she most yearned to be.

The worst thing about England was the weather. It was always chilly, and at night she often wrapped herself in her coat for warmth. The sun had not emerged all week, and that, Bea said, was quite usual for November. Madonna, save us . . . But . . . Peter was here. Peter, Peter, Peter; the train seemed to echo his name.

"What exactly do you plan to do, my dear?" Bea had asked. She was all for telephoning the family, if they had a telephone number that could be obtained. But Flavia had no intention of doing such a thing.

"I see him face-to-face," she said. "It is the only way. I go to house."

"To the house," Bea said distractedly. "Just like that? With no warning? Do you honestly think—?"

"Yes." Flavia nodded.

Bea had regarded her with what looked like admiration. "You're a plucky little thing, I'll give you that," she said. And then, "Should I come with you, I wonder?"

"No." Flavia shook her dark curls decisively. This was her journey, and she must do it alone.

"Then, after you have been to the house," Bea said, "you must telephone me. And I shall expect you back within three days. Agreed?"

"Sì."

But as the stations were eaten up by the hurtling train, Flavia felt her certainty waver. What if he no longer lived there? What if after all this time it emerged that Peter had never made it back to England . . . ? What if his family were cold or cruel or didn't want to speak with a girl from Sicily? Peter, Peter, Peter, echoed the train.

At last they drew into the station, and Flavia picked up her bag, squeezed the lever to push open the heavy door, and made her way up the platform. Once again, she hailed a taxi (she was getting quite good at this—a decisive gesture was the way); once again she sat in the cab, her bag hugged to her chest, and watched a city pass by her eyes . . .

Exeter was very different from London. There was less traffic; it was greener, smaller, and less daunting, though it, too, showed its legacy of the war years. They passed several fire-blackened ruins and sites of rubble and demolition. Peter . . . thought Flavia. There were also signs of rebuilding. Bea Westerman had told her that England was rebuilding its entire future. Was it possible, Flavia wondered? And yet it was true that with this new construction there was a sense of hope in the air, a new energy after the war years. She saw a coal truck making deliveries, the men in caps with their blackened faces and grimy clothes. She noted a large canal, too—with barges, a big church, a gas station in what looked like the main street, an ABC cinema. It seemed a pleasant town; she had known somehow that it would be.

The house, when she arrived, was not grand like Beatrice Westerman's house. But it was newly painted and had a nice front garden with a gate and a neat path. Flavia's heart was hammering like a wild thing. She took deep breaths. She didn't stop to think. She lifted the heavy brass knocker. Peter, *she thought.*

She heard footsteps, saw a light go on, heard a voice, saw a female form getting closer. A girl of about sixteen opened the door. She held it not wide open, but just ajar—to keep in the heat, Flavia supposed. She had brown hair and very blue eyes. Flavia blinked at her, but they were not Peter's blue, not at all.

"Can you help me?" she asked politely, for she had rehearsed this speech. "I am looking for Peter Rutherford. I am a friend from Sicily."

The girl stared at her as if she were from not Sicily, but another planet. "Peter Rutherford?" she echoed.

"Yes." Flavia crossed her fingers in her woolen gloves behind her back.

"Oh, Rutherford." She frowned. Turned and yelled. "Mum? Who were the people who lived here before us? Was it Rutherford?"

"Yes." An older woman came into the hallway. Her hair was encased in rollers and a tight net. She wore a pinafore

apron and was holding a dishtowel in her hand. She surveyed Flavia. "Which one were you after?" she asked.

"Peter," answered the girl for her.

The woman nodded. "The younger son? Mid-twenties? Fair hair? Tall?"

Flavia almost exploded with relief. He was alive, then. He had made it.

"Sì," she said. "Yes. That is Peter."

The woman nodded, still eyeing Flavia with curiosity.

"Can you tell me, please? Where is he now?" She held her breath.

"Living only two streets away, I believe." The woman slung the dishtowel over her shoulder. "I see him sometimes in the grocer's."

"Two streets away?"

"I'll write down the name of the road." The woman went to fetch a pen and paper.

"Thank you."

"I don't know the number, mind."

"It does not matter." Flavia was so excited, she could hardly speak. Peter. So near.

The woman wrote down the address. "Silver Street," she said. "That's where I've seen him walking to."

"Thank you. Thank you." Flavia took the scrap of paper— she felt like kissing it, kissing the woman, too.

"They're a nice couple," the woman remarked. "Nice little kiddie, too. Well, good luck, love," she said. "I hope you find them."

Chapter 50

At three p.m. the tangerine-colored VW was outside waiting for her, drawing lots of admiring glances, her father looking very calm at the wheel.

Ginny climbed in. Her father . . . It was a sensation she wasn't used to.

"Where to?" he asked.

"Pride Bay." She directed him. "They do the best hot chocolate there."

In the café he ordered a coffee latte for himself and hot chocolate with whipped cream for Ginny.

"I guess you're wondering about a lot of things," he said, sitting down opposite her. He spoke slowly, as if he was putting a lot of thought into the words. "Like why I suddenly turned up like this—out of the blue, as your Nan almost put it."

"Yeah." Ginny sniggered. She liked his accent—the Australian twang—but she wasn't going to make this easy for him. He'd been gone all her life—that was eighteen years he'd missed out on birthdays, Christmas, and day-to-day contact. A lot. A hot chocolate wouldn't do it—even with whipped cream.

He tapped his nose. "A windfall," he said. "I expect your mum told you that I was a bit of an old hippie . . ."

Ginny shrugged. She had imagined they both were. Only her mother got catapulted into the world of children and responsibilities, while he'd bummed off to Australia and continued the hippie dream, she supposed. All right for some.

"Well, I never had any money to come over to England until now."

Weak, thought Ginny. What about contacting her via the Internet? Or by post? Even a phone call would have been good.

He seemed to read her mind. "It's easy to let the opportunity go by," he said. "And there's a point where it seems as if it might be too late. Unless . . ."

"Unless?" she prompted. She thought she knew what he meant about opportunity and it being too late.

"Unless you feel you can do something. Make a difference."

Ginny was lost. What sort of something did he intend to do now?

He stirred sugar into his latte. "And I guess you're also wondering why I ran off in the first place?"

That was simpler. "Because you didn't want the responsibility of a baby?" Ginny suggested. She could understand that. Thank God she wasn't pregnant. Thank God.

He looked straight at her. "I was scared shitless, to be truthful with you," he said. "I was so young. A kid was the last thing on my agenda. No offense."

Ginny nodded. "None taken." He was honest, she'd say that for him.

"Your mother was so cool about it, so together. Seemed like it was no problem for her." He was lost in reflection now. "But I was terrified. Truly."

"So what did you do?" Ginny sipped her chocolate. It was hot and sweet, and the cream was melting into it in just the way she liked it to.

He continued to stir his coffee. "Took off to Australia. Did fruit picking, worked in a bar, traveled around, smoked too much weed. You can lose decades smoking that stuff. Sheer bloody lethargy."

Ginny was a bit surprised at his admitting this, but she supposed he wasn't your regular run-of-the-mill parent. She had tried a bit of weed herself, but though it made her giggly at first, and spaced out in a good kind of way, after a while she'd started to get paranoid and wanted to throw up.

Her father was still talking. "I joined a commune of New Age travelers in Western Australia," he said. "There were a lot of spiritual things going down. It was creative, too, you know, music, poetry, painting, all that kind of stuff."

All that kind of stuff. . . oh God. It was quite thrilling, to have a parent who had done *all that kind of stuff*. But the best thing was that he was so laid back about it, like it was normal. The Ball was being a bit sarcastic about this. "Listen to him," it jeered. But Ginny wanted to at least give him a chance.

"I met a Dutch couple there a while ago," he went on. "We bonded. They fancied going prospecting in the desert, and they asked me to go along for the ride. I've always been handy with engines. You don't want your transport to break down in the middle of nowhere, do you?"

Wow. Prospecting. "You mean for gold?" Ginny was well impressed now.

"Sure." He spooned up some froth from his latte. "Loads of people have a go at it. You never know, do you?" He laughed.

Ginny found herself laughing, too. "And . . . ?"

He stopped laughing. "We struck lucky, didn't we?" And at that moment he looked so young and uncertain, as if he hadn't really wanted to, as if now, he didn't know what to do with it. God. It sounded like she'd found herself a reluctantly rich father. Maybe a very rich father.

"So you came back to England," she said. And yet it was all too easy, too glib. She thought of her mother coping for all those years, bringing up Ginny on her own, and suddenly she wanted to lash out at him.

It must have shown in her eyes.

"I realize you've got no reason to even give me the time of day," he said. "I've let you down, I've let your mother down, and I've let myself down even more. I took off when your mum needed me the most. I never even contacted you—for eighteen years."

"Exactly." She eyed him over the rim of her cup. That could hardly be explained away as a lost opportunity.

"I wanted to," he said. "More than you could ever guess. God knows how many times I picked up a pen to write to you."

Ginny waited.

"But I was bloody useless," he said. "I had no money, I made no contribution to your upkeep, I had nothing to offer you. Honest to God, you were better off without me, Ginny."

The way he said her name made her soften—slightly. "You could have tried," she said. "You could have let me make that choice."

"Yeah." He nodded. "I could have been different. I should have been different. I should never have brought a kid into the world, for a start." He paused. "Let that be a lesson to you."

She blinked at him. It was as if he knew . . . That was how easy it could be; how easy it almost had been for her and Ben . . . And she couldn't help warming to him—for his directness, she supposed.

"You've probably hated me for years," he said.

"I hated you for a while," she agreed. And then . . .

"I don't blame you." He shrugged.

Ginny had finished her hot chocolate, and she pushed the cup away. "So what do you want from me now?" she asked.

"Nothing you don't want to give." He was regarding her intently. "I'd like the chance to get to know you a bit . . . that's why I came. But also to try and make things—not right, but better. To give something back."

"Money?" She shot this at him in the most disparaging tone she could manage. Money could never make things right. Nothing could.

"Money buys you freedom," he shot back. "Money's not everything, I agree. Jesus, I turned my back on things material a long time ago, believe me. But money can give you choices; money can make you more comfortable. Maybe your mum could use some—even after all this time?"

"Guilt money?" Ginny asked. She didn't want him to be able to shrug off his guilt so easily.

"Call it what you like." He leaned closer toward her and waggled his eyebrows. "Late payment of alimony?"

She giggled. There must be something in the stars sending windfalls her mother's way—first the house in Sicily, now this.

"Tell me about you." His eyes were intent. His face reminded her so much of her own. It was weird—like looking into a mirror that traveled in time. "I've wondered so often. About you."

It was over an hour later that they finally got up to go. She had told him about her life—it was easy, perhaps because he was a bit of a drifter and seemed to understand, or perhaps because he was a stranger, and it was easier to tell a stranger. At any rate, the Ball had lessened its grip on her— just a bit—in the telling.

"What do you want, Ginny?" he asked her, as they left the café.

The million-dollar question, that was. "I want to do . . . something unsuitable," she said. "I want to see things. I dunno, really."

"And what don't you want to do?"

That was easier. "Study. Do psychology. Go to uni. Stay in Pridehaven."

He laughed. "Anything else?"

"I don't want to do what other people want me to do," she said, feeling vaguely guilty about her mother. "I want to be free." From the Ball, she meant. And everything it stood for.

He nodded. "Sounds like you need to get away."

As if it were easy . . .

He unlocked the door of the VW. Ginny couldn't imagine him with her mother, not now. She thought of the photograph in the living room at home. If they'd stayed together, they would have split sooner or later—it was obvious. One more broken family . . . So what did it really matter that he'd left before she was even born?

He dropped her back at Nonna and Pops's.

"How did you get on with him?" Nonna asked her, the second she walked in the door. She was still wearing her suspicious look. And something else that Ginny couldn't identify.

"I liked him," Ginny said. And she heard the surprise in her own voice. "I liked him a lot."

And then her cell bleeped. She dug it out of her pocket. Looked at the screen. MUM. Oh, glory . . .

CHAPTER 51

IT WAS THE NEAREST THING TO A HEART-TO-HEART they'd had for a long time, Tess reflected a few days later as she walked to the Hotel Faraglione to meet up with Millie for coffee. She supposed a part of her—a selfish part, she had to admit—wanted Ginny to tell her father to get lost. *Where have you been all my life?* That kind of thing.

But Ginny had surprised her by being more considered, more thoughtful, she supposed. "It's good for me, Mum," she'd said.

"Why?" Had she been such a bad mother? Had she not been enough for Ginny all these years?

"Because he can answer some of my questions," her daughter said. "Questions that I've wanted to ask him for years."

The sun was already hot and hazy in the blue Sicilian sky as Tess made her way along the narrow streets and dusty cobbles. How could it not have occurred to her, she thought now, that Ginny would have questions to ask David? That there would be things that she, Tess, could not explain? Mainly, she realized, because she didn't know herself.

"I'm going to come back home right now," Tess told her. "I need to see David. You shouldn't have to deal with this alone."

"But, Mum," Ginny said. "I want to deal with it alone. I want to have time with him. Can't you see?"

Tess had tried to see. But all she could see was that Ginny didn't want her to come back. She wanted to be with her father. All their life together up to now seemed to have been canceled out—as if it counted for nothing.

"Not because I don't love you, Mum," Ginny had said, as if she knew exactly what her mother was thinking. "Not because I don't miss you. Because I do."

It had been a long time, Tess realized, since her daughter had said anything like this to her. It made her want to cry. "Okay, darling," she said. "But if you need me, just call."

"I will."

"And Ginny?"

"Yes?"

"I love you, too."

Loving your child, Tess reflected, as she entered the cool, tiled foyer of the hotel, was sometimes about letting them go. It might not be easy—but she had to try.

Because Millie was busy with the hotel and Pierro was away a lot on business—he seemed to have irons in a multitude of fires—Tess had not seen quite as much of her new friends as she had hoped to. Nevertheless, it was good to have a woman friend to speak English to, and Pierro had been very helpful with her ideas for Villa Sirena. It wasn't easy, Tess had discovered, being a woman on her own in a run-down villa in Sicily.

"Are you okay?" Millie asked her, as she poured coffee for the three of them. "You seem a bit distracted." They were sitting on their private terrace which was full of bright flowers in pots—trailing jasmine and purple and orange bougainvillea—and shaded by a linen canopy. Today Millie was wearing a bright-yellow sundress. With the red lipstick and nail polish and her black hair she, too, looked like some exotic flower, Tess thought. Perfectly lovely, but so brittle that if you touched her, she might break.

"There have been a few issues at home," she admitted. She was tempted to tell her the whole story—but it was a long one.

"Teenagers." Millie smiled. "I can imagine."

"And I had a few words with Tonino," Tess added. "About this ridiculous family vendetta."

"Vendetta?" Millie's perfectly plucked eyebrows rose. "Sounds thrilling. Do tell."

Tess hesitated, but it was hardly a well-kept secret, since most of the village seemed in the know, so she sketched out the gist of it. Even Pierro seemed interested and stayed outside to listen.

"Gosh." Millie's eyes were wide. "So what is *il tesoro*, do you think?"

"Search me." Though Tess was beginning to wish it didn't exist.

"And where do you suppose it disappeared to?"

"I have no idea," said Tess. She accepted another almond *biscotti* from the plate Millie offered to her. They were perfect dipped into *caffè latte*. And she could always diet later, back in England . . . "Giovanni seemed to have some idea it was hidden in the villa—when I first arrived, he cross-questioned me about it."

"Really," drawled Millie. "I wonder if *he* knows what it is."

Tess wasn't sure if it was her imagination, but she thought Pierro gave his wife rather a sharp look. Their relationship was hard to fathom. Pierro seemed to adore his wife, but Millie . . . Sometimes she was very offhand.

"But wouldn't it be exciting . . ." Millie really had the bit between her teeth now. "To find out? Where it is and what it is, I mean. Didn't your mother give you any clues at all? Have you even asked her?"

"No, I haven't." Tess had to laugh.

Millie leaned forward conspiratorially, and Tess caught the aroma of her perfume—musky and sweet. "Perhaps you should," she suggested. "It might make all the difference with Tonino if you can find out more about it. Who knows?"

"Muma doesn't want to talk about those days," Tess reminded her. How could it make Tonino change his mind? For him, what was in the past could never be erased. And, besides, she had her pride. If Tonino didn't want her because of some stupid old family quarrel, then she wasn't going to run after him.

"For the Sicilian," Pierro said, "the past is always woven into the present."

Millie rolled her eyes.

Tess had some sympathy. Sicilian men were all too fond of telling her about the idiosyncrasies of their race. Still, "Like Tonino with his fairy tales and folk stories," she said. Past and present. Sometimes they were so tangled up it was impossible to pry them apart.

"You like him a lot," said Millie. Her eyes were sharp and penetrating.

"I suppose." Though Tess could still hear Giovanni's voice in her mind. *He is good at tricking women.* The last thing she needed was to get involved with another player.

Pierro smiled. "You are well suited," he said. "It would be perfect. Millie and I would no longer be the only English-Sicilian couple in Cetaria."

Millie frowned. "Tess is half-Sicilian," she reminded him. "So it isn't the same." She put her coffee cup to her lips, and Tess was surprised to see her hand tremble. She was about to say something, but then Millie flashed her a bright smile, and the moment was gone.

"Yes, of course you are," said Pierro. He slapped his forehead with the bridge of his hand. "For a moment, I forgot."

Tess had not really felt half-Sicilian while she was growing up. Her mother was a little different, yes, but apart from Muma's cooking, she'd had a very English upbringing. Now though, being here, she did feel as if she had a part of Sicily in her blood, and as if she always had.

"Anyway, there's no chance of us getting together," she told Pierro, pushing her cup away. "I'm the enemy, and for Tonino the past has the louder voice."

"Then he is an idiot," said Pierro gallantly. "And did you know, dear Tess, that this place was originally owned by one of Tonino Amato's ancestors?"

"It was?" Tess looked around them. The mauve stuccoed hotel with its colorful grounds was very sleek and upmarket. She couldn't quite see it somehow.

"Although, then, it was only a bar and restaurant," he said.

"Ah. Luigi Amato." The great uncle who had died of heart failure—significantly after a visit from Enzo Sciarra, though Tess decided not to mention this.

"Yes. He ran it with his sister," Millie said. "He was gay, though he kept it pretty hush-hush in those days, I imagine."

"Really?" That was another fact that Tonino had omitted to tell her, Tess thought. Not that it was necessarily relevant. But still.

"And what about Villa Sirena?" Millie changed the subject, rather to Tess's relief. "What's happening there?" She offered more coffee, but Tess shook her head. She was drinking so much of the stuff that she was on a permanent caffeine high.

She told them her plans. She wanted to make the entire bedroom area into four bedrooms en suite, with a private living area for whoever might be running things. The kitchen had to be completely refurbished and the villa decorated throughout. Plus a bit of landscaping wouldn't go amiss. That was the absolute minimum if she was going to run it as a B&B—with a manageress in charge, perhaps.

"Why not run it yourself?" Pierro poured himself more coffee.

"My daughter's only eighteen," Tess reminded him.

Millie shrugged. "Then she's almost off your hands." You could tell, Tess thought, that she and Pierro had not had children of their own. "Before you know it, she'll be away at university or married. And where will you be, Tess?"

"Stuck in England, probably," Tess admitted.

Pierro glanced at his watch and got to his feet. "I feel you will come back one day," he said. "All the answers—they are here in Sicily."

"Perhaps not all the answers," Millie interjected. "It's a huge leap—from taking a holiday here to moving lock, stock, and barrel. Maybe Tess will never be up for it. She has family in England, remember."

Pierro grinned. "They will love coming out for visits," he said.

Tess wasn't so sure about that. "My mother couldn't wait to leave Cetaria," she reminded them. If she could ever get Muma out here—especially at her age—it would be a miracle. But a wonderful miracle, she realized.

"Ah." Pierro moved away from the table. "*Cu nesci arriniesci.*"

"Come again?"

"A Sicilian proverb," he explained. "You have to get out of Sicily to succeed."

"Unless," Millie added, wagging a finger, "you get into the tourist industry."

Tess smiled. They'd certainly done okay. But Millie was right. It was a big, big step—not one to undertake lightly. And no way could she leave Ginny.

"As for Tonino Amato," Millie went on, "he's not the only fish in the sea round here, you know."

The problem was, thought Tess, that he was the fish she wanted.

She left soon afterwards, knowing that Millie and Pierro both had to get back to work. Something Millie said was bugging her—but she couldn't quite pin it down.

Should she ask her mother about *il tesoro?* She didn't want to get involved any further than she was already, but something told her she had to be. She was here for a purpose—Edward Westerman had seen to that—and maybe that purpose included solving the mystery.

She thought of what Santina had told her—that her mother had found the airline pilot and that she had never forgotten him. Tess frowned. It was difficult to accept that Dad had never been the one and only for her mother. But what did this tell her? That the airline pilot had moved on by the time her mother found him? That Flavia had been too late . . . ?

CHAPTER 52

A NICE COUPLE. A NICE KIDDIE . . .

The words had been resounding in Flavia's head for the past hour. And yet still she had come here to Silver Street, as if she needed to see for herself, as if she still hoped it would not be true.

She sat down in a tearoom on a corner, watching, waiting. Always waiting, she thought. Always waiting. There was a red-and-gold poster on the wall opposite advertising a panto-mime. Jack and the Beanstalk, *she read.* At the Theatre Royal.

There was a young man behind the counter watching her. "You all right, love?" He'd asked her a couple of times. He had kind blue eyes. Not like Peter's, but nice . . . She realized now how many people in England had blue eyes. But Peter's were still special.

"Yes, thank you," she replied, cradling the white mug of cocoa between her cold palms. She heard the clattering of crockery from behind the counter, the hiss of steam. A nice couple, a nice kiddie . . .

"Only, I've got to close in a bit," he said. "You got anywhere to go?"

"Go?" she echoed.

He seemed embarrassed. He stood there fiddling with the cuff of his shirtsleeve, visible under his white bartender's apron. He moved the glass salt and pepper pots to one side and wiped the table with a cloth. "Tonight. You look like you might be a long way from home."

The laughter exploded from her. Hysteria, she thought. She had finally broken, then. But . . . A long way from home? Yes, if Sicily was home, could ever be home again.

The young man frowned. "Can I help?" he asked. "Only . . ."

And then she saw him. Through the misty café window, walking up the street toward her. He was older, heavier, and there was a slight hunch to his shoulders that hadn't been there before, but even in the dim light of a yellow streetlamp, she could see that it was him.

"Peter," she muttered. And she was out of her chair and through the door in seconds.

She stood on the pavement not ten feet from him. "Peter." She said it so quietly that it was almost silence. His face was drawn; she remembered the faint frown, the sharp angle of his cheekbones, the lightness of his eyes. And that mouth, his lips . . .

He must have sensed rather than heard her. He looked around, frowned, saw her—all in the same moment. She saw confusion, disbelief, elation cross the mobile features.

"Flavia?" Only Peter could make her name sound so romantic. "Flavia?"

She flew into his arms. She couldn't help it. It had been so long, and now he was here. And . . .

"Yes, it is me," she said.

He held her for a moment that seemed to last forever and yet no time at all. And she felt it. She felt his need, his love, his desire, like amber light winging around her soul.

Until he broke away. "Flavia? Is it really you? Good God. What the blazes are you doing here?" He was flustered. He pushed his hair back from his forehead. Flavia remembered that gesture. He looked nervously up the street. People were hurrying home in their belted coats with scarves wrapped over their noses and mouths. It was cold. But it wasn't yet completely dark, and the streetlights gave the sky a strange orange glow. "How on earth did you know where to . . . ?"

"I went to the house," she said. "To the address you gave me before." Before—in another world.

"But you traveled all the way here—from Sicily?" He stared at her almost as if he didn't want it to be true.

"Sì," she said. "To find you." It was the simple truth—most of the truth.

He swore under his breath. Looked up the street again.

Which house did they live in, she wondered. The nice couple with the nice kiddie? Was she inside waiting for him even now? "But you did not wait for me," she said. This was what she had not been expecting. That Peter would have found someone else. And yet it was so obvious. Why else would he not have written? Why else would he have not come back for her?

Peter grabbed her hands. At his touch, she felt a current of longing streak through her. Peter . . .

"You didn't write to me," he said. "You didn't answer any of my letters." His eyes were wild now. He held her hands so tightly that it was hurting her.

She wanted that, though. It took her mind from that other pain. And then she realized what he had said. It was her turn to stare at him.

"I did not receive any letters," she said after a moment, in a flat monotone. "But I wrote to you many times."

Suddenly, she knew what he was going to say.

"I never received them."

She was silent; thinking, trying to understand.

"I thought you weren't interested," he said. "I thought I was just a novelty."

"A novelty?" With her gaze, she traced a path from his head—his fair hair was still short and would be soft to the touch. If she could . . . Down to the full lower lip and the slightly crooked upper lip, to his jaw—slightly shadowed. His face was fuller now it was no longer wartime, now he was completely well.

"The novelty of a stranger," he said. "An English stranger passing through." He hung his head. "I know that the way we met and everything . . ."

She knew he could not bring himself to say "fell in love."

". . . is not how these things are done in Sicily."

Those were not his own words. Flavia knew it, like she knew that this was a cold December night and that they were in Exeter, England, and that she was lost. Lost.

"You didn't come back for me," she whispered.

"I did."

The words sliced through her. "When?" But even as she asked him, she knew that, too. There had been only the one time. She knew everything now.

"Four years ago," he said. "I saw your father."

Slowly, she nodded. Four years ago, yes.

"He seemed to know I was coming."

Well, he would, Flavia thought, if he had intercepted the letters. Papa had friends who had friends in the right places.

Like Enzo. He would know what to do. In Sicily, everything could be bought, every person corrupted, it seemed.

"He said that you had married, damn it." *Fiercely, he clenched his fist.* "That you were away somewhere with your new husband. That I should forget about you and marry one of my own kind. It is not done this way in Sicily," *he said.* "You were his daughter. You had to marry a Sicilian man. A man that your family approved of."

Flavia nodded once more. She had been sent to visit her Aunt Paola in a neighboring village—just to help out for a while, as her aunt was feeling unwell. At the time, she had not thought it strange. But . . . Flavia closed her eyes. Peter had been there in Cetaria, and she had missed him. Her father had destroyed her life.

"I will never forgive him," *she told Peter.* "As God is my witness, I will never forgive him."

He let go of her hands. "You didn't marry?" *he asked.*

"No."

"You were waiting for me?"

"Yes."

He had put his hands in his pockets now, as if that would stop them reaching out for her. There was a long pause.

"I have a child," *he said at last.* "A son, Flavia. He's called Daniel."

She nodded. But she didn't want to hear about his son.

"I am so awfully sorry," *he said.* "What can I do? I . . ."

His eyes were full of pain. It reminded her of when she had first found him by the broken glider, in the tangled wreckage.

"Please do not worry," *she said.* "I will be perfectly all right." *To herself, she sounded like a machine speaking, but Peter clutched onto her words like a drowning man onto a life raft.*

"Are you sure?" he said. "Because you could come back to the house. Molly—"

"No." Flavia reached up to kiss his cheek. Not that. His skin was cool and damp. With her fingertip she touched his lips. "Good-bye, Peter," she said.

And she turned to walk away, upright and strong—at least for the first few steps, for she knew that he would be watching her, and she knew how it hurt to let her go. Because he had come for her . . . He had come all the way to Sicily for her. And she had never, never known. So he mustn't guess how hard this was.

Around the first corner, she crumpled. The tears were hot in her eyes. "Papa, I hate you," she muttered. "I hate every bone in your body."

From nowhere, a man stepped out of the shadows. His arms were raised and Flavia stepped back instinctively, raising her own arms in defense. Close by, a train chugged down the line. And the moon slipped out of its cloud cover, full and luxuriant and ready for a night out on the town.

"Oh," said Flavia, with a kind of choked surprise. "It is you."

Flavia stared at the words in the notebook. When Tess read this she would finally understand why she, Flavia, had never returned to Sicily and why she disliked even talking about the place. She had forgiven neither her father nor her mother for what they had done. The bitterness had burned inside her for years.

Only now . . . Only now, with a daughter and a grand-daughter of her own, could she begin to comprehend her father's belief that he was doing the right thing, his certainty that he was the best judge of his own daughter's future happiness. Only now that she was writing these words, telling this story that she had thought she would always keep locked in her heart . . . Only now that he was gone, could she feel the first stirrings of forgiveness in her heart for Papa, for Mama, for Sicily.

The young man from the tearoom had taken her firmly by the arm and escorted her back to the house where he lived with his mother. "Don't be scared," he said. "I won't hurt you."

Flavia had nodded. She wasn't scared. She didn't care enough. About anything.

"You can stay here for the night," he said, in his kind, caressing voice.

So she had.

She could hardly remember that night—she'd cried most of it away. And in the morning, she'd taken the train back to London, with their address written on a piece of paper in her bag. When she got back to London, she had written a polite note to thank them for their kindness, and that—she had thought—was that.

She continued working for Bea Westerman—although it was some time before she could tell her what had happened with Peter that night.

And then, when she'd been there for almost a year, Bea made the proposal that would change her life and give her a new passion—something to live for and something to work for.

She had much, Flavia reflected now, to thank Bea Westerman for.

* * *

Sicily—an island surrounded by sea. Living in Cetaria there was always the smell of the sea and always the taste of the fish that came from it. Fishermen like Alberto Amato who went out to sea every day in all weathers and who rarely returned empty handed. They would take a cart round the village to sell their catch.

Flavia remembered the fish market in Trapani, the grizzled fishermen, the fish—so many varieties—laid out on slabs, some already filleted, shiny and gleaming, their scales a rainbow of color and light. Tuna, sardines, anchovies . . . Scorpion fish, eel, mackerel, and squid. Clams, cuttlefish, red mullet, swordfish. *Each fish has its time. The question you ask at the market is not how much, but how fresh . . . ?*

So much had changed in the fishing industry. More fishing, fewer fish—it made sense. Drift nets taking too much from the sea; the bloody drama of the *mattanza . . .*

There were many recipes to include. Anchovies, for example—small, but big in flavor. *Pasta con le acciughe. Heat gently,* she wrote, *for they can easily become bitter.* Tuna cooked sweet and sour with vinegar, *a sfinciuni* with anchovy and onion, or stewed with garlic, mint, and cloves. *Sarde a beccafico*: the most famous recipe using sardines, a specialty of Palermo. *The name comes from the small bird—* beccafico*—with the tail feathers that stick up in the air. Use pine nuts, bread crumbs, and parsley to stuff. The sardines are rolled from top to tail, packed tightly, and presented so that the bay leaf stalks and the sardine tails point up like the tail of the* beccaficio. That would make her daughter smile . . .

A taste of the sea. Of lightness and movement and liquid and sun.

Sicilian food is playful, and above all, it is given respect. Sicilians understand what it is to be hungry. They always have.

CHAPTER 53

GINNY STILL STRUGGLED WITH CALLING HIM "DAD," though since his appearance in her life she had seen him most days. ("We're bonding," she had said to Becca, "but it's more glue stick than superglue.") They quite often went off somewhere in the VW—stopping for a pub lunch or coffee and having Philosophical Discussions.

"Whatever you plan to do in life," he said, "just remember that you can change your mind."

Which sounded a bit wishy-washy to Ginny. She could just see Nonna picking up an oven mitt and saying, "Lack of drive, my dear," in her clear, firm, accented English.

"Yeah?" she said doubtfully.

"It's called going with the flow," he said.

The Ball had insinuated more than once that her father's philosophy was one of cowardly self-interest, but Ginny had to admit that it had some appeal.

"What if you disappoint other people?" she'd asked.

"It's your life."

"What if you regret it later?"

He shrugged. "It was your choice."

"But how do you know?" she said, "if it's the right thing at the right time, or the right thing at the wrong time, or the wrong at the right, or whatever?"

He blinked. "You don't."

"Oh." Ginny wasn't used to the notion of uncertainty. She wasn't sure if it was a good thing or a bad. Although in her father's philosophy, she supposed, it wouldn't be either. It would just be.

"The thing is," he explained, "when we make ourselves do something we don't want to do, or someone else makes us do what we don't want to do, it makes us feel bad."

Too true. Ginny knew the Ball wouldn't question that one. It was a parasite. It fed off such things.

"So the simplest answer," he said, "is not to do it."

"The easiest option," murmured Ginny.

"Not necessarily." He met her gaze, and the expression in his eyes told her that he was thinking of the time he went to Australia and refused to be a dad. "It may be the most honest, and it's the only way to be true to yourself. But it's not easy."

Ginny considered this. It was true that if she refused to go to uni—which was academic, as she wouldn't get a place anyway—then it wouldn't be easy. She would upset people—her mother and Nonna, especially—but at least she would be true to herself. And when she came to think about it, she realized that no one could or would make her go. Oh, her mother might have a lost-opportunities rant, but in the end she couldn't do jumping jellyfish about it. And she wouldn't. At the end of the day, her mother wanted her to be happy.

"I love my mum," she said to this man who had also loved her mum and had also let her down.

He nodded. "Sure you do."

"But I need to get away from her for a while," she said. "She keeps me too safe."

He raised an eyebrow. "It's good to be safe."

"Yeah." And she laughed, because this was about the first normal parental thing he'd said to her. "But I need to . . ." It sounded stupid.

"Discover yourself?" he said.

"Well, yeah. Sort of." Find me, she was going to say. Find a different sort of me. The sort of me who can live without a mother looking after me the whole time, the sort of me who can vanquish a Ball.

"I know how you feel," her father said. "You don't have to hold it in." And he reached over and touched her arm, and she believed him. And she felt its grip relax, like a loose tentacle, as if the Ball had been expecting something else, as if it were disappointed, for the first time in Its life.

CHAPTER 54

FLAVIA HAD TO CONCENTRATE HARD TO REMEMBER the order of events. It seemed important. She wanted to make her account as accurate as possible for Tess. But it was easier to recall the emotions than the facts. Perhaps that was always the way.

A few months after she'd seen Peter in Exeter, Flavia received a letter from the young man in the tearoom who had taken her home to stay with him and his mother that night.

"I'm coming to London," he wrote. "Could we meet?"

Flavia wasn't sure; she didn't want any reminders of the night in Exeter, but Bea persuaded her that it was only common courtesy. "And think," she said. "What would you have done that night without him, my dear?"

This was true. So Flavia met him, and he bought her fish and chips from a café in Shepherds Bush and a half pint of Guinness in the Royal Crown. It was a foggy winter's night at the end of February and hard to imagine that spring might be around the corner. In England, she guessed, spring would be a long time coming. And the fog . . . Smog, they called it, in London. Flavia saw it as a mysterious cloak—a shroud— that covered the city while cars and buses crept and grumbled by and silent trolley buses glided through the grainy yellow light. She knew it caused health problems, but still—there was something she liked about its strange and heavy silence.

"It will pass when the weather warms up," Bea Westerman had told her. "It's pollution—from the coal smoke." Flavia could believe this. It was like trying to breathe through a thick layer of muslin, and it made everyone look pinched and gray. Not him, though. He looked red faced, healthy, and smiling. Like a breath of fresh air.

He didn't refer to what had happened in Exeter, but he asked Flavia how she was liking life in London.

"It is different," she confessed. She looked around the pub; this, too, was a revelation to her. Its beery smell, its dinginess, the big mirrors advertising the ales, the posters about the latest election campaign, the stained carpet, the men in suits stand- ing at the bar—it was nothing like the bars of her homeland.

Part of her longed for the warmth of Sicily. And yet . . . Here she was so free. She had begun to explore the city. She had visited the market of Petticoat Lane and the Bengali shops in Brick Lane with their dusky spices, bright silks, and Indian sweetmeats. She had bought flowers and vegetables from Cov- ent Garden. She had found an Italian quarter around Holborn with a church—St. Peter's—at its heart, and she came here every Sunday to think and to pray. Her God had not given her what she wanted most in the world . . . And she wasn't entirely sure that she even believed in Him anymore. But the sense of God was a comfort to her; it seemed to give her strength.

She discovered Soho, too—a maze of narrow streets in which she felt strangely at home, perhaps because the area was such a mishmash of European and African street life, cafés, and jazz clubs. She was not stupid—she knew about the more dubious nightclubs and sex trade, but in the daytime there was a vibrancy about this area that drew her. She even found an Italian coffee bar—with an espresso machine, arty decor, and a jukebox—and she stayed there for an hour on her day off, drinking espresso, soaking up the atmosphere, and wondering . . . What would she do next?

"So," he said, "what will you do next?"

Precisely. "I do not know," she confessed. She couldn't envisage working for Bea Westerman forever. What she wanted more than anything was to open her own restaurant—she had seen what passed for restaurants in England, and she knew she could do better—if she could only find produce of sufficient quality to cook with. There were Italian restaurants in London—though some of them were rather seedy. And she had walked past an Italian trattoria on Gerrard Street that looked a lot more promising. She knew now that others like her had come not only from India, Jamaica, and Pakistan, but also from Sicily to England to make a living. They were willing to work hard, and they often worked in nurseries and restaurants—because who knew more than the Sicilians about food? And it was becoming easier all the time to procure ingredients such as balsamic vinegar, parmagiano, and good olive oil. But . . . she still wasn't sure that England was ready for what she had to offer.

She told him this.

"Then do it," he said. "Make them ready for it. Give them what they don't even know they want."

"But how can I?" She spread her hands. "To start a business you need money. I know this. And I have so little saved."

"Nothing's impossible." He seemed very serious. "I'd like to run my own café, too. I will one day." He hesitated for just a second. "Maybe we should join forces."

Flavia laughed. But somehow she knew even then that he meant what he said.

After that meeting, he wrote to her regularly, and she wrote back. Their letters were polite to begin with, and Flavia knew hers were stilted and awkward—her English was improving, but sometimes it felt like one step forwards and two steps backwards, as the English might say.

But gradually she loosened up, and he got braver, and letters streaked back and forth between them—letters packed full with their lives, their sadnesses, their hopes, and their dreams. He was three years younger than Flavia; at times he sounded like a man, at other times a boy. Perhaps, she thought, she had grown old before her time.

"Will you ever go back to Sicily?" he asked her.

"No." Flavia didn't have to think about it. England might be cold and damp, but this was where her new life was. England was still recovering after the hard war years; there was much reconstruction. But more than that—there was that feeling of hope in the air. And Flavia needed that. She still wrote to Santina, but she hadn't answered any of her parents' letters. There was no going back.

Every so often he traveled by train to London to see her, and she came to look forward to his visits. He was never pushy—she couldn't have stood that—but he was kind, and he was good company, too. He became a friend.

It was in September that year that Bea Westerman took Flavia to the Dome of Discovery, whose exhibition was part of the Festival of Britain. The banks of the Thames had become a haunt of Flavia's during the summer—Tower Beach was the nearest London got to the seaside, and on warm days the sandy banks were full of people sitting in stripy deck chairs and children paddling in the river. It was a far cry from Cetaria—but Flavia liked to sit and watch these English families, though there was a part of her that couldn't help but recall that other family, in Exeter . . .

According to Bea, the South Bank had been an area of shabby warehouses and near-derelict housing, but this had been cleared and developed to create a site for the 1951 Festival of Britain and the Royal Festival Hall. Just the outside of the Dome and the floating, needle-like Skylon tower standing next to it were mesmerizing for Flavia—and she could have stared at this vision of modernity for hours. But Bea was a woman with a mission. "Six million pounds," she murmured. "A million bricks."

"Truly?" Flavia followed her in.

Bea was philosophical. "It is meant to raise the nation's spirits, my dear," she said. "After this war we've lived through, something has to, you know."

They were carried in with the rest of the crowds by an escalator, the interior of the building concealed until their moment of entry. Then . . . Da-daa! All was revealed—the magnificent tiers of galleries, the massive curving roof, latticed with rafters. There were gasps of wonder. "Ooh" and "Ahh" and "I say!"

Flavia, too, was entranced. This was, she had heard, the largest dome in the whole world. And she was walking through it. They began with the land of Britain—how Britain's natural

*wealth had come into being—and plowed on, through land-
scape and wildlife, agriculture and minerals, shipbuilding
and transport . . . The list of Britain's achievements was endless, thought Flavia, as they moved on to sea, sky, and space.
It was a world power such as she had never dreamed of. Compared with Britain, Sicily was a poor relation indeed. She
stood straighter—proud that she, Flavia Farro, was here in
London, witness to such a grand sight.*

*Bea was not impressed by the television exhibition. She
had never seen the need, she muttered. And this, frankly, was
almost beyond Flavia's imagination. And then there were the
British people . . . symbolized by the Lion and the Unicorn, the
strength and the imagination. She cast surreptitious glances
at those around her. These qualities were not altogether in evidence. But still . . . There had been men—explorers like Cap-
tain Cook and great scientists like Charles Darwin—who had
such qualities in abundance.*

*At last they retired to a nearby tearoom. "Did you enjoy it,
my dear?" asked Bea. "It's supposed to be very educational."*

*"Oh yes!" Flavia assured her. "You were so good to bring
me."*

*Bea's expression softened. "I have grown very fond of you,"
she said. "And that is why . . ."*

Flavia felt a sliver of foreboding.

*And sure enough, Bea took her hand. "I am leaving Lon-
don, my dear," she said. "I'm going to live with a woman friend
of mine. In Dorset."*

"Dorset?" Flavia frowned.

*"It's a small house," Bea continued. "And I'm terribly sorry,
my dear, but—"*

"I can't come with you," Flavia said. "You don't need me."

Bea lowered her head in acknowledgment. "My friend is very independent," she said. "She likes to cook and clean for herself." She stayed Flavia's hand and poured the tea with her own.

"I understand," said Flavia. She watched the golden liquid stream into the porcelain cup. But what would she do now? What could she do without this woman who had been so kind to her?

"Like me, Daphne has never married." Bea was still speaking. "She wants a lady companion." She stirred in milk and a small ration of sugar.

"Yes, of course." Though Flavia did not want to hear any more about Daphne.

"It will suit me very well," Bea said. "London, after all, is for the young."

It was true that after Cetaria, London was crowded, noisy, and frightening. But Flavia had grown accustomed to it. And now she would have to get a real job— it had only ever been a question of time.

"However," Bea said, taking a delicate sip of her tea. "I have a proposal for you, my dear."

The proposal turned out to be that Bea would put up a sum of money for a business. "I will have a reasonable sum to invest now that I'm moving out of London," she said. "And I rather like the idea of investing in you, my dear." They would purchase, she suggested, a café or a small restaurant in a place of Flavia's choosing, and Bea would become what was called a sleeping partner. Flavia would be a partner, too—a working partner—and as such would be manageress and get a share of the profits. And she could live in.

"We would need more staff, though," Bea said, pouring more tea.

Flavia stared at her. She could hardly believe what was happening. First the Dome of Discovery and now this. It was an extraordinary day indeed.

"Perhaps even another partner," Bea said. *"A man?"*

Flavia realized at once from the glint in Bea's eye that she'd been talking to a certain someone.

"Do you imagine that he'd be interested?" Bea asked, as if she didn't already know.

"I do," Flavia said.

And he was. After initial discussions, they decided to look for somewhere in Dorset—so that Bea could keep an eye on her investment and so that he wasn't too far from his mother. *"But not Devon,"* Flavia had stipulated.

"Not Devon," the others agreed.

It had taken more than a year to move and set up, but in March 1953 they finally opened the café in Pridehaven. Flavia was cook, he was host, and a young waitress helped wait at table.

To start off, with they served English food peppered with a few Italian dishes, then gradually introduced more Sicilian specialties. People tried Flavia's pasta and pizza, and they came back for more. Flavia got more adventurous, and she found good suppliers of vegetables, meat, and fish. And so the café gradually grew its own identity, which had evolved over time. The Azzurro was born.

Right from the start, Flavia found it easy to work with Lenny. He took a room in Pridehaven, but he was always at the Azzurro and willing to work just as hard as she did. That was hard.

Every Sunday they closed the café and took the day off, and that was when they went out—to the pictures, sometimes to a dance or even out for a meal. On the day of the queen's coronation they organized a street party, and when the day turned out cold and wet ("As you would expect of England in June," Flavia muttered to Lenny), they opened their doors to the entire street and celebrated the Sicilian way with a spread fit for the queen herself.

They seemed to move so seamlessly from being friends to being a couple that, thinking about it now, Flavia couldn't remember exactly when or how it had happened. He was younger than her, yes, but he possessed a quiet inner strength that calmed her.

And then on the first anniversary of the Azzurro's opening, as they toasted each other with a glass of champagne after they'd finished for the evening (in those days, they finished at eight but later stayed open till midnight sometimes), Lenny literally dropped down onto one knee.

"I know I'm not the one you'd have chosen," he said, looking up at her with those blue-violet eyes of his, "but I can tell you, Flavia, my darling, you're the one for me."

It was the only time he had ever referred to Peter, even by implication. She knew that he had seen them outside the tearoom in Exeter and that he probably even knew Peter and his wife, since they lived so close to where he had worked. God knows what Lenny had thought that night . . . She didn't tell him the whole story, though. She didn't want to relive it. And it was true—he was not the one she would have chosen. Santina alone knew what she felt for Peter— what she would always feel. But Lenny was the man who loved her and who worked with her and who would lay down his life for her.

"Is this a proposal?" she asked him, putting her hands on her hips.

"Yes, Flavia," he said solemnly. "Will you marry me?"

"Of course I will, Lenny," she said.

She never wrote to Santina again. Her old friend was part of it, of Sicily and the past. Flavia only wanted the future now.

The seasons go by and the seasons cannot lie. In the Sicilian kitchen you use what is available. In spring there are almonds, asparagus, and early peaches. In summer there are figs, melanzane, *and zucchini.*

To the ancient Romans, the globe artichoke was believed to be an aphrodisiac. Protect by its outer leaves or the heart will wither and perish . . .

The season was from November till April. At festival time it was possible to go to a restaurant and eat artichokes with every course . . . The best artichokes were from her village and the countryside nearby. Everyone knew that Palermo wore the Artichoke Crown. Flushed pink and purple, long stemmed, rough leaved, their globes small and tender; Flavia remembered them being sold from barrows, piled high.

The dishes range from antipasto to risotto, from caponata *to* frittedda. *Stewed, braised, roasted, barbequed, fried, or grilled. Baby artichokes raw in salads. A light stuffing slipped between their petals. Simple is best.*

There is an art to cooking the artichoke, Flavia wrote, imagining as always that she was addressing Tess. *Like everything that is good, it requires patience . . . First, prepare. Cut off the stem; remove only the tough outer leaves, cut away any prickly collar, the stalk, and the top. Take a cut lemon . . . Squeeze . . .*

Of seasons that go by and seasons that cannot lie.

* * *

From her writing room, Flavia heard a shout from the garden.

She made her way outside. Lenny had apparently left his fork and his bucket on the lawn and appeared to have vaulted the dividing wall into Cathy and Jim's garden. How else could he be running across their garden even now? Flavia's stomach was churning. Lenny . . .

Cathy had heard the commotion, too, and came out of her back door just as Lenny tipped himself over the wall into Edna's garden. What on earth . . . ? As if he was thirty-something, not seventy-something. He had always kept himself fit with gardening and walking, but this was something else again. Had the man lost his mind?

CHAPTER 55

TESS WAS WALKING BACK TO THE VILLA TO GET changed. She was due to meet up with Giovanni for more discussions about the loan to fund the refurbishment of the villa. She had to get things moving, but did she want to be obligated to Giovanni? If Tonino was to be believed, the Sciarras were not a pleasant family. Apart from Santina, of course, who was lovely. And Giovanni? Well, Tess couldn't make her mind up about Giovanni. And then her cell rang.

"Muma?"

"It's your father." Her mother didn't mince words.

"What about him?" Scenarios fast-forwarded through her brain. Her stomach catapulted to her feet. "Is he ill? What's happened?"

"He had a fall."

Oh God! "Is he hurt? Is he okay?" She held on to the wall of the *baglio* for support. Her father wasn't the one she ever worried about. He was always there, stable, keeping the status quo.

"He went to the hospital. He has some cuts and bruises. And his wrist is broken." Tess noticed how shaky her mother's voice sounded, how vulnerable.

"Oh, Muma." But Tess exhaled in relief. Cuts and bruises and a broken wrist weren't life threatening. "Any other damage?" she asked. She was thinking stroke and heart attack and trying not to.

"No, darling. I just wanted to let you know."

But Tess was already making plans. "I'll catch the next available flight. You shouldn't be on your own. I need to see him. I—" She hurried up the steps from the *baglio*. She'd pack, get to the airport, go on standby; that would be the best thing.

"Tess." Her mother's voice grew stern. "He's fine now. Really. He is already back at home. Do you want to speak with him?"

Did she? "Of course, yes please, Muma," she said. She put her key in the lock. "Dad?"

"I'm all right, sweetheart." Thank goodness . . .

"What have you been up to, then?" She tried to keep her voice light.

"Oh, you know. Trying to be a hero."

Tess smiled. He had always been her hero. She remembered following him round the apartment above the Azzurro, while he did whatever DIY job was on the agenda that day. *My little apprentice*, he used to call her. She remembered fetching and carrying in the Azzurro, too, doing errands, wiping tables, fetching pastries from the kitchen. He always had time for her. When she had a problem at school, she could always tell him, when she was lost, when she didn't understand . . . "It'll work itself out, love," he would say. "You'll see."

"I think you should put away your cape, Dad," she said. "Don't you reckon it's time to slow down a bit?" She walked through the kitchen, slung her bag over a chair, grabbed some mineral water from the fridge, and poured herself a glass.

"You could be right." He chuckled. "And I don't need you to come rushing back, my girl. I'm fine. I've got your mother clucking around me like an old hen. Not to mention your daughter."

"You should be so lucky." But Tess smiled.

"I'll pass you back, love. Muma wants to talk to you."

"Okay. You take care now. Big hug." Tess went out onto the terrace. Down below, the sea looked cool and inviting. She wished she could dive in from here . . .

Her mother came back on and filled her in with more of the details.

"For God's sake," she said, when her mother came to the end of the story, "he's almost eighty. He's got to stop doing this sort of stuff. He's an old man." Though it hurt to say it.

"No need to rub it in," said her mother. "You know your father—if someone needs rescuing, he will step into the brooch."

"Breech," said Tess absently. But she was right. "So he's really okay?"

"How many times? He is really okay."

"And Ginny?"

"Ginny is fine."

"And David?"

"David?"

"Come on, Muma." Tess took another sip of water. "What does he want? Do you have any idea? Do you think I should come back to see what's going on?"

"He has written to you," her mother said. "Perhaps you should wait to hear what he has to say."

"Written to me?" That didn't sound like David. Tess transferred her cell to the other ear. She got to her feet once more and walked down the terraced garden, past the broken fountain and the hibiscus, listening to her mother's voice as she talked about David's reappearance in their lives.

"Ginny needs to spend time with him," her mother was saying. "I think it is doing her good. You know, maybe our daughters need their fathers more than we want to believe, Tess, hmm?"

Tess stared out toward the ruin of the cottage her mother's family had lived in. Just a pile of stones . . . Thought of the Sicilian girl and her English airman. "That's all very well, Muma," she said, when her mother paused. "But David chose to leave in the first place, if you remember."

She had accepted from the start that she was a single parent who'd have to manage alone—or at least without a man. And she'd never asked David for a thing—it would have been pointless, since he never had anything. She had always resisted the impulse to bad-mouth him to her daughter, and in any case she didn't have anything against him apart from the fact that he'd run away. But . . . Turning up now—when she wasn't around and when things were difficult with Ginny, annoyed her. It was so typical, so careless.

"I know that," her mother said. "Only perhaps it was not as easy for David as you thought."

"Yeah, well it wasn't easy for me either." Her mother knew that better than anyone. She was the one who was there for Tess after Ginny was born, who helped her through the postnatal tears, the loneliness, the sheer terror of looking after a baby alone. What would Tess have done without her? She went back to the wrought iron table and took another long swallow of her mineral water. She was still tempted to get on the next available flight—what with her father and David. And now that everything had backfired with Tonino . . . But on the other hand, she should stay and get the building work on the villa underway at least. And she needed to talk to Giovanni.

"What is the harm in letting David spend time with Ginny?" her mother asked.

She was right. What harm could David do? He wasn't unkind, and Ginny was his daughter. Ginny was old enough to look after herself, and she did have her grandparents to watch out for her. Added to this, none of her family seemed to want Tess to come home . . .

A thought occurred to her. "Would Ginny come out here, do you think, Muma? For a holiday? Would you and Dad come, too?"

She heard the intake of breath. "I do not think so, Tess," she said.

"But wouldn't you like to see it all again, Muma?" She looked around the dilapidated terrace. "The villa, the *baglio*, the village . . . ?" It was hard to comprehend. Whatever her mother felt about the place, Cetaria was still where her family had lived, where she had grown up. And the longer Tess stayed here, the more she could sense the fabric of her mother's life, the more she was beginning to understand her. She had been made tough by her experiences; Tess understood that now. It was a matter of survival, and of love.

"I am not sure that I could," her mother said at last. "It may be too much of a journey."

Tess thought of the pile of rubble on the other side of the garden wall. That might be hard. "Will you at least think about it?"

There was a long pause.

"There are days," her mother said, "when I hardly stop."

CHAPTER 56

FLAVIA THOUGHT SHE HAD COME TO THE END. NOT the end of their story—but that was part two, and Tess had been around for much of that, so what was the need to write it down? Did she really need to know the rest?

But there was something unsatisfactory about the story—she'd realized that even before Lenny's fall. It was unfinished, it left too much unsaid, it wasn't the whole truth. If she died tomorrow, Tess wouldn't know—just as it turned out Lenny hadn't known.

It had been a shock. They never had much trouble in Pridehaven. It was an area with a low crime rate, and most of the young people were nice enough, though some were a bit noisy. Most looked far fiercer than they really were. It wasn't a bad place.

When Lenny first heard the shouting and Edna's voice raised, he should have called Flavia, or the police, instead of resorting to DIY.

In Edna's garden, their neighbor told Flavia later, were two youths. One was trampling her flower beds at the bottom of the garden; the other was halfway across the lawn.

"Kindly remove yourself from my property, young man," Edna told him. "Or I'll call the police."

"Aw, I'm so scared," said the boy, just as Lenny launched himself heroically onto the lawn.

"Come here, you little toe-rag," yelled Lenny. ("He was very masterful," Edna added). "Let me at you."

Boy One now had a muddy foothold on the back fence and was scaling it like a rat up a drainpipe. And despite the fact that he was being threatened by a red-faced elderly man wearing sunflower-yellow gardening gloves, Boy Two was legging it down the garden.

"Run away, would you?" snarled Lenny and gave chase.

"He didn't see Tabitha," said Edna, when recounting the story to Flavia. "She was in her favorite spot by the nasturtiums. But she's such a nervous cat. She streaked in front of Lenny, and he tripped right over her. Fell face down on the path."

Fortunately, by then, Boy Two was already disappearing over the fence, unaware that his adversary had fallen.

"I'm so sorry," Edna said to Flavia. "Tabitha was terrified, you see."

"It wasn't your fault," Flavia reassured her. "Or Tabitha's." Flavia couldn't even blame Lenny. How could you blame someone for being who he was?

Edna got to Lenny as soon as she could. She thought at first he'd had a heart attack—so she performed artificial respiration and put Lenny in the recovery position before phoning for an ambulance. She'd watched *Casualty* enough times, and the temptation was just too much. "Anyone," she said, "would have done the same."

By the time Flavia arrived by the more conventional route of the pavement, the garden path, and the front door, Lenny was sitting up with a cut lip, gingerly examining his wrist.

Flavia had been shocked at the state of him. His face was cut, too, and there was a big lump on his temple. His arms and legs were badly grazed, and his hand was limp and twisted. She went with him in the ambulance, held his hand, and prayed to the Madonna she had last prayed to in Sicily when she was a girl.

"It's just a fall, love," he kept saying to her.

But to Flavia it felt like a warning.

"We've been happy, haven't we, Flavia my darling?" he said as they arrived at the emergency room.

Flavia stared at him. "You said it was just a fall. Why are you talking as if you're at death's window, for the love of God?"

"Door," he said. "Death's door."

"Door, window, wherever . . ." Flavia clicked her tongue.

"Tell me," he said. "Tell me we've been happy."

"Yes, Lenny," she said. "We have been happy." Yes, it was only a fall. But sometimes a fall could shake everything up.

And that's when Flavia knew.

CHAPTER 57

GINNY HAD A LOT OF STUFF TO TELL BECCA WHEN they met up for pizza and a long-overdue girlie chat.

They started with Pops's fall.

"Until it happened," Ginny told her, "everything was going tickety tigers." The Ball had been keeping a low profile. Ginny guessed It was only sulking and that pretty soon it would show Its face again, but for now, she was enjoying the reprieve.

"That's life," said Becca in a philosophical un-Becca-like way. "It's all swings and bloody roundabouts."

Ginny had been working in the Bull and Bear early Saturday evening when the call came through. Magic Fingers had just started their set; lots of rhythm, lots of juice, and Albie was looking dark and sexy and as bemused as ever. Not for long, she decided.

Ginny could serve drinks in her sleep now. She was so fast, she almost knew what they would order before they asked for it. She could do shots while a pint was pouring, crack open a beer while she ladled out ice. She knew who'd been waiting longest, and while they were waiting she could keep them in line.

She'd met up with Albie a couple of times so far. He was nice. She reckoned that he'd be easy to fall in love with or run away with or give up anything for. So she was holding back. She didn't want to start what she couldn't finish. Not yet anyway. And she had places to go. Someone to find. While Albie—who had his music and his songwriting and the band—seemed okay with that. For now.

"I'll have a pint of best, please, Ginny, my darling." That was her father, who had come to hear the music—and probably to check out Albie, who she'd mentioned at dinner the other night.

The phone in the pub rang and rang, and at last Brian answered it. Ginny could see that he could hardly hear: he covered his other ear and yelled into the receiverl then he lasered a look straight at her and Ginny flinched.

"What?" she mouthed at him, continuing to serve a customer.

He came up to her, put an arm round her shoulder. "Better get your coat, love," he said.

"What? What's happened?" In the busy, noisy pub, Ginny's eyes looked for her father's. He was some way from where she stood, but he saw her immediately.

"Dad," she said.

"Wow," said Becca. "So you had a sort of Dad moment?"

"Yeah." Ginny sipped her Coke. Her first.

"And your Granddad's okay?"

Their pizzas with garlic bread on the side and large fries to share arrived. Ginny's was Margherita with extra pepperoni, and Becca's was a four-cheese special.

"He's fine." Ginny bit into the garlic bread. It was crisp, deep, and pungently perfect. His wrist was splinted up and his arm was in a sling. But apart from the blue-yellow bruises creeping around his mouth and jaw, he was fine.

Becca loaded chips onto her pizza and cut a slice. "What does your mum say about your dad turning up, then?" she asked, before wrapping her mouth around it.

"She's been pretty cool," Ginny admitted. Lately, she'd had a chance to see things from a different point of view. And she'd come to the conclusion that her mother was a bit special.

She knew that her dad had written to Mum, too, and she had an inkling what it might be about.

"Now," said Becca. "Tell me about Ben."

Ginny obliged.

"What a dick," said Becca, when Ginny finished. "It's not you who should have been doing something else in bed, Gins, it's him. Come here."

And as Ginny leaned closer, she instructed her in some of the finer details of sexual artistry and expectation, both of them punctuating the lesson with mouthfuls of Coke and pizza. "For next time," she said with a wink.

Ginny thought of Dark and Bemused. "For next time," she agreed.

"So what's on the agenda now?" Becca sat back at last, her plate empty.

"I'm going traveling," Ginny said. "To Australia."

"Blimey, Gins," said Becca, "I was talking about dessert."

Over chocolate brownies and whipped cream, Ginny told her what her father had said.

"I've got a place in Sydney you can use as a base." Bought presumably since the windfall, Ginny thought. "Just say the word, and I'll hand over the keys."

"Would you be there in Sydney?" she'd asked him, not knowing if she would want him to be or not.

He shrugged. "I was thinking of doing some traveling of my own," he said. "In the van. Europe maybe. I kind of missed it out before."

"Cool," said Becca. "Is it easy to get work in Australia? Is it easy to travel around?"

Ginny was savoring the taste of melted chocolate and cream. There was nothing like it. "Simple Simon, my dad says. The hostels give you all the info you need about jobs and stuff and where to head for next. Some of the back-packers do bar work, some do telemarketing, some do fruit picking."

Becca didn't comment on the "my dad" stuff. And that was good because sometimes Ginny couldn't get her head round it either. Like one minute she was fatherless, and the next he was there, being, well, being what she seemed to need. Ginny kind of understood now that he hadn't turned his back on her; he had turned his back on fatherhood. Which was bad, but maybe not as bad. She wouldn't forget the lost years, though. How could she?

"Amazing," Becca said, spooning the last of the dessert into her mouth.

"The brownies?"

"Your dad."

"Yeah, well . . ." He had made a lot of mistakes. He wasn't perfect or even near perfect. He was different, that was all.

Becca's father wore suits and worked in a bank, and her mother was a lunch lady in a school. They were never going to compete.

"Do you need a traveling buddy?" Becca asked, finishing her Coke.

"You are joking?" Ginny stared at her. She hadn't wanted to admit to anyone that this was the aspect of the trip that worried her the most. It was all very well to go off to find yourself, but who would count to ten and then help you look?

"I'm deadly serious." Becca wiped her mouth with a napkin. "I'd love it. Seriously, Gins, we'd have such a good time."

Well, they would, but, "What about Harry?" she asked.

Becca pouted. "Who's Harry?"

"You haven't—?"

"No." Becca shook her head. "But he's not the whole world, Gins. He's taking off to uni soon. And then what?"

"We'll have to do some serious saving," Ginny said. Her father might help her out, but she wanted to do some of it for herself.

"I've got some dough coming my way on my eighteenth next month," Becca said. "Courtesy of rich Auntie Margaret. She doesn't have any kids of her own."

"Done!" So that was it, Ginny thought, joining Becca in a high five. She had a plan, she had a base, she had a buddy. And she had a rich father, too. Just think—not so long ago, the only remarkable thing about her life was that she might be pregnant.

CHAPTER 58

THE LETTER ARRIVED A FEW DAYS LATER. EVEN AFTER all this time, Tess recognized David's writing immediately —thin and slopey, just like him.

She resisted the urge to rip it open at once. Instead, she made coffee, took it out onto the terrace, and admired the view down into the bay (the sea was like a millpond today, the sky that deep dark Mediterranean blue that she loved), allowing the envelope to sit unopened on the table for a while. Let him wait.

Down in the *baglio*, the day was taking shape. Beneath the silver spread of the eucalyptus tree, she could see a group of men sitting on the bench by the stone fountain, playing dominoes or cards, probably, and a few people wandering out of the café and across the cobbles. She could see Tonino's studio and Tonino himself. Moving back and forth, shifting bits and pieces from one place to another. Restless, she thought. And stubborn. Why did she have to meet a man who was so damned stubborn?

Yesterday, she had gone diving again, but it was like running the gauntlet, getting past him and his dark, angry face. Was he angry because she was still diving alone or because she was the sole representative of her mother's family, who had once dishonored a member of his family? God . . . Whatever—it was a criminal waste of time and good chemistry.

She almost stamped her foot, she was so cross, then laughed out loud at herself. It was all so ridiculous. She took a last look at the turquoise bay, *i faraglioni*, the tall pinnacles jutting from the sea, and returned to The Letter.

What was happening back home? She had spoken to Ginny and Muma and Dad in the past couple of days, and everyone seemed calm. *We're fine*, they all reassured her. *Everything's fine* . . . No wonder she was worried.

And now David. She slit the letter open with her thumbnail and unfolded the top section, as if it might be dangerous to look at it all at once.

"Dear Tess," he had written. "It's been a while."

Typical understatement. She unfolded the single sheet properly. and something dropped out. A check. She picked it up, stared at it, turned it over in her hands. A check for fifty thousand pounds. God in heaven . . .

Putting it aside, she turned back to the letter. Now it had her complete attention.

"I hope you don't mind me turning up like this," he wrote, "hoping to see our daughter." *Our daughter* . . . That rankled. In the list of absentee fathers, he'd be top.

"But something happened to change my life. I came into some money, Tess."

In spite of herself, she smiled. His voice, emerging in the words he'd written, hadn't changed one bit. He was still the David she'd first met walking barefoot on the beach at Pride Bay. The David who sang songs to her and strummed on his guitar. Who talked of far-off places and how he was going to take her there. The David she'd fallen head over heels in love with, knowing that he was nothing but a dreamer. She'd known he wanted her. But she'd also known—from the start—that he didn't want responsibility, he didn't want commitment, and he certainly didn't want a baby.

Tess hadn't planned it; though she had been as careless as he. But once it was done, she couldn't undo it like he wanted her to. Simple.

"Now you know my thoughts on money . . ."

Easy come, easy go, thought Tess.

"But this is the sort of money that changes lives."

Clearly. She snuck another look at the check. Where had it come from—had he robbed a bank or just won the lottery?

"I don't want to change your life," he continued. "But I do want to pay up what I owe you. I hope you'll take it, and I hope it'll be useful."

Jesus wept . . . Tess picked up the check again. It really was fifty grand, and it really was for her.

But how could she accept it? Wasn't it, well, unethical or something? And what would he want in return? Nothing, she realized. David wouldn't want a thing—that was one of the nicest things about him.

"I would have liked to see you, Tess," the letter went on. "I would have liked to do this face-to-face. I suppose I wanted to find out if you could forgive me—for not being there for you, for not being a proper father to our kid, and all the rest of it . . ."

All the rest of it, she thought . . . But in a way, she would have liked to have seen him, too. Not to resuscitate old feelings—they could never do that. But just to say "hi" for old times' sake.

"I expected Ginny to be angry. To—I don't know—hate me. But she doesn't seem to. She seems to be okay about spending time with me. And I'm trying real hard not to say the wrong thing to her."

Tess smiled at this.

"And then there's you," the letter continued. "I know you (or I used to), and I reckon you'll be big hearted enough not to mind me seeing her and not to mind me helping out. Better late than never, huh?"

Tess wasn't too sure about that. She had minded him seeing Ginny, but from a purely selfish point of view. Now she did a rethink. Why should she deny her daughter the right to get to know her own father? What David said was true. Better late than never. And he was no threat to her. How could he be?

So should she take the money? Probably not. She'd done all right alone up till now.

There was a P.S. "You've done a great job with Ginny, by the way. She's beautiful. And she has your smile."

Tess folded the letter and replaced it with the check in the envelope. Had she done a great job with Ginny? She had made herself more distant than she had to be—by succumbing to the pull of Sicily instead of being there for her. Did Tess have any right to all this me-time? First and foremost, she was a mother. But . . .

She'd done what she felt was right at the time. And no one was trying to make her feel guilty for it. So. She probably shouldn't take the money. She smiled. But then again . . .

CHAPTER 59

IT WAS, FLAVIA THOUGHT, THE SCENTS OF *LA CUCINA* that were at its heart, that kept it alive, that she had tried to replicate in her English kitchens—first at Bea Wester-man's, then in the Azzurro and finally in her own kitchen too. Cardamom, cloves, broom and honey—aromatic and heady . . . Sun-dried tomatoes, plaits of garlic bulbs, strings of waxy red chili peppers—hot, dusty, and spicy . . . Caramel, vanilla, apricot, and peach—sweet, rich, and fruity, resonant of *dolce*. *Cannoli* was the *dolce* most ancient and most associated with Sicily—and with weddings, too, as it happened.

This pastry tube filled with ricotta, honey, and candied fruit was considered phallic and was originally served at wed-dings as a fertility symbol. Canna, *meaning "cane" also means the barrel of a gun. The* scorza *(the crunchy casing of the can-noli) must be deep-fried for one minute in very hot oil—to seal in the sweetness. When they have drained and cooled, fill and sprinkle with icing sugar. Decorate with candied peel.*

Flavia smiled to herself. It was so rich and heady, almost too much for the palate. But she must include it here. No gaps. There were to be no gaps for Tess.

And so, for the rest of the story, thought Flavia.

* * *

The first time Peter turned up at the Azzurro was less than a year after Lenny and Flavia were married.

Flavia happened to be working in the front of the restaurant, as Lenny had gone out to organize a delivery.

She couldn't believe her eyes. She knew now exactly how he had felt that night in Exeter. He was standing at the counter. She stared at him, and he stared right back at her. He looked just the same—blond hair a little longer and wispier, angular cheekbones, those eyes . . . He looked hardly older, although he must now be heading toward thirty. Was it possible that so much had happened since she saw him last and yet he could have changed so little?

"How did you find me?" she asked at last.

"It wasn't easy." Their gazes were still locked. Another time, she thought. Another time, another place. He held out his hand, and she put her hand inside his palm, where his fingers curled around it like flames.

Some customers came in and broke the moment. Flavia served them, conscious all the time of Peter's steady blue gaze, the question hovering around his mouth.

He sat in the corner by the window, and she brought him Italian coffee and a pastry. She sat down opposite him for a moment, to drink him in. Outside, it was raining. It was February. Always the most depressing month in England. But Peter was like sunshine; he always had been.

"I made a terrible mistake," he said. "It was just such a shock—seeing you, I mean."

"No." She thought of his wife and child. "You did the right thing."

He shook his head. "We were never happy," he said. "How can you be happy when you're still in love with someone else?"

Flavia thought of Lenny. He was a good man. He would be back soon, and she wouldn't hurt him. "You can live a decent life," she said. "You can be content." But inside, she longed to reach out for Peter, to stroke his face, to touch his hair, to kiss those lips. She longed for the feel of his body, long and lean against hers. She had never really had that, and she was conscious of the bitterness of regret.

As if he'd read her body language, he put out a hand toward her and teased a dark curl around his index finger. He cupped the side of her face in his right palm, and she leaned down, resting into it. Just for a second, she told herself.

"I've left Molly," he said.

She sat up straight. "And your son?" Her voice sounded ridiculously formal to her own ears.

He sighed. "I see him when I can. But I don't live there. I can't live there."

Gently, she touched his hand. "I am married now," she said.

"Yes." He nodded. He didn't seem surprised. "Of course you are, my beautiful Flavia. Any chap worth his salt would want you."

She felt something stir inside. The memory of this man when she had cared for him in Sicily swam to the surface, hot and liquid. "I am sorry," she said.

"Do you love him?" His blue eyes blazed into her. "Tell me that."

Not like I love you, she thought. "Yes, I love him," she said.

He left soon afterwards, left with a touch on her arm and the softest of kisses on her hair. "Good-bye, Flavia," he said.

Seconds later, Lenny appeared, back from Dorchester. He gave her a strange look, but said nothing. Perhaps he had not seen Peter; perhaps he would not remember who he was. He said nothing when Flavia wept silently into the pillow that night. But his breathing was heavy, so perhaps he was already asleep.

But when he said what he did in the ambulance, when he asked her to tell him that they had been happy—she realized that he had always known about Peter's visit, and had always wondered. And so, she thought. And so . . .

CHAPTER 60

As arranged, Tess went to meet Giovanni in the bar at the *baglio*. It was an airless day, and the sky felt heavy as if a storm was imminent. Tess pulled her hair back from her face; she felt warm and clammy. Giovanni was late (weren't Sicilians always?), so she bought a *caffè latte* and a *cannolo* and found a seat that did not have a view of Tonino's studio. She set to brooding about David's letter. And the money. Such a lot of money.

How could you calculate child support payments, she wondered, over eighteen years? She tasted the coffee—it was creamy, the final swirl of the espresso punctuating the froth of the milk. There were so many factors. Inflation and interest; school trips and holidays; Christmas presents and the mortgage. Not to mention food. And then there was the twenty-four-hour child care a mother did without thinking. Still . . . Fifty thousand pounds. She bit into the crisp pastry shell; inside, the filling was sweet, thick, and smooth on her tongue.

"Tess. *Ciao*." Giovanni had breezed in without her noticing. He looked hurried and slightly flushed, which was unusual. Where had he been hurrying from, she found herself wondering.

He kissed her, ordered espresso with a dash of hot milk, and sat in the seat opposite. He was carrying a slim black leather briefcase, and from this he extracted a manila folder.

All very businesslike, she thought, wiping flakes of pastry from her fingers. "What's this?" she asked.

"A simple contract for the loan," he said. "You will be glad to know that it is all arranged."

Tess sipped her coffee. It tasted bitter after the cloying sweetness of the *cannoli*. She wasn't glad. In fact she felt a tinge of anxiety. How could she put this, so he wasn't offended? "That's great, Giovanni," she said. "And I really do appreciate everything you've done to help me, but—"

"It is nothing." He waved his arms to indicate the amount of nothingness involved. "I am delighted to help." He hit himself on the chest for emphasis. "It is not so easy, always, to find the backing for these projects. And so I am overjoyed that I can do this thing for you."

Oh dear, thought Tess. It was all so extravagant, so theatrical. Though he didn't look overjoyed. And was that a smear of lipstick on his collar? *Should she, shouldn't she?* It was just that with David's letter coming when it did . . . It seemed like fate.

"The sooner we begin, the sooner we finish." Giovanni took charge of her plate and his espresso—pretty much like he took charge of everything, Tess observed—moving them to one side of the table. He laid out the contents of the envelope. "I have spoken to the builder," he said. "He is free to start next week."

Tess blinked at him in surprise. She hadn't even approved the builder—in fact she'd thought his quote rather high and she'd asked Pierro to recommend another company so that she could compare estimates. The other builder was coming over to the villa tomorrow. Also . . . There was something she hadn't liked about Giovanni's builder. Something about the way he wouldn't quite meet her eye. He was shifty.

"I'm not sure about the builder," she told him.

"What is wrong with him?" Giovanni grabbed his coffee and took a gulp.

"Well, I'm sure he's a good workman," Tess began.

"The best," said Giovanni.

"But his quote was rather high." Tess dug the estimate out of her bag as evidence.

He snatched it from her and began to study it, hemming and hawing, tutting and muttering: "That seems more than fair . . . This is fine . . . Hmm, good, yes . . . That is definitely right."

He came to his conclusion. "It is a very reasonable quote," he said.

Now why wasn't she surprised at that?

"Other builders may *estimate* less," Giovanni explained slowly, as if he were talking to a rather stupid child, "but they eventually charge *more*, Tess." He made the gesture of money in the hand. "We are in Sicily, now, remember." He let out a bark of laughter. "There are many different truths here. Nothing is simple."

Tess sighed. "I do appreciate your help, Giovanni," she repeated. "But I want a few more estimates—for comparison."

His face darkened.

"And don't forget what I said," she tried to sound firm, "about this being my project. I'm supposed to be making the decisions. Remember?"

His face fell. "Tess, Tess . . ." He took her hand and began playing absent-mindedly with her fingers.

She tried to extract them, but his grip only tightened. For some reason—though it was absurd—she felt a shiver of fear.

"Do you not know," he said, "that I wish only the best for you?" He brought her hand to his lips and kissed it.

Tess felt more uncomfortable than ever. She nodded. "Of course. You've been very—"

"And do you not know that our two families are like this?" He crossed the two fingers of his free hand together as he had done before. "Have always been like this?"

"Yes, I know," she said, thinking he protested too much, wishing he'd let go, wishing she'd never let him talk her into anything in the first place. Wishing she was somewhere else.

"So . . ." His voice was caressing. "Why worry your pretty head about these things, hmm? Let me take care of what I know best. I know this town, I know these builders. I can be your representative. It is no trouble."

Yes, but why, thought Tess. Why did he want to help her so very much?

"Do you know what it was?" she asked abruptly. "*Il tesoro*? This . . . *thing* that was stolen way back when? This theft that you told me about—supposedly carried out by Tonino's grandfather? Do you know where it came from?"

For a moment, his eyes flickered, and then he let go of her hand as if it had burned him. "Why?" he demanded. "Why do you want to know? Why does everyone want—?"

"*Everyone* want to know?" Tess pounced on this. "Who? Who wants to know?"

"No one." His mouth was a thin line. "No one, Tess. And no, I do not know what the artifact was, only that it was valuable. *Il tesoro.* Nor do I know where it is now. Do *you* have any idea?" His eyes seemed to bore into her. "Did your mother tell you? She must have known."

"No," she said. "She doesn't." She was not much more than a child. Why would she?

He folded his arms. "We will go ahead with this builder," he said. "Or . . ."

"Or?" Tess didn't like to be threatened—or blackmailed, if that was what he was doing.

"Or there will be no money," he said. "No money, no deal." He collected the papers into a pile and shuffled them into order. He looked very different now that he wasn't smiling. Hard and . . . well, ruthless.

Tess thought of the check, snug in her purse now. Thank you, David.

"Fine," she snapped. "No builder, no money, no deal." She got up, scraping back her chair.

Giovanni looked really angry now. But also confused—as if someone had outguessed him at poker. "You cannot do anything without the money, Tess," he said.

She leaned in close to him. "Watch me," she said.

He laughed. "No one else will lend it to you. I can guarantee that."

Tess opened her purse and put a few coins on the table to pay for her coffee and *cannoli.* "I don't need the money," she said.

He grabbed her wrist. "What do you mean, Tess? Why don't you need the money?"

She winced. "You're hurting me, Giovanni."

But he didn't let go.

She saw the waitress hovering—one look from Giovanni, and she disappeared behind the counter and out back. The only other customers got to their feet and left without seeming to notice anything out of the ordinary. Great. Tess might as well be invisible.

"You think you know the story, Tess." Giovanni's voice was a soft purr. "But ask your precious boyfriend where all his family's money came from. How a poor fisherman's son finds the money to buy business premises in the *baglio* at Cetaria." He got to his feet, still holding her wrist, and clamped his other hand on her shoulder.

"What are you saying?" She tried not to sound scared. She looked out of the window, but suddenly there was no one around.

"How convenient for that family to come into such a large sum of money at the same time as the disappearance of *il tesoro*," said Giovanni.

Tess decided she'd had enough. "None of this has anything to do with me," she said. "He has nothing to do with me." But even as she spoke, she felt a dart of betrayal. Tonino.

"Let me tell you something else, Tess." Giovanni's face was close to hers now. Too close. "It isn't only the money. My grandfather Ettore Sciarra disappeared just after the war, too. Just disappeared. At the same time as *il tesoro*. What do you make of that, eh? Eh?" His voice was rising.

Jesus. The plot thickened. Was Giovanni suggesting someone had murdered his grandfather? Certainly, he looked almost fanatical now, close enough for her to smell his sweat, to see the red veins in the whites of his eyes. "I have no idea," she said firmly. If she could only keep calm, she wouldn't enrage him further. And he would let go of her wrist and shoulder. She would give him another minute, she thought, and if he still wouldn't let her go, she'd kick him in the nuts. Hard.

"But I will tell you who knows," he snarled. "I will tell you who knows what happened to him."

Somehow, Tess wasn't surprised at this juncture to see Tonino come strolling into the *baglio*, looking as if he didn't have a care in the world. She saw him glance toward the bar, glance away, glance back again.

In three strides, he was in the doorway. In three more, he was by her side. "What in God's name are you doing?" He wrenched Giovanni's hands away.

"Are you all right?" he asked Tess.

She was. Nevertheless, she wanted him to wrap his arms around her, and she wanted to cry. Which was a bit pathetic, so she just nodded.

He grabbed Giovanni by his very slightly lipstick-stained collar. "Keep away from her," he growled.

For a moment their eyes locked, and for the first time, Tess tangibly felt the force of that old family rivalry; she saw and felt the hatred. It was as black as the land they came from, as dark as the shadows of Sicily. Giovanni clenched his fists, and Tonino tensed, both men ready to fight. But instead, as Tonino let go of him, Giovanni staggered slightly and made for the door. When he reached it, he turned.

"Do not imagine you have heard the last of this," he said, addressing Tess, and then he spoke very fast in Sicilian to Tonino.

Tonino swore softly in reply.

"*Sì, sì, sì. Scopilo . . .*" With a final curse and a gesture that looked worryingly like somebody's throat being cut,

Giovanni slammed the door and strode away and out of the *baglio*.

Tess turned to Tonino. "Thank you," she croaked.

He nodded stiffly. "Stay away from him," he said.

"Tonino . . ."

But already he had crossed the bar to the door and was gone.

*   *   *

She followed him out of the building and across the *baglio*. The sky had turned leaden while she was in the café, the swell of the sea was like rolled steel, and the line of the horizon was a heavy purple. Even the air seemed to be pressing on her shoulders, her head. It was an effort to move, to drag one foot after the other.

"Tonino," she said, to his retreating back.

The rain began to fall then—slow, thick drops—and in that instant there was a tangible release of pressure as a jagged crop of lightning streaked the sky. Almost immediately, the thunder rolled like a drum.

A storm. The gray sky was illuminated by another dazzling fork of light; it reflected, glaring and gold, on the surface of the sea. It was as if something that had been simmering below the surface was now coming to the boil.

The bar and café owners were rushing around retrieving chairs, tables, parasols—dragging them under cover. People were huddling in doorways, pulling up hoods, donning scarves, holding their hands ineffectually over their heads. Running for shelter, for home.

At last he turned to face her. "Go back, Tess." He looked tired. "Go back home to England."

She stood her ground, though the rain was still falling, and inside she was weeping, too. Not that she'd let him see. "Why?" she countered. "Don't I have a right to be here? Don't I have the same right as anybody else to be here?"

She had raised her voice, but still her words were half-drowned by a gust of wind and the roar of the waves crashing onto the rocks in the bay. She could hear the undercurrent, too, dragging them back as the tide receded.

Tonino shook his head. "Bad things happen here," he shouted. "And it is not yet finished. If you stay . . ." He let this hang. "I cannot always protect you."

Tess was stung. Had she asked for his protection—had she? She could have dealt with Giovanni alone if she'd had to. He wouldn't dare hurt her—would he? And, besides, all these things had happened so long ago. They had nothing to do with her, with the present. What was wrong with them all?

The rainstorm was so complete, it seemed to drown everything. Already the cobblestones of the *baglio* were awash, and the buildings had taken on a sad and derelict air.

Tess was soaked to the skin. But still she stood there, while Tonino sighed, shrugged, and started taking all his things inside. He was working on a much larger design now, she could see, made up of turquoise and sea-green glass. The pieces of glass and stone were shiny and jeweled from the rain, glittering like treasure.

"I am keeping the house," she yelled. "And no one can stop me." Who was she telling? Herself? Tonino? The whole of Cetaria? "I'm not frightened of Giovanni Sciarra."

"You should be," Tonino muttered as he went past, flinging open the door of his studio.

Well. She was angry with him. He'd given up, hadn't he? "And where did the money come from?" she yelled. "Tell me that." She just wanted to get his attention, that was all. But she knew immediately that she'd gone too far.

He froze. "What?"

She should have kept quiet. And yet he infuriated her with his withdrawal, his refusal to face up to the past, face up to her and whatever it was between them. "Your grandfather's money. Your money. The money for your business." She couldn't look at him. "You told me the Sciarras had taken all your family land."

He swore softly. Came toward her. And as another streak of lightning seemed to strike the ground behind him, he lifted her chin and shook his head sadly. "Not you, too, Tess," he said. "Not you, too?"

She met his gaze. "How am I supposed to know," she said. "What's true, what to believe? You and Giovanni . . . You're so damned dark and mysterious all the time!"

Once again, he sighed. His hair was damp now and clung to his forehead; he blinked the rain out of his dark eyes. "I told you it was an inheritance," he said. "An uncle from another village who worked hard and died childless. That is all. Because it happened at the same time as . . ." He hesitated. "The rest of it, everyone assumed there was a connection." He looked at her. "There was no connection."

She nodded. She believed him. She would probably always believe him, always trust him, infuriating though he was. But, "A man disappeared, too," she whispered.

"Yes. A man disappeared, too. Ettore Sciarra. A man with so many fingers in so many affairs, who could guess how many had reason to murder him . . ." He was very close to her now. As he bent toward her, as she knew for certain that his lips would touch hers, as she felt the sweet anticipation . . . She also felt a shiver in the earth beneath her, like a vibration passing through the very cobblestones of the *baglio*.

As one, they took a step apart. She heard some glass tinkling in Tonino's studio, as if a giant hand were shaking the shelves. And while she watched in disbelief, a crack split a pathway up the stone wall beside them.

Tonino was motionless. He seemed to be listening, waiting for something to happen. The sea in the distance was still wild and rolling, but the wind was abating now; the storm had shifted and was moving away down the coast. Once again, the earth shivered as if it were stretching after a long sleep, and then all was quiet; all was still. From somewhere in the village, a church bell tolled.

Tonino visibly relaxed. He took her arm. "Do not worry," he said. "Go back to Villa Sirena now."

Tess could hardly conceal her bitter disappointment. "What was it?" she said. "Was it the storm?"

He shook his head. "An earthquake," he said. "They are not uncommon. But it is finished, I think. Go."

The steps up to the villa had never seemed so steep.

At the top, Tess turned and stared out at the rocks, *i faraglioni*, at the lonely fishing boats there in the harbor, at the faded and disused cannery. Could you love a place and a man and be scared of them at the same time? Could you be drawn to them—half against your will? If you could, if it were possible, then that was how it was for her.

CHAPTER 61

About six months after that visit, Peter sent her a letter. Flavia examined the neat handwriting on the blue envelope and somehow knew it was his. It reminded her of all those other letters that she hadn't received. What had her father done with them? Thrown them in the brazier, probably. He must have read them first, though; otherwise how would he have known that Peter was coming to Sicily to get her? And since Papa spoke no English, he must have shown them to someone else, someone who translated for him Peter's words, Peter's love letters to Flavia.

Even now, this fact made her burn with anger and shame. Who else had read them? Enzo? She thought of Enzo's dark, cruel face, and she shivered. Should she have warned Tess about the Sciarras?

This wasn't a love letter, and Flavia was glad. It began "My dear Flavia" and ended "Yours, Peter." Though of course, he wasn't. In between, he asked after her health and the café, told her where he was living (alone), that he had found a job selling insurance, and that he saw his boy once a week on Sundays.

Once a week on Sundays . . . It wasn't much, for a man who had been so proud. She remembered. I have a son, Flavia. His name is Daniel.

He hoped, Peter wrote, that she might find time to write to him one day—as a friend. And if she ever needed anything . . . He had let the words hang.

As a friend . . . Flavia had never imagined when she came over to England that Peter would be her friend. Her lover, yes. But friend . . . ?

Still, she was touched that he cared enough to make the gesture of friendship. So she replaced the letter in the blue envelope and put it in her bedroom, in her stockings drawer.

A few weeks later, when Lenny was due to visit his mother one Sunday, she made her excuses and stayed home. In the afternoon, she replied to Peter's letter. She told him how the Azzurro was doing and how good her English was getting. She told him about Pridehaven and told him that Lenny was a nice man, one of the best. "I, too," she wrote, "will be your friend."

It was an erratic correspondence, but Flavia received perhaps four or five letters every year. When he had a problem, when his ex-wife found someone else and Peter was worried about the effect this might have on Daniel, or when something went wrong at work and he wasn't selling as much as he should, he wrote to her and told her. Sometimes he mentioned another woman. There was a Katherine, whom he took out for some months, and an Audrey, whom he was seeing for quite a while. But he didn't remarry, and he continued to live alone.

Was he waiting for Flavia? Waiting—for all these years? He never said, and she tried not to think about it. Still, she made it a habit to look out for the postman—just in case.

Her life was good, though she and Lenny had to work hard. Flavia made all her own dough for fresh pasta and pizza, and they had bought some nursery land so that they could grow tomatoes, too, big beefsteak tomatoes and small, tasty cherry tomatoes under glass.

They were a team. But what of love? Lenny was not a romantic—he never had been, and now with the Azzurro, there was little time for romance in their lives. But he was a good man, a kind man, and for this, Flavia was grateful. Romance, though . . . That was for the girl she had once been; she had left that girl behind.

She knew that Lenny wanted children, but it didn't happen for them, and in a way Flavia was glad. There was so much work to do, and she had never felt herself the maternal type. She was too ambitious; she had never wanted the Sicilian way of womanhood—house and children.

When it did happen, she was in her early forties and didn't believe it at first. It couldn't be. Not after all these years . . . But it could be, and it was, and it seemed like a small miracle when Tess was born, a tiny bundle of life and warmth, already squalling as if she knew quite well what she wanted. Flavia smiled. And as if she would fight for it.

"Do you want to hold her now, Mum?" the midwife asked Flavia.

Mum. Flavia wanted to laugh. She would never understand the English; they were a strange race indeed. But, "Yes, please," she said meekly. "I would like to hold her."

They called her Teresa Beatrice.

Now, even more than before, life with Lenny was not just life with Lenny and the Azzurro. They became a family, a real family at last.

Yellow for the durum wheat glowing in the sunshine, yellow for saffron, yellow for lemons, and yellow for golden, warm, runny honey.

Honey, known to the most ancient civilizations, has been produced in Sicily for thousands of years, but its flavor has changed over the centuries. The flowers have changed, and the honey known as millefiori *("thousands of flowers") reflects this heritage. These days, most Sicilian honey is made from orange blossom or eucalyptus nectar.*

Flavia's favorite honey was Sicilian orange blossom. She put it in all her *dolce*, she told her daughter. It was light and fresh and tasted of spring. Of hope and of new beginnings . . .

CHAPTER 62

TESS WAS GLAD WHEN SHE RECEIVED A SURPRISE invitation to go to Millie and Pierro's for lunch. She'd just received a text message from Ginny, too. Nothing earth shattering, but Tess was trying to give her some space—to be there, but not obtrusively there. And it seemed to be working. Ginny was communicating.

Lunch was laid out on their private terrace—a small spread by Sicilian standards, but it looked delicious. There was a simple green bean salad with bread and various seafood antipasti artfully arranged on white plates.

Pierro was darting about doing jobs connected with the hotel: one minute dealing with a difficult customer; next, finding a pair of pliers for a workman; then taking a phone call . . .

Millie, in contrast, was relaxed as ever. Her "girl" Louisa was on reception, and Millie was happy to take a couple of hours off. "I deserve it," she told Tess. "Come here and let me look at you."

Tess obliged, and Millie reached to kiss her on both cheeks, the Sicilian way. Today she was dressed in a fuchsia-pink top, with black cotton culottes and black pumps with a tiny fuchsia bow. Her lipstick, though, was as bold and red as ever—a clash that only Millie could pull off so success-fully, Tess thought.

"How are you both?" she asked. "How's business?"

"Good." Millie waved her to a chair. "And your father? I hear he's doing well."

Tess was faintly surprised. "Well, yes. Though according to my mother, his superman days are definitely over."

Pierro came over just in time to catch Tess's quizzical look. "What?" He too bent to kiss her.

"Just that in Cetaria everyone seems to know what's happening to everyone else." Tess shrugged and tried to laugh it off. After all, they were her friends and it really didn't matter . . .

"They do." Pierro sat down in a chair opposite her. "And my wife is the biggest gossip of them all."

Millie pulled a face. "Don't listen to him," she said. "Good news travels fast, that's all."

"And bad news travels faster," said Pierro.

Tess smiled. He was right there. She remembered some-thing. "This morning, I could have sworn someone was watching me when I left the villa," she said. It was the strangest sensation; she had almost been able to feel the scrutiny, like the beam of a flashlight on her back.

"They probably were." Pierro poured out three glasses of iced lemonade from the jug on the table. "In Sicily someone is always watching you."

"Really?" That was worrying.

Millie clicked her tongue and told him to shush. "He's kidding you," she told Tess.

Tess wasn't convinced. But who was always watching? And why would they watch *her*? She thought of Giovanni Sciarra, and she shivered.

Pierro passed her a glass. "How were the builders yesterday?" he asked. "Did they give you a good quote?"

Tess sipped the lemonade. It was homemade—from Sicilian lemons, no doubt—and delicious. "Not bad," she said. This builder had taken a lot more trouble looking around the villa; had commented on her plans in comprehensible, though pidgin, English; and had given her some useful advice. Oh, and then there was the minor point that his estimate was ten grand less than Giovanni's outfit's.

"So will you go ahead?" Millie looked worried. "Can you afford it?"

"Yes to both questions." Tess accepted some bread from the basket Millie handed to her and helped herself to some *calamaretti*—baby squid with pine nuts, parsley, garlic, and bread crumbs—which she had first tasted at one of her lunches with Giovanni. If she was going to keep the villa and make it into a business, then the work had to be done, and she was damned if she was going to let Giovanni railroad her or Tonino frighten her away. She was a big girl now. She could make her own decisions.

"They did an excellent job on converting the hotel," Pierro said, turning round to survey his pride and joy. "And if anything should go wrong, they are always reachable."

"Probably because we always pay on time," Millie commented. She crossed her legs, letting one of the black pumps fall to the floor.

But Tess couldn't help feeling that Pierro's recommendation was worth a hundred of Giovanni's . . .

Millie popped a stuffed mussel between her red lips and chewed it thoughtfully. She frowned at Tess. "But how will you manage to pay for it?" she said, as if talking to herself.

Pierro shot her a look. "That is not our business, my love . . ." But before he could say more, his cell rang, and he got up with a gesture of apology to answer it, wandering away from the table and talking in rapid Sicilian that lost Tess completely.

Millie leaned forward confidentially. "Have you come into some money, darling?" she inquired. "How wonderful." Her eyes—green and gleaming—seemed to invite confidences.

But Tess was wary. That sensation of being watched when she'd left the villa this morning had unnerved her. And it wasn't the first time. She'd paused on the steps, looked around. Life was continuing as usual in the *baglio* (though Tonino was nowhere to be seen), and there were just a few people down in the bay. She thought she saw the glint of something—the sun on a camera lens, maybe—on the hills behind the village, where she had walked with Tonino in the olive grove. But . . .

It was probably her imagination. Still, after Giovanni had threatened her in the café, after Tonino had told her to go home, she had decided: she would tell no one here about David's money. Not Giovanni, not Tonino, not even Millie. It wasn't that she didn't trust them, it was just beginning to irritate her that here in Cetaria everyone seemed to know everyone else's business.

So, "Something like that," she told Millie, and gave her a secret smile. She helped herself to some bean salad and *gamberoni*.

Her friend looked a bit put out, but thankfully Pierro returned to the table at this point, and she let the subject drop.

During lunch they talked of other things—the weather in England, what had been on the world news, how Tess was planning to manage the B&B, and finally of Pierro's mother, who was threatening to come and stay with them—indefinitely.

"A fate worse than death," said Millie, rolling her eyes.

Tess didn't mention Giovanni—she'd already decided to keep quiet about that, too. She didn't want to make too much of it, didn't want to cause any more trouble with him. She knew how much damage an unthinking word could do.

At two p.m. Pierro excused himself and Tess made to go, but Millie kept her there for another forty-five minutes, chatting aimlessly, with *dolci*—homemade almond biscuits—and fresh coffee. You would never imagine that she had a hotel to run, Tess thought.

"I really must be off," Tess said at last. "I need to contact the builders and get things moving." Plus she wanted to do another dive. After the storm and the earthquake, the sea had looked fresher, brighter, more inviting than ever. Once the builders got started, there'd be less time for diving. And anyway, who needed an excuse—Tess wanted to be in there.

She tore herself away from Millie, who suggested that she call in on the builders pronto and even gave her directions to the office, which was only a few streets away. "Sicilians prefer to do business face-to-face rather than by phone," she told her. "Better to strike while the iron is hot, as they say."

But once she'd left the hotel, Tess changed her mind and decided to return to the villa and do the dive first—even builders had siestas in Cetaria.

The *baglio* certainly was sleepy in the early afternoon heat, the shops (including Tonino's studio) all closed. But again, she felt it. That sensation of someone watching.

Ridiculous, she told herself, starting up the steps. Finding her key, she let herself in the side gate and walked round by the white jasmine to the front of the villa, her mind already planning the dive she was about to do.

She opened the front door, stepped inside the hall, and stopped abruptly. Listened. Something wasn't right. She frowned, took another step inside. She could hear a noise— like a drill, then a hammer, then the soft murmur of voices. Someone was here in the villa.

She hovered by the kitchen doorway. She should leave immediately, get help (but no one was in the *baglio* . . .), perhaps even run back to the hotel for Pierro if Tonino wasn't around. She remembered his words: "*I cannot always be here to protect you.*" No. She couldn't ask Tonino.

And besides . . . she took another step inside. All her instincts were telling her not to leave, to find out who was here, to find out what was going on. This was her house, damn it.

"Who's there?" she called. Silence. "Who's there?"

CHAPTER 63

THE FOOD WAS THE SECURITY AND THE SENSE OF continuity.

Granita di caffè, Flavia decided. *Put the water and sugar into a pan, heat until the water dissolves. Boil for one minute, simmer, add the coffee, blend, take off the heat. Add the vanilla pod and the cinnamon. Mix well. Cool. Freeze for two hours, taking out to stir every fifteen minutes. It should,* she wrote, *be a fine granular consistency, almost mushy at the end. Whip the cream and icing sugar until stiff. Divide your* granita *between however many glasses, add the cream, and serve with warm brioche.*

One day, when Tess was three years old, Flavia received one of Peter's letters.

"I don't know how to tell you this, Flavia," he wrote. "I even thought about not telling you at all."

Even after all this time, Flavia felt icy fingers clutching at her heart.

And she was right.

"I have cancer," he wrote, "lung cancer. Should have given up the weed years ago, but . . ."

She'd never even known he smoked. Flavia blinked at the words on the page. How could she not have known such a small, such a fundamental thing?

He hadn't smoked in Sicily, had he?—at least, he never said. He hadn't smoked when he came to the café that day.

I never knew him at all, Flavia thought. I don't know him now.

"I want to see you," he wrote. It was the first time he had suggested a meeting in all these years. "Could you? Would you?"

Could she? Yes, she could. Lenny had never been a possessive man. He didn't question her movements (though to be fair, they were usually around the kitchen of the Azzurro), and he respected her privacy. Would she? That was another thing. She did not want to betray her husband. She did not want to lie to him either. But where was the harm? And Peter . . . Peter was ill. Peter needed to see her. Could she refuse him?

She met him in Lyme Regis in a tearoom on the seafront. The tide was high, and the waves were wild and gray; anything less like a Sicilian sea she couldn't imagine.

She told Lenny she was going shopping with a friend. Alice, a woman she'd met at Tess's nursery school, someone Lenny hardly knew. Lenny would pick up Tess from nursery school and look after everything at the Azzuro. Flavia cooked the day's meals in advance and arranged cover. Lying to Lenny was the worst part. But . . . She hated the guilt that settled over her as she tried to meet his frank and open gaze. "Of course you should go, love," he said, making it easy for her. Oh, Lenny . . .

She could—she supposed—have told him she was meeting Peter. She could have told him about the letters, too, and that Peter was ill and that he wanted to see her. Lenny—being Lenny—might have understood. But he might have understood too much. He might have understood why she had agreed to go, and Flavia didn't want to hurt him. He was a good man. He didn't deserve it.

Peter was thinner. His hair was thin, too, fine like baby hair. And soft, she thought. His face had new lines and pouches of loose skin—especially round the eyes—and his mouth was harder. His eyes were as blue as the sky, as blue as they had always been.

"Thank you for coming," he said. And he held her hands across the table as if they were lovers.

They drank tea and ate toasted tea cakes and talked—for hours. it seemed like. Not just about his life and her life over the past years, but about the cancer. When he talked, she thought she could detect a shortness of breath, and her heart went out to this man she had loved. They were both in their forties now—middle aged, she supposed, though she didn't feel it, especially with a young daughter to look after and a business to run. But Peter's life had not worked out the way he hoped. And now it would be cut short before he was fifty.

"I must go," she said at last. "Lenny will worry . . ."

He shook his head. "Who would have thought it? My Flavia, so English . . ."

My Flavia . . .

"I have been here twenty-five years," she reminded him. "I think in English these days."

"And do you think—my lovely Flavia—that you would do me one last favor—for old times' sake?" he asked. He had hold of her hands again.

She knew she couldn't refuse him. She might never see him again. He was staying at the big hotel on the hill.

"I'm not asking you to let me make love to you," he said. "But I can't die without holding you. Just once. I can't, Flavia."

She knew exactly how he felt. Hadn't she thought the same thing years ago? So she walked up the hill with him to the hotel. She waited by the reception desk as he collected his key, and she went up in the elevator with him to his room.

Inside the room, he turned down a corner of the sheets and quilt and left her.

Shivering, Flavia took off her clothes—her warm black overcoat, her suede boots, her thick skirt, and her stockings. She took off her cardigan and her blouse and the silver cross Lenny had given her when they married. Silently, she asked her husband to forgive her for what she must do. She took off her underthings, she slipped under the covers, and she waited for Peter, just as she had waited for him before.

CHAPTER 64

THEY CAME THROUGH THE DOOR ON THE OTHER SIDE of the kitchen, the door that led through to the living room.

Giovanni Sciarra and another man, older, wearing a grubby shirt and overalls. Giovanni himself looked cool in jeans and a white linen shirt. As if he'd been invited round for Sunday tea.

"Giovanni," she hissed. "What the fuck's going on? What do you think you're doing?"

A myriad of expressions passed over his face, as if, she thought, he couldn't decide who to be.

"You are back early, Tess," he said. He shook his head mournfully.

Back early? What was he talking about?

"Too early for your own good."

She tried to push down the fear that was rising in her, making her legs weak. He wouldn't dare. Not with a witness. "What do you want?" she demanded. "What are you looking for?"

But she knew—of course. And she knew why Giovanni had been so angry that she didn't want his builders. He thought it was here, in the villa. *Il tesoro.* He was convinced of it. That's why the place had been in such a state when she first arrived. Edward Westerman hadn't left it like that—Giovanni had.

"Where is it hidden?" he muttered. "*Il tesoro?*"

So he'd never believed that story he fed her about *il tesoro* being handed in to someone by Tonino's grandfather in return for money. He'd just been trying to cause trouble between them. "Giovanni," she said. "You seem to have forgotten something—this is my house and you are trespassing."

He muttered something she didn't understand.

"Please leave. Now." She watched them as they came farther into the room. The guy in the overalls was holding a pneumatic drill, for God's sake . . . So, Giovanni had already searched in the obvious places, and with the prospect of the building being refurbished, he had been hoping to dig deeper, so to speak. Now that she'd rejected his builder . . .

"Ah, Tess," he said.

Again she felt the sliver of fear. "It must be very special," she said. "*Il tesoro.* But what makes you think it's here?"

Giovanni shrugged. He spoke to the man beside him, who slunk away past Tess, into the hall, and out of the front door.

Tess let him go. Now they were alone. She was scared, and she was angry. But she wanted to get to the bottom of this. She wanted the truth.

"Where else could it be?" Giovanni was watching her closely. "It is the obvious place to hide it, no?"

"I don't see why," she snapped. "It could be anywhere."

"For example?" Giovanni's voice rose. "*Scopi questo!* Wherever it was hidden, it would have been found by now."

Tess had spent enough hours already thinking back over the story. Alberto Amato had been asked by her grandfather to hide it during the war. But why? Why hadn't her grandfather just hidden it himself? That way he could have been sure of not being betrayed; that way, only he would have known its whereabouts . . . It didn't make sense.

"Even if it was here," Tess said, treading carefully now, "what gives you any claim to it, Giovanni?"

He swore softly. "It was owed to the Sciarra family," he said. "It is our right."

A piece of the jigsaw clicked into place. He had told her this before, hadn't he? About the debt owed by the Amatos—which would be a debt owed by Luigi Amato in particular. Protection money for his business. But why would Edward Westerman end up with *il tesoro* if it had originally belonged to Luigi Amato? And then she got it. Millie had told her, without meaning to tell her. Luigi Amato was gay. Edward Westerman was also gay. This gave them at the least a common bond and possibly even a relationship. Was Edward Westerman the only person Luigi could trust? Did he give it to Edward for safekeeping because the Sciarra family meant to have it?

"Where did Luigi get it from, Giovanni?" Tess asked. She'd gone too far to back off now.

"Clever girl." He smiled. "It was unearthed when he was building the foundations for his stupid little restaurant," he said. "But we have eyes everywhere, you know, and even if we didn't, his gossiping sister could not keep her mouth shut. Like most women." He scowled. "So. It belongs to Sicily, to Cetaria." And he straightened up, looked almost proud. "To the brotherhood," he said, so quietly, she almost missed it. The brotherhood?

"And you would give it to Sicily, would you, Giovanni?" she asked. Because she would gladly give it to Sicily. To be truthful, she had no interest in the bloody thing; it had just caused a load of trouble as far as she could see.

"What do you know," he spat, "of Sicily? Some English tourist, walking in here like she owns the place . . . ?"

He seemed to have forgotten that she was half Sicilian, Tess thought. That her mother had grown up here just as his had, had played with his own aunt in the same streets. And that she did own the place. This place.

"That's enough." She held out her hand, palm up.

He looked at her enquiringly. "What?"

"The key, Giovanni. Give me the key to my villa, and we'll say no more about it." She didn't feel scared now, just angry.

He grinned, took a step closer. "Come and get it, Tess."

"Oh, for God's sake." She turned away.

"No, I mean it." Closer still. "Come and get it." He raised his hands. "Come on. I'll make it easy for you."

She glared at him. "Who do you work for, Giovanni?" She couldn't imagine that he was a one-man band. He was far too self-assured. And he knew too much—how had he known she'd be out today, for example?

Giovanni hadn't bothered to answer her question. Or perhaps he already had. *The brotherhood . . .* He was still grinning, laughing at her. The poor Englishwoman, just a tourist and utterly out of her depth . . .

"I suppose you've been having me watched?" She fired a shot in the dark.

He raised an eyebrow. "Now, why would I do that?"

"To see when I go out—so that you can break into my house?"

He laughed. "No need, my dear Tess."

Ah, yes, because he had a key.

"I have other ears," he continued in a whisper. "And other eyes. And we care about *il tesoro*. We want it. It cannot have simply disappeared."

"Well, I don't have it," Tess snapped.

"Hmm." He regarded her thoughtfully. "The problem being that we do not entirely believe you. Which is why we cannot leave you alone, *no?*"

Tess thought of Tonino. Did he, too, want *il tesoro*? It had, after all, once belonged to his family. Was that why . . . ?

But it couldn't be. If that were so, he would never have broken off with her, would he?

"The key is in my shirt pocket," Giovanni whispered. "Here." He pointed.

Tess could see the shape of the heavy metal outlined under the white linen. The shirt was undone at the neck, his dark chest hair visible, the faintest sheen of sweat on his olive skin.

"Take it," he said.

Tess's gaze fixed onto his. She knew he was goading her. Nevertheless, she reached up for it.

He snatched her hand as she did so, pulling her roughly toward him. He grabbed a handful of her hair.

"Get off me." Her voice was shaking. His face was almost touching hers, his eyes cruel and cold.

"Do you think I want you?" he muttered. "After that bastard has been there?"

And he pushed her away, so hard that she stumbled and almost fell. She grabbed the back of a chair. "Give me the key, Giovanni," she said.

He was already at the door. He turned for a moment, plucked the key from his shirt pocket, and threw it on the floor between them. It landed on the flagstones with a dull, metallic ring. "Take it," he said. "It makes no difference."

He opened the door.

"And don't come here again," Tess yelled at his retreating back. "Or . . . Or . . ."

But she was wasting her breath. He was gone.

CHAPTER 65

YES, THOUGHT FLAVIA. SICILIAN FOOD EMBRACED contrast and discord—it had always been so. Sweet and sour, hard and soft, sweet and salty, hot and cold . . .

In *cassata*, for example, there was the hard density of the candied fruit, the sweetness of the icing over rich, cheesy ricotta. A cake as well as an ice cream. By 1300, Arab Sicily was a thing of the past, and *cassata* became an aristocratic dessert, its recipes jealously guarded by monastic nuns or the chefs of the aristocracy. Even today, she knew, not many people outside the culinary profession were ambitious enough to make it at home.

However, *cassata* was a specialty of Flavia's home village. And it would not do to let traditions and recipes die out. It was part of her story for her daughter.

The candied fruit should be stored in a cool place in a covered jar. The true flavor of the fruit is preserved underneath the sugar coating.

She began to write the recipe in the back of the book.
Just so . . .

*He undressed slowly, as if every movement was an effort; tug-
ging off his sweater, pulling at his shirt, looking at her all the
while. A sad look, a look of love. Were those looks so different,
Flavia thought?*

*She lay there under the crisp white sheets, trying to control
the trembling of her body. It wasn't fear. It wasn't anxiety. It
wasn't even desire. It was just emotion, she realized. The emotion she had once invested in this man bubbling up again like
lava inside her.*

*And then he was naked, standing next to her by the bed.
"We wasted so much time, Flavia," he said.*

*His body hair was a fair down—thicker than she remem-
bered, but golden and hardly visible on his shoulders and, as
he half-turned—on the small of his back. He was too thin—
that was the disease, she realized. There was already a wasted
look about him, and his skin was too yellow pale, glistening
with a light sweat.*

*She pushed back the sheet and coverlet. "Come here," she
said.*

*He bent toward her, climbed into the bed, and opened his
arms, and she lay inside the circlet he had made, her head in
the hollow between his chest and shoulder, her arm around
his back as he turned to face her.*

*They were silent. Two separate hearts beating. She could feel
the pulse of him, thumping against her skin. For a moment,
her thoughts flitted to Lenny. He was a different shape—a
stockier, shorter man, with dark hair on his chest and legs, but
also with a pale skin, not honey pale like Peter's, but white-
pink pale like the blush on an apple. She had become used to*

Lenny's shape, Lenny's body, and it felt strange to be in anyone else's arms—even Peter's. But . . . "So good," she murmured.

Because they fit. They breathed in the same rhythm. The hollow between his chest and shoulder was the exact right shape for her head, and her hip fitted neatly into the curve of his waist and groin.

And, as he held her, he stroked her hair and began to murmur, "Flavia, Flavia . . . I have never stopped loving you."

"Nor I you, my love," she said.

And she relaxed; until the trembling stopped and she slipped into a peaceful semihypnotic state that was almost sleep . . .

For how long they lay there, holding one another, she had no idea.

Afterwards, when she had left him and was waiting for the bus that would take her home, she thought about it. She could still feel his skin against hers; still smell the scent of him— tobacco woody mixed with something slightly chemical. Had he started chemotherapy? She hadn't even asked.

But she didn't feel guilty—about Lenny. This was separate from Lenny, something that would not affect him. She would not allow it to.

And she realized that she did know Peter after all—it was in him and in her and in the fit of them. It was in the love between them that they had never lost. In the way he held her and the way she felt in his arms.

CHAPTER 66

TESS WAS STILL NUMB WITH ANGER AS SHE GATHERED the gear together for her dive. She knew perfectly well that she was not in the right emotional state to go diving—it was important to be calm and use minimum energy to conserve air and deal with the whole underwater experience.

But she was not going to let Giovanni Sciarra spoil her day. She'd planned this dive, looked forward to it, checked the tide times, everything. So she would go ahead. And if he—or any of his bloody *brotherhood*—were watching her, they would see how much she cared.

Tess put on her bikini and wet suit, leaving the top half unzipped for now, as it was still pretty hot and she had to get all her stuff down to the water's edge. She had thought she was coming to Sicily to discover her mother's story, and she had uncovered so much more . . . She put on her weight belt, picked up her mask, her fins, her flashlight, and her little diver's knife.

All the time, during her preparations, a small part of her was thinking—*was* it hidden here in Villa Sirena? *Il tesoro*? Had it been here all the time? Tucked away behind the old stone fireplace, perhaps, hidden in the ancient well, buried in the terraced garden: five paces from the dwarf palm, three from the purple hibiscus, *X* marks the spot . . . ?

Down in the bay, there was a sense that everything had been rinsed clean by the rain and the storm—even by the earthquake, perhaps. The air was clear, and the aquamarine water beckoned. *Come on, Tess. Feel me, touch me, taste me* . . .

Down the steps, a quick look around, but no one was taking any notice of a woman in a wet suit with a scuba tank strapped on her back. Across to the stone jetty; Tonino's door flung wide open, but no Tonino. (And what could he do? What would he do? Nothing, that's what).

Tess shook her head. No. She had to deal with it herself: Giovanni for one, and the villa, her gorgeous pink villa, which seemed now to hold only a legacy of betrayal. And maybe *il tesoro* . . .

The sun was hot on her head and on her shoulders; she was overheating in the wet suit, with the weight on her back and round her waist. She couldn't wait to get in that water. She did the usual checks and waded in, feeling the sweet relief of the cool liquid, a body quencher; an increasing weightlessness as she relaxed into the waves. She knew already that she didn't have far to swim from the shore before she would find those amazing rock formations, coral, sponges, and underwater life. So she felt safe. You could dive without a boat, and you could dive without a buddy. *Just stay safe* . . .

She knew exactly where she was heading. In the near distance were the rocks, *i faraglioni*, rust and cream, with bits of moss, earth, and algae stuck to their jagged surfaces.

She slipped under. The water was still slightly murky after the storm. The seabed had been stirred up, hadn't yet entirely settled down from all the disruption. A bit like her, Tess thought, trying to still herself, to reach that point of calm, to get into the rhythm, her rhythm that was also the pulse of the tide.

The rocks, when she got there, seemed unchanged at first, but there were more fish than usual—maybe because of the storm. She saw salps, bream, and parrot fish, plus a few she didn't recognize and would have to look up later. She used a gloved hand to etch a line along a crack that seemed fresh . . . as if recently disturbed.

Something was different, as if some of the rocks had shifted or been dislodged somehow. And there was a hole, a gap, where before . . .

Tess examined the rocks more closely. Where there had before just been rock, boulders piled together, there was now an opening. She looked more closely. More than an opening, more than a hole. An entrance—easily wide enough to take a human being. Wide enough for her.

She shone her flashlight, directing the beam through the opening. The area on the other side seemed bigger, and the water was a distinct bright turquoise, as if illuminated by more than the beam of her flashlight.

Once an explorer . . . She didn't really have to think about it. She eased herself through the gap and found herself in a natural tunnel of rock.

Oh my God, she thought. This hadn't been here before. Surely? She couldn't have missed that hole, wouldn't have swum right past it . . . The water was turquoise, because of a thin shaft of light, she realized. And as she kicked herself gently forward, the tunnel of rock widened out. Some shrimp and small weed particles scampered past her in the water. And after a few moments . . . She broke surface.

She was in a cave. An underwater cave. God . . . And although it was quite dark, that thin shaft of light was shining down on the water. There must be a narrow chimney letting in sunlight from above. Too narrow, presumably, for access from the surface. So the only way in was the way she had come . . . Underwater.

Tess took the valve out of her mouth. Because there was air. A little stale. But nevertheless, breathable air. She took off her mask, too, so she could see more clearly.

The cavern was deep and the rock shelved on various levels, forming platforms going up to the ceiling of the cave. She could make out the water level from the dark color of the rock and could see that high tide would leave the top section of the cave dry.

Jesus . . . Slowly, she swam across the surface. She could hear an interminable *drip drip drip*, and every ripple of the water with every stroke she made seemed to echo around the stone. It was eerie. Scary. And . . . why hadn't she found this before?

Simple. She paused at the other side of the pool. The earthquake. The one that had seemed to shake the cobblestones of the *baglio* as she stood there with Tonino two days ago. The day of the storm. That was why she hadn't seen the entrance to the cave on her previous dive. Because it hadn't been there before. The cave had been there—but there hadn't been a hole to swim through; there hadn't been access. The opening had been created somehow by the earthquake. A fissure in the rock may have been forced open; a rock or two could have shifted. What had Tonino said? Rocks are always moving here in Sicily; they may be solid, but they don't always stay in one place.

She breathed in deeply and coughed, the sound reverberating around the cavern. The air was breathable, yes, but dank and musty, the atmosphere chill. Tess directed the beam of the flashlight around. The rocks near the surface of the water were slimy with green moss, and from the flashlight she could see mineral deposits on the rocky platforms and calcified growth coming down from the ceiling—stalactites—and . . . Jesus! she jumped as something fluttered and flapped overhead. Something dark with broad webbed wings. A bat.

That was it. She was getting out of here. She groped her way among the rocks near the water's surface and saw some black crabs scuttling for cover. Black as death, she found herself thinking. *Stop it, Tess . . .*

Wait till she told Tonino about this place . . . Whatever had happened between them, she had to tell Tonino about this.

She was just about to put away her flashlight and put her mask back on, when she glimpsed something on a high platform ledge above her. It looked like some sort of old earthenware pot . . . Which was weird. And then something else caught her attention—something white and gleaming that seemed to catch in the light. Like a pile of . . . It couldn't be, could it? Tess didn't want to look again, but she had to.

Bones. A human skull and white human bones. A skeleton.

Bloody hell. She didn't want to be here a second longer. Tess didn't know what had happened here, but she knew she'd had enough.

Quickly, she shoved the regulator back in her mouth and pulled her face mask back on. Cave diving was potentially hazardous, and she didn't have the necessary training. She shouldn't really be here—especially not on her own. But, it was too late for that now, so—slowly, *take it slowly, Tess*— she moved back toward the tunnel. Toward the tunnel of rock and the opening. Toward the sea. There was no need to panic. She must get a grip.

Someone had died in there. A long, long time ago. It happened. So . . . As she'd suspected, the underwater cave had always been there. But the entrance had got closed up—by an earlier quake perhaps. Some rocks could have fallen from above and sealed the entrance. And now it had reopened, thanks to the recent earthquake. The rocks had moved again.

She was close to the opening now. She shone her flashlight. She could see it in front of her, just where the rocks were overhanging from above, just where the tunnel was at its most narrow.

Her theory was possible, even probable here in Sicily. After all . . . She reached out her gloved hand. This looked like some sort of fault line and . . .

It happened so quickly. One minute she was edging toward the opening, still examining the rocks in the tunnel as she went, her brain speeding while she kept her rhythm slow.

The next minute there was a sound and a sensation from just behind her, a kind of shiver in the rock and a dull, heavy, splashy kind of a thud.

And then she couldn't move at all.

She felt no pain, which was confusing. But as she twisted round as far as she could, she saw that a boulder—still unstable from the quake perhaps—had fallen, become displaced. And somehow, she wasn't sure how, it had trapped her leg.

But . . . She could feel her leg; it hadn't done any damage. So she mustn't panic. All she had to do was ease her leg out from under it. It shouldn't be too difficult.

She tried. She could move her leg an inch or so to either side, but she couldn't get it out from under the rock. Shit. *Don't panic, Tess.*

She couldn't help glancing at her air gauge. Fifteen bars of air left. Okay. Fifteen minutes. No problem.

She twisted the top half of her body again, pushed ineffectually at the boulder. It was bloody heavy. She pushed and pushed, but it was hard to twist far enough round to get the angle right, to get any kind of a grip. She couldn't shift it.

Bugger. Fuck. *Don't panic, Tess.*

She tried to move her leg again. Nothing. She could feel the boulder pressing against it now, but her leg was actually trapped against the side of the rocky tunnel, she realized that now. Nothing was broken. She was pretty sure that nothing was broken. But . . . What use was that if she couldn't move?

She thought of Tonino. The story about his diving buddy getting trapped in a torn fishing net and no one being there to help him. Tonino not being there to help him. *Don't dive alone, Tess. It's not good practice. It's . . .*

Bloody stupid, she thought. No one was here. No one could help her. She was on her own. So there was no point conserving her air supply. She had to go for it. She had to move the rock or her leg.

She thought of Ginny. And she thought of her mother's journey to England, her own journey to Sicily.

She had twelve minutes left to get out.

CHAPTER 67

SHE HAD BEEN SHORTSIGHTED, FLAVIA THOUGHT now. Shortsighted to imagine that Lenny wouldn't know, wouldn't guess, wouldn't sense something. And shortsighted not to realize how he felt—how he had always felt. She had thought that her feelings for Peter were nothing to do with him. But they were. He was her husband.

"You know I love you," she had told him when he came out of the hospital. "You know how much you mean to me?" It felt odd even saying such things after all they'd been through together. Flavia had never felt the need before, never realized there was a need. But now she knew she had to. Sometimes emotions should be voiced. Misunderstandings, apparently, could last a lifetime, and they could be fed and nurtured without a woman being any the wiser.

"You've stuck by me, Flavia, my darling," he said. "That's all I could have asked."

She held his good hand. It felt limp and helpless. She hated to see him this way—her strength, her rock, Lenny...

"You read the letters," she said, watching his face. "You know we wrote to each other."

He hesitated. Nodded.

"He came here, you see." She told him about the first visit. "And I met up with him one day, when I knew he was very ill."

"Thank you," said Lenny.

"For what?" Flavia was confused.

"For not leaving me, of course. For not going off with him."

She was about to protest, about to say, how could I leave you when I loved you . . . ? But she realized that he was right. That it wasn't that simple. That when Peter first came to see her, she had loved them both. So she could have gone to him; it wouldn't have been hard—the right look, the right touch, the right time.

"I know how you felt about him," Lenny said. "I saw you, don't forget. In Exeter. I saw how much you cared for him."

"It is true," Flavia said. "But I have also cared for you." She put her hand to his cheek. He hadn't shaved for a couple of days, and there was a rash of coarse gray stubble on his jaw. She would do that for him later. She wanted to do things for him, to make him see . . . "We made our life together," she said. "You and I. I loved you. I still do."

"And Peter?" His face twisted.

It was funny, she thought. When you were seventeen, you thought love was reserved for the young. But when you grew old, it still mattered just as much. It mattered, even though Peter had died so many years ago.

"Oh, Lenny," she said. "What matters is what we have, you and I."

"Yes?" He seemed to be hanging on to her every word.

"Because what love really is, is caring for another human being, living with them through the good and the bad, working with them, wanting to grow old with them. That is true love. Not hearts and flowers and romantic dreams. Love is what we have, you and I. It is not second best. It is the real thing." Perhaps, she thought, you could fit in different ways with different people. Perhaps there was no one and only, just different possibilities. Or perhaps . . .

Yes, a part of her would always love Peter. But she had been wrong to imagine that he'd haunt her till her dying day, wrong to think she'd never be free.

He nodded and closed his eyes. "You're a wonderful woman, Flavia, my love," he said. "I couldn't have asked for more."

"And neither," Flavia had said firmly, kissing him on the head, her Lenny, and knowing every word was true, "could I."

For every recipe there is a reason, wrote Flavia. *Trade, social change, the season, the weather. Food is warmth. Food is identity.*

The final *dolce* was Flavia's personal favorite. And so she had left it till last.

The fig—like the pomegranate—was an ancient fruit, and some might say that the best way to eat them was from the tree—ripened and warmed by the summer sun, velvety to the touch. Sinking into the taste of a ripe fig was to bite into musk and be rewarded with the sweetest, most intense flavor imaginable, seedy and honeyed on the tongue. The fig was sensuality epitomized, sexuality symbolized in a fruit of the earth . . .

Bake in the juice of oranges with red wine. Add cloves, nut-meg, cinnamon, vanilla, and honey to taste. Sprinkle with toasted almonds. Serve. Wallow . . .

She had a dream that night—a memory dream. They were in a ballroom. In the center of the ceiling was a revolving mirrored globe, its surface sparkling as it turned. Illuminating the bronze light fittings, the posters on the walls . . . She remembered the pompadoured, slicked-back hair, the tiny waists, the stiletto heels, stockings, and full skirts.

Lenny was teaching her to dance, to waltz. *One, two, three; one, two, three.*

"I'll never get it," she said. She stamped her foot. "Never. It is too hard." *One, two, three; one, two, three.*

"It's easy if you just keep going," he told her. "And suddenly . . ."

Yes, you are enjoying it.

Flavia put down her pen and closed her notebook. And that was the end of the story—more or less.

CHAPTER 68

IT WAS NO GOOD, TESS REALIZED. THE BOULDER hadn't moved. Her leg hadn't moved. She hadn't moved.

She was going to run out of air and she was going to die. Here in this bloody underwater tunnel, alone and afraid. And it was her fault, for being irresponsible, for taking stupid risks, for not thinking . . .

Sorry, Ginny. Sorry, Muma. Sorry, Dad.

Ten minutes left. And still Tess continued to struggle, couldn't give up without a fight, for God's sake. She even thought—one almighty push—it might have given just a tiny bit.

And then she saw the other diver. And he saw her.

He was through the entrance in seconds, checking she was okay, glancing at her air gauge, assessing the situation, the weight on her leg, the position of the rock.

Tonino. No wet suit. Just black shorts and full diving apparatus.

He pushed with all his strength, once, twice . . . The rock budged. It budged enough for her to slip her leg free, inch out, and ease through the gap in the rocks, back to the open sea.

He was with her. He pulled her to him and put the spare breathing tube he was carrying, that all divers had to have with them, in her mouth. "Okay?" He was signaling. "Are you okay?"

She nodded, though she didn't feel okay. She felt weak and dizzy and spaced out. But she was alive. She clung to him. She was alive.

"I cannot believe," Tonino said an hour or so later, as she sat in his studio, shivering, two towels and a blanket wrapped round her, a hot coffee and a brandy on the table beside her, "that you want to go back there."

He had brought her up to the surface, back to his studio, understanding instinctively that she didn't want a fuss. She needed quiet, warmth, privacy.

And he hadn't—thank God—said "I told you so." He hadn't said much, but he had stared at her with his dark eyes, and he had held her close, and he had looked after her.

"How did you know I was in trouble?" she had asked him, once they were on dry land and she was beginning to recover from the shock.

"I saw you go out." His expression was unreadable. "You looked upset."

Tess nodded. "I was." She told him about finding Giovanni in the villa.

He shook his head. Said something she didn't understand. "What, Tonino?"

"This thing must be taken care of," he said. "Once and for good."

She couldn't agree more.

"So, you thought I looked upset . . . ?" she prompted. He'd given her two brandies already. Any more and she'd be comatose.

He shrugged. "I waited forty minutes," he said. "I was worried."

He waited for her? He timed how long she was in the water, and he was worried about her? Didn't that suggest that he cared?

"I suppose I was lucky," Tess said carefully, "that you happened to have your diving equipment close to hand, after all this time." He lived practically at the water's edge, but he must have got his act together in minutes in order to get to her so quickly . . .

He avoided her eye. "I was thinking," he said, "about diving again. Maybe, after all, it is time to put the past to rest."

Hallelujah! thought Tess. He might not have been there for his friend—though from what he'd told her, that was hardly his fault—but he'd certainly been there for her. Without him . . . But when he said he was ready to put the past to rest, was he talking about diving? Or did he have something even more personal in mind?

"Did you know there was a cave there?" she asked him.

Tonino frowned. "My grandfather told me of that cave," he said. "He called it the Grotta Azzurra."

Because of the light on the turquoise water, she guessed. She thought automatically of the Azzuro—her parents' restaurant. Was that simply a coincidence? Of course Tonino's family would know about the cave. They had always been linked to the sea. Spear fishing, tuna fishing . . . Tonino used to make a living from diving, too.

"But I did not know there was still a way in," he said.

"There wasn't," she told him. "But now there is."

Of course, he understood immediately. He knew how these things worked. He nodded. "The earthquake," he said. "A rockfall."

"Uh-huh. And that's not all." She told him what she'd seen in there. The pot and the bones.

He was surprised—but not as surprised as he was when she said she wanted to go back there.

"Why get involved?" he asked. "Why not leave things be?"

He was being remarkably dense, Tess thought. But then, she'd had longer to consider it properly, time when she was struggling for her life, the sort of time when revelations sometimes occur.

"Your grandfather was a spear fisherman, wasn't he?" She sipped her coffee. It tasted of caramel, nuts and vanilla.

Tonino raised an eyebrow. "So?"

"So he knew this area underwater better than anyone?"

He folded his arms. "Yes?"

Did she have to spell it out? "So, my grandfather asked him to hide *il tesoro*," she said. "Any idea why?"

"Because he was his closest friend?" Once again, he shrugged. He wasn't really trying.

"Because, Tonino, he knew where it could be hidden and where it would be safe. And what's more, he had the skill to get it there."

She watched understanding dawn.

"You think he hid the treasure in an underwater cave?"

Yes, it sounded crazy. But, "Why not? The top part of that cave is always dry. It would be safe, no one would ever find it, no one would even guess. You didn't." Even Tess hadn't guessed—until she saw the pot.

"You think *il tesoro*—whatever it is—is hidden in that pot you saw?"

"It might be." There was still something she didn't understand. "But if *il tesoro* was hidden in the cave and your grandfather realized that the entrance to the cave had been sealed up by a rockfall," she said, "then why tell everyone that the treasure had disappeared?"

Tonino frowned. "Maybe he didn't put it quite like that," he said. "Maybe he said he could not locate it. Maybe he even told them about the cave, but they didn't believe him."

That made sense. And even if Enzo Sciarra had believed him, he would have made damn sure that Tess's grandfather didn't.

"The foundations of Sicily," Tonino murmured. "That is where he said it was hidden. Where no one would find it." He looked at her. "You could be right."

"Damn sure." Well, Tonino was the one who'd told her the story of Colapesce . . . She finished her coffee. "Any chance of another cup?"

Over in the corner she saw the large design that Tonino had been working on. It was coming together. There was no illumination, and yet still the turquoise and luminous greens on their transparent glass backing seemed to glow.

He saw her looking. "I cannot finish it."

"Why not?" She wasn't sure yet what it was supposed to represent.

He avoided her gaze. "There is an important missing piece," he said.

He could say that again. The making of mosaics wasn't the only jigsaw going on around here. "And don't forget the skeleton," Tess reminded him.

"Ah, yes." He was looking at her as if she might have imagined it.

But she hadn't. Who was it that had met a watery death down there? It must have been a long time ago—if her theory was right, it would have been before 1945, sometime before Alberto Amato went back for *il tesoro*. So someone else knew where it was hidden. And if it was in the days before diving apparatus was readily available . . . Had someone—without the underwater experience of Tonino's grandfather—gone for it and failed?

"Perhaps," said Tonino, "we should tell the authorities?" He went over to the stove to fetch more coffee.

Tess stared at him. Was he mad? "Would that be the authorities who tend to have close links with the Mafia?" she asked. And maybe Giovanni Sciarra, too.

He poured the coffee, glancing over at her. "I see your point."

"Which is why we have to go back there and check it out first," Tess said.

"We?"

"We, as in you and I." Which bit didn't he understand? Which way would he go?

She waited. She couldn't do this without him. Wouldn't do it without him. And she had to do it—no question. She had never really understood why Edward Westerman had insisted she came to see the villa before she inherited it.

Perhaps he thought it was the key to bringing her family back where he thought they might belong; perhaps he himself regretted not going back to England—to his own roots. Perhaps he just wanted to give them the chance. Or perhaps, she thought, he had hoped she could solve the puzzle of the missing *il tesoro* and uncover the truth. So . . . "Will you be my diving buddy?" she asked.

He grinned. "Try and stop me," he said.

CHAPTER 69

GINNY DID THE RELAXING BREATHING EXERCISE that her psychotherapist Jayne had shown her and then she phoned her mother.

"We need to talk," she said. Jayne had convinced her of the benefits of conversation. If you communicate, Jayne said, you have a chance of being understood. Ginny had been trying this lately and found it to be true.

"Of course, darling," said her mother. "Anytime, you know that." She sounded pleased to hear from her and kind of distracted at the same time.

Ginny wondered exactly what was going on in Sicily. Her mother certainly sounded different.

"What's up?" she asked.

So Ginny took another deep breath, and she told her. She told her about how she had flunked her exams so that she wouldn't have to go to uni, she told her about her pregnancy scare, she told her about her plan to go to Australia, and she told her about Jayne.

There was a short silence. Ginny knew it was a lot to lay on her in one helping. But she had always been close to her mother. Until . . . Well, she wasn't sure exactly when. And so her mother had earned the right to know what was going on.

"Why do you need to see a psychotherapist?" Tess asked at last in a small voice.

So Ginny told her about the Ball.

It was her father who had suggested she go talk to someone. He had suggested it because one day he was driving her back from Pride Bay, where they had spent a whole day together doing not much more than staring at the ocean and eating ice cream, when she flipped.

It came out of nothing. Ball rising.

"That was a top day," he said.

"Yeah," she said. "And where were you?"

"What?"

"Where were you on sports day?"

"Er . . . When the dads were doing the sack race, and I fell over in the egg and spoon?"

His hands were tense round the steering wheel. He pulled over. "Ginny . . ."

"Where were you on the night of the hurricane?" Her voice was rising, and she could hear the emotion underneath, like the turquoise underbelly of a surfing wave. "When a tree blew over and crashed into the front bedroom window, and Mum screamed, and we thought the world was coming to an end?"

He shook his head.

"Where was Father Christmas?" Her voice was a whisper now.

He didn't reply. He looked down.

She hit him on the shoulder. "Where were you when I had chicken pox? And nightmares and exams and food-poisoning and there was a spider in my bedroom . . ." Her voice faltered, and he looked up at last.

"And Mum had to get the next-door neighbor in to get rid of it." She sighed. "Where were you?" And sat back, crumpled and spent, in the passenger seat.

"I'm sorry, Ginny," he'd said. "I truly am." He put his hand on her arm, wiped what might have been a tear from his eye, and started the VW.

When he dropped her at Nonna's, he got out to hug her. "If I could turn the clock back . . ." he said.

"I know."

The following day he gave her a business card. *Jayne Cartwright. Psychotherapist*, she read.

"What's this?" she asked him, holding the card out in front of her as if it might bite.

"I thought you might want to talk to someone," he said. "It could help."

Ginny was about to snap his head off; then she thought—maybe it would.

"I can make you an appointment," he said. "And I'll take care of the bill—obviously."

"A Ball?" her mother said.

"Jayne thinks it feeds off my anger," Ginny told her. "On pressure, repression, confusion, anxiety, you name it, really."

"Oh, Ginny." Her mother sounded heartbroken. "I never realized you felt that bad."

Neither had Ginny, really. She only knew it now because she felt so much better. In three sessions with Jayne she had talked and she had breathed and she had written (often from the perspective of one or other of her parents—which was weird); she had drawn and visualized and imagined. She had given up smoking, too. And the Ball . . .

"It rolled into a corner at first," Ginny said. "Shamefaced. Its voice getting a bit muffled and faded."

"And now?" asked her mother.

"It still seems to be lying low. I think . . ." She hesitated, afraid to say it almost. ". . . It's disappeared."

"Well. Great . . . ," said her mother, sounding completely shocked.

It was, thought Ginny. And if it came back, Jayne had shown her what to do to make it go away again.

"I shouldn't have come to Sicily," her mother said.

"Oh, it's been around for ages," Ginny told her. "It wouldn't have made any difference."

"Even so . . ."

She could tell her mother was grappling with the old guilt. "It's not your fault, Mum," she said. "You have a life, too—not just me. Please live in the now."

"I'm coming back right away. I'll book a flight for tomorrow," her mother said in her determined voice—the voice that always did what it said. "You come first, Ginny. You always have."

"Mum . . ."

"Don't tell me not to come, Ginny," she said. "I need to see you."

Ginny smiled. "And I need to see you. So I was thinking. Can I come over—to Sicily, I mean? I'd love to see the place where Nonna grew up."

"Darling, of course you can!" She sounded delighted. "Come over for as long as you like, and we can travel back together. We need to talk properly. We need to make a plan."

"Okay," said Ginny. "Sounds good." And it did.

CHAPTER 70

THE FOLLOWING AFTERNOON, TESS GOT READY FOR the dive with mixed feelings. It was like falling off a horse, she told herself—you had to get straight back on . . . Which was why when Tonino had said: "When?" she had said: "Tomorrow?"

She would have canceled it to go back to Ginny, but now she didn't have to. Tomorrow had become today, and as she pulled on her wet suit, all she could think of were those moments in the tunnel, trying to pull herself free. The sense of entrapment, the powerlessness . . . She tried to shake it from her head. She had to put it behind her now.

Down in the bay, Tonino was waiting for her, already wet-suited up. They had decided to go at siesta time. "The *baglio* will be at his most quiet," he had said, as if he, too, thought he was being watched, with someone recording his every move.

He, too, was banishing his ghost, Tess thought, as she gave him a quick wave and made her way over. They might, of course, be completely mistaken about the cave and *il tesoro*. The pot she had seen might contain nothing more than a few stones, shells, and sand. The skeleton . . . She shivered at the memory of it . . . Could have been anyone.

But they had to find out. And if it proved a fruitless exercise, what did it matter? They would both feel a whole lot better just for trying.

In his studio yesterday afternoon, when she had finally stopped shaking, when she had drunk his coffee and his brandy, and after they'd decided to do this dive together, today, she had at last—reluctantly—got up to go.

He didn't hold her; he didn't kiss her. But he put one hand on her shoulder and fixed her with that look. "Promise me, Tess," he said. "Promise me you will never do it again. Never dive alone."

"I promise," she had said. And it was a promise she intended to keep, advice she would pass on, if any of her plans ever came to fruition.

Only then had he let her go home.

"You are sure you want to do this?" he asked her, now, at the water's edge.

She clasped his hand. Thought—not of the dive, but of her daughter, who had been traveling on her own journey, most of which Tess had been unaware of. She couldn't say she was glad about the exams and Ginny's decision not to go to university—what parent would be? It had been a shock to hear what Ginny had done and what she'd been going through—but she was glad that she would see her soon. And glad that Ginny had at last told her how she felt.

"Yes," she said to Tonino. "Are you?"

He nodded. They checked their equipment and waded in side by side.

It was so much more rewarding, she thought, being with a diving buddy, sharing what you saw. Because although they were on a mission, heading back toward the cave, there was still lots to see on the way. Gray stripy salps, anthias, and bream; an octopus with swirling tentacles and a funny little pulsating cuttlefish, like a brown-and-white slipper in a skirt, that made her smile, despite everything. And the sea was clearer today; the silt and sand had settled on the seabed after the storm; visibility was good.

The rock face was vibrant with sponges of white, yellow, and orange, and the patches shaded by overhanging rock had attracted groups of silvery-black-pronged cardinal fish and sea anemones. When they reached the gap in the rocks, the hole that had formed the new entrance to the cave, Tess hesitated. Could she really go in there again?

He hesitated, too, as if aware of what she was feeling.

Go for it, girl . . . She nodded and slipped through, kicked herself gently along the tunnel, even recognizing the gray boulder that had trapped her yesterday. *Don't think about it.* He was right behind her, a sleek, lean figure in his wet suit, gliding effortlessly through the water.

They broke surface together and pulled off their masks. He shone his flashlight around, swearing softly, clearly impressed with the size of the cavern. And it was beautiful, she supposed, the contrast between the dark rocks and turquoise water, the skinny beam of sunlight filtering through. *Grotta Azzurra.*

"Where?" he asked.

She shone her own flashlight in the general direction of the platform where she'd seen it. For a moment, she thought both pot and skeleton had disappeared. But no. There they were, clear as day.

He nodded, eased himself out of the water onto the slippery boulders, pulling off his fins. He scaled the rock wall barefoot up to the platform, with the beam from Tess's flashlight lighting the way.

As she watched, he stepped gingerly over the bones. God . . . She was glad he wasn't contemplating taking those back with them.

Then he stooped to pick something up from the floor. He examined it briefly and tucked it in the pocket of his wet suit. He grabbed the earthenware pot—which was the size of a large pumpkin—with both hands and called down to her. "It is heavy."

The words echoed around the cavern. *It is heavy . . . heavy . . . heavy.*

Tonino was carrying a waterproof bag attached to his weight belt. He unhooked the bag, placed the pot inside this and half jumped, half stepped down to the lower level, holding the weight of the bag in front of his body.

Tess winced. "Careful . . ." But he was agile and seemed to have perfect balance.

He put his fins back on, reattached the bag to his belt, and slid back into the water. "*Andiamo.* Let us go," he said.

And Tess was happy enough to follow him.

* * *

They let the tide take them away from *i faraglioni* and back to shore, paddling lightly with arms and feet, finally pulling off their fins so that they could walk out onto the beach.

They emerged by the stone jetty, dripping but triumphant. Tess pulled off her face mask. Tonino had already done the same and was grinning at her.

"And now," he said, patting the bag at his waist, "we will see."

She nodded, aware of a lurch of anticipation inside, following his gaze as he scanned the beach. But all was quiet.

"Come."

Tess, too, didn't want to hang around. Without even unclipping her belt, she followed him, trudging past the old boathouse and rusty anchors, negotiating the steps to the *baglio* toward the safety of the studio. They had been discreet. But that feeling of someone watching—it never quite went away.

Tonino unlocked the studio door and pushed it open. Silence. He unclipped his belt, placing it with the bag carefully just inside the door, and began to unstrap his tank. Tess followed suit.

She didn't know what made her look up; the faintest of sounds, the premonition that they were not, after all, alone. But as she glanced toward him, a shadow fell across Tonino, who had bent down to put his scuba gear on the floor.

"Toni!" she shouted.

The man had come from the side of the studio and was standing in the open doorway. One arm was raised above Tonino's head. He was holding something . . .

"*Diantanuni*? What the devil?" Tonino blinked.

It happened so fast. Tess lunged forward, pushing Tonino to one side. The weapon—a slab of driftwood, she realized—destined for Tonino's head, fell instead onto his shoulder.

Tonino whipped around and was on his feet in seconds. "You."

It was Giovanni.

For a moment Tess was frozen to the spot. It felt as if they were, all three, caught in a tableau echoing one from the past. She scrambled to her feet.

The two men faced each other. Tonino in his wet suit, his eyes dark and angry, the scar on his face as raised and livid as she had ever seen it. And Giovanni, his face twisted with hatred, his mouth curling back into a sneer.

"What the fuck . . . ?" yelled Tonino, rubbing at his shoulder and letting loose a torrent of furious Sicilian.

Giovanni just laughed. He kicked the door shut behind him. Held out his hand. "Give me the bag."

She'd been right. He had been watching; he'd seen them go out diving this afternoon—he knew all their movements, for God's sake. He probably knew what was in the bag. He knew everything. And God knows who he was in league with.

Tess was the closest to the bag. She stood in front of it. No way.

But the two men were still eyeing each other like a couple of Sicilian wild dogs guarding their own territory. And so it was, she realized. Did Tonino know that Tess's theory was correct—that the treasure had originally belonged to his family? Giovanni certainly believed that it was Sciarra property; ancient protection money as demanded by the Mafia.

Giovanni threw the first punch, catching his opponent off guard. Tonino backed off, rubbed at his jaw, squared up to his opponent.

Oh my God, thought Tess. What could she do? What should she do? She didn't want to be some helpless female on the sidelines of this battle. But . . .

They were flinging insults and fists at each other, much as they probably had in the playground. It was an old and bitter rivalry, and somehow she had found herself in the center of it. It was not her battle. But as Giovanni let loose a vicious punch to the face and as Tonino buckled, Tess realized her mistake. This was no playground fight. This was the culmination of what had been festering for years. It had started with their ancestors and simmered in the deep, dark cooking pot that was Sicily. And now—with these two men—it had reached breaking point.

Tonino . . . How could she help him?

But even as she looked blindly around, Tonino seemed to recover his balance. He swung a fist and—more by luck than judgment, she guessed—it landed on Giovanni's nose.

"*Ouf.*" Another torrent of angry Sicilian.

Giovanni struck out again and again and suddenly they were both flailing wildly, each at the other, fists flying, punches connecting—with faces, eyes, throats.

"Stop!" she shouted. "Enough!" But she might as well be invisible.

Tonino was the slighter of the two and hampered by his wet suit, but he was also the faster and more agile, more adept at ducking and dodging punches. Thank God. And in some strange way as they fought on, Tonino's wet suit seemed to help him: it made him slippery and hard to catch.

Both men were breathing heavily now—though still able to fling insults at each other, she noted—and slowing down a little. There was nothing to choose between them. It was a fair fight, and something told Tess that she couldn't, shouldn't intervene. She had to stay out of it. This was something they had to finish for themselves.

Then something changed.

As they grappled together up close, Giovanni got Tonino in a headlock. He smashed a fist into his face.

Tess screamed. She lunged toward them once more, but Giovanni shoved her roughly away.

"Stop! No!" Surely someone outside must hear her? But no one came. Just as in the café that time. No one came.

Tonino elbowed Giovanni sharp in the ribs, and he grunted with pain and loosened his grip. Like a seal, Tonino slipped from his grasp, but his face was now bloody and raw.

"Tonino . . ." Tess realized her own face was wet with tears.

His gaze flicked toward her, and in that second, she saw Giovanni reach into his pocket. She screamed again.

Something glinted in Giovanni's hand. The bastard had a knife. He had flicked it open and was swishing and swirling it through the air.

Shit. Now the fight really was unfair. Tess had to do something. She grabbed her scuba tank which was still on the floor and heaved it up, swinging it at Giovanni—hard.

It caught him a glancing blow on the arm. He swore loudly and shoved her away, harder this time. The tank clattered to the floor and Tess fell back, hitting her head hard on Tonino's wooden workbench.

For a moment, everything was a blur. Tonino was yelling at him now. But the distraction had enabled him to regroup. He was in a better position—and in his hand was his own diving knife, normally kept in a clip on his shin. Hardly a lethal weapon like Giovanni's flick-knife, but at least he was no longer unarmed.

Both men's faces were tight with tension. The air was still and heavy. Tess could hardly breathe. She edged farther away on her backside and then stumbled to her feet.

Giovanni lashed out, catching Tonino on the back of his hand and then slitting the wet suit at the shoulder. Tess saw a flash of crimson. He moved in for the kill, plunging the knife toward Tonino's upper chest. "Now you are finished!" he bellowed.

Tess screamed, Tonino ducked, and the next moment he was up, behind Giovanni now. He seemed about to strike, but Giovanni twisted around just in time to parry the blow.

Tess breathed again. But it wasn't over yet. Again they circled one another.

"Enough!" she pleaded. "Stop it, both of you! Haven't you done enough?"

But again they ignored her.

Tess shuddered. There was something about the look in their eyes. It was animal. She was terrified. It was as if they had agreed. A fight to the death was the only way to end it after all.

All of a sudden Tonino gained his first hit—a nick in Giovanni's forearm. Tess saw the shock on the man's face as he registered the sight of the blood. And she also saw the new determination. He lunged. Tonino twisted away. And then he had him. Tonino had a grip on the hand that held the flick-knife and he had his knife at Giovanni's throat.

Tess blinked. No, Tonino, she thought.

"Drop it," he said.

Giovanni had no choice. The knife clattered to the floor, and Tonino kicked it away. Again, she held her breath.

Tonino was muttering into Giovanni's ear now, still holding the knife to his throat.

"*No, no . . .*" Giovanni was begging. His expression had changed. His voice had changed. He would never forgive Tonino for this, Tess realized. If he lived.

Tonino raised his arm, the knife drew closer.

Then he pushed him away. "Go," he said. "Don't come back. It is over."

Giovanni half fell, half stumbled out of the studio.

"Tonino . . ."

He looked at her. "Are you hurt?" In a few steps he had reached her.

Her breath caught. How nearly she had lost him. And then he pulled her into his arms.

Tess removed the top half of her wet suit, slung a towel around herself, and made Tonino sit down while she bathed his face. Fortunately, his wet suit had protected his body, so his wounds weren't as bad as she'd thought. Then she held the waterproof bag while Tonino removed the earthenware pot.

She took it from him. "It is heavy," she agreed. "Shall we look inside?"

Gingerly, he began to towel his hair. It hung in tendrils over his forehead and neck. "It is why we brought it here," he said, a gleam in his eye. "Why we have gone to so much trouble, you and I."

"Okay." The pot was the color of faded terra-cotta, and the lid seemed to be crusted on—with glue, salt, or just with old age, perhaps. In the end, Tonino had to work at it with his diving knife to free it.

"Please." He gestured to Tess to do the honors.

She was holding her breath, she realized. She breathed out and pulled off the lid with a flourish. They peered inside. Weird. Inside the pot was another pot. "Like Russian dolls," she said. Carefully she eased the second pot out. It was old and fragile, the top of it a shallow cup.

"Some sort of Greek urn," said Tonino.

"Is this *il tesoro*?" Tess couldn't help but feel disappointed. She had expected . . . Well, something more.

"Perhaps." He shrugged, but she could see he felt the same.

"What else did you pick up?" she asked him, remembering how he'd stooped to retrieve something from the shelf of the cavern.

"Ah yes." He dug it out of his pocket.

It was a ring. They both peered at it. Maybe a wedding band, Tess thought.

Tonino fetched some cleaning fluid from a cupboard and a rag. He took it from her and polished it gently. Gradually the scrolled initials *ELS* were revealed. "So . . . ," he breathed.

This time the understanding was simultaneous and mutual. "Giovanni's grandfather?" they said together. "Ettore Sciarra?"

It made sense. Enzo's friendship with Tess's grandfather would make it likely that he shared the secret of the whereabouts of the treasure. So . . . What if he tried to get to *il tesoro* before Tonino's grandfather had the chance? What if he sent his brother, Ettore, down there—but Ettore couldn't get out again? He could have run out of air; he could have fallen; maybe he was even trapped by the original rockfall, retreated to the cave, and eventually died of starvation. Whatever. When Ettore didn't come back from his mission, Enzo must have known or guessed the truth. He had lost his brother, but that wouldn't stop a man like Enzo Sciarra putting it about that someone else was responsible for his death.

Tonino picked up the old Greek vase and examined it more closely. It had a handle in the form of a lion flanked by snakes and was certainly beautiful in its own right. Still . . . "He must have wanted it very much," he said. "They all did."

And you? Did you, too, want it so much? Tess wondered. "But your family found it first," she murmured.

He raised an eyebrow. "What do you mean, Tess?"

"Luigi." But he still looked confused, so she explained her theory.

"Ah." He held the casket at arm's length. "That could explain a great deal." He frowned. "I wonder if my grandfather knew it was Luigi's treasure. Perhaps he did . . ."

"Maybe he would have asked Edward Westerman about it," Tess chipped in, "when he got back from England after the war. If he'd been able to locate it from its original hiding place, that is."

"Maybe." Tonino felt the weight of the casket. "It is so heavy. I wonder . . ."

He laid it gently on the table, sideways, and she could see immediately that on the underside there was a ridge. He jiggled it a bit, and it moved, just a fraction. They shared a quick, complicit glance. There was more to this than they'd thought. Tonino jiggled it a bit more, until finally it shifted and opened. The larger part of the urn, under the shallow cup, must be hollow. And filled with . . . ?

He let the contents spill out onto the table.

Tess gasped. Old bronze coins decorated with images of horses and grapevines, Greek warriors, doves, serpents . . . She ran her fingers through them, awestruck. Some coins felt thick and heavy; some were as fragile as a dry leaf. The decorations were blunted with age but still clear; the edges uneven but true. Gold leaves, medallions, and finger rings: she picked up an oval ring embossed with the image of an old man, bent and leaning on a stick, with a dog who appeared to be leading the way. The picture was so complex, the work so delicate . . . A narrow gold armband, the thinnest of jeweled hairpins, golden spiral earrings, and decorated pendants—one of a boy on a dolphin, another of a naked woman.

"It's fabulous," said Tess. "Just fabulous."

Tonino let the ancient coins and the golden jewelry slide through his fingers. "And what do we find hidden inside," he said, as if to himself. He raised an eyebrow at Tess. "*Il tesoro*, I presume," he said.

CHAPTER 71

TESS HAD BEEN LOOKING FORWARD TO THIS MOMENT for weeks—and at times it had seemed impossible that it would come. But now they were here in Cetaria—Muma, Dad and Ginny. They had come for a holiday and the plan was that Tess would return with them to England until Ginny left for Australia. After that . . .

"What finally persuaded you to come back?" Tess asked her mother.

The four of them were sitting at a high raised table in the *baglio* restaurant on the other side of the old stone fountain.

"It was time." Her mother's lined face was weary but flushed with excitement. Carefully, she extracted a thick red leather-bound notebook from her bag and laid it on the table by her side plate.

"Aha," said Ginny, who was sitting opposite, though she didn't elaborate further. Her plane tickets for Australia were already bought, the visas taken care of. She and Becca had it all planned—she'd been telling Tess this afternoon on the way from the airport. The hostels and the fruit picking, the stay in David's house in Sydney.

David . . . That was another thing. She hadn't yet had a chance to ask Ginny much about David. But she sensed that David had entered her daughter's life at a good time. Not the right time—that would have been when Ginny was born. But a good time—when Ginny was floundering. Tess smiled to herself. Perhaps meeting another flounderer (or should that be flounder?) had helped her daughter. Perhaps it was unreasonable even to expect a girl of eighteen— especially in this world of multiple choices—to know what she wanted to do with her life? Tess was pretty sure that at thirty-nine, she'd only just decided.

"So tell us more about your plans, love," her father said on cue.

Tess managed to tear her gaze from the red leather-bound notebook. They had already discussed her plans for Villa Sirena—Muma walking round room to room with this look on her face—as if she couldn't quite believe she was here, seeing it all again, the villa of her childhood. Once they all left at the end of the week, the renovation project would begin in earnest, and the next time Tess came to Cetaria it would hopefully be complete and ready to go. Thank you, David, thought Tess. Because it was his money—minus what she would be giving to Ginny—that was paying for it.

"Is it just like you remembered?" Tess had asked her, catching hold of her mother's arm. There had been a bad few minutes when Muma had seen the ruin that used to be her family's cottage, but Tess had prepared her for that, and in a way it was the mermaid's villa, the grand villa of her mother's childhood, that resonated with her more.

"No," her mother said. "And yes."

Tess had laughed. She knew exactly what she meant. Memory was a strange creature. It was selective, and it could play strange, unexpected tricks. Sometimes it was impossible to untangle what had really happened from what you had wanted to happen, what you had dreamed of happening, and what you had been told had happened. And yet you thought you knew . . .

"Well, there's all the B&B stuff, obviously," Tess told them now.

She and Ginny had talked long and hard about how Ginny would feel about her mother being based in Sicily—at least for a while. Would Australia work out for her? Would she end up spending more time with her father? Or would she go back to the UK sooner than she expected? Even move to Sicily, perhaps? None of them had any idea—but they'd cross that bridge when they came to it, Tess had said, trying to be philosophical. She was quite prepared to move back to England if she had to—she would rent out the house in Pridehaven so that she could reclaim it if need be. It was hard not knowing when she'd see her daughter again, but she wouldn't stand in her way. She had learned to give her space; to be there and yet let go, she realized. "I love you, Mum," Ginny had said. "And I'll miss you. But . . ."

"This is something you have to do." Tess nodded. And she was proud. They were strong again. And Ginny had embarked on her own journey now.

"I'll probably get in some domestic help when I can afford it," Tess continued. But to start with, she'd cope alone. "I'm going to learn the language. And I'm planning to start up a diving center." Cetaria was so rich underwater that it was screaming out for one. And yet no one seemed aware of the potential—not yet anyway. The nearest diving center was about thirty kilometers away en route to Palermo and the airport. There were hotels and B&Bs in the area—apart from Tess's—that could accommodate tourists. A diving center could provide equipment for rent, tuition, underwater photography diving trips, and maybe whole scuba-diving vacation packages. Why not? It was ambitious, but it was exciting. And she'd discussed the aims of such a diving center with Tonino already—to protect the submerged environmental and archaeological heritage of the area.

"A bit different from the water company, love," her father said when she'd finished enthusing. "Though they do have something in common." They laughed. "Are you up to it?"

"Of course she is." Muma surprised Tess with her emphatic tone. "She's my daughter, is she not?"

Everyone laughed. She'd have to reassure her dad later, Tess thought. He was a worrier and she'd been shocked at the airport to see how old he seemed—his hair surely thinner, his back more bent, his eyes more faded than before. When they'd hugged and she smelled that familiar smell of her childhood, she'd felt like she couldn't let him go.

"The fall upset him," her mother had whispered to her. "It will take a while to heal."

"He really hurt himself?" But they'd told her it was nothing more than a fractured wrist and a few cuts and bruises.

"His dignity." Muma had nodded. "Suddenly he knows he is an old man."

Tess had to turn away then, to hide her emotions. She didn't want them to be old; she didn't want them to ever leave her.

"And did you know, my darling," Lenny turned to Flavia now, "that when our daughter went running off to Sicily, she would also fall in love?"

Fall in love? Tess blushed.

"It scared me," her mother admitted. She clicked her tongue. "Sicily is a seductress."

Sicily . . . ? Ah, yes. It was true that she'd fallen in love with the place. But more than that—it felt like home.

"And will you do all this alone, Tessie?" her father asked her, his eyes wise as ever.

"We'll see," said Tess. She had seen a fair bit of Tonino since their recovery of *il tesoro*, but she couldn't tell what his intentions might be. Was she—could she ever be—just a friend?

"And now," said Ginny. "Tell us about the treasure." Her eyes shone.

So Tess launched into the story just as she'd launched into it to Millie a few days after she and Tonino had made their find. Yes, it could be worth a lot of money; yes, it was beautiful—gold jewelry and coins, possibly Greek; and yes, it was first discovered by Luigi Amato.

"But where is it now?" Millie had asked, her eyes wide and greedy. Tess knew she was poised, cell at the ready, eager to let someone know. And she knew which someone it would be.

"You can tell Giovanni that we no longer have it," Tess had told her. "So there's no point in him breaking into the villa again. It isn't there."

For the first time since she'd known her, Millie looked uncomfortable. "What are you talking about, Tess? Surely you don't imagine that I—"

Tess laughed. "I saw you, Millie. So you're wasting your breath." The day after the dive with Tonino she'd hotfooted it to the hotel, couldn't wait to tell Millie and Pierro what they'd found. Pierro was away on business, apparently, Millie wasn't in reception, so she'd gone round to their private rooms. Just as she got there, the door to their apartment had opened, and Giovanni came out, looking somewhat rumpled and worse for wear. And as if that wasn't evidence enough— Tess had dodged behind a potted palm, feeling like a character in a cheap detective movie—Millie had followed him, giggling and tugging at his arm until he turned to give her the sort of kiss that left Tess in no doubt of their relationship.

It was Millie's business, she had told herself, taking a different route out of the hotel and back to the *baglio*. But she remembered the lipstick on Giovanni's collar, and she remembered the prolonged lunch with Millie at the hotel the day he'd broken into the villa. And that's when she realized. Everything she'd ever told Millie . . . Well, she'd as good as told Giovanni, too. Millie wasn't her friend—she never had been. She was Giovanni's mistress, first and foremost. She'd seen Tess with Giovanni at the market, got jealous, and decided to befriend her so she could find out what was going on. Then she'd become Giovanni's spy. It sounded ridiculously melodramatic—but it was true.

Millie had sat back in her chair and regarded Tess coolly. "So why are you here?" she asked. "To gloat?"

Tess shook her head. "We wanted Giovanni to know that he could finally give up on getting it back."

Tonino had been adamant about what he wanted to do. "*Il tesoro* never belonged to the Amatos," he said. "Not truly. And it has only ever caused bloodshed for our family. It belongs to Sicily, and she shall have it."

Not all the authorities in Sicily were corrupt. By letting the right people know what they had found, Tess and Tonino were pretty sure that *il tesoro* wouldn't fall into wrong hands. That it would go to a museum that celebrated its heritage, not into some greedy, grubby, corrupt organization.

Millie had gone very quiet.

Tess reached into her bag and withdrew the ring, wrapped in tissue. "And you can give this to Giovanni as well," she said.

After a moment's hesitation, Millie unwrapped it. She turned it over in her fingers. Tonino had made a good job of cleaning it up, and the engraved initials *ELS* shone out from the gold. "Who . . . ?" she began.

"We think it belonged to his grandfather," Tess said. "Ettore Sciarra. You know, the man who was supposed to have been murdered by Tonino's grandfather?" She paused. "I know Giovanni has a similar ring engraved with his initials. It's a family tradition, I suppose."

Millie nodded.

"It was in the cave," Tess said. "Alongside *il tesoro*. And a skeleton."

"A skeleton?" Millie flinched.

Tess got out of her chair. "Giovanni might want to think about what it was doing there," she said.

When Tess had returned to the *baglio*, she'd told Tonino about Millie and Giovanni—why should she bother to protect Millie's reputation?

"I guessed already," he said.

Tess stared at him. "How?"

"Millie Zambito chases after every man."

Tess considered this. "You as well?"

"For some months," he admitted. "The woman—she does not give up so easily."

Tess remembered what Millie had said about him. How she had looked. "Were you tempted?" she asked. She realized it must have been Millie, too, who had told Tonino that she was Flavia Farro's daughter the night he turned up late and drunk, the night she'd expected to make love with him and ended up breaking up with him.

He shrugged. "I am a man," he said.

She'd noticed.

"But no. Millie is too brash. A man-eater.""And what about Pierro?" Tess felt sad about Pierro. He was a lovely man. He didn't deserve what Millie was doing to him.

Tonino made a sign. The cuckold. "Maybe he knows. Maybe not. Maybe he, too, has someone. Maybe not. Millie Zambito is a very unhappy woman, Tess."

Tess knew that he was right. She thought of the brittle brightness Millie seemed to exude. And she was sad because she had hoped Millie could be a friend. Could she stay in Cetaria when it also housed Millie and Giovanni? Yes. She had the feeling they might leave her alone from now on.

In the restaurant they raised their glasses in a toast. "To *il tesoro*," said Ginny. "The famous treasure returned to Sicily by my mother!" They all laughed.

"They say the *Grotta Azzurra* is very beautiful," Flavia murmured.

"Oh, it is." Tess stopped abruptly. Had she told them the name of the cave? Definitely not. "Muma . . . ?" She caught her mother's eye. "You didn't know about the treasure and where it was hidden—did you?"

Flavia clicked her tongue. "Do you think those men would have told me?" she asked.

No . . . But Santina had told her how Flavia liked to listen . . . And as Tess looked into those wise old eyes, there was an unmistakable twinkle . . . "Muma," she breathed.

Flavia smiled and shrugged. "It was your pathway, my darling," she said.

"To Edward Westerman." Tess looked around at them all, her family, here with her in Cetaria, where—for Muma, at least—it had all begun. She thought she was beginning to comprehend at last—why Edward Westerman had left her the mermaid's villa. There was a lot to lose, when you lost sight of your roots. She had come to Sicily in order to understand her mother, but in coming, she had learned to understand her daughter, too. Mothers and daughters . . . It had been quite a journey.

"To Edward," echoed Flavia. She glanced across at Lenny and smiled. "And to his sister, Bea."

"So when are you going to tell us what this is, Nonna?" Ginny pointed to the red book. "I've seen you writing in it, you know."

"It is my story." Looking suitably modest, Flavia handed it to Tess. "It may fill in some of the gaps, my darling."

Tess took it from her. She opened it. Her mother's handwriting filled the pages—neat and sloping. She felt a lump in her throat. "Muma . . ." How brave she was. Tess put a hand on hers.

"And at the back . . ."

Tess looked. There were pages of recipes, all in her mother's handwriting. She started reading one. *A pinch of this, a handful of that, a few of the other* . . . She flicked through. *Antipasto and meat and fish and dolce* . . . All Sicilian; all the recipes that she had grown up with.

"I started writing it for you, my dear," said Flavia. "But I ended up writing it for myself, too."

"Thank you, Muma . . . ," Tess said. *Food is your identity . . . Food is where you have come from. The place you call home* . . . This was it, she realized. This was the real mother-and-daughter stuff. This was the real treasure.

CHAPTER 72

In bed that night, Lenny turned to Flavia. "What do you think of our girl?" he said.

"She has done well." Flavia smiled at him.

"D'you reckon she'll be happy here?"

"As a rabbit in clover." Flavia had seen Tess talking to the man who made the mosaics in the *baglio*. He was Alberto Amato's grandson. A fine man. She would trust that one.

"And you, my love?" He opened his arms, and she crept inside, resting her head on his shoulder. "Are you happy to be back here—even if it is just for a holiday?"

"I was going to talk to you about that," said Flavia.

"Which part of that?"

"The holiday part."

"Ah."

They were quiet. Flavia felt his familiar warmth, and she was content. This afternoon she had visited Santina, and they had both wept copiously.

"I thought you would never return," Santina said, over and over, hugging Flavia close and then propelling them apart. "So that I can look at you, my friend."

My friend . . . Santina had shown her the sampler they had embroidered together, too. It was funny—Flavia had almost forgotten about it, but when she saw that piece of faded linen, well, it brought everything back.

Sometimes home is about forgiveness. And sometimes you have to search for home. Over the years England had become home to Flavia. But . . . As she'd told that young man down in the *baglio*, Flavia had come back because it was time to put the past to rest. Time to end the journey. Time to forgive her family. And Sicily, too. She had finally let it go.

CHAPTER 73

WHEN THEY WERE ALL IN BED, TESS MADE HER WAY down to the *baglio*. It was midnight, and Tonino was in the bay waiting for her. He had lit a wood fire and was grilling fish and prawns. The fragrance of the burning wood filled the night air, mingling with the sweetness of the seafood, salt, and wet stone.

She sat on the wall by the jetty. He had brought a couple of oil lamps down to the bay, and these were propped against the stones, letting off a yellow-blue light from the flames, which combined with the glow from the fire and the full moon to illuminate the scene. He had laid a rug down on the pebbles and set out white wine, ice, glasses, and bread in a basket.

"Have you finished it yet?" she asked. She knew that the mosaic he was designing was special, but he hadn't revealed what it was or why. He was waiting, he kept saying, for the missing piece.

"Yes, it is complete," he said. He squeezed some lemon juice over the fish.

"Really?" And then she noticed that he had propped something—a large flat object—up by the jetty, covered in a tarpaulin. "Is that it? Is there going to be an unveiling?" she teased.

"Of course."

He made her wait until they had eaten the last of the fish and prawns with hunks of Sicilian bread and drunk the last glass of white wine, until the fire was dying and they lay back against the rocks, looking out toward *i faraglioni*, the shadowy cliffs, and the moon gleaming on the waves in the bay.

He got up, positioned it until it was directly in the moonlight, and moved the oil lamps closer. He pulled back the tarpaulin.

Tess sat up, stared at the mosaic. It was beautiful. She was beautiful. For it was a mermaid, designed in profile, holding a mirror in one hand, a comb in the other, her long seaweed-colored hair hanging down her bare back, her gorgeous tail curved and pointing behind her. She reminded Tess of the motif on the villa, the mermaid she thought of as her mermaid. Though the mosaic mermaid's face was tranquil rather than sad; she looked as if she had discovered a secret; it was as if she knew much more than she would say.

"She is all sea glass," Tonino said.

"Because that's where she came from." Tess could make out the shades of the glass now; the turquoise and sea greens of the body; the lilac sheen to the hands, arms; and face; the yellows and browns of her hair.

"And the missing piece?" she asked him.

He pointed to the perfect almond-shaped, blue-violet eye.

"So you found it!"

"It wasn't easy." He grinned. "But it is worth the wait, do you not think? It is a special piece. I found it right over by the far rocks."

"Well, yes, it's lovely." Tess had the feeling she was being teased. "So what does the mermaid signify? When are you going to tell me her story?"

He rested on his haunches, seemed to deliberate for a moment. "The mermaid was sighted out on *i faraglioni* by a fisherman from Cetaria," he said. "She was looking in the mirror and combing her long brown-and-yellow hair." He pointed and smiled. "It seems she only appeared when the moon was full."

"Like tonight," murmured Tess, looking out to the rocks at sea.

"Like tonight," he agreed. "Her mirror reflected the surface of the sea. He was drawn to her irresistibly. He sat on the rocks and listened to her song. It was the most beautiful sound he had ever heard."

He paused, and Tess strained to listen. But all she could hear was the lap of the water on the rocks and the soft splash and hiss as the waves broke and drew back from the shore.

"But he was not satisfied to listen to her only once a month," Tonino went on. "He wanted to listen to her every night. He wanted more."

Tess nodded. Didn't they all? "So what did he do?"

"He tried to keep her. 'You must stay out of the water,' he told the mermaid." Tonino's voice changed. He seemed to become the fisherman as he took on his words. "'You must come and live with me and let me love you.'"

Tess waited.

"'If I stay out of the water,' she said, 'my song will die.'"

Tonino got up and approached the mosaic, continuing the story, "The fisherman did not believe her. 'I can only catch fish when I hear your song,' he said. 'The rest of the time the water is barren. Come to me, and there will be fish aplenty. and we shall feast and love and be merry.'"

"What did she say to that?" asked Tess.

He glanced across at her. "Still she held back," he said softly. 'If I leave the sea,' she said, 'the fish will leave, too, and you will be hungry.'" Tonino paused. "For the third month the fisherman threw himself on the rocks at her feet. 'When you are with me,' he said, 'I am safe in the water. My raft will not fail me, my harpoon will stay straight. Without you, the sea is my enemy.'"

Tess looked up toward Villa Sirena. From here she could not see the mermaid motif. But she could see that she had been faced with a difficult decision.

"The mermaid could not bear to think of the fisherman drowning," Tonino said. "So she put away her comb and her mirror, and she came to live up there on the land." Tonino, too, looked up toward the villa. "He named his cottage after her. *Sirena*. But she was trapped. She was not free. The tides changed and winter came, and there were no longer fish in the sea. The mermaid—she lacked the strength to sit out on the rock. Slowly her song faded to silence."

His voice was hypnotic, as before. It seemed that when he told these legends, he slipped so easily into that other world. "No wonder she looks so sad," Tess murmured.

"At last the fisherman saw what he had done. One night when the moon was full, he took his raft, he placed her on it, and he took it out to sea. 'Be free!' he cried, and she slid from the raft and into the waves, her tail flashing like liquid silver."

Tess could almost see her. She looked at the mosaic he had made with so much care. Yes, she could see her.

Tonino bent his head. "The fisherman, he was heartbroken," he said. "It did not matter that fish returned to the sea or that he heard her song when the moon was full. 'I should not have expected her to live in my world,' he told himself. And the next time the moon was full he went out to the water's edge and waded into the sea."

Tess gazed at him. "And . . . ?"

"He saw her by the rocks in the moonlight," he said. "He looked into the blue-violet eyes. He listened to her sing the same beautiful song that he had heard before. And when at dawn she slipped once again into the sea, he followed her."

Tonino crossed his arms in front of him. "*Finito*," he said.

Finito? Tess wondered if Edward Westerman had ever heard that story. "What does it tell us?" she wondered aloud. "To give up everything for love? Or that we all need to be free?"

Tonino ran a caressing hand over his mosaic. "Perhaps it tells us something about relationships," he suggested.

But what about us, she wanted to shout. Had he created this midnight moonlit picnic simply in order to show her his latest design and talk about mermaids?

"The mermaid, Tess, *La Sirena*, she is for you," he said.

"For me?" She was so beautiful. Tess didn't know what to say.

"And I have spoken with your mother."

"My mother?"

"Like me, she thinks that it is time," he said.

"Time?" Tess hoped that she wasn't turning into one of those people who just constantly repeated what other people said.

Tonino came to stand beside her. Very close. She was conscious now of the scent of him—glue, dust, stone, and Sicilian lemons. It was a heady mixture. He put out his hand and helped her to her feet. His eyes were so dark, but unlike before, they seemed to be trying to tell her something. The old scar on his face, the curve of his cheek, his jaw . . . Yes, it did remind her of someone—or something. For some strange reason, it seemed to remind her of home. Wherever or whoever that might be . . .

He let his hands rest on her shoulders. "Time to put the past to rest," he said. He bent closer. Almost touching. "I do not think that we live in such different worlds," he said, "you and I."

Tess realized what he was trying to tell her. "You mean . . . ?"

Even closer. "That is exactly what I mean," he said.

Acknowledgments

I READ LOTS OF FICTION AND NONFICTION AROUND the subject of Sicily to prepare for this book and have done my best to be historically, geographically, culturally, and linguistically accurate. However, this is a work of fiction, and I have adapted some things for the purpose of the story. Any errors I have made are my own.

Heartfelt thanks go to my lovely agent, Teresa Chris, for her support and belief in me as a writer. Thanks also to every one at Quercus, especially to Jo Dickinson, who is a brilliant and sensitive editor.

I'd like to thank Grey Innes for his help throughout the writing process, particularly for providing his expertise on diving matters and for his perception and listening skills. . . . Thank you also to Margaret and Leo in Castellamare for help with matters Sicilian. Thanks to my lovely friend Jane for advice on psychotherapy, and also to friends who have read sections of my work for me—Sarah Sparkes, Caroline Neilson, June Tate.

I would also like to thank my dear friend Alan Fish, who is always supportive, always interested, and always willing to read my work and tell me what he really thinks! In this novel he also helped me with some research when I was in danger of running out of time and energy . . .

I wrote a lot of this book while traveling around Europe, and so special thanks go to my dearest friend Caroline Neilson, who looked after things while we were away. She has been a fantastic support in very many ways.

Love and thanks to my beautiful daughters, Alexa and Ana, and to my son, Luke. And much love to Grey, who is the best traveling companion and ideas stormer a writer could hope for!

Rosanna Ley has worked as a creative tutor for over twelve years, leading workshops in the UK and abroad, and has completed an MA in creative writing. Her writing holidays and retreats take place in stunning locations in Italy and Spain. Rosanna has written numerous articles and stories for national magazines. When she is not travelling, Rosanna lives in West Dorset by the sea.

THE VILLA
READING GUIDE

Reading Group Notes

Do you think Flavia made the right decision to leave Sicily?

How does Rosanna Ley explore fundamental human relationships—that is, the relationship between mother and daughter, lovers, et cetera?

Who is your favorite/least favorite character and why?

What do you feel is the central theme of the book?

Landscape is used to portray emotion in this novel—how successful do you feel this is?

How did you feel Ginny changed over the course of the book?

How would you compare and contrast Tess's and Flavia's experiences of love?

Q&A with Rosanna Ley

How did you start writing?
From a young age I wrote poems about everything—from my parents not understanding me to my feelings about my teddy bear! I wrote a play at school in history about Henry II and Thomas à Becket that filled a whole exercise book. I poured out teenage angst in verse. And I dabbled with creative writing as part of a college course when I was eighteen.

Some years later, in my mid-twenties, writing grabbed me again, quite by chance, when I tried to sign up for an adult education pottery class that was full. Flicking through the brochure, I found creative writing. Why not?

In a matter of days I was hooked again. I poured out poetry, articles, short stories, journals, you name it. The first article I published (in *Mother and Baby)* was about my four-year-old son's unshakeable belief that he could fly. As you might imagine, it was funny but scary at the same time . . . he seemed so *sure!* I went on to write short stories for women's magazines and eventually a novel, and after a couple of years it was me tutoring that creative writing class! My first novel was typed on a manual typewriter and returned by a literary agent as reading more like a psychological dissertation. Hopefully, I've come on a bit since then . . .

What is your working day like?
My main aim is to avoid looking at e-mail and social networking sites until I've got some work done!

If I am in the middle of writing a novel, I deal with anything urgent first thing and then try to work in the mornings planning a scene—often longhand—or thinking something through. This might involve going somewhere like a café or a beach (depending on the weather) to write in a notebook. Then I get onto the computer and do a long stretch until lunchtime.

After lunch I try to have a walk—it's too easy to sit hunched over a computer all day; it's important to stretch out, exercise, and take some thinking time—and then I'll either do some revisions or some research, depending on what stage I'm at. The Internet is incredibly useful for research, but it is a distraction. Sometimes you can lose hours that way!

If I'm doing mentoring work, I'll spend a lot of time reading and also writing up reports for authors or chatting with them. If I'm traveling and doing research, then I'll be out and about with my notebook all day, and I'll try to write things up in the late afternoon or evening.

Once I feel I've achieved a day's work (and this doesn't always happen!), I'll sort out post, admin work, e-mails, and so on. I usually have a list of tasks to be achieved that day, and I take great pleasure in crossing off each one when it's done.

Last thing at night before I go to sleep, I try to think about the scene I'll be writing in the morning so that it can start composting in my head . . . Unfortunately, I'm often so tired that I don't get very far with that one. But who knows what's going on in your subconscious while you sleep?

Where do you write?
Wherever the mood takes me. I love writing longhand into a notebook, and so I'll take that to a café or a park bench or a clifftop and just get inspiration that way. It's especially important for me to write scenes in the actual setting of the novel. If I'm working on my computer, I'm at home at my

desk and then I'm fully focused on the words rather than the inspiration.

Have you been to Sicily?
Yes. It's a magical landscape. I was fascinated by the contrasts: the darkness and light; the tranquil with the undercurrent of menace; the beauty next to the undeniably rather seedy. These contradictions intrigued me. When I read up on the history of the island and the Sicilian fairy tales and myths, it all started to make sense, and I decided to use Sicily as a setting for the novel. And then of course there was the Sicilian food . . .

Your novel describes the bonds between mother and daughter beautifully—how did you approach writing this?
Thank you. The mother-and-daughter bond is very special to me. I've always had a good relationship with my own mother, and I have two amazing daughters with whom I've always been very close. I'm lucky in that they have talked to me a lot over the years about their lives and their feelings, and I suppose I've absorbed a lot of that and been able to express it on the page. Not that any of the characters are based on my daughters, but you do get a general sense of voice.

In the book, Flavia is a strong character who has suffered great disappointments in her life—some of them due to the behavior of her own parents. I wanted to convey her strength and her vulnerability. She wants Tess to have a different life, one of her own choosing, and yet she still can't help trying to protect her from things she perceives as dangerous due to her own experience. I think that this is one of the dilemmas that mothers face. Another dilemma is what happens when our daughters shut us out—because they think we won't understand, or because they're trying to assert their individuality and independence. As mothers we need to get through that stage—it's a case of damage limitation really, and that's what happens between Tess and Ginny. Ginny shuts her out, but equally, Tess doesn't confide in Ginny. Lack of trust like this can often signal the beginning of a breakdown in any relationship. If we keep talking, we're communicating and there's more chance of being understood!

Did the writing of The Villa bring any surprises for you?
The writing of every novel hopefully comes with its own surprises, which is one of the things that makes writing such fun! This one started off in my mind as being somehow linked with volcanoes—but that never really happened. I hadn't intended Flavia's recipes to feature, but after tasting the Sicilian food, it seemed a great way of allowing her to pass on a legacy to Tess. The novel became more historical in flavor, too, and I became much more caught up in Flavia's past story than I had expected. I got interested in Sicilian fairy tales during my research, and I like the idea of myth and legend being used symbolically within a story—so that went in. And when we were traveling around Italy—while I was also writing the book—we came across a beautiful pink villa with a stuccoed mermaid above the front door, which gave me the idea for La Sirena—the mermaid's villa. Finally, my husband began using sea glass as a material for his artwork (just like Tonino!), but in this case I'm not sure which came first—the chicken or the egg . . .

What advice would you give to aspiring writers?
Never give up! Write a bit every day. Listen to the feedback of others (preferably those who know what they're talking about) but ultimately listen to your own heart.

For more news and updates, visit Rosanna Ley's website at www.rosannaley.co.uk